The
Answer
Is Yes

Also by Sara Lewis

BUT I LOVE YOU ANYWAY

HEART CONDITIONS

TRYING TO SMILE
and Other Stories

Sara Lewis

The
Answer
Is Yes

Harcourt Brace & Company

New York   San Diego   London

Library of Congress Cataloging-in-Publication Data
Lewis, Sara.
The answer is yes/Sara Lewis.—1st ed.
p.   cm.
ISBN 0-15-100326-2
I. Title.
PS3562.E9745A84   1998
813'.54—dc21   97-46079

Text set in Galliard
Designed by Camilla Filancia

Printed in the United States of America
First edition   E D C B A

For Kees, Caroline, and Paul with love

acknowledgments

MY NAME on the cover of this book might make it seem as though I did all the work myself. I didn't. Several people deserve gold medals and thunderous applause for their important contributions. I offer this page of thanks to

Binnie Kirshenbaum, Melinda Knight, and Mona Lipman for reading drafts of the manuscript and for their indispensable comments;

Geri Thoma of the Elaine Markson Literary Agency for her insight, diplomacy, and unyielding optimism;

Christa Malone, Dori Weintraub, Mary Grey James, Dan Farley, Beverly Fisher, Lynne Walker, Jenny Mueller, Tom Knapp, Camilla Filancia, Marianna Lee, Schuyler Huntoon, David Hough, Lisa Holcombe, Marsha Brubaker, and many others at Harcourt Brace for years of hard work and support.

And with all my heart, I thank booksellers at Barnes & Noble, Del Mar; A Woman's Place, Salt Lake City; The Bookloft, San Diego; Dutton's Brentwood Books, Los Angeles; Thidwick's, San Diego; and Esmeralda's, Del Mar, for their passion about books in general and their enthusiasm for mine in particular.

The
Answer
Is Yes

MAKE A WISH. In this course, you'll watch for shooting
stars, search for heads-up pennies, throw coins into fountains,
blow out candles on a cake. Make as many wishes as you
want, then tell of their fulfillment to the class. Field trips
include a walk to a shopping-center fountain, a shooting-star
watch, and a penny search. Mondays, beginning August 4.
Course cost: $15. Materials: Please bring birthday candles,
a wishbone, and pennies to share with the class.

I WAS ON A LADDER on the stage, resetting a light. I
had a wrench to turn the knob and was trying to loosen it while
at the same time maintaining my balance on the ladder. The knob
was resisting, either because it had been tightened by someone
stronger than I was or because it was old and rusted. Most of the
equipment in our theater was old because we had bought it used
or borrowed it from someone who didn't need it. The tech run-
through was in two hours; the only dress rehearsal was the next
day, and the day after that was our opening. I remember thinking
that I had about four minutes to get these lights where they need
to be. I took hold of the wrench with both hands and put more
of my weight against it. The ladder wiggled. Many things that
were meant to move here didn't, like the knob I was fighting with;
other things that weren't supposed to move did, such as the ladder
I was standing on. I regained my balance and looked down to see

if there was someone standing around doing nothing who could hold the ladder steady for me.

Priscilla and Edward were on the stage, Edward on his knees pinning Priscilla's costume together. Tiffany was going over a speech that she hadn't quite memorized. Clara was collecting props. If I asked one of these people to hold the ladder, I would be slowing down another person. We might not be ready on time. As I remember it, Edward and Priscilla seemed to look up at me at the same time, to say something—to warn me?—but then they looked down again and went back to what they were doing.

Michael walked across the stage in his purple bike shorts, sweatshirt, and pink ballet shoes. He glanced up for a second and said, "Be careful up there."

I said, "I am being careful."

Then I fell off the ladder.

I FELT PAIN in my head before I opened my eyes. Michael was next to me. I looked at him, closed my eyes again. I looked at Priscilla and Edward on the other side of me, then at the white sheet that covered me, at a woman I didn't know, a nurse. Slowly I realized that I was lying in a hospital bed. Michael said, "Jenny, you're all right! Are you all right?"

"I don't know," I said. "It's hard to tell." I tried wiggling my fingers and toes, moving my legs, my arms, turning my head. There were some sore spots, but everything seemed intact. "Yes," I said to Michael. "I'm all right." My voice sounded quieter, more tentative, than I expected. The small smile that I managed to produce hurt something on my face.

Michael looked across the bed at Priscilla and Edward. "She's OK! She talked to me. You heard her!" He started kissing me all over my face. "You're my angel! You know that, don't you?" he said. "I love you, Jenny!" He laughed with relief, held my hands, and kissed them. I closed my eyes again, feeling his warm breath on my skin, his soft lips touching me over and over.

Someone else was standing at the door of the room. I heard the nurse say, "No more visitors, please. We're taking the patient down to X-ray now that she's conscious. You'll have to wait. Are you a family member?"

Michael paused for a moment to turn and see who was at the door. I looked, too, but all I could see was the nurse, her white uniform top stretched tight across her broad back.

"A family member?" I heard the visitor say, "I'm her husband!" Then Todd pushed past the nurse into the room. He looked down at me, lying in the bed. His hair was plastered to his forehead, as if he had been running a long way. His mouth was slightly open, and it seemed to me that we all waited a moment for him to say something more, to ask a question. Michael's hands were still in my hair; my face was still damp in the places where his lips had touched me.

When Todd didn't speak, I said, "What time is it?" I looked at a big clock on the wall. "Oh, no!" I said. "We're supposed to be in the middle of a run-through! I've got to get out of here!"

Todd stood there for a minute at the side of the hospital bed, not saying anything. I tried to get up. "Jenny, don't!" Michael said. "Just rest now." He pressed a hand hard on my shoulder.

Todd opened his mouth to say something, closed it again, then walked quickly out of the room.

Priscilla, Edward, and Michael stood there looking at the door without saying anything. I was still a little slow, trying to piece together what was going on. Too late I said, "Wait." Todd was probably halfway to the elevator by then.

t w o

COOKIES FOR CASH. Our own local Cookie King started out selling from a counter inside a photocopy store. Since then he's franchised thousands of counters in 11 states; developed his own successful brand of frozen cookie dough, available in supermarkets everywhere; and written a national best-seller about helping yourself to the cookies of life. His secret? A blend of spiritual openness and real butter. Learn how you can franchise a cookie counter or develop your own secret recipe under the guidance of the Guru of Goodies. Friday, August 15, 7–10 P.M. Course cost: $15.

*N*OW I'LL TELL you how I got up on that ladder in the first place.

One day as soon as the front doors of the bank were unlocked, a woman walked up to my desk to speak to me. I evaluated loan applications in a shopping-center branch of a big bank chain. The woman was in her forties, wearing jeans and a T-shirt. Ignoring the fact that I was on the phone, she said, "I want you to explain this to me." She said it loudly because she was upset. I could see the security guard straighten up, not exactly springing into action, but listening for what was coming next. I didn't have an office with a door that closed, just an L-shaped desk in the middle of the floor with a chair in front of it for applicants to use while they talked to me. Some of the people I worked with slid their eyes in

4

my direction while pretending to go about their business. The woman put her purse down on the chair in front of my desk and took out a piece of bank stationery, a letter with my signature on it.

Into the phone, I said, "I have to go," and hung up on my husband, Todd, who was at a molecular biology conference in Colorado. To the woman in front of my desk, I said, "I'm sorry, I—"

"You don't remember me," she said in a voice much too loud for a bank. "Let me refresh your memory. I'm Marion Randall. I applied for a loan. I'm a newly divorced mother of three, who put on a dress and good shoes because I wanted to make a good impression on you. I did that, instead of just filling out a form and dropping it off, because I wanted to be a real person to you, a human being instead of a little number in the corner of a loan form. I sat here in this chair and told you about the custom cake business I was starting in my home. I said I wanted to do something that wouldn't require being away after my kids get out of school. Do you know what you said? 'That must make them feel good, knowing you're there.' You *said* that." She paused, allowing time for me to take this in. " 'I can do any kind of cake,' I told you. Remember? No, of course you don't. 'Barbie, Batman,' I said, 'a wedding cake decorated with fresh flowers, a cake in the shape of any number you choose, for anniversaries and birthdays and what-have-you.' And you said—I remember this clearly, even if you don't—you said, 'I'm sure they're wonderful. It sounds like a great idea for a business, especially in a growing family area like this.' You seemed to like me, Ms. Brown. I thought we made a connection. I didn't call and pester you about my loan, did I? No, I waited without a word all those weeks because I had faith that you were seeing to my application promptly and fairly. Then I get *this* in the mail." She held a denial of her loan, a form letter, very close to my face.

I started to tell Mrs. Randall that she had me all wrong. She didn't have to dress up for *me*. The person she saw behind this desk wasn't who she thought at all. I did remember her. Of course I did. She wanted to borrow money to buy a station wagon for delivering her cakes to parties. I took a breath to speak, but she cut me off again.

"*Why?* I just want you to tell me why," Mrs. Randall said. "You owe me at least that much."

I said, "Here, let me show you something." In about half a minute, I typed her numbers into my computer to show her how they added up to a poor risk. I was going to add that to me, personally, the amount she asked for seemed quite modest. If it had been my own money, I would have written a check on the spot. I would have said, "Take it, and good luck to you! Come back and let me know how things are working out." But it wasn't my money. It's the people who really need the money you have to turn down. The people who already have a lot can get more with no trouble. It's like trying to buy a padded bra, if you're familiar with that process: It's almost impossible to find a one with a double-A cup. Padded Bs and Cs are no problem. But then if you're a B or C, do you need padding? Do you even deserve to have more than you've got already? This was the crux of what had been bothering me lately about my job; the essential unfairness of it was gnawing at me from the inside, making it harder and harder to come in every morning and sit there at my desk all day. I wanted to explain my true feelings about loan evaluation to Mrs. Randall—I would have to speak very quietly or ask her to step outside for a minute—but she didn't let me.

She said, "Can't you just look at my face and see that I would pay it back? Can't you *see* that?"

I looked at her. She had curly brown hair, beginning to gray, and hazel eyes. I would bet anything that she was the fun kind of mother who went on scary rides with her kids and didn't mind a lot of noise in the house, who let them play with the hose sometimes without making them change into their bathing suits. This was the kind of mother I would have tried to be, if Todd and I had not decided that we weren't going to have children. I said, "I'm sorry, Mrs. Randall. I'm very sorry." I was going to try to talk over with her other ways she might try to get the station wagon, not as part of my job, but because I wanted that cake business to happen. I was sure we could come up with something together if the two of us went over the situation systematically. But she didn't give me a chance.

She said, "I bet you're sorry. I just bet you're as sorry as you can be!" She started to choke up and stopped talking. Without looking at me again, she picked up her purse from the chair and left the bank.

I watched Mrs. Randall back her old two-door Toyota out of the parking lot. Then I sat there, staring at my computer screen, trying not to cry myself. The screen went black while I was looking at it, the screen saver turning it off automatically, letting me know that I had sat there a full ten minutes without making a move. I looked at the black screen a second or two longer, then stood up and walked out of the bank.

I did not love my job. But as I used to tell myself every morning on the way to work, not everyone does. Millions of people do what they do all day, not because they have a burning need to but because they have to make a living and this is where they end up. They try not to put in a lot of overtime or work weekends if they can help it, and they make the most of holidays and vacations. I was one of those people.

I don't know if you've ever felt this way, but at that moment, I didn't like myself very much, didn't even want to be near the kind of person I was. I didn't like the house I lived in, my face, what I knew I would have for lunch. I felt like taking my clothes off right there in the middle of the shopping-center parking lot and setting fire to them, walking away to start over as a different kind of person. I didn't, though. Instead, I bought a frozen yogurt, looked at it for a while as if it might speak to me, answer all my questions, then threw it out. I stared into shopwindows at all kinds of clothes and gifts and food that I didn't want to buy. Then I started walking back to the bank because I couldn't think of anything else to do with myself. I was looking in the window of the video store and not watching where I was going when I bumped right into someone. "Excuse me," I said, as a man backed away from me.

"Sorry," he said. "I mean, excuse *me*. I don't know where my head is at sometimes. You OK?"

"My fault," I said. "I'm fine. You?"

"Perfect," he said.

He started walking backward in the direction he had been going, while he continued talking. "Hey," he said. "Have a nice day!" He was wearing a red T-shirt. Across the front, it said, THE ANSWER IS YES.

I said, "Thanks. You, too." He turned around to walk forward. On the back of the shirt, it said, NOW, WHAT'S YOUR QUESTION?

I went back to the bank and sat down at my desk. I got to work right away, but I wasn't working on a loan. I was working on a way to go home early. A dentist appointment? A sore throat? A family emergency? As it turned out, I didn't leave early. I even stayed a little late, finishing up, filing. Todd was still at the conference, so there was no need to rush.

When I did go home, I put some leftover take-out lasagna from the night before into the microwave. I took out an old mug with a picture of a dog on it and filled it with water. Sometimes you can get a really beautiful thing that you love and break it or lose it the first day. On the other hand, there are ugly, pointless things, like this cup, that can stick with you forever, whether you like it or not. Todd's mother sent this cup to him in a box of kitchen things when he moved into his first apartment during college. I couldn't seem to get rid of it. Somehow, I couldn't bring myself to just drop the cup into the garbage can when there was nothing wrong with it. I sipped water from the dog cup and put my lasagna on a plate.

After I'd eaten, I called my mother in Connecticut, but she was out. My mother was a nurse. Lately she worked as a consultant to medical care facilities. She traveled a lot.

My husband, Todd, and I had not lived here in San Diego very long, not quite three months. We had been living in Cambridge, Massachusetts, when Todd was offered an assistant professorship at a university here. The house Todd and I lived in now belonged to the university, where he spent most of his time. We got it rent-free for a year as part of the deal Todd made when he was hired. For this neighborhood, it wasn't a very big house, but coming from an apartment, we didn't have nearly enough furniture to fill it. There were two empty bedrooms upstairs that we never went in.

To give myself something to do after I ate my lasagna, I decided to go for a walk. I put on a special outfit—shorts and a shirt with reflective stripes, shoes designed for walking long distances, specially constructed not to give blisters or bunions. The shoes reminded me of what I was trying to forget, Mrs. Randall putting on her good shoes to come to see me.

The answer is yes. Now, what's your question? That T-shirt slogan kept repeating in my head, like some Top 40 song I'd heard too many times. "Yes" was probably some kind of surfing or stereo equipment, I thought, or maybe a shampoo with built-in conditioner or a no-fee checking account. The T-shirt must have been advertising for some product I didn't know about, but I liked the sound of it anyway. *Yes,* I said to myself again. It was certainly a very positive slogan, whatever it was promoting.

I set off down the street. To build strength and endurance, I looked for hills. In a few minutes, I came to a shopping center I had never seen before, then a lot full of new town houses just being framed. I hoped I could find my way back. I kept walking and came to an older neighborhood I hadn't seen before. I had been walking for about twenty minutes when I started to get thirsty. That lasagna was way too salty, I thought. I didn't have any money with me, so I would have to find someplace with a drinking fountain. I walked some more until I saw a building that looked like a school. When I got a little closer, I saw that letters had been pried off the concrete front wall, leaving rusty shadows that still spelled out CORONA VISTA ELEMENTARY. The lights were on inside. If it was open, maybe there was a fountain or a bathroom where I could get some water.

On the door of the building was a piece of cardboard with the word SCHOOL written on it with a black marker. I pulled on the handle and the door opened. I could hear people talking inside and some loud music coming from one of the rooms. There was

9

another hand-lettered sign on a door, saying, REGISTRATION AND INFORMATION. I went into the office.

An elderly woman was sitting at a desk. She was having trouble with a computer. She was hitting it, banging it on the side, and frowning at the dark screen. Without looking at me, she said, "Down the hall, last door on your left."

I said, "Pardon me?"

"You're acting for the first time, aren't you?" she said.

"I'm sorry, I—"

"Didn't bring your checkbook? First class is free. See me next time."

"Thank you, but I was just—"

"You've got *two minutes!*" She almost shouted at me. She shook the computer. The screen suddenly brightened and filled with words. "Ah. There we go!" She looked up at the acoustic ceiling. "Thank you!" she said. She began to type. I went out. "Have a good class!" the woman barked after me.

"Right. Thanks," I said. Maybe there was water down the hall somewhere. I glanced into some classrooms on my way. Loud music was blasting from giant speakers in one room. I looked in. Some old people and some very heavy younger ones in exercise clothes or shorts and baggy T-shirts were doing small jumps and slow turns. The teacher, a man, who was a lot younger and thinner than most of the students, was wearing purple bike shorts and a sweatshirt. He had a baseball cap on backward and battered pink ballet shoes with holes in them where his big toe was sticking out. "Woo!" he yelped to the class, clapping his hands. "We're kickin' some butt now!"

An old man in front let out a cry of enthusiasm, "Yeah, *baby!*"

A very heavy woman at the back said, "Somebody stop me!" and did a pirouette, pausing several times on her way around to put a foot down and steady herself before continuing.

The floor was buzzing under my feet from the volume of the music. I would have stood there longer, but the teacher noticed me then. He waved, calling out, "Glad to have you!" I smiled

10

and walked on down the hall. In the next room, a woman who looked about sixty was learning how to hold a violin. I saw a drinking fountain at the end of the hall.

As I passed the last classroom, a woman stepped out. "There you are!" she said. "We're all in here waiting for you!"

I looked around. There was no one in the hall but me. I said, "No, I just came in to get a drink of water. I was on a walk, and—"

"OK, get your drink, and then we'll start." She went back inside the classroom. "She's here," she said to a roomful of people.

The fountain was very low, as if it might have been designed for kindergartners. I bent and drank for a long time, planning to sneak away while the woman was occupied with her class. I looked for a red EXIT sign over a back door. I didn't see one. When I finished drinking, the teacher was standing in the doorway, giving an opening speech to the class, starting it there so that I could hear. "You're going to learn a monologue in this class, perform it several times for the class, then work with a partner on a scene and perform that, too." Her hair was dyed a purplish red and pulled up into a ponytail on top of her head. It bounced around enthusiastically as she spoke. She had on earrings that were small globes twirling on their axes, and she was wearing a pair of blue-green overall shorts with white cowboy boots. She motioned me into the room. I didn't want to interrupt, didn't want everyone staring at me while I explained that I didn't belong here, so I went in silently and sat down. Maybe there would be a break and I could tell her that I wasn't supposed to be in the class.

"You're all going to surprise yourselves," the teacher went on. "You may not believe me now. That's OK. I know what I know. I'm Rory, and this is Acting for the First Time. Anybody in the wrong room?" I realized that this was my chance, but she didn't leave enough of a pause for me to say anything. "Good," she said. "Let's begin. These are the speeches we're going to be working on first. They're from *Spoon River Anthology*. Some of you probably remember this from high school. Doesn't matter if you don't.

It's dead people talking about their lives. No plot, just people taking turns talking. I want you to memorize your speeches before the next class."

She handed me one of the photocopied speeches. I took it. I did remember it from high school, from some English class. Rory talked about acting for a little while, then some of the class members got a chance to read their speeches, just to get a feel for what we would be working on. My hands got sweaty worrying that she might choose me to read. After each reading, Rory talked about what the character might be trying to express in the speech, what it meant. Before I knew it, an hour and a half had passed, and the class was over. Rory looked at me and said, "Next time." She thought I was disappointed about not getting a turn to read my speech.

I went out, taking the paper with me. After I'd sat there the whole time, I couldn't very well return it and tell the teacher I wasn't enrolled. It had gotten dark outside. I walked home, surprising myself by remembering the way with no trouble at all. I wouldn't go back there, of course. I wasn't going to take an acting class. What for? I worked in a bank.

t h r e e

LIVING ALONE AND LOVING IT. Celebrate your solitude by collecting recipes for one, learning where to buy household and grocery items in small quantities, exploring the real estate market for the small-home buyer. With tips on screening phone calls, how to turn down well-meant but unwelcome holiday invitations, and rejecting with love. Saturday, August 3, 10 A.M. to 2 P.M. Course cost: $20.

THE DAY AFTER Mrs. Randall yelled at me, I sat at my desk all day, wishing I were somewhere else. I didn't get very much done. I considered quitting my job. What stopped me was the idea of being home by myself all day with nothing to do.

After work, I drove to the university to see Todd. He was back from the conference, but as usual, he had gone straight from the airport to his lab. Whenever he went to a conference, he always felt he had slipped behind in his work, though, of course, attending the meeting was part of it. I circled the parking lot for a space, but there wasn't one that I was allowed to park in. There were plenty of available spots with purple triangles on them, but the triangles meant faculty. Or was that the yellow trapezoid? Maybe purple meant support staff or maintenance crew. Whatever it was, I didn't have a sticker for it. I needed a spot with no colored painted shape and a meter. I circled the lot one more time before I realized that there were no meters at all in the parking lot of Todd's building. All the other times I had come here, I was with

Todd in his car, which had a faculty sticker. I would have to find another lot.

I drove over to the one by the faculty club, where there were a few meters, but they were all taken. I went to the lot by the swimming pool, and the spaces there were all occupied, too. I saw a man come out, holding a towel. I tailed him slowly in my car. He didn't look at me or point to where his car was so that I would know where to go. I followed him right to the other side of the parking lot. He kept walking. I had followed him this far, so I decided to keep on going. All the way down at the end of a driveway, under a group of eucalyptus trees, the man stopped at a bicycle rack, bent down, and began to unlock a bike. Now he turned to look over his shoulder at me, smiling.

I smiled back. "Thanks a lot, creep," I said through my teeth.

I drove back to the faculty club and found someone pulling out of a metered space. I pulled in, searched my wallet for quarters. I didn't have any. I looked through my purse, hoping to find one at the bottom of it somewhere, but didn't. I looked all over the floor of the car, even lifting the floor mats. Nothing. Finally, I found two dimes and a nickel in the ashtray of the backseat. Three students, a man and two women, were passing on their way somewhere. "Excuse me," I said, "does anyone have a quarter?"

Obligingly, the three of them searched their pockets and backpacks. "Sorry, not me," said the man.

One of the women said, "Nope."

"I thought I had one, but I don't," said the third student.

"Thanks anyway," I said as they walked away.

In the next row of cars, a man was unlocking his trunk. I walked over to him. "Excuse me," I said, holding out the coins. "Do you have a quarter?"

He reached into his pocket. Wordlessly, he handed me a quarter and took my change.

"Thank you very much," I said, as he slammed his trunk and walked away in silence.

I put the quarter in the meter, turned the handle. I had fifteen minutes of parking time. I would get some more quarters from Todd. I started walking fast over a hill, past the cafe, through some trees and some kind of art installation or fence on wheels, past some tennis courts and a dorm, and arrived at Todd's lab.

He wasn't there. I checked his bench. There was a tray of tubes there and a pad for phone messages, some pipette tips, and a box of latex gloves. "Todd?" I said. "Todd?"

"Hi," said a voice, not Todd.

I turned around and there was a young man standing there. He was as tall as Todd, over six feet, with light brown hair that stood up on one side as if he had slept on it wet. He had on a T-shirt with the name of a brand of kids' bubble bath, shorts, and sandals. "I'm Drew," he said. "I think Todd's in the tissue-culture room."

"Oh," I said. "Jenny. I'm his wife."

"Cool," he said, nodding, shaking my hand. "I'm his graduate student."

"Nice to meet you," I said.

He looked at me a few more seconds without saying anything. This was my first experience being the boss's wife, being checked out for that reason. I looked away at a garbage can with a yellow sign on it saying that it was for biohazardous waste. A phone rang. "I have to get that," Drew said, and hurried away.

I stood there a little longer, looking around. There were a lot of cardboard boxes addressed to Todd that he hadn't opened yet. Others had been opened and rummaged through, but not all the way unpacked. I sat down on a stool in front of a microscope just as Todd came around through the door, fast. He was wearing jeans and a button-down shirt that I had given him five or so birthdays ago and a pair of disposable gloves. "Hey, Jen," he said.

"Hi," I said. "How was your trip?" I stood on my tiptoes and kissed him.

Carefully, he held his hands out to the sides away from my body so as not to contaminate me with whatever was on the gloves. "Good," he said. "I saw Winston and Smales and those guys from Jim Farmer's lab."

I nodded. "How were they?"

"Good. They filled me in on their stuff," Todd said. "And I met that German guy who did that thing with transgenic mice that I told you about. But I'm so far behind now, I almost wish I hadn't gone. I've got to find someone to inject my mice today, or I'm not going to make it."

Todd worked on identifying the genetic properties of a certain kind of brain tumor. As a graduate student, he collaborated with a group at Harvard School of Public Health who did family studies of patients with a predisposition for developing these tumors. Todd had identified the gene responsible. Now he was looking at how mutations of the gene contribute to the development of this type of malignancy.

Did that sound like I know what I'm talking about? Years ago, I pieced these phrases together and memorized them so that I would have them ready to pop out whenever anyone asked me what my husband did. Actually, I didn't understand a thing about it, except that it took a lot of intelligence, time, skill, patience, perseverance, and faith that the experiments might be getting somewhere despite potentially catastrophic setbacks, ruthless competition, and nearly overwhelming technical difficulties.

"Tonight, you mean," I said. I pointed at the clock. "You've got to find someone to inject your mice tonight."

"Oh, *man,*" Todd said. "I've got to hurry up." He started to walk toward the bench where he was working.

"Do you have any quarters for the parking meter?"

Todd glanced at me, peeled off his gloves, dropped them in the trash, checked his pockets. "Sorry."

"It's OK. You probably don't have time to have dinner with me anyway."

"Dinner?" Todd said. "Ha! No way."

I shrugged. "OK. Well. Guess I'll go, then."

"Sorry," Todd said. "Hey, you knew I would have . . . See, if I stop now—"

"Never mind," I said. "I know I should have called. I'll see you later."

"Sorry. I'm just trying to hurry so I can get—"

"I know. Really, it's OK. I'll keep my fingers crossed for the mice. See you later," I said again.

At the door, I turned around to wave, but Todd was already pulling a new pair of gloves out of a box, anxious to get back to work.

I hurried back to my car, but I didn't make it. The time on the meter had expired four minutes earlier, and an attendant was just putting a ticket on my windshield. I took it off and looked at it. Twenty-four dollars. I unlocked my door, put the ticket on the empty passenger seat, and drove home.

As soon as I got back from the university, I wanted to leave again. I didn't want to stay alone in an empty house all evening. But I didn't know many people here yet, so I decided to take a walk again. I changed into my walking clothes, went out the front door, and took off in a different direction this time. I passed a park with a playground, a different shopping center, some big brand-new houses overlooking a canyon. The builders were extending the backyards of the houses with landfill and cinder blocks so that squares of artificially constructed property stuck out into the canyon. I kept walking past a shopping center with a movie theater and a row of fast-food restaurants, then a health club and two more new developments that I didn't recognize.

I was just starting to wonder if I was lost when I recognized a building: the school where I had ended up the night before. I couldn't figure out how this had happened when it seemed that the streets I took had led away from here. I stood still a minute, reorienting myself, looking back in the direction I'd come from and concluding that the streets must have been more curved than they appeared.

At least, I knew the way home from here. And now that I knew where the drinking fountain was, I could go straight to it and come right back out again. I went inside and glanced into the classrooms as I passed. A room I hadn't looked in the last time I was here was full of people typing on computers and typewriters or writing with pens and pencils on tablets or notebooks. A sign on the door declared the time and name of the class:

An instructor, a tall woman with short hair, was telling a young man with a ponytail, "Don't worry about whether it's any good or even what it says. Just get it on the paper."

Next door, there was another dance class going on with the same teacher I had watched before. He didn't seem to notice me, so I stood there for a long time. Some of the students were the same ones that were there the night before, concentrating hard on moving their feet and arms the way he did, causing him to say, "Now you've got it, Joe!" or "Ellie, that was awesome!" Grins and blushes spread across the faces of the students as the instructor praised them.

I looked into the music room, where there was a private piano lesson in progress. The student looked about eighty. She was wearing a bright yellow T-shirt like the one I had seen on the man in the shopping center. I could only see the back of it, where it said, NOW, WHAT'S YOUR QUESTION? Slowly, she was working her way through "Twinkle, Twinkle, Little Star." When she finally got to the end, the teacher, a young woman, laughed and hugged her.

Maybe this student had always wanted to play the piano, but when she was growing up, there wasn't any money for lessons. Now, long after her children—maybe even her grandchildren— were grown, she got the idea, *I can do whatever I want*. She signed herself up for private piano lessons, paid with a check.

In the room closest to the drinking fountain, it wasn't the acting class that had been there the night before. On a chalkboard at the front of the room was a list of words:

HAPPINESS!

LOVE!

IDEAS!

MONEY!

All the chairs were pushed to the back of the room. The students were sitting on rectangles of carpet on the floor. They all had their eyes closed. Only the teacher had a chair. He sat with his eyes

18

closed, too, talking in a low voice to the class. "Happiness," said the teacher.

I waited to hear what was coming. There was a very long pause. I sat down on the floor next to the door.

"Think of a perfect day in your special place. Everything you see fills you with contentment and delight."

I closed my eyes. I had missed the part about the special place, but I did my best. In my head, I saw the inside of a house with framed photographs on the walls: children smiling in Halloween costumes; adults who looked alike hugging each other. A group of people were singing a song they all knew. There were a lot of big vases with red, white, yellow, and purple flowers crammed into them. A roomful of people were eating from full plates, talking, laughing, singing.

The teacher went on. "You have all the love you need."

In my mind, I stayed in the house where the party was going on. As a matter of fact, I lived there. A man was reaching for me. He put his arms around me and kissed me on the mouth. He said, "Jenny, I love you." The people at the party clapped and cheered. Deep within me, I felt a soft glow of joy, like the gentle, reassuring radiance of a night-light in a dark hallway.

The teacher spoke again. "You have original ideas, solutions come to you, creative energy flows through you endlessly."

I had to work a little harder on this one. I was holding something, a unique creation that I had made myself. It was a toy, no, a kitchen gadget, or a way to organize your work. Anyway, this thing did its job well, whatever it was, and it was the only one like it in the world. I had invented it myself, and now it was available for sale everywhere.

I found that I was finished with this part too soon, before the teacher was ready to move on. I wanted to go back to that house, the man. He was holding me, whispering to me, dancing with me.

Then the teacher started speaking again, interrupting my nice dream. "I want you to imagine yourself surrounded by riches," he said. "Imagine wealth."

The picture that came into my mind was a cave full of treasure, something I'd seen with Todd on the Pirates of the Caribbean ride at Disneyland when we first arrived in California. In my head, I saw a treasure box filled with enormous, glittering jewels—necklaces of emeralds, rubies, diamonds, sapphires—dripping over the sides, gold coins piled high all over the floor.

"All the money you can use," the teacher continued.

I imagined our checking account balance, adding several zeros to the end of the figure.

"All right," the teacher interrupted again. "You've traveled far, and now it's time to return. I'm going to count backward from twenty to give you time to reenter our class. Twenty... nineteen..." He counted slowly all the way to one. "Now," said the teacher. "You're going to notice some changes. Open your eyes, open your mind, open your heart! There are surprises waiting for you!"

I opened my eyes and saw the dirty green-and-yellow linoleum I was sitting on and the gouged, grimy plaster of the wall opposite me. I looked into the classroom. The teacher was smiling, as though he had left presents for all of his students under their pillows at home. I got up off the floor, took a long drink from the fountain, and walked out the front door with some of the people who were leaving the class.

A man stopped suddenly in front of me, stooping to tie his shoe. "Excuse me," I said as I nearly tripped over him.

"That's OK," he said. "Great class, huh? Hey, what's this doing here?" He picked up a twenty-dollar bill from the sidewalk next to his foot. The man looked around to see who might have dropped it. I looked, too, but there was no one else around. He finished tying his shoe and stood up. "Wow," he said. "Twenty bucks."

Several more people from the class came out of the building.

"Hey, you guys!" said the man. "I just found twenty dollars on the sidewalk!" He waved it in the air. Three women and two men came over to see the money. "I found this right here. I did this intense visualization about money, and then there it was, just, like, waiting for me!"

The rest of us scanned the sidewalk to see if there was any

more. One of the women crouched down to look under the cars parked at the curb.

"Irwin's amazing, isn't he?" said the man with the money.

"Irwin?" I said.

"His meditations really work. Weren't you in Happiness Love Ideas Money?"

"Sort of," I said.

Another man pointed to the twenty. "That is exactly what he means by the changes you should expect."

A young man in a business suit said, "See that? It's already starting to happen to you, man. You're lucky. Some people totally resist goodness."

The man with the money put it in his pocket, smiling. "See you guys next week," he said. "Who knows what else I'll find between now and then."

Maybe there was something to this visualization thing. Maybe something like that would happen to me, too. I could use a nice surprise like that. And I had done the visualizing right along with everybody else.

I walked home, humming "Twinkle, Twinkle, Little Star," thinking about the old woman playing the piano and the money on the sidewalk. I can do anything I want, too, I told myself. I guess it's possible that things could start to change just by adjusting the way you think. I went back over what I had visualized. *Happiness, love, ideas, money,* I thought to myself. *Happiness, love, ideas, money.*

Just then I felt something squish under my foot. Without even leaning down to investigate, I could already smell what I had just stepped in. I wiped off what I could on the grass nearby. It was going to be really hard to get the rest of that out of the deep grooves in the soles of my walking shoes. Maybe changing your thoughts didn't necessarily work on the external world right away; or maybe you had to be officially enrolled in the course and pay before you saw results.

When I got home, I took the dirty shoe off outside the front door. Todd was sitting on our futon couch, reading a scientific journal. The TV was on, tuned to one of those emergency shows where real people tell about gruesome things that have happened to them, sometimes breaking down as they get into the details of their crisis.

"Hi," he said, glancing up. "Where's your other shoe?"

"Outside. Did you finish?" I said. "Did you get it done?"

"What? Oh, yeah." Todd looked down again at what he was reading.

I went to the refrigerator to find something to eat. "I met that guy you hired. Drew? Was today his first day? It must be nice to have someone there with you after being alone in the lab for all these weeks."

Todd didn't answer. Sometimes when he was reading, he didn't even hear me speaking to him; his concentration was that good. There wasn't much in the fridge: a quart of milk, a coffee-flavored nonfat yogurt that I had bought by mistake, wilted lettuce, and a garlic slowly drying out, nearly new bottles of ketchup, mustard, mayonnaise. I stood there, holding on to the refrigerator door handle, and closed my eyes. I tried to picture the food I'd imagined earlier, but here in my own house, I couldn't quite get it back. I opened the freezer: bagels and ice cubes. "Did you eat dinner?" I asked, closing the freezer door. "Todd? Todd, I'm talking to you."

"Me?" he said.

I said, "I'm going to order something. There's a new Indian place at the shopping center. They deliver."

"Indian? Isn't that going to be spicy?"

"Probably," I said. I ordered for both of us without asking Todd what he wanted.

While I waited for the food, I filled a bucket with soapy water and took a plastic knife and some paper towels out to the front step to work on my shoe. Just as I thought, the deep indentations were really hard to get to. I held my breath and scraped. At least it's only one shoe, I thought. Could be worse.

Just as I finished, a car pulled into the driveway, and a woman got out carrying the food. "Oopsy-daisy," she said. "New shoes?"

"Pretty new. Almost done now," I said. "You were faster than I expected." She was holding three warm bags with grease spots on them. "That looks like a lot of food. Maybe I overdid it. I hope I have enough money."

"Sixteen-twelve?"

"Oh," I said. "Just a minute." I went inside and washed my hands. Then I dug in my wallet, pulling out a five, four ones, four quarters. "Do you take checks?" I called to the delivery woman.

"Cash only."

"Uh-oh. Wait a sec, OK?" I said, and went to the family room.

"Ma'am, I'm kinda on a schedule here."

"Be right with you," I said. "Todd, do you have any money?" Todd handed me his wallet. I went back to the front door, took another five and two ones from Todd's wallet, all the money he had, handed it to the woman with all of my money. "Keep the change?" I said.

She looked at it skeptically. "Are you sure you can spare it?"

"Sorry," I said. "It's all I have."

"Right." She turned away. "Whatever," she snarled over her shoulder.

"Sorry," I called after her. "Next time I'll be sure to—" Her car door slammed and she started backing fast down the driveway.

Now, if it had been me who found that twenty, the food would have been free, tip included.

I closed the door, gave Todd his wallet back, went to the kitchen, and started opening the bags. "This looks good." I divided the food between two plates.

Todd came to stand beside me. He frowned at the food. "Is it spicy?"

"I don't know yet," I said. "I'll tell you in a minute." I tried some cauliflower and peas. "Mmm," I said. "It's a little spicy. Not too. This is *so* good. I wish I could cook like this. Maybe I could take a class or something. Remember those Indian places in Cambridge?"

"Oh, God," Todd said, holding his stomach. "That's one thing I don't miss about Cambridge. The dirt, the sleaze."

"I miss the restaurants. And the people. I knew so many people there."

Todd looked at me, eating. "Drew started last Monday, and he's fine," he said. "He'll be fine. He's young, you know."

"He started that long ago, and you didn't even tell me?" I said. "I didn't think you heard me before." Still standing up at the kitchen counter, I put a big forkful of food in my mouth.

"I sort of did. I was thinking about this experiment I have to do tomorrow. Sorry. I'm going to bed. Drew and I are going to be working in another lab for a couple of days. We have to use some equipment we don't have. I want to get started early."

"Wait," I said. "Don't you want some of this food?"

"I already ate. I told you."

"No, you didn't. I asked you, but you didn't answer."

"I thought I did. Sorry. Night." He clicked off the television and went upstairs.

Even if I had stopped eating that very second, if I had dumped all the food straight into the garbage can and run up the stairs two at a time, when I got there, Todd would be under the covers already, with the light off. If I whispered to him, softly touching his skin, kissing him, he would say, "Jenny? Jenny, stop. I'm too stressed-out right now. I'm tired. Do you mind?"

I would say, "No. It's OK. Fine." And eventually, I would fall asleep.

So I didn't hurry up the stairs after him. I stood there and ate my dinner instead. Then I ate Todd's dinner. I threw away the containers, washed the plates, and went upstairs. I brushed my teeth, put on my nightgown, and climbed into bed. "Good night, Todd," I said, "I love you." I didn't wake him up, didn't even break the rhythm of his snoring.

I closed my eyes and saw the treasure box, the man, the flowers, the money on the sidewalk. I opened my eyes and looked at my husband. I thought of the things I said to him that he didn't hear, the things he seemed to hear then forgot immediately, the things I didn't bother to tell him in the first place because I knew he wouldn't listen. And it was this emptiness that had opened up between Todd and me that I couldn't stand anymore. *I am going to leave him,* I told myself, one part of me informing another. *Soon I will be gone.*

f o u r

IN-LINE SKATING FOR ADULTS. Leave your ego in the car, and come prepared to fall on your butt. We promise not to laugh at anyone but ourselves! This course meets daily until *everyone* can skate around the block as well as stop without mishap. Begins Sunday, August 17, 10 A.M. Course cost: $20. (You may bring your own safety equipment and in-line skates or rent them from the instructor at an additional charge.)

*I*N THE MORNING, I got ready for work the way I always did. I didn't want to go, but I couldn't stay home, either. I still didn't know anyone very well here, so I couldn't call in sick and take off somewhere with a friend for the day. Just getting my clothes on seemed difficult and took a long time. The bagel I ate for breakfast settled in my stomach like a stone coming to rest at the bottom of a pond.

As soon as I got to work, Bruce, our branch manager came to my desk. Quietly, he said, "Jenny, may I see you in my office, please?"

I followed him. Up to now, Bruce and I had had just one conversation. During my interviews with the bank when I was applying for my job, one of them was with Bruce. I remembered him asking me what I wanted to do in five years. I had looked at the ceiling for a moment before I answered, saying that analyzing loan applications was a rewarding experience for me, that five years from now I wanted to be processing a higher volume of larger loans. I tried to say all this so that it sounded sincere. I couldn't tell from his expression whether or not he believed me, but I did get the job.

Bruce left the door to his office ajar now, and I sat down in the comfortable chair opposite him. On his desk was a professional portrait of his five daughters, all blond, all dressed in white, and their dog, a yellow Labrador retriever. This was new since the last time I was here; I would have noticed a picture like that.

Bruce cleared his throat, folded his hands on top of his desk. "Jenny, I am going to have to let you go. I hate to do it, but I have no choice."

At first, I thought of Mrs. Randall. He was firing me for being heartless. I deserved it, I thought. I should have given her the money on the basis of human trust and a gut feeling that her idea was sound and that she was a good risk. Bank rules were not supposed to be applied literally; I should have known that. That's what Bruce was about to tell me, I thought, that I should have been more generous, more yielding.

Bruce said, "We've been very pleased with the work you've done, so I want to put those questions out of your mind right now. You've caught on quickly, worked hard, and fit in very well here. But I'm afraid the bank, on the corporate level, has mandated that all branches scale back. You see what kind of position that puts me in, I'm sure. We'll miss you. I know you haven't been with us long, but we're a family here, and we don't like to lose anybody." He explained about my severance package and what would become of my health insurance policy.

I couldn't take my eyes off the picture of his family, his real family. I said, "Wow, even your dog matches."

I guess he thought that was an odd thing to say for someone who had just been fired, that I was upset and thrown off balance. Bruce said, "Will you be all right? Can you get home by yourself?" He said this as if I had been drinking and it might not be safe for me to drive.

I said, "Oh. I see. You mean, I'm all finished? I can leave right now instead of tonight. Is that what you're saying?"

26

"Yes," he said. "Would you like some help with your things?"

"No, thanks," I said, standing up. "I got it."

Bruce went with me anyway. I got my coffee mug off my desk, some pictures of my mother and of Todd. I looked through all the drawers, but I couldn't find anything else that belonged to me. Bruce walked me to my car, giving the appearance of a caring send-off. But I wasn't sure. It might have been part of his job to make sure that I didn't steal anything or commit any acts of sabotage before he had a chance to revoke my computer password. As I drove off, I waved to him and tooted my horn, like a houseguest saying good-bye after a nice visit.

I went straight home and packed a suitcase.

MY MOTHER picked me up at Palomar Airport the next day. It's a small one north of San Diego, used by corporate jets; a few American Airlines and United flights, shuttling back and forth between there and Los Angeles; some helicopters; and a lot of small private planes, like my mother's. Hers is just four seats, including the pilot's, and no bathroom. She didn't own the whole plane, just a fifth. Four doctors she knew owned equal shares, but she was the one who used it most.

It was a clear, windy day, and I could see her coming for several miles. Her plane was a dot in the sky at first. Then, in a few minutes, it grew to look like a blue-gray radio-controlled toy, before lining up with the painted lines on the runway and bouncing a little as the tires hit the blacktop. My mother taxied to where I was standing, then climbed out to hug me.

As she put her arms around me there on the airfield, I thought to myself that no one at the airport would ever guess that we were mother and daughter. My mother and I are not alike. We do not eat alike, think alike, or look alike. While I am short—just under five feet two—my mother is five ten and a half. Her ancestors were Irish and English as far back as she knows, about four generations. Before her naturally curly hair started to turn white, she was a pale redhead with fair skin that she had to protect from sun and irritants like wool and bubble bath. My hair is another thing that separates me from my mother, not only because it is just shy of black with only the slightest bend of a wave to it, but also because it is so long. Since I was little, I have worn it the way it is now, in a single braid down my back that I frequently sit on and close in doors by accident. Sometimes I think about cutting my hair and switching to a more current style, maybe layered to my shoulders or a short wash-'n'-go cut that you might see in one of the women's magazines. But I know I won't do it. I have dark brown eyes to match my hair. When my mother and I stand side by side in front of a mirror, she looks pink and orange to me, while I see myself as on the yellow-green side of the complexion spectrum. Mexicans, Puerto Ricans, and Argentines have come up to me asking questions in Spanish, which I don't speak. Italians, Turks, Greeks, Egyptians, and Israelis have all guessed that I was one of them. And once, as I was watching a demonstration of Native Americans in Harvard Square, a participant asked me which reservation I was from. I could have belonged to any one of these groups. As an adoptee, I just didn't know anything about my own heritage.

I should have mentioned this earlier. I try to talk about the fact that I'm adopted as soon as I meet someone. I don't know if I feel this need to talk about it because I think being adopted is the most important fact about me, or if I just don't want anyone to think, later, that I've avoided talking about it.

You can see how it's always been a tricky subject. When I was little, several friends' mothers, on meeting mine, had said with surprise, "Oh! Jenny's father must be very dark." And my mother would say, "We assume so," creating an awkward silence followed by a flustered apology or a quick change of subject. "Jenny's adopted," my mother always added, though never quickly enough for me.

As a kid, I was usually the shortest and lightest in my class. In private, my mother had explained to me again and again why she didn't know more about the sources of my physical features. "They didn't tell us anything about the birth parents. They genuinely believed they were doing the right thing, that it was best for the children, the adopting families, and the birth mothers not to know anything about each other. They thought they were protecting everybody. I'm sorry, treasure. That's just the way they did it then."

"It's not your fault, Mom," I had to keep telling her.

If you woke my mother up in the middle of the night and said, "Quick! What was the happiest day of your life?" she would say without hesitation, March 19, 1962, the day I brought Jenny home." My birthday is March 10, but we always celebrated twice, first on that day and then to commemorate the day she got me—two batches of presents, two cakes, right up until I went away to college. Even now, she always sends me two packages and calls on both days.

"Isn't this nice?" my mother said now, looking around the airport. "Let's put your bag in the plane. I just want to activate my flight plan, then I've got to go to the bathroom. Is there any place to eat here? I'm starving. Have you had lunch?"

"I waited for you," I said. "There's a place over there." I pointed to the Runway Cafe.

"Cute," she said. "Let's go."

I followed her to the inside to a desk, then to the bathroom, then up the stairs to the cafe, the same way I'd trailed her around airports all over the country as a little girl and as a teenager. My mother started flying lessons when I was in third grade and gradually worked toward getting her instrument rating by the time I finished high school. Now she was certified to fly in any weather conditions. When I reached her the night before, she was working at a failing HMO up near Yosemite somewhere, finishing up several days of meetings. "Sure, I'll come and get you," she said. "What's the occasion?" When I didn't answer, she said, "I'll be there around noon."

After lunch, we climbed into the plane and took off. As soon as we reached our cruising altitude, my mother said, "So. Jenny. What's the problem? What happened?"

"I lost my job," I said.

"I see," said my mother. "But it wasn't exactly the ideal—"

"And I left Todd," I said. For as long as I can remember, the inside of an airplane has been the best place to talk to my mother about problems. Everyone should have one. It's easier to deliver bad news when my mother is scanning the sky for other aircraft or looking at her instrument panel and not at me. I waited for my mother to say something, to ask me a question. She didn't, so I went on. "Being with him was lonelier than being by myself. I couldn't stand it anymore."

"I see," she said. This was what my mother always said when I told her about a problem. She didn't believe in telling people what to do. "I suppose you've gone over all your choices together and decided that this is your only option." I looked at some clouds in the distance. "I'm very sorry, of course," she went on. "I'm sad to hear this. I love you both, and I hate to see any couple break up. But I know you wouldn't take this step unless you'd exhausted every other possibility. Having been through a divorce myself, I wouldn't wish it on anyone."

I said, "This isn't like you and Dr. Brown." I always call him Dr. Brown, though if you want to be technical about it, he is my father. William Brown, M.D., was head of the cardiology department in the New York hospital where he and my mother once worked together. For a well-connected doctor with a low sperm count, finding a healthy baby to adopt was not difficult. Making a family was harder for him, in fact, impossible, as it turned out. Just a year after they adopted me, my mother's husband left her, and she never remarried.

My mother says it was too humiliating to stay in that place, where Dr. Brown started dating other nurses even before the divorce was final. She moved the two of us to suburban Connecticut and got us settled in an apartment within the boundaries of the best school district she could find. Then she looked for a job. At first, the position she found was beneath her abilities, experience, and training, and she struggled for a while on her low salary. My mother would not accept alimony from Dr. Brown, only child support, and nursing has always been an underappreciated profession. But she stuck with it and worked her way up until she became head of the nursing department in her hospital. When I went away to college, she took a leave of absence from her job and spent a year in Alaska. She flew a plane (a different one then) to remote regions and provided medical care to people isolated by weather. Her specialty was bringing medical services to isolated areas, particularly places cut off by snow and mountains. She liked that kind of nursing, the independence she had, and the appreciation she received from the people she worked with. She used to tell me, "You get out in the middle of nowhere, and that's where nursing gets interesting, that's where you get the deep rewards." These days, she didn't work with patients much but as a consultant for new and existing medical-care facilities in remote regions.

"No two situations are alike," she said to me now. "But tell me, how is this different from my divorce?"

"No baby," I said. "No broken hearts."

"Are you sure?" she said. "About the hearts?"

I started to cry.

My mother pretended not to notice. "So what are you planning to do?"

"I'm moving back to Cambridge," I said, sniffing. "All my friends are there."

"You and Todd have had a lot of years together."

"He doesn't even see me anymore," I said. "It's like he's blind to anything you can't see through a microscope. I swear he'd be more interested in me if I were an aberrant piece of DNA. He'd listen to what I had to say." I sniffed again.

My mother pulled a tissue out of her jacket pocket and handed it to me. "And you've decided you don't want to give it more time?"

"I'll tell you what will happen," I went on, blowing my nose. "He'll stay in the same house, but he'll work even harder because I'm not there to make him feel guilty about not coming home. He'll probably get tenure a year or two ahead of schedule. Then one day he'll get to talking with one of his women postdocs. By then he'll have a whole lab full of them. They'll stay up all night, telling each other the stories of their lives. Todd will tell her that

I left him flat with no warning whatsoever. He won't mention all the time he forgot to look at me and didn't hear me talking to him. She'll be all sympathetic and understanding. They'll have the science to share between them. Eventually, he'll realize that the two of us had never been right for each other. He'll marry the postdoc and be much happier."

"And what about you? Have you made up a story for yourself, too?"

I said, "I need someone who talks, someone who listens. I just couldn't stand being there one more day. I was too lonely." I swallowed. I didn't mention the way we almost never touched anymore, hadn't had sex in who knew how long. Even in an airplane, it's not the kind of thing I'd care to talk over with my mother. "I might go to cooking school," I said, the thought just coming to me at that instant out of the clear blue sky, so to speak.

My mother said, "I see. Cooking school?"

We kept flying until we got to Phoenix, where we had to refuel and go to the bathroom. I thought I remembered this airport from another trip a long time ago, but I wasn't sure. "Call Todd," my mother said as she went to check on the weather. I scowled at her, but she insisted. "Go on. He'll want to know where you are," she said.

I didn't mention that I hadn't discussed my leaving with Todd, but my mother seemed to know this. I looked at my watch. "He won't be home yet."

She just looked at me and waited for me to go to the phone. I called Todd at the lab. There was no answer. He might have been in the cold room or the warm room or the tissue-culture room or some other room with a heavy door that shut tight. Then I remembered what he told me two nights before. "He's working in another lab today," I said to my mother at the airport manager's desk. "I don't know the number."

"Let's eat something, then you can try again."

After we ate, Todd still wasn't at the lab. I hung up and called again, in case I had dialed the wrong number. This time I let the phone ring twelve times. Still no answer. I called him at home, just so I could tell my mother I had tried everything and we could

32

get going again. The only time he ever went home early was when he spilled something radioactive on his clothes.

To my surprise, he answered on the first ring. "Jenny!" he said. "Where *are* you? Drew died in a car crash on his way to meet me this morning. My student, Drew. He's *dead!*"

"Oh, God," I said. "No. How awful." I could feel the blood leaving my head. I put my hand on the wall. My mother, watching me from the table, straightened, looking worried, alarmed at my expression.

Todd said, "I had to identify the body and call his parents, tell them their son was dead. They got here a couple of hours ago, and they're arranging to take the body back to Chicago." His voice sounded shaky and small. I don't think I had ever heard Todd's voice sound that way. "Where *are* you?" he said. "I called the bank, and they said you don't work there anymore. I've been going crazy trying to figure out where you were. I didn't even know where to start. I was worried. I thought maybe you—"

"I got fired yesterday. I didn't tell you. They're scaling back. I'm in Phoenix with my mother."

"Phoenix," he said, his voice flat now, as if he couldn't take in any more.

"She picked me up at Palomar Airport."

"I don't understand," he said. "You just decided to go on a trip without telling me?"

"I was just calling to tell you, to let you know where I was. When you weren't in the lab I—"

"Jenny, come *home,*" he said.

There was a clenching feeling in my throat. I squeezed my eyes shut tight. "I'll be there as soon as I can," I said to him. After I hung up the phone, I had to stand there a minute, to reorganize my thinking. A few minutes before, I had already left Todd. I was miles into my new life. Now I had to turn around.

I went back to my mother, who was waiting to hear what had made me turn pale and shaky after all my bold talk in the plane. I said, "I found him. I have to go right back. Could you fly me home, or do you have to be somewhere?"

"What?" she said. "What happened?"

"He had a graduate student working for him. He just started. Drew. I met him once. He seemed nice. He was only twenty-three or so. This morning, on his way to meet Todd, he was killed in a car crash. Drew was."

"What? Oh, *no!*"

"Yeah. Todd is completely freaked out. Understandably. So I have to go right back. I have to get home quickly."

"Sometimes, Jenny, life has a way of—"

"Don't," I said sharply.

"OK." She got out her wallet to pay our check.

f i v e

BOOGIE WITH YOUR BABY. It's never too early to
learn to dance! You and your infant will move to the beat of
rhythm 'n' blues, rock, and rap. Ages newborn to 6 months
(participants must be accompanied by an adult). Mondays,
3:00 to 3:30 P.M. on a come-if-you-can basis. Course cost:
$3/session.

*M*Y MOTHER had an important meeting the next day
and couldn't fly me back to Palomar. I had to wait a long time
for a flight to San Diego, paying a lot for the ticket because I was
only going one way and hadn't bought it in advance. It was
eleven-thirty by the time I got there. Todd was waiting for me at
the gate, his face pale and tight. He held me without speaking for
a minute. If I told you how long it had been since Todd touched
me this much, you'd be shocked. He said, "Let's not go home.
Let's go somewhere else, a hotel. I want to go someplace I've
never been before."

"All right," I said. "We'll just drive up the coast until we find
something."

I drove. Todd slumped in his seat and stared out the window.
After an hour or so, we came to an exit for Dana Point, and I
took it. There was a big hotel on a hill overlooking the ocean. I
went in and registered. Then I parked the car near our room. As

soon as I unlocked the door, Todd went in and dropped facedown on the bed.

TODD AND I had been together a long time. I met him when I was in college. He was almost finished when I still had more than a year to go. It wasn't a problem that I met him just as he was about to graduate because he wasn't leaving. He had years and years of graduate work ahead of him. When he got his degree, he just moved from MIT, where he had been an undergraduate, to Harvard Medical School for his graduate course work, and then went to work in a lab for a couple of years. For his postdoc, he moved to a lab at Tufts.

I met Todd at a conference for adoptees in Cambridge, the first event like that I had ever attended. Todd is also adopted. I should have told you this before. His story is a little different. Some disaster or series of them—poverty, illness, death, abuse, addiction—had caused him to be given away by his birth mother or taken from her at the age of two. He was adopted then by a couple in Iowa, owners of a small farm. They look like they could be his birth parents. Both are tall and blond like Todd, though it turned out that, while his adoptive parents are of Swedish descent, his birth mother's background was probably a mixture of Polish and German. For one of the years he was an undergraduate, he was also trying to find his birth mother. He took a semester off to give his search his full attention. I met him when he had just completed his search. The woman at the end of the trail had died when Todd was ten, in Detroit, of medical complications resulting from alcoholism.

I didn't know if finding out about the birth mother who died was the end of it for Todd. If he ever fantasized that he had ended up in the wrong place, that there was someone else out there, his *real* birth mother, someone healthy and strong, who wanted to find him, he didn't talk to me about it. He would never say that; it's just that I think it's the way I would feel. To me, one of the problems with searching is that often what you find is not what you wanted. After he got the information about the woman who died, he started putting all his energy into science, accelerating his years of course work, research, and his postdoc, more than making up for the time he had lost.

At the conference where I met Todd, he was speaking to small groups about databases and how to use them. I went because I always felt lonely and disconnected. It was possible that everyone else felt this way, too, and no one had ever thought to mention it to me. Or maybe the fact that I was an only child or the child of a divorced couple made me feel more isolated than people who grew up with brothers and sisters and their parents' marriage intact. But it seemed most likely that I felt lonely all the time because I was adopted. I decided to go to an adoptees' conference to find out if there was anything I should know, anything going on there that could make me feel better.

As an adoptee, I had always thought about my birth mother. I longed to look like someone. I had had all the adoptee's fantasies about my birth mother: that someday she would come and find me, that I had been stolen from her, that she was looking for me all the time, that she was my fourth-grade teacher, that she was someone famous on TV, that she was the perfect mother who never yelled or got tired or had to work. I'd also had the other kind of fantasies: that my birth mother was a drug addict or a prostitute; that she couldn't wait to get rid of me the second I was born; that she had some fatal hereditary disease, which I had inherited but didn't know about yet; that she had forgotten all about me. A lot of other people were searching for their birth mothers, not just scanning rows of faces on buses and trains and comparing themselves in the mirror to pictures of movie stars, but deliberately and systematically demanding their non-identifying information, going over hospital records, and joining services and groups devoted to searching.

As soon as I got to the conference, I regretted going. In small discussion groups and large auditoriums, people were talking about issues like genetic heritage, birth mothers searching for the now-grown children they had given up years before, the need to establish an identity. After about two hours, I had had enough. In a panel discussion of birth mother searches-in-progress, my cheeks got hot, my hands went clammy, and I felt light-headed. I thought I might be sick to my stomach, and I had to leave.

I met Todd on my way out. He followed me to the lobby of the conference center. "Excuse me? Miss?" he called as I reached the door.

I didn't turn around. I felt as though I were ditching school and a teacher had caught me.

"Hey, wait!" Todd said more forcefully.

I stopped and looked back at him. Standing there was a very tall guy with flyaway blond hair, wearing old blue jeans that were a little bit too short. "Yes?" I said. It may be that, as a group, adoptees are particularly attracted to people who are their complete opposites: You choose someone who appears as genetically dissimilar to yourself as possible, eliminating any possibility of finding out later that you've slept with a sibling. All Todd's girlfriends before me were small and dark, and all my boyfriends had been tall and blond.

Todd said, "Where are you going?"

I said, "I have to leave."

"Oh," he said. "I was hoping you'd come to my seminar. It starts in ten minutes."

"No," I said. "This really isn't for me. I have to go. I think I might throw up or faint or something."

"Really?" he said. "I hope not. Let's get you outside so you can get some air." We stepped out. It was one of those fiercely cold days in Cambridge with wind that lashes your cheeks and makes your eyes water, and snow that has turned to gray ice sculptures that seem ancient and forever. It felt good to have the cold scratch at my face and clutch at me through the loose stitches of my sweater. I didn't put my coat on right away. "Better?" Todd said. "OK now?" He didn't have his coat with him, of course. He put his arms around himself but didn't go back inside yet. "I know how you feel. It's kind of overwhelming sometimes. Could you just give me your phone number so I can call you in case you decide you don't want to come back to the conference? Could you do that? Please? We could get together for, um, coffee, or something? Do you live here in Cambridge?"

"Yes," I said.

"Are you a birth mother or adopted?" he asked me.

"Adopted."

"Already, we have a lot in common." He smiled at me. I remember his face, the way the right side of his mouth went up a little more than the left and the front tooth that overlapped its neighbor just a little; the way his cheeks flushed pink; and that his eyes were as blue as the cold, bright sky. I gave him my number.

In the beginning, being with another adoptee was like meeting someone from your home country after living for years in a foreign land among natives whose language you were still trying to learn. We moved in together after just two months. Even back then, I remember thinking that it would be difficult for Todd to leave me or for me to leave him because of the fact that we were both adopted. Knowing how vulnerable we both were to feelings of abandonment, our relationship seemed sealed forever, complete and irrefutable. At the time, I found this gave me a feeling of security and belonging, which, of course, was exactly what I wanted.

One of the things Todd liked most about me when we first got together was that I was not a scientist. He used to pick up whatever I was reading and look over the pages, even if it was a magazine article about how to make the most of your cheekbones. He let me choose the movies we saw, as if this were more my area. It didn't seem to bother him that I was unfocused and directionless about a career. As a matter of fact, I think that was one of the things that attracted him to me. As a scientist, there was such a predictability about his career: first the undergraduate degree, then the graduate course work, followed by working in a lab and publishing a few papers, the postdoc and some more publications, the assistant professorship, tenure, several levels of associate professorship, full professorship. There was always a great deal of tension about whether or not he was going to make it to each subsequent step, but that was part of it, too. Todd liked the way that even up to the last year of college, I was still considering changing my major and the way I wasn't even sure what kind of job to look for after I graduated.

For a couple of years after college, I was a waitress at a hamburger restaurant in Cambridge. I liked the closeness between the waitresses who worked there. But I didn't like having people I didn't know touching me and calling me honey, and being obliged to indulge their food hang-ups—that the mayonnaise should be on one side of the bread only or that there should be no more than three ice cubes in the glass. Eventually, I decided to go to graduate school myself. Everyone else we knew had or was working on some advanced degree. My field was going to be psychology. Todd thought psychology was slightly comical because it was not a "real" science, like biology, chemistry, or physics. But it was not the research part of it that interested me anyway. I was attracted by the idea of understanding the way people think, figuring out where they get off track, and helping them find a way back. But my program had more to do with personality testing and statistics than helping anyone who was in trouble. I quit after less than a year.

I took a word-processing course. I worked for a law firm until the partners decided to move their offices to the suburbs, then for a small business magazine, which folded after six months. Briefly, I considered a law degree, and then I thought about a master's in journalism. I also considered more computer courses. In Cambridge, you can study just about anything you want. But you do have to decide what it is you want to learn, and that was the part I was having trouble with.

Finally, I decided not to decide. What I really wanted to do was to search for my own birth mother. I had thought about her every day of my life since I was old enough to think about such things. Now I wanted to take some real steps toward finding her. I signed on to a couple of databases, giving all the facts of my adoption so that if she were searching for me that way, now she could find me. I knew that for a lot of people the search process took a long time or never succeeded. But I remember feeling optimistic, convinced that all I had to do was make the decision that I wanted to find her or be found, and it would happen.

It didn't happen. I had pictured my search taking about a month, maybe two at most. After three months, I started going to conferences regularly, networking with other adoptees and birth mothers, sometimes traveling to New York or Philadelphia or Washington, D.C. I read all the adoption literature I could find. I used up the little money I had saved from my jobs, and then I got some from my mother. I kept thinking, if I can just have another month, I will find her. Then everything will settle down, and I can figure out what I'm supposed to be doing with my life. I imagined myself having a career, moving systematically up some professional ladder, rung by rung. I thought that once my birth mother was a known quantity in some not-too-distant city and with my mother within reach in Connecticut, birthday presents arriving precisely on time from both of them, I would be all set. If I found my birth mother, my professional path would also become clear to me.

Todd and my mother were very supportive about the search. "If it's that important to you," my mother said, "I'm happy to help."

I kept searching for two years. It was all I wanted to talk about, all I thought about. Being an adoptee was my occupation, my hobby, my passion, my obsession, all at once. I talked about it at parties, at home with Todd. I never doubted for a moment that my search was as interesting to everyone else as it was to me. I was on the phone all the time with other adoptees and anyone who could help me search.

We had a big phone bill. Before I knew it, I had spent a lot of time and money and still hadn't found my birth mother. For about the first year and a half or so, my friends were pretty tolerant. When they asked me how I was, I gave them an update on my search. In the middle of a meal, a conversation, a movie, I would get up and call our answering machine. I always worried that someone (my birth mother or someone with information about her) might have called me in the fifteen minutes since I had last checked.

My best friend Kathy was the first person to suggest that I give up. We were having lunch in a restaurant in Cambridge. Right after we ordered, I said, "I have to go use the phone."

Kathy said, "We just got here."

I said, "This will only take a second."

She said, "Jenny, how long are you going to do this?"

I bristled. "Until I find my birth mother."

Kathy said, "But what if you don't find her?"

I just looked at her. I couldn't believe she was saying this, knowing my search was vital to me.

"I'm just afraid you're going to feel bad in a couple of years if you end up with nothing to show for this period in your life," she told me quietly, and I could tell she had been planning to say this, working up her nerve. "You're not working. Other people are moving ahead in their jobs, and you're not doing anything."

"It may not seem like anything to *you*," I said. "You've got your mother's cheekbones and your father's widow's peak. You've got four brothers who look just like you, two complete sets of grandparents, and jewelry and anecdotes from a great-grandmother! I don't have any of that. I *am* doing something. It's something to *me*!" I stomped out of the restaurant.

I knew that, in part, she was right, though I wasn't about to admit it. I kept having this feeling that if I just got one lucky break, I'd find my birth mother, that I might be just a phone call away from locating her. On the other hand, I might not; I might be waiting for a lucky break for the rest of my life.

I talked to Todd about it. He said, "Some searches take a long time."

"And some are never completed."

He said, "You have to decide. If you want to keep going, you should."

"You don't think I'll find her, do you?"

"Jenny, I have no idea," he said, taking my hand, placing it against his cheek. "How would I know that?"

I said, "I heard about a woman who looked for her birth mother every day for *ten* years. Finally, she found her living two streets away. And another woman I talked to was sixty-one years old when she found her birth mother, who was eighty, still healthy and spry and so happy to be found!"

"Yeah," Todd said. "There are a lot of stories like that to keep you going." He rubbed my back. Neither of us pointed out that there was a huge number of people who searched for years and years and never got close to finding their birth mothers.

"Does it bother you that I'm not working?" I said.

"Not really."

"You mean it does."

"What? I said 'not really.' "

" 'Not really' means not very much, so it *does* bother you. Even if it's only a little bit, it's there. It does bother you to some extent."

Todd sighed. "I understand what you're going through. I've been there myself, so I get it. Sure, it would be great if you were working and we had more money, but that's not our story right now. OK? I can live with this."

"Fine," I said. "Great. Perfect. I'll stop searching. I'll do something more productive, if that's what you want. I'll get some *job*."

"It's up to you," he said. "All I'm saying is you decide."

I stopped searching. For quite a while, I had felt guilty about all the time and money and attention it was taking. And if I were really honest about it, which I rarely was, I had this feeling that my search was consuming me, eating me alive. I was becoming nauseatingly narrow, even to myself. And lately I was starting to believe that my birth mother really was one of the ones who would never be found. Maybe she was in another country or dead or unreachable in some other way.

A few days after Todd and I talked about it, I decided to make a clean break, start something big and practical that would get me somewhere, that would eventually lead to a job, maybe even a career. I signed up for some business courses at BU, planning to go for an MBA. Before the classes even started, I got a job in a Cambridge bank. I put off the degree program temporarily, then never got back to it.

Working in a bank never felt right, either, though I worked my way up several steps until I was evaluating loan applications. I even felt like an impostor in the clothes, someone in a costume.

The small talk and the superficial relationships that developed at work seemed almost intolerable. But I was relieved of a tremendous burden of guilt just by earning a modest salary, and I forced myself to get used to all the rest of it, believing that most people didn't love their jobs. Most people were not like Todd with a talent to solve a certain kind of problem, with a passionate belief in the importance of doing so and the drive to get it done as quickly as possible. Those were the things that I loved most about Todd, his ability to focus completely on achieving a goal and his unyielding drive, exactly the qualities that I lacked.

THE DAY AFTER we checked into the hotel in Dana Point, while Todd was asleep, I went out on the balcony with my book and sat there reading until the sun disappeared and goose bumps rose on my legs. I ordered dinner from room service. Even when I talked on the phone, Todd didn't open his eyes. Whenever he was depressed, he slept as if he had been forced to stay awake for months. Our dinner arrived, and I ate. He rolled around a little but didn't get up. I watched television, took a bath, went to bed.

Sometime after I had fallen asleep, I heard him get up and go to the bathroom. He got back into bed and held me close. "What's the point?" he said. "What's the point of anything? He wanted a skateboard," Todd said. "He wanted to learn to do the ramps and the turns and all the fancy stuff. We had a talk about whether twenty-three was too old to learn. I said twenty-three wasn't too old for anything. I said twenty-three was just the beginning. He listened to me. He went out and bought full gear, knee and elbow pads, a helmet. He brought them to the lab to show me. It mattered to him what I thought. He was about to buy a used board. He was just deciding which one. I had to pack the helmet and pads with his other things and give them to his father." Todd started to cry. I cried with him. After a long time like that, holding each other in the dark, Todd telling me every little detail he had learned in the short time he had known Drew, we fell asleep.

When we woke up, it was after ten in the morning. We ate

breakfast and went down to the beach, though it was foggy and cool. We spread out towels in the sand. Todd was staring at things—shells, rocks, the water, lumps of sand—as if angry that they dared to exist. Then his face would crumple like an exhausted child, and he would cry again. In all my years with Todd, I had only seen him cry a couple of other times. "Life is so lonely, Jenny," he said.

"I know," I said. "I'm adopted, too, remember?"

He laughed. I reached for him, took his hand. "We only have each other," he said. He squeezed my hand. "That's the only thing that means anything to me."

"That's not true," I said. "You have your parents. You have your work."

"Empty," he said.

We took a walk down the beach. He kept his arm around me the whole way, his fingers tightly gripping my T-shirt, as if I might try to jerk away and run, as if he wanted to be ready to catch me, hold me back.

WE WENT HOME late that afternoon. Because Drew had been his only student so far, there was no one back in the lab waiting for his input or needing to be kept on track. He had a few other students coming, but they weren't expected to start for another few weeks.

That whole day, Todd kept touching me, warily keeping me in sight. As we got ready to go, he seemed a little better. He bought me a magazine in the lobby and helped me pack our things into the trunk of the car. After he slammed it shut, he held my upper arms and looked straight into my eyes. He said, "I'm a jerk. I don't pay enough attention to you sometimes. But if I try to do better, will you stay with me forever? I love you. Do you know that?" He pressed my body tightly against his.

I don't think he knew that I had tried to leave him, but what he said made me shiver. I said, "I love you, too." I drove us home.

———

WHEN WE PULLED into our driveway, I had a kind of sinking feeling, knowing that everything was about to go back to normal, something like the feeling of returning to school in the fall after a summer of freedom. I cheered up a little when I remembered that I had been fired. I pulled up on the parking brake, and Todd said, "Jenny, I know what! You could come and work with me in the lab! Yeah, I need somebody, and that way, we could be together all the time!"

I got my suitcase out of the trunk and carried it inside. Upstairs, I started putting my things away. Todd followed me up. "Well?" he said.

"Well what?"

"Will you come to the lab and work with me? It's perfect. I have money for a technician in my grant."

"I don't want to be your technician. I don't want to work in a lab. I don't know the first thing about it."

"I could show you what to do."

I shook my head. "I don't even like the smell. I know you're lonely there, but soon you'll have more students. I have to find a job I like. I'm sorry, but I can't go work there just to keep you company."

"Fine," he said, pressing his lips together.

I flung my braid around my neck: a boa. "It would be all wrong for me. I wouldn't like it at all." I pulled upward on the end: a noose.

Todd looked at his watch. "I understand. I'm going now. I have to refresh my cells."

"Oh, great!" I said. "Just wonderful. See you about midnight, then." I flipped my braid to the back and went to put my toothbrush and shampoo away.

"What?" Todd said. "You knew I had to go to the lab. If I don't go, all my cells will die. I'll have to start all over. Don't act like this."

"Sorry," I said. "I'm just crabby because you have somewhere to go, and I don't. Go ahead. I'll see you later."

He left. I went for a walk.

I walked to the school in my best time yet, twenty-four

minutes. I planned to pick up a course catalog. Maybe there was a course in getting a stuck marriage to work again. I started to feel a little more optimistic as I walked. I would meet other people in a similar situation, develop strategies, work through this step by step.

When I got to the building, the doors were locked. I had forgotten it was Sunday. I walked home.

THE HISTORY OF THE UNIVERSE. Our instructor
will tell you his theory of how everything started and what
happened after that; then he'll listen to yours. Monday,
September 8, 7–8 P.M. Course cost: $5. Refreshments
included.

*L*EAVING SOMEONE is more complicated than walk-
ing out the door with a suitcase. I wasn't going anywhere, after
all. Maybe I had always known this and was just admitting it to
myself now. I had to find ways to make myself feel better without
abandoning Todd. I set about my search for happiness the same
way I always had, by trying to surround myself with more people.
I remembered that I had the phone number of someone I knew
from my waitress days, Melissa Halloran, who had moved here
several years before. All the waitresses had gotten together to give
her a party at the restaurant when she left, presenting her with
sunscreen, sunglasses, a beach towel—everything in a beach bag
with her name on it.

I dialed the number, rehearsing the message I would leave on
her machine: "Hi, Melissa. This is Jenny Brown. My husband,
Todd, and I moved out here a few months ago. I thought maybe
we could get together sometime. My schedule is pretty open."
Then I'd give my number and hang up.

Melissa herself answered on the second ring. "Hello?"

"Hi," I said, startled, unprepared. "This is Jenny Brown."
There was a pause. "I'm sorry," she said. "Who?"

"We used to work together? At the Burger Thing?" I said.
"In Massachusetts? It was quite a while ago."

"Oh," she said, "Long braid, right? Now I got it. Sorry, I
was thinking more in the present, more locally."

"Sure," I said. "Anyway I called because my husband and I
moved to San Diego a few months ago. I remembered that you
lived around here, too. I don't know many people here yet, and
I thought maybe you and I could get together sometime."

"Uh, sure," she said. "Why not? Let me just get my calendar." When she came back, she said, "So what are you doing out
here anyway?"

"My husband, Todd, got a job at the university. He's an assistant professor. I was working at a bank, but I just got laid off."

"Too bad," she said. "So what are you going to do now?"

"I'm not sure, yet," I said. "I'm thinking of changing jobs.
I never really liked banking. I might take a class or something
before I decide."

"A class?" she said. I heard paper, the pages of her calendar
turning.

"I'm enrolled in an acting class right now," I said. It just
popped into my head, something to say next. There was a silence.
I went on, explaining, "I mean, I've never done it before, but I
thought—"

"Acting?" she said. "*Acting?* You're going to start acting at,
what are you, thirty-five?"

"Oh. Is that bad?"

"Do you have any idea how many actors there are in this state?
Do you have even the vaguest notion of how many attractive, well-
trained people with years of experience are out there looking for
acting jobs right this very second?"

"No," I said. "How many?" Then I remembered that Melissa
had been a theater major in college, before she worked in the
restaurant, that she originally came out here because she wanted
to do something in movies. I couldn't remember what—screen

writing, directing. Now that I thought about it, maybe it was acting. I said, "I don't think any of those people should feel the least bit threatened."

"Well," she said, disgusted with my naïveté. "Do what you want. And about getting together—"

I said, "Come to think of it, I'll have to call you back. I just realized I left my calendar at the, um, Laundromat."

"Right," she said. "OK, call me back."

"Sure thing," I said, and hung up fast.

WHEN I WENT BACK to the acting class, the teacher wasn't there yet. There was a note on the blackboard in the classroom. It said, WAIT. DON'T LEAVE.

I sat down. I went over my speech one more time, and I noticed a couple of other people doing the same thing. The students didn't seem to know each other; there was no talking. About twenty minutes after the class was supposed to start, the dance teacher I'd seen twice in the room down the hall came in. He was wearing black bike shorts this time, and he was a little sweaty. He must have just finished teaching a class. "I'm Michael," he said. "Rory had to go out of town on short notice and couldn't make it. Just for tonight, you've got me. Rory said you all had your speeches memorized, and we could listen to them. So that's what we'll do. But don't ask me anything technical because I've never done this before. We'll start with you. You can sit in this chair in front here, and we'll be the audience. Unless you want to stand up. Would that be better? What's your name?"

He was looking at me. "Jenny," I said. Of course, I had planned to go last. I was going to explain that I had never even thought of taking an acting class until I got into this one by mistake, that I'd managed to memorize my speech, but I didn't really know what else I was supposed to be doing. But now that I was here, everything I had planned to say seemed inappropriate. The thing to do would be to say all the words of the speech and then get back to my seat again quickly without thinking about any-

50

thing. Before I knew it, my turn would be over and everyone would be looking at someone else.

I sat down in the chair in front of the class. I started. With the words memorized, it wasn't so hard. It felt almost as if someone else were speaking, the character I was pretending to be, this other person I had no responsibility for. I came to the end. Michael stared at me silently for a long time. He had greenish brown eyes and wavy brown hair that was on the long side with a little gray scattered through it.

I didn't know what to do next. Was I supposed to wait for him to make a comment? Was I supposed to say something myself? I just sat there, feeling myself turn red as he kept looking at me.

"Well!" Michael said suddenly. "Thank you!" Then he looked around to choose the next person. I got up and went back to my seat.

A man named Edward sat down in the chair that I left vacant. He was in his late forties, maybe fifty. Halfway through his speech, I thought, This is not the right monologue for him; he would be more convincing as someone younger. I even had the speech in mind. The day before, I had checked out *Spoon River Anthology* from the library and read it straight through. I was unemployed; I had plenty of time.

When the class was over, I got up to leave.

Michael said, "Excuse me, Ginny, was it?"

"Jenny," I said.

"Sorry. Jenny. Could you stay just a minute? I want to talk to you."

I stood up and joined a group of class members waiting to ask Michael questions. When my turn came, I couldn't imagine what he had to say to me. He looked at me as a pause opened up between us. "I was wondering." I looked at the paper I was holding with my speech on it, rolled up now into a tube. "Would you like to teach a course?"

I stared at him. "What?"

"I was just thinking, since you're so poised and comfortable in front of a group, you might like to teach. All you have to do is give me a title and a course description. I'll get it in next month's catalog. Or maybe if you want to start sooner than that, I could put up signs for you. Let me give you something. Here." He reached down and rummaged in his bag at his feet on the floor. There was a bottle of water in it, shoes, a book.

"Teach?" I said. "Teach what? I don't know how to do anything." This place was even stranger than I thought.

He pulled a wrinkled T-shirt from his bag. "School shirt," he explained. "Take it. It's for you."

"Oh!" I said, suddenly understanding that the wrinkled thing he was handing me was new, a gift. I held up the shirt. It was yellow and huge, size XXL. I read the writing on the front: THE ANSWER IS YES. I turned it over. NOW, WHAT'S YOUR QUESTION? I said, "Thank you. I've seen this before. I didn't know it was from here. What's the name of this place anyway?" I turned the shirt over, looking for the name of the school in small print somewhere, but there was just a phone number.

"I wanted to call it the Yes School, but people talked me out of it. No one thought it sounded official enough. We call it the Institute of Affirmation. I guess it works. That's our slogan there on the shirt, you know, and our philosophy. Is that the right size?"

I held it up. It hung down past my knees. "It's a little big."

"Oops. I gave you the wrong one. I meant to give that to one of the larger gals in my dance class." He dug around in his bag again. "Here's one." He handed another shirt to me, purple with white letters.

"Thanks," I said. "So this is your school?"

"I started it," he said, nodding. "I had to think of something to make my place stand out. You know there are quite a few adult education places to choose from in this area. But at the Institute of Affirmation, every idea you have is a good one and no one ever tells you no. There are plenty of places out there to say that your idea won't work, that you ought to start over at the beginning, that other people can do what you want to do better, that will tell you over and over that it's a competitive world with no place in it for what you have. I saw right off that the no field was already pretty crowded. So we say yes." He smiled at me. "We don't make an issue of talent or ability. You just have to be willing."

"Willing," I said.

"I liked your speech. You've done a lot of acting. I could hear it."

My ears burned. I folded up the shirt neatly.

"No, listen," Michael said, "it's OK that you're in a class for beginners. That's not a problem. I didn't mean that. I'm just saying you're very good. Interesting to watch."

"That's nice of you to say." I imagined that, in keeping with the school's philosophy, he always complimented people on whatever they did. I wondered how he made his voice sound so convincing, his face look so sincere. "I got into this class by accident one night," I found myself saying. "I was on a walk and came in here looking for a drinking fountain. I've never done anything like this before. Acting, I mean. Ever. I'm not sure why I came back, what I was—"

"You must come from a theatrical family, I guess," he said.

"Maybe," I said. "I'm adopted, so I don't know." For once, I had the perfect opening and got this out right away. Of course, this was one time when it was not necessary. I could have just shaken my head and said no and that would have been plenty. I went on. "Maybe my birth parents are circus performers or politicians. Then again, they might be postal workers or party planners, writers of defense software. I really don't know."

Michael opened his mouth to say something, but I wasn't finished. "Teachers, executives, sanitation workers, housecleaners. They could be anything." I shrugged my shoulders and gave him an opening to say something. He didn't. "My mother's a nurse," I went on. "My adoptive mother. No theatrical background in my upbringing at all." I didn't know why I was blabbing along this way. I looked at the shirt again. "I like it," I said. "I should go."

"So bring in your course description, and we'll get you set up with a room and a time."

"No," I said. "I'm not going to teach anything. What would I teach?"

Michael said, "Oh, it could be anything. Sewing? Wilderness

survival skills? Window-box gardening? Here, have a copy of our catalog." He reached into his bag again. "Maybe it will give you some ideas."

"I don't think so." I took the catalog and shook my head. "But thanks for the catalog. I've been meaning to pick up one of these. Do you want the shirt back because I'm not going to teach a class?" I said.

"No, no. Please wear it. It's advertising. I try to give away ten a day. I set myself a goal and try to follow through on it. It's almost nine-thirty, and I've still got three more to give away, not counting the one I gave you."

"Oh," I said. "OK. Sure. If you think it will help."

"It does. Really," he said. "See you soon. Come to my dance class sometime. First class is free."

I was backing out of the room. "Thanks, but I—"

"No experience or sense of rhythm? You can't even touch your toes? It's OK. Really," he said. "Nondancers are my specialty. Nice talking to you."

"Thanks for the shirt," I said, and set off for home.

I GOT A JOB interview. The bank was just ten minutes away, near the beach. It was a small bank, not one of the monster chains. The people seemed friendly. There were a couple of women my age. The manager, Sharon Armstrong, didn't ask me any open-ended questions designed to test my personality. She stuck with where I'd worked before, whether I would mind staying late on Wednesdays when the bank was open until nine. We talked a long time. There was a good chemistry between us. I could picture shopping for shoes with her or going to the movies; I could see us becoming friends.

The next day, I went back for a second interview with a district manager. That went well, too. He and Sharon took me to lunch. We had a nice conversation at an Italian restaurant, and I even laughed a lot without feeling forced or fake.

I bought a couple of new outfits I could wear to work and some things I'd been wanting to get but had felt too guilty about spending the money for, pillows for the couch and a couple of CDs. I wasn't really happy about going back to work at a bank, but I was relieved that I wouldn't have to feel bad anymore about not having a job.

AT THE NEXT acting class, Rory was absent again. Michael came in late, carrying a clipboard. "I'm happy to report that Rory got a directing job in L.A.," he said. "Everyone here at the Institute of Affirmation is very excited for her." He sank into a chair and rubbed his forehead.

One woman seemed ready for a fight. "Are you canceling the class? We're getting a full refund, I hope. She only showed up the one time, remember."

"Could you get another teacher?" suggested a teenage girl. "Could we still take the class with someone else?"

A boy behind her said, "Maybe you could teach it."

Michael said, "As I mentioned last time, I don't know anything about acting. Zip. And there are scheduling problems. My Hip Hop for Elders class goes another fifteen minutes after this one starts. I had to dismiss them early these last two sessions. That class has been going for eight months, and I really don't think a change of schedule would be fair to my people." He looked at his watch. "In half an hour, I've got Big Bodies Bounce."

"Great, just great," said a man near the back of the class. "You finally get everything organized so you can do something you've always wanted to, and it gets canceled on you." This was Edward, I remembered from last time, a tall man with a pot belly and a bald spot in the center of his dark hair. I could imagine him getting a lot of other things under control before signing up for this class: a job, a family, a mortgage, a sprinkler system—practical and worthwhile things whose management didn't necessarily leave a person feeling unique or special.

There was some whispering and a murmur of disgruntled talk among the class members.

Michael sat there for a few minutes, letting the class talk. Then he said, "What I was hoping—I thought if we could all put our heads together, maybe we could come up with some way to work this out. Some idea, something..." He trailed off and looked around the room. "We should keep the class, and maybe ... a new idea, something exciting that we hadn't expected to ... uh ..."

There was a silence. Maybe he had just heard about Rory's leaving for Los Angeles and hadn't had time to give the problem much thought. "Here's an opportunity," Michael said. "Someone in this room has a great idea, something we hadn't planned on that will turn out even better than the class we thought we were going to have." He looked around, waiting for someone else to speak. They don't have the money to offer a refund, I thought.

Another grumble rippled through the class. I thought I heard the phrase "Better Business Bureau" coming from somewhere near the back of the room.

"Instead of a class on technique, what about all of us working toward a performance, a production of this same piece we were working on, but one that friends and family could come and see." Everyone turned in their seats to face the middle of the room and see who was speaking. They were looking at me; I was the one talking.

Michael said, "Well, I—" and then I interrupted him.

"We wouldn't really need a teacher. It's a pretty straightforward piece. But we would shift the focus of the class to practicing for a performance, rather than centering on the craft, since, at the moment, as far as I know, we don't have anyone qualified to teach that."

The room was quiet. I looked around. Everyone was looking at me, waiting for me to go on, to hear what else I might have to say.

I stood up and continued. "We could use this room right here, put some chairs here for the performers, more chairs over here for the audience. We could invite the other people taking classes here at the school. If no one shows up, then we could perform it for each other."

I found that now I was walking to the front of the room, picking up a piece of chalk from the tray in front of the blackboard. I looked at it a second, wondering what I was about to do, then I drew two semicircles on the chalkboard, representing the chairs the performers would sit in and the chairs the audience would occupy.

"If you had the actors' chairs here and the audience's chairs there, you'd have hardly any distinction between us and them, you know, actors and audience. It could look like a group therapy session or some kind of twelve-step meeting." Or an adoptees' support group, I thought to myself. "This way, you would suggest a context for all these people standing up and talking about themselves. I mean, you wouldn't *say* it was a self-help group, but the presentation could suggest that. Now, I realize these people are dead. So let's say it's self-help in the afterlife. Whatever. It's kind of a loose concept. We could put a video camera here, tape the whole thing, and sell copies to anyone who wants to buy one, maybe make a little money for the school. I was thinking that for costumes, we could—" I stopped. Some of the people in the class were taking notes on what I was saying. Michael was leaning forward slightly, waiting to hear the rest. "But then, maybe someone else has another idea." I put the chalk back.

"I like it," said Edward, beginning to copy my simple diagram.

A woman in the back spoke next. "This sounds like it could really go. I think we should charge admission, don't you, Michael? Just a couple bucks. Because, I mean, who's going to come if it's free? That would seem a little desperate, wouldn't it?" The woman was tall and about fifty years old. She wore a lot of lipstick and blue eye shadow and a hot pink jogging suit in some kind of slippery material. I could see her as a school principal or a state senator, someone highly competent who had the ability to get people to do things they didn't necessarily want to.

Michael was still looking at me, lips parted. He seemed poised to jump. "Yes!" he said, standing up so fast he knocked his clipboard to the floor with a bang.

The noise startled me, and I felt self-conscious standing there with the chalk in my hand. I sat down. Some of the class members nodded, smiling at me.

Michael said, "Now, we're going to need a director." He was looking at me expectantly.

Quickly, I looked down at the floor, put my hand to my brow as if shielding my eyes from a bright light.

"Or," Michael said, "not." He thought a minute. "Actually, we don't need anything like a director at all. What was I thinking? Because you're all in this together, right? Everyone will help each other. We won't have anyone in *charge* or making *decisions* or anything like that. We'll just need one person to set the rehearsal schedule, jot down the performance times for the office, that kind of thing. Nothing major, no responsibilities, pressures, or, you know, duties." He wasn't looking at me anymore.

He sat down, picked up his clipboard, and wrote something. "Unfortunately, *I* can't do this," Michael said, pointing to his chest, shaking his head. "If the class time were different, I'd be fine with it. Even a person like me with no experience at all could handle this. But I've already explained the problems." He looked at the class, and we did our best not to look back at him. "I can't be here for your rehearsals." He lifted his hands, looking around the room helplessly. "You can decide everything as a group with nobody telling anyone else what to do. Easy. I'll just need to check in with one person every now and then to see how it's going." Eyes went down; the room became silent. It seemed as if everyone was being careful not to move in case the slightest gesture might be taken as sign of volunteering. "I wouldn't ask anyone to take charge. No way. That wouldn't be fair, would it? You're all beginners. It would be unreasonable of me to expect any of you to put a lot of extra time into a production, even a small and simple one like this. And we wouldn't ask any one of you to act as an authority over the others, deciding that one idea is more practical, say, than another one. We don't even need that. We just need somebody to be the link between the school and the production. A liaison between the class and the office. Just anyone willing to jot down rehearsal and performance schedules and hand them in up front so we know when you're using the room. That's all. Nothing much, right? No big deal. You'll just be the scheduler.

Anyone who wouldn't mind writing down the rehearsal schedule and leaving it in the office for me?"

I felt my hand going up, fingers rising toward the ceiling, as if hoisted up by an invisible string. "I guess I could do it," I said. There was movement and sound in the room again. A couple of people exhaled loudly. "If it's just writing down the times we—"

"That's all it is," said Michael quickly, standing up. "Sure. Absolutely. Perfect. Any questions, just ask Jenny here." He picked up his clipboard from the floor.

I said, "Well, I don't know if I can answer any *questions,* or—you know, I've never done anything—" The class was giving me a round of applause now, and no one heard what I was saying.

From the door, Michael said, "I have a class. Gotta go. Good luck."

After he left, there was another hush in the room. Everyone was looking at me. I froze for a minute. What was I doing, volunteering like that? Now they were going to expect a lot of things from me that I didn't know how to do. I couldn't do this. Maybe I should quit right now.

Edward stood up. "Chairs in a semicircle, you said?" The others in the class joined him in moving the chairs. "This right, Jenny? This it?"

"Yes," I said. "That's fine." I stood up and walked to the chair in the center of the semicircle they were making. "This chair will be the one each person sits in to speak. We'll try that, see how it works. We may end up just standing at our places to say each piece. It might make the whole thing too slow to have people changing seats all the time. We'll have to try it both ways, see how it looks." I stopped and looked around. "Of course, if anyone else has any other ideas, we'll try them. Anybody?" No answer. "OK, for now, let's do it this way."

We went through all the parts and reassigned the ones that didn't seem to work. Some people who didn't like their speeches traded with others. I had a couple of ideas about people I thought were in the wrong roles, and I switched them around until I felt everyone was in the right part. I gave mine away to a teenager named Tiffany. The part was too young for me, and I thought I might be more useful staying outside the piece and listening to the other actors. Tiffany glowed with happiness at being chosen for mine and got started learning her new role right away. When we had settled which parts everyone got, the actors read the play straight through, taking turns in what we called the Hot Seat. When we decided to stop, it was long after the time the class was supposed to end, but no one seemed in a rush to go. I said, "Meeting once a week doesn't seem like enough to me. What do you guys think? Should we schedule some more rehearsal times?"

The actors agreed that if they were going to perform the piece for an audience, they should rehearse a few times a week. We set some rehearsal times, and I took down everyone's name and phone number.

The woman in the jogging suit who had suggested charging admission said, "Honey, let me photocopy the phone list and the schedule for you. Can I get you anything while I'm down there? A Coke from the machine? I'm Priscilla, by the way."

"Jenny," I said. "Nice to meet you. No, thanks, nothing for me."

She took the papers out of my hand and went down the hall to the office, came back in a few minutes with copies and distributed them.

Another thing you should know about me: I attract mothers. They're drawn to me. In fourth grade, my teacher offered to take me home with her after school every day until my mother could get back from work at the hospital. In junior high, my friend Margo's mother invited me to spend the night on school nights when my mother worked a late shift. Margo's mother taught Margo and me how to make fudge and knit. The fact that these women singled me out for extra attention made my own mother feel that they had sniffed out some deficiency in her care and moved in to fill a void. It kept happening even after I grew up and went to college and later when I was with Todd. A woman my own age, a friend from work, say, might bring me soup when I had a cold or drive me home so I wouldn't have to wait for the T in the rain. Sometimes it was an old lady living in our building, who would do things like not switching off the porch light until I got home from a party with Todd.

I felt it was something about me—my wide-eyed expression, my small size, my hesitant hand gestures—that in some way suggested a baby left in a basket on a doorstep. In reality, I was not much like a waif. I had always been wiry and strong. I did well in track in high school. I was a good swimmer. I had stamina. I'm small, but I could outlast almost anyone at studying through the night or stripping wallpaper or putting in calls to a radio station to win concert tickets. Now at the Institute of Affirmation, I saw that Priscilla was kind and capable, and I appreciated her stepping in to help me.

An hour after the class was supposed to end, I said, "For next time, bring some clothes you think would work for your character." Some people wrote this down. "Or, I mean, does anyone have ideas about costumes?"

"No," said Edward. "We'll do what you just said. Right, everybody?" There were a lot of nods and some more note taking.

Taking charge was new to me. At the same time, it was as if somehow I saw this coming and had been secretly preparing myself for quite a while.

KAMPER KITCHEN: RV RECIPES. Cook sumptuous feasts from canned goods and prepared convenience foods in the tiny kitchen of your RV or your home microwave. Thursday, September 18, 6:30–9:30 P.M. Course cost: $15. Materials required: one package dried soup mix (any flavor, any brand), one canned meat or fish, one cake mix.

W HEN I GOT HOME, Todd was there, reading a journal article on the couch and scribbling arrows and letters on a piece of paper.

"Where were you?" he said, still writing.

"I was at my class."

He didn't say anything.

"The acting class I signed up for? Tuesday nights? Anyway, the teacher took another job, so she's not going to be doing it, after all. And guess what!" I said.

"What?" he said. He looked back at the journal, copied something down.

"We're going to be performing a play."

Todd looked up. "You're what?"

"I know," I said. "Me! Who would've thought? I even have a little job. I'm the liaison between the show and the school office. I'm not sure how that happened. I just sort of raised my hand all of a sudden. I didn't plan to. Well, I don't have to actually *do* anything, if I don't want to, just kind of get the rehearsal schedule written down so they know when we need to use the room. It's *Spoon River Anthology*. Remember that? We're going to rehearse several times a week until we have it ready to present to an audience. We're going to sell tickets. I'm getting to know these people. Edward is in his late forties, maybe, and there's Priscilla, who's a little older. There are some younger people. Tiffany is in high school, and—"

Todd said, "What kind of place is this you're going to? Who are these people?"

"They're just, you know, people. When the teacher of our class wasn't going to come anymore, I had this idea. Why not do a performance? You know, instead of just practicing away for nothing. So I suggested it to Michael—it's his school—and he said yes. Actually, they say yes to everything there. It's kind of their policy. But anyway, they're doing it. My idea."

"Jenny?" Todd said.

"Yes?"

"Did you hear from that bank yet?"

"Not yet," I said. Todd asked me this every night. I was glad they hadn't offered me the job yet. I would be happy to be employed again, but I wasn't looking forward to doing the work.

"Because, I mean, I'm not saying we're broke or anything, but maybe you better send out some more résumés."

"It's only been—"

"Anyway . . ." Todd closed his journal. "As I said, we have enough money right now. You should do what you want. It's just that I remember when you were searching for your birth mother and not working. It wasn't the happiest I've ever seen you. But I guess that wasn't only the fact that you didn't have a job. But listen, just because you've had this little setback with your most recent job doesn't mean you should give up, you know?"

"I didn't give up," I said. "Come on. I just found something fun to do."

"I'm worried you're going to get distracted again by something that's leading you nowhere. You know what I'm saying, don't you?"

"Rehearsals are at night. When that bank hires me, I can start right away and still do the play. Anyway, I like these people. This is going to be a great project. I've never done anything like this before. I'm excited about it."

"But maybe that's because it's not a job. Maybe it's because there's no responsibility attached to it. I'm just saying it might not be a good idea to spend a lot of your time and energy on something that won't get you anywhere. At the end of all this, what will you have to show for it? Money? A line on your résumé? A more secure future? You see what I mean?"

"What the—" I sputtered. "I mean, what are you saying? Does everything you do have to have a point? A *purpose*? That's kind of limiting, don't you think?"

Todd rubbed his hair and looked confused. "Limiting? No, I don't think so. To me, it really helps if what I do has . . . well, yes, a point."

"Well, there you go. There's one of our differences right there."

He waited to see if I was going to say anything more, if maybe this was the beginning of a long speech. When he realized it wasn't, he stood up to go upstairs, passing me where I was standing in the middle of the room with my hands on my hips.

I sat down on the couch and rummaged in my bag for the course catalog from the Institute of Affirmation. I looked in it for courses that could help me save my marriage. I checked the relationship section, one of the longest lists of classes. But most of those courses focused on how to meet someone to fall in love with or how to plan a wedding. So I looked through the whole catalog from the beginning. The kind of class I wanted existed only in the automotive section (Resurrect Your Wreck) and the home-improvement section (Dump to Dreamhome in Just Days). There was another course for cultivating a flower garden in a yard full of rocks, weeds, and bad soil; and one for reworking a wardrobe full of worn and outdated clothes. But there was nothing that would help my situation with Todd. I looked up marriage in the index, and it wasn't listed. Marriage Makeover would have been about right, or Renovating Your Relationship. Scanning the *M*'s, I noticed Making Magic and Miracles, with a cross-reference to Happy Endings. Since I didn't feel like going upstairs anyway, I turned to these course descriptions.

> MAKING MAGIC AND MIRACLES. Instructor Glenda
> Wick has developed a three-step system for achieving happy
> endings in every part of life. Glenda promises that her system
> will work on your problem. Just don't tell her what it is; she
> doesn't want to hear about it! Thursdays, 10–11 A.M. Come
> just once or weekly for as long as you want. Course cost: $5
> per session. (See also HAPPY ENDINGS.)

When I looked up Happy Endings, the description was the same, except for the time, which was Mondays, 8:30–9:30 P.M. What could the three steps be? I tried to picture the kind of person who would come up with three steps to solving every kind of problem. You'd have to be a little nutty to participate in a class like that, or at least completely desperate.

ON THURSDAY, while I walked to Making Magic and Miracles, I planned that if I were the only one who showed up, I would pretend that I had come to the wrong room and walk out very quickly. I didn't want to be trapped alone with some eccentric woman for an hour. But when I got there, the room was packed with people. In fact, there were no seats left. I had to stand by the windows. The room was warm, crowded as it was with fifty or sixty expectant bodies. I tried to let in some fresh air. The window had a little crank that fell off in my hand. I put it back on, but it wouldn't turn. I tried it the other way, pushing with all my strength. It didn't move. A man with a big notebook in his lap turned to me and said, "You're the fourth one to try that."

"Oh," I said. "Maybe someone ought to put a sign on it."

The instructor came in. All the talking stopped and there was some rustling, people getting comfortable and ready to listen. A big woman with a wide-brimmed straw hat was standing in front of me, so I couldn't quite see the instructor at first. I just heard her high, crackly voice. "Hello, everybody!" she said. "Anybody have a problem?" Several hands shot up. "Now, none of that," said the instructor in a scolding voice. "I don't want to hear about it. I got enough stuff of my own going on." She giggled softly to herself. "Can't hear any of your troubles. Don't have time. Besides, I wouldn't know the first thing about it. But whether it's getting the money to buy a house or some sickness in the family, don't worry. It's going to turn out right."

I had to lean way to the left to see around the big woman with the hat. The instructor was old, probably in her late seventies. Her long white hair was twisted, puffed, and sprayed so that her head looked like a soft tornado with a face. She wore glasses on a chain around her neck and white stirrup pants with a pale yellow sweatshirt that said WE ♥ GRANDMA. There were a lot of handprints in different colors and children's names scrawled all over it. She set a big white purse on the front desk.

"Maybe the problem is something of a romantic nature," she said, lowering her voice, her eyes softening.

She seemed to be looking at me, but I was way in the back of the room, so maybe I was wrong. I ducked back behind the hat lady.

"You have nothing to worry about anymore."

Hearing her say that, I got a lump in my throat. My eyes filled with tears. I hate when that happens.

"Let's go over our three steps, the secret to getting everything to work out right. I know some of you know 'em already. I recognize you guys who keep coming back!" She laughed again. "I'm better than TV, don'tcha think? And some of you don't believe a word I say. That's fine. OK, here we go. Number one."

I stood on my tiptoes to make myself taller and looked over the big woman's shoulder and under the brim of her hat. The instructor made a big number one on the blackboard. She said "Pray for divine intervention, or a miracle, to get what you want." She looked around the room as if to give this time to sink in. She wrote the word PRAY next to the one on the blackboard. "Why not?" she said. "What's it going to cost you? Don't believe in God? Oh, go ahead and do it anyway. It's not going to kill you. And it might work! The very next second after you say your prayer, it might be answered. Or the next day or week. So start praying right now and don't stop, no matter what." Some of the class members were nodding. Others made a note of this.

The instructor wrote a big two on the board. "You didn't think we were just going to sit back and let the Almighty do all the work, did you?" She looked around. "No, sir. The next step is to work like a dog to get what you want." She wrote WORK next to the two. "You do every darn thing you can think of to reach that place where you want to be. If it's more money you need, you think up a scheme—or ten schemes—and put them into action. Stay up all night, sacrifice everything to get them going. Sell lemonade on the corner, if you have to. Have a garage sale, ask for a raise. Work, work, work on getting yourself where you want to be. Don't let up for a single second. Now, here again, it just might happen for you. That combination of prayer and effort might be enough to solve your problem. You're going to lose the weight or convince your girl to marry you or finally have enough for the down payment just because you've prayed and worked so hard. Isn't that nice? Congratulations." She smiled at us as if we had all just won a big prize.

Then she stopped and looked at the class. "It would be nice if we could get everything we want by praying to the Lord and making a sincere effort, if the harder we tried, the further we got; the more we believed, the quicker our prayers would be answered. But it doesn't always work that way. And what if prayer and hard work don't give you results?" She looked around the room, as if knowing for sure that every one of us had had this experience more than once. "Now, here comes the hard part." We waited. "When you've tried everything you can think of, exhausted every possibility, you're worn-out and discouraged and disappointed, there's one more thing you've got to do." She paused again, then wrote on the blackboard: 3. GIVE UP. Then she turned around and said it out loud, "Give up!" She lifted her hands and then let them drop to her sides.

"Here's where the magic happens," she said with a twinkle. "You give a sigh of frustration or defeat or despair—let's all do that together now. A big sigh on three. One. Two. Three." There was the sound of the class heaving a collective sigh, which sounded more like a groan, then some laughter rippling through the room. "Good," said the instructor. "You did that very well. Now you let go of that idea of what you wanted or what you thought you should have and move on. You can't have everything. You know that as well as I do. You say to yourself, 'Well, I didn't make it.' And get on with something else. And if you've really given up, let go with both hands, so to speak, you're going to be surprised. One of two things will happen. Either that thing you've wanted all along is going to come and find you after you've stopped looking for it or something better is going to happen, something you didn't even think of, something you couldn't have dreamed up if you tried. Why, instead of that promotion, you get an offer from another company where the pay is better and, on Fridays, you don't have to wear a tie. Or you forget about the girl you thought you couldn't live without and someone better comes along. Or you fail to come up with the down payment on the house you wanted and it gets sold to someone else. A month later, your aunt Betty dies and leaves you her house. I've seen it happen a thousand times."

Glenda put the chalk back in the tray. "All right now, anybody have a question about the three steps?"

Several hands went up. "What if you've done all that and still have your problem?" a young man in shorts and sandals wanted to know.

"Either you didn't really give up, you were just pretending, or you didn't wait long enough. How old are you?"

"Twenty."

Glenda nodded. "Sometimes it takes a long time, my love," she said softly.

There were some more questions about how to pray, what words to use, and whether it was necessary to attend religious services. Then Glenda gave examples of her system at work: tumors disappearing, people winning money, homeless and disconnected people finding love and shelter, her granddaughter's fifty-seven warts that suddenly disappeared. After years of prayer and treatment, one day her granddaughter told everyone to leave them alone, she had decided to keep them. Within a week, the warts were gone. Glenda Wick had a lot of these stories. I could have listened to them all day, but there was another part of the class that she had to get to before the hour was up.

She pulled what looked like a stack of crumpled paper out of her huge purse. "Listen carefully, everybody," she said. "I'm going to pass out notebooks. This is a very important part of our system. I want you all to write down three miracles, three wonderful things that you would like to happen to you. You write the number one and a miracle. Write it as if it's already happened. For instance, 'I have more money than I can spend.' Or, 'I am enjoying my perfect health.' You write three of those things, leaving a big empty space under each one. Now listen up. That space is very important. Sometimes we forget to do this. When your miracles happen, go back to your notebook and write down how it happened. Now, do we all agree to do this? Raise your hand if you don't." She looked around the room. No hands went up. "Oh, I like this class," she said. Some people laughed affectionately. She passed out the little books, which turned out to be three sheets of notebook paper jaggedly cut in half and held together on the sides with two crooked staples.

"Everybody got a Miracle Book? In my other class, we call it a Book of Happy Endings." She shrugged her shoulders. "Same thing. Call it what you want. Now you need to write down your three miracles before you leave this room. Get busy. I've got other things to do today." She sat in a chair in the front of the room with her arms folded across her round stomach, like a high-school teacher giving a test, watching for misconduct.

I hadn't expected to have to actually come up with miracles on the spot. Some of the other people were already writing. Maybe I could just fake it, write out my address a couple of times and then leave.

"As soon as you're finished," said Glenda, "bring me your books. I'll check your miracles for you and then you can go."

I looked around to see other people's facial expressions, to try to read what they were thinking. Most people near me were busy, either looking for pens or writing. They didn't look as though they felt silly or shy about showing this woman the miracles they wanted. I wondered if I could leave now, just walk out the door without saying anything. But I didn't dare. She might just let me go; but on the other hand, Glenda Wick might be the type to yell at me, to chase me and bring me back, to haul me up in front of the room to have me explain myself. You just didn't know, with a person like this, what she might do. I reached into my purse and got a pen. I put my notebook on the windowsill and tried to think what to write.

A man in a business suit was finished. He walked to the front and handed Glenda his little book. She read his three miracles, handed it back. "Lovely, dear, don't forget the three steps. Every day, all day." He left the room folding his notebook and putting it into his jacket pocket.

Someone else was finished, a young man who got up and handed his book to the teacher. Then a woman stood up with her book. A line started to form and I hadn't even started. I looked at my paper. I wrote the number one. I couldn't decide: Should I write real things that I wanted to happen or make something up just to show her and get out of the room? I sat still a minute longer before I wrote:

1. I am happily married to the right person.

I got a lump in my throat again and took a deep breath. Now for the other two. I only came for that one, of course, but I could think of more if I really tried. My mind went blank for several minutes. Then I wrote:

2. I love my new job.

The line in front of the teacher was shrinking as people left the class. I took one of the empty seats. What other miracle could I ask for? I stared at the floor. Now most of the people in the class were already in line. Glenda was checking their notebooks quickly. "Beautiful!" she was saying. "Good!" The room was emptying fast. Only two other people were still in their seats, an older woman who seemed to be writing a lot and a man who was shaking his pen to get it to work. He stopped shaking the pen, wrote something on the last page of his notebook, and stood up to get in line.

Hurry, hurry, hurry, I told myself. Then I thought, What the heck, just write anything. Just to have something on the page, I wrote:

3. My birth mother and I are reunited.

I got in line. The woman who wrote a lot got up and stood behind me. At least I wasn't last. When it was my turn, Glenda looked over my pages and said, "Wonderful!" She clapped her hands twice, smiled, and reached for the next notebook.

Even after looking at her up close, I couldn't tell whether Glenda was an eccentric grandma who had decided to teach a course or someone who just looked like an eccentric grandma but was actually deeply wise.

WALKING HOME, I got started on the first step, *Please let my marriage be happier. Please let it be better.* Was I doing this right? I wondered. I had no religious training. My mother had never been interested in church. I thought she believed in God in some way, but she had never shared her ideas on this with me. Todd had gone to a little bit of Sunday school as a kid, but I knew for a fact that he did not believe in God now. Instead, he believed in the natural order of the universe—in the laws of physics that governed the largest stars and planets down to teeny hadrons and quarks; in evolution; and in the immune system. He preferred to rely on laws and principles he could trust to be consistent, rather than volatile forces of human psychology or a possibly all-powerful spiritual being which might behave any way at all with regard to his own particular predicament.

I could see his point.

I stopped at a shopping center to buy a magazine with tips on window treatments and six showstopping meals to make in thirty minutes. I got a shopping cart and collected the ingredients for one of the meals. As I stood in the checkout line to pay, I thought, I will give my marriage my full effort and concentration.

Things might start to improve right away, tonight. You couldn't tell.

I followed the recipe in the magazine, including the salad and dessert. Even though the food took more like an hour and a half, not thirty minutes, it was still only two-thirty in the afternoon when I finished. I put everything in the fridge with Saran Wrap over it and set the table with place mats and candles. *Please let Todd like the dinner.*

I took my notebook from the class out of my jeans pocket and put it upstairs under a pile of sweaters in my closet. I wouldn't want Todd to find this and ask me about it.

The phone rang, and I felt sure I knew who it was. My heart started pounding. It was going to be Sharon from the bank, offering me that job. About the right amount of time had passed since the interview. I was just starting to get comfortable with not working. *Maybe I can ask for another week,* I thought as I lifted the receiver. *Maybe I'll really like this bank; the nice people might make all the difference.*

"Hello?" I said.

"Esther from down at the school," said a woman's voice.

"Oh," I said. "School?"

"Institute of Affirmation. Michael asked me to call you— Is this Jenny? The director of the show, right?"

"Uh, director?" I said. "No, I'm just the scheduler. He said I just had to write down the rehearsal schedule. That's all I have to do, he said."

"Aren't you the one in Acting for the First Time? The one who had the idea of doing a show and inviting families?"

"Yes, that was me. It's just that I'm not *the director.* I'm not *in charge* of anything. We really don't need one, he said, because we're just going to—"

"Is this Jenny?" she asked sharply.

"Well, yes, it is. I—"

"Fine. Michael said to tell you not to spend more than twenty-five dollars on costumes. That's the absolute limit, so don't go crazy on clothes."

"Oh. Clothes? Go crazy? I wasn't even thinking of—"

"He said he forgot to tell you how much you could spend."

I said, "I get to spend money on costumes?"

"And if you want my advice, you better get on this quick."

"Oh, uh, really? You think so?"

"Darn right. You've got a big group there."

"Well, thank you," I said. "Thank you for calling."

"You're welcome."

As soon as I hung up, I looked up Clothing, Used, in the Yellow Pages. I made a list of thrift stores and their addresses and got in my car. I spent the rest of the afternoon collecting clothes for the play. I really enjoyed myself, looking through the piles of stuff, imagining who might wear a particular dress or hat or sport coat. For that much money, you can get a lot of pretty interesting stuff, if you look around. When I got home, I put the clothes in a big box for people to dig through. Then I called everybody in the class and had them each bring a chair from home. I said it could be anything other than a brown metal folding chair, which was what we had at the school.

I prayed about Todd and me at the same time I was doing the other things. *Please let it be better. Just a little better, not even perfect or anything, just a slight improvement would be fine. Please. Please. Please.* It might work, I thought. You can't tell.

Todd came home. He looked at the place mats and candles. "Whoa," he said, "what's going on?" Then a little flash of panic crossed his face. He probably thought he'd forgotten some occasion he should have brought home a present for.

"Surprise!" I said. "I cooked something!"

"Hey," he said. "What?"

"Chicken Fiesta with Confetti Rice." I pointed at the food.

"OK." He took his seat. "You made a lot. What are you going to do with it all?"

"I don't know. I guess it's designed for having people over, which we're not. I'll put some of it in the freezer." I took a bite of the chicken. "It's kind of good."

Well, he ate it. He didn't complain that it was too spicy or say that he'd already eaten at work. So that was something. We talked.

Todd said, "There was an accident on the freeway. It was all backed up. So I went the other way."

"You weren't even late."

"Nope."

OK, it wasn't the greatest conversation in the history of human communication or anything, but words went back and forth, and we didn't argue. He asked me what I'd done all day.

I said, "This, for one thing. I made this dinner." I didn't tell him about the class I'd attended, of course, because that was just the kind of thing that would get Todd going, if you know what I mean. I could just imagine him saying, "I can't believe you paid money to have someone tell you to pray!" and slapping his hand to his forehead with exasperation. I skipped the part about shopping for the play, too, just to be on the safe side. I said, "I did some reading." I didn't mention that I read an article on how to get your husband to take more time with foreplay, one about 101 bright new storage ideas, and another about how to make your house a charming and inviting *home* he'll never want to leave with colorful touches that cost next to nothing. I just said, "I read some articles."

"Mm-hmm," he said, trying the rice. "What else? Did that bank call?"

"No," I said. "I'll tell you when they do. Would you mind not asking me all the time? Thanks." It just slipped out. I didn't mean to snap that way. My brain scrambled for something pleasant to say next, something that he would like. I came up with "I sent out a few résumés." I was lying.

I know it was wrong to say that when it wasn't true, but Todd's answer was just as wrong. "Good for you!" he said, sitting up straight and looking into my eyes. "That's my Jen!" He squeezed my hand.

A knot formed in my stomach. The right answer, of course, would have been, "Please, no more bank jobs when they make you so unhappy! You need to find something that you love."

Todd let go of my hand and patted my shoulder. "What banks?" he wanted to know.

I swallowed a piece of chicken without chewing it. I coughed.

"Some big banks downtown," I said, taking my plate to the sink, scraping the food into the disposal. "I don't really want to talk about it." He looked at me. "I mean, you know, until something comes through."

"I can understand that. But don't worry. Something good will come of this, I'm sure. I'll wash the dishes. Good dinner," he said, turning on the water.

"Glad you liked it."

I cleared the table, while he rinsed the dishes. When I was finished, I sat up on the counter and watched his hands scraping bits of food into the garbage disposal, depositing plates into the dishwasher rack. I waited until he had done the last one, rinsed the sink, and was just about to turn off the water. Then I took his hand and put two of his fingers into my mouth. "Try being spontaneous," the magazine had urged me.

Todd looked flustered and took his hand out of my mouth. "Jenny," he said with a little laugh. He turned off the water and gave me a kiss on the cheek. He dried his hand on the dish towel that was hanging from the handle of the oven door. *Pray,* I told myself. *Work hard. Please let this happen,* I said inside my head.

Todd turned around and reached for me, rubbing his hands on the tops of my thighs. He kissed my neck, licked it. I touched his cheek while he was kissing me, stroked his back, tipped my head back to give him better access to my throat. Todd held me around the waist and lifted me off the counter. I put my arms around his neck as he began to carry me across the kitchen, kissing me on the mouth as we walked. *It's working,* I was thinking. *Thank you, thank you!*

Then I heard something snap; something in Todd's back actually made a cracking sound. He let out a groan and dropped me fast to the floor. "Oh, my God," he said.

"What? What happened?"

"My back," he said. He was holding on to the counter now, leaning over at the waist. "It hurts," he said. "It hurts so much."

"Todd," I said. "What should I do?"

"Just a second," he said. "I'll be OK. Hold on."

I stood there quietly and waited for him to tell me what to

do. When someone is hurt, it's not a good idea to talk a lot, I always think. After a few minutes, I said, "Do you want me to rub it?"

"No!" he almost shouted. "Really, don't touch me whatever you do."

"Ice," I said. "I think you're supposed to use ice."

"OK, let's try that."

"Can you get to the couch?"

"Yeah, I think so." Todd started to move toward the couch. All hunched over and with one hand on his hip like a fourth grader acting the part of an old man, he shuffled with tiny steps to the couch.

I put ice cubes in a plastic bag and wrapped a clean dish towel around it. "Here," I said, offering it to Todd.

He was lying on his side and put the bag of ice against his back, then rolled back on it. "God," he said. "Jesus."

"What else can I do?"

"Nothing," he said. "Except can you just move that up a little bit?"

"You mean like this?" I adjusted the ice.

"Not that much. Yeah, thanks, like that. Now, if I could just move this leg—God, that hurts! OK, there."

With a lot of effort, he got himself settled on the couch. "I can't believe this," he kept saying. "This never happened to me before."

I patted his back, careful not to touch the part that hurt. "This can happen to anyone. You just made a strenuous movement that you're not used to. I guess you'll have to sleep here. You're in no shape to move upstairs. Good thing we have such a hard couch. Soft mattresses are terrible for bad backs. Are you sure it wouldn't help if I massaged it for you?"

"No, no," he said. "Please don't touch me. Really. I don't want you to do that."

"I was going to be very gentle. Do you think you need to go to the hospital or a doctor or something?"

"No," he said. "I don't think so. Jen?"

"Yes."

"Sorry we didn't get to—"

"Never mind," I said. "Do you want the remote?"

"Yeah, OK."

I got it for him. "Anything else?"

"No, I think I'm all set."

"OK, then, see you tomorrow," I said.

"Night, Jen."

"Night."

I gave him a kiss on the top of his head. His smell could still do things to me. Todd turned on the TV. I went upstairs by myself.

This was only the first day of praying and working hard, I said inside my head, way too early to get discouraged.

"MAYBE YOU should *call* that bank," Todd said from the couch the next morning. His injury was severe enough to keep him home for the morning, but he could now stand up and shuffle around the house a little bit. And he had some cells that needed another four hours to grow before he could do anything with them. "Find out what's going on over there," he urged me.

"I thought you weren't going to bug me about this anymore. And sometimes things take a long time within a corporation," I said. "Really, you don't realize how long it takes to get one simple thing accomplished when you have all these people involved. It's almost as bad as a university."

Todd said, "If they're as nice as you say they are, they should at least let you know what's going on."

"All right, all right," I said. "Then will you stop pestering me?"

"Yes," he said. "I will. Promise."

Even though I didn't want to do anything to cut into my time off, I called the bank and asked for Sharon. When she came on, I said, "Hi, this is Jenny Brown."

"Oh," she said, a little flustered. "Oh, hi."

"Is this a bad time? Do you want to call me back?"

"No," she said. "Go ahead."

"Um, I was wondering, I don't mean to rush you, but what's happening with that job opening? It's not as though I need to start right away or anything. I could wait a few more weeks, even a month. I just wanted to know what—"

"Yes," she said. "I really should have called you."

"Oh, that's OK. I was just—"

"We filled it."

"You did?"

"Yes," she said.

"Someone else got the job?"

"I'm afraid so. I should have let you know. Honestly, I was hoping my assistant had called all the candidates back. But we had a very long list, and maybe your name just fell through the cracks somehow. I apologize."

"I see. Thanks anyway," I said.

I hung up. A sharp grabbing feeling started in my stomach. "Now what am I going to do?" I whispered to the toaster oven.

"What?" Todd said from the couch. "What did she say? What happened?"

"I didn't get the job."

"Oh, no," he groaned. "You really should have gotten that one. How much longer do you think this is going to take?"

I didn't tell him that he was making me feel worse than I already did. I just held very still, waiting for the toaster oven to answer me.

eight

ANOTHER YOU. Create a whole new look for yourself with different makeup, hair, and clothing. Change even those features you thought were permanent—eyes, nose, cheekbones, chin, height—with fun-to-apply plastics and gels. Our instructor swears that changing your appearance will change the way you think, speak, and behave. Your best friends won't recognize you! Better yet, you might not recognize yourself! By appointment. Course cost: $45 per session.

*A*T OUR FIRST real rehearsal, we set up the semicircle of chairs again, this time using the ones the actors had brought in. No two were alike. There was a vinyl-covered chrome kitchen chair dating back to the sixties; a few office chairs, including one that swiveled; some straight-backed wooden ones; two plastic patio chairs, one white, one blue. The clothes I brought for the actors were just as varied. Some were bold fashion statements from another era; others were hardly distinguishable from their everyday clothes; some were dressy; some were exercise outfits.

I pulled a black vinyl shoulder bag out of the box of things I'd brought. The strap was a chain of big gold circles. "Tiffany, this goes really nicely with the vinyl minidress. Want to try it?"

"Thanks," said Tiffany. "Oh, I love this. And my mom said you might want to use these two dresses she was going to give away."

"Oh, thank you," I said. I draped the dresses she gave me—a denim jumper and a long flowered knit—over chairs so people could see them.

I said, "Any of you men interested in a tweed jacket with patches on the elbows?" Jason, a high-school boy, tried on the jacket, decided to use it. I handed it to him from the box.

Clara, an elderly woman I had pictured as a librarian or schoolteacher type, had brought a gauzy powder-blue strapless party dress. "Oh," I said when she asked my opinion. "Where did you find that?"

"I don't really remember where we got it," she said. "My girls used it for Halloween years ago. It was in a plastic bag in the garage. Let me show you!" Clara went to the girls' bathroom down the hall to change. In a few minutes, she was back to model the dress for us. Her arms had a lot of loose skin on them, all the way down to her wrists, where her little gold watch made a deep indentation. She did a twirl. I saw that the skin of her back hung down a little over the top of the dress. She almost looked like a fairy godmother or a good witch, somebody with magic powers. Clara giggled. "It brings out the prom queen in me, don't you think?"

I said, "It looks great. Perfect."

"Go for it, Clara," said Edward, who was modeling a tuxedo jacket he had brought over his T-shirt.

"Nice," I said to Edward.

Priscilla labeled all the costumes with the names of the actors who were to wear them. She marked names on the chairs with a piece of masking tape across the back.

When almost everyone had chosen something, there was a lull in the activity. The actors began to look to me expectantly. My throat got dry, and my hands got sweaty. I went to Priscilla and whispered, "I don't know how to— What do I—"

"Listen up, everybody!" Priscilla bellowed to the room. "Jenny is going to hear each of you say your speeches, one at a time, and tell you what to work on. She'll call you when she's ready for you. The rest of you, pair up and move over by the

80

windows. Practice saying your speeches to one another. Keep your voices low so you can hear Jenny when she calls you." Obediently, the actors paired off and moved over to one side of the room. She turned and winked at me. "I've done a lot of amateur theater," she whispered.

"Jason!" Priscilla said. "You're first." She dragged two chairs over in front of the chalkboard. "Sit down here, sweetie," she said to me. She pressed down hard on my shoulders until I was sitting.

Jason sat in front of me. He had wiry red hair and a lot of freckles all over his face, neck, and arms. He wore a Padres baseball cap on backward. A lock of hair stuck out the hole in the front above the plastic band for size adjustments.

"Sh-should I j-just s-start?" he said.

Priscilla moved away to a pile of costumes she was labeling.

"Yes," I said. "Go ahead."

Jason began. He was about seventeen and had a severe stutter. He had his lines learned perfectly. I listened to his speech through twice. The first time, he got hung up every few words; the second time, he got through with only a few brief pauses.

"You've done a lot of work on that, Jason. I like it. For next time, think about what he was like as a small boy, as a teenager. What would he have done with the rest of his life if he hadn't died? See if that changes your speech for you for next time. Nice work."

"OK." He smiled, turning. "Thanks, J-Jenny."

He stood up. I looked at the list of actors to call someone else. "Tiffany?" I said.

Quickly, she walked over to the seat Jason had just left. She had dark brown hair to her shoulders. She was wearing overall shorts with a flowered T-shirt and sandals. She and Jason were about the same age; maybe they even went to the same school.

"Ready?" I said.

"Yeah," she said. "Um . . . What, like, from the beginning?"

"Yes," I said. "Please."

"I'm not very good at memorizing," she said.

"We'll just see how far we get," I said.

She said her first two lines, then stopped. I prompted her. She repeated what I'd said, plus two words, then stopped again. She blushed and bit her lip, as if she might be about to cry. I said, "All right. Why don't you just read it this time."

She exhaled. "Sure, I can do that."

As soon as she reached the end of the speech, she said, "See, I've always wanted to be in a play so bad." She squeezed her eyes shut tight as if anticipating a blow. She opened them and looked at me. "At school, I keep trying out, but I never get into the plays. There's a group of kids who get the parts every time. They already know each other, and the teachers don't seem to let anyone else in the group."

I said, "That's the way it was in my school, too. I guess that's the point of this place. You get a chance, no matter what. It's a few weeks until the performance. You have plenty of time. Do you want to try it again?"

She smiled at me, relieved. She tried her part again, often looking down at a pile of cards she held on which she had copied all her words. The cards were becoming limp in her tight, warm grip.

"Good," I said when she was finished. "Keep practicing."

Tiffany said, "I will."

Valerie, in her early twenties, kept her head down while she spoke and was so quiet it was hard to hear her, even sitting directly in front of her, not three feet away. "I don't know if I can do this," she told me when she finished. "Do you think people will laugh?"

"No," I said, "people will listen. It's not going to be you talking up there, remember. You're someone else when you're saying these words. Remember when we said our speeches for Michael? That was what helped me, the idea that it wasn't me but the character, this other woman. Then I didn't worry so much that I might make a mistake. And I didn't."

She rubbed the tight lines across her forehead.

"Let's hear it again," I said. She spoke louder this time, looking up at me more than once. "Good. This is going to be lovely."

Valerie smiled and stood up to join the others.

"Edward," I called.

Edward had been in some community plays when he was younger. Like several others, he wasn't really acting for the first time at all. He gestured broadly and projected his lines so loudly that I had an urge to move my chair to the other side of the room. The second time through, there was a knock on the door.

A tall woman with very short hair was there when I opened it. "Hi," she said. "I'm Ruth from Write It Down, next door. I know your actors are rehearsing, but do you think maybe they could speak a little more quietly? We would appreciate it so much."

"Sure," I said. "Sorry. We've just started working on this piece, and we didn't realize. By the way, we're going to be doing part of *Spoon River Anthology* on the tenth, seven o'clock right here in this room."

"I'll tell my class. Good luck, or I guess I mean, break a leg!"

When she was gone, I had Edward start again. "Just say it to me," I said. "I'm right here. And I'm listening."

"OK, boss," Edward said. This time, he was much quieter.

Only a few of the actors seemed stiff and uncomprehending of the words. I made certain to encourage every sign of effort. "Lovely moment there, Denise," I said when an actor paused slightly before going on with her speech.

"Oh," she said. "I just stopped because I remembered about this video I forgot to take back. Was that good?"

"Let's keep that pause," I said. "It seemed right to me. Some of the best discoveries happen by accident." The second time she did her speech, there was a big gaping pause in the middle followed by a little smile afterward because she was pleased to have followed my direction.

I had just finished listening to the last actor when Priscilla's voice rang out. "That's it, people. It's nine o'clock. End of rehearsal."

"Is it nine o'clock already?" I said. The actors started for the door.

Priscilla said, "Hold it, everybody! Not so fast! Line up your chairs here along this wall. Costumes go in these boxes. Thank you."

"And we'll see you at six-thirty on Thursday," I said.

FOUR WEEKS of rehearsals went by quickly. When the performance was just two days away, I got another phone call from the school. "Esther here. Michael says your dress rehearsal is Saturday afternoon. He'll meet you at nine tomorrow morning to go over what you have left to do."

"Dress rehearsal?" I said. "Do?"

"Nine sharp," she barked, and hung up without saying goodbye.

The next morning, Michael was waiting for me by the water fountain with his clipboard. He said, "OK, you've got this room all day tomorrow. Sorry I couldn't get you in there tonight, but Waltzing Without a Partner is at seven, and the instructor was pretty adamant about keeping the room. But I bumped tomorrow's classes for that room into different locations because I knew you'd need the full day to get ready." He made a circle around something on his list.

"I do? A full day? Well, OK. Sure. I guess we could use— Right." I nodded, trying to look as if I knew exactly what I was going to do in a full day's rehearsal.

He looked at his clipboard again. "How many people are you expecting from the press?"

"Press?"

"I'll block off some good seats. You invited newspapers, right? Radio people?"

"Uh, no, I honestly never even thought of that. I was thinking more like friends, family—"

"OK," he said, a little taken aback. "Well, fine then. Yeah, OK. I was kind of thinking maybe the publicity ... But it still might be all right." He drew a line through something on the list.

"It might?"

84

"Of course. You don't need newspapers. Sometimes word of mouth can work even better. Absolutely." He checked his clipboard for the next item. "And what were you thinking about using for the refreshment stand? Because I've got you a table, unless you had something else in mind."

"Uh . . . a table . . . well, I—I'm sorry. I just hadn't thought about selling refreshments."

He looked at me briefly without saying anything. Recovering quickly, he said, "Oh. I see. Fine. That's—makes it simple, doesn't it? I guess in such a short evening, refreshments aren't necessary. The benefit to the school would probably be small anyway. And so many people are dieting these days, it certainly wouldn't be doing anybody any favors to have a bunch of gooey, high-fat, sugary treats just waiting to throw people off course. Smart." He crossed out another line of his own handwriting on his list. "How much was the video camera rental?"

"Yes, well . . ." I hadn't given the video camera a thought since I suggested someone make a tape. I suppose, as it was my idea, Michael thought I was going to be the one in charge of it.

"Or do you have your own?"

"No, I—"

Michael said, "I see. OK. Of course, these are inexperienced actors, so maybe it's better not to throw too many distractions at them." He crossed out one more item. "I've got tickets for you and a cashbox. You can pick them up in the office before the performance. Who's going to be cashier?"

"I am," I said quickly, so that he wouldn't know this was another thing I hadn't figured out.

"Good." He made a circle around something. "That's all, then. I've got a class right now, so I can't stay and talk. Sounds like you've got everything covered, all organized." He started off down the hall. "Break a leg tomorrow."

"Same to you," I called after him, then realized this wasn't the right thing to say.

I stood there a minute, reviewing the things he had mentioned. He looked so disappointed, so let down. It was just a small production after all, just people in a class performing for friends and family. No need to overdo the preparations, make it into a bigger deal than it was.

I drove home and went straight upstairs to the computer. I wrote a paragraph about the play, giving the date and time, name and address of the school. I put the words *Press Release* across the top. "Free refreshments with press ID!" I added as an after-thought. "Giant Chocolate Chunk Brownies handmade by a local bakery." At the bottom, I said I would leave two tickets at the box office. I faxed a copy to each of the local newspapers.

Then I got started on the brownies. While they were in the oven, I called three stores about a video-camera rental. The rental fees seemed fairly reasonable. I was about to call Esther in the school office and ask how much money was available for this. But, of course, it would be better not to spend anything at all.

I called Edward, who I remembered had children. "Do you have a video camera we could use to tape the play?"

"Sure do," he said. "Top of the line. Just got it a month ago. First grandchild on the way. All yours. Who's going to be the cameraman?"

"I am," I said. "I'll be doing that."

When the brownies were cool, I wrapped each one in plastic wrap and put them in the freezer so that they would stay fresh until the performance.

I SPENT ALL the next day at the school. Priscilla brought her sewing machine and worked on fitting the costumes. Tiffany brought in a book about makeup, and Michael provided her with a box of makeup that Rory had left behind. Tiffany practiced on the people in the class, looking at the open book in her lap for ways to make scars, age lines, a crooked nose. When Edward looked in the mirror at Tiffany's work—a pointed chin an inch longer than his own, cheekbones like two small mountains, eye-brows fit for a werewolf—he said, "Amazing!" Priscilla got cheeks as red as lollipops and long false eyelashes. She said, "Tiff, I think you really enjoy makeup. You like the way it feels to smear it on thick."

Tiffany blushed with pride. "Yes," she said. "I sure do."

"Well, it shows," Priscilla said. "OK, everyone, get into place for the dress rehearsal. Right, Jen? If we don't get started, we're not going to have time to go home before the show."

"Right," I said, looking at my watch. "We need to start now."

Edward said, "It's bad luck to have a rehearsal on the day of the show."

"Help me with these chairs," I said, "and I promise I won't whistle backstage."

The rehearsal seemed slow to me. And even after all the times we had gone over it, the actors were confused about the order of their speeches. When one stopped speaking and left the Hot Seat, two, sometimes even three, people started to stand up to go next. Several times I had to call out whose turn it was, and once there was an argument about it. When the last speech ended, an hour and a half behind schedule, I said, "Go home now and rest a little while. I'll see you back here at six-fifteen. Edward, are you sure you want to wear that chin home? You guys did great this afternoon—really—and tonight will be even better!"

"Thanks, chief," Edward said. "See you at seven."

"Six-fifteen," several people said. "Didn't she say—"

"Six-fifteen," I repeated, and wrote it on the blackboard.

I went home and called Todd at the lab. "Don't forget. The performance is tonight."

"Performance? Oh, that's right," he said, "your thing. Uh, what time do I have to be there?"

"Well, you don't *have* to come, but it starts at seven. I'll reserve a good seat for you."

"But I don't have to? Because this experiment I'm doing is—"

"Sure," I said. "I understand. It's just a little thing anyway. No big deal."

"You don't mind if I work? Really? Because I could stop and

then go back. Part of it would be ruined and I'd have to go back until two or three in the morning—"

"Skip it," I said. "Don't come."

"Really?" he said. "You don't mind? You're not just saying that?"

"Not at all. See you later." I hung up.

It was better not to have him there. This way, if the play went badly, he would never know; he would never be able to use that to support his view that I had wasted a lot of time. I put on a dress, my own costume.

I went back to the school early. I set up the chairs and put a small table in the hall outside the door. I picked up the cashbox and tickets from Esther in the office.

"You going to get us back on our feet?" Esther said without looking up from typing on her computer.

"Pardon me?" I said.

"We owe everybody." Her fingers stopped abruptly, and she gave the computer a shake.

"I didn't know."

"We could use a little shot in the arm around here." She slapped the top of the computer. "Work!" There was a pause while she narrowed her eyes at the machine. Then she said, "Thank you," and began to type again.

I set up a table outside the door of the classroom and beside it, a table for my brownies. I made a sign: CHOCOLATE CHUNK BROWNIES $1.00. If they didn't sell, I'd bring the price down.

As soon as all the actors were there, I spoke to them about how good they were in their parts, how no one would ever guess that, for some of them, this was their first experience of performing. The actors clapped for me and several of them hugged me. When I got back to the refreshment table, Priscilla was looking at my sign.

"I know it's a lot," I said. "I just thought that since the school needs the money—"

"They look good," she said. "How about cutting them in half and charging two-fifty. I can do it in the office." Priscilla hurried away with my basket of brownies while I made a new sign.

HUSBANDS, WIVES, PARENTS, and children of the actors lined up to pay for tickets. Michael had to go to the other classrooms and bring back more chairs. While I sold tickets at the door, my heart was pounding. I smiled and my lips stuck to my teeth because my mouth was so dry. No one asked for press comps, and I felt guilty about not trying harder and earlier. The room filled up pretty well anyway. Michael had his dancers from Hip Hop for Elders perform a short, funny dance as an opening act.

Then our piece started. I was too busy videotaping to worry about how it was going. I made sure that I got each actor centered in the frame, that I had a close-up and also a medium shot.

Jason got stuck on a word for what felt like a very long time. It seemed the audience was collectively holding its breath until he got it out. Then, finally, he did. There were a few more times that he stuttered, but these occurrences were minor in comparison. Tiffany got a third of the way through her speech and then jumped to the last sentence, concluding abruptly, then taking her seat again. She didn't seem aware that she had left out most of her words. After weeks of relaxed practices, Valerie, the one who started out speaking too quietly, seemed to retreat into herself in the performance, speaking in a barely audible voice, staring intently at her hands in her lap.

For Edward, Priscilla, and a few others having an audience seemed to bring something new to life in the characters they created, and they did their best work ever. Clara somehow transformed herself into an angel who had done a brief stint on earth as a human. I almost expected to be able to see through her, prom dress and all, to the back wall of the classroom. My throat choked with emotion, watching her.

During intermission, I sold all of the overpriced brownies and made almost a hundred and fifty dollars for the school. I wished I had baked twice as many. When the last one was gone, I rushed into the classroom to flick the lights and get the video camera started again.

After the last speech, which was Denise's, all the actors lined up and held hands. A few of them bowed just once, while several others bowed repeatedly. The applause went on almost as long as they were standing there.

When it was all over, the actors were energized and happy, if a little let down. Jason came to me and said, "I had a bad moment there. I j-just couldn't g-get the w-word out."

I said, "But, you know, it was on the word *death*, which is a theme in the play. When you stopped there—just for that tiny moment—you made the audience reflect on this theme. I think that little pause heightened the meaning of the whole evening, don't you, Michael?"

Michael looked up from stacking chairs. "Uh," he said, pausing to look at me, "I do, yes, I do, very much so."

Valerie slumped in a corner. "I liked what you did," I said to her. "Some actors get their points across by exaggerating everything, being bigger than life. But you gave a subtle, understated performance that demanded our attention."

"I did?" she said quietly, studying the fabric of her dress.

"You have your own style."

Valerie looked up. "Style? I do?"

"Very compelling," I said. "It had an intensity. You had a focused, introspective approach."

"Really? Thanks," she said, brightening.

Tiffany rushed up to me with greasy goo all over her face to remove the makeup, which was now blurred streaks of gray, red, and blue. "Did I forget anything?" Tiffany said.

"You got in everything you needed to," I told her.

"This is my mom," Tiffany said.

Tiffany's mother and I smiled at each other. "Your daughter did an excellent job," I said.

"We're very proud of her."

Some of the actors gave me little presents—candy, a bouquet of flowers, some homemade bubble bath in a basket. "You guys," I said, laughing. "Thank you. This is embarrassing. I didn't do anything but listen to you say your speeches and ask you to bring chairs!"

Priscilla said, "Jenny, I want you to meet my daughter. This is Chelsea."

"Hi," said a teenager with blue nail polish and matching lipstick. "I liked your play. And the brownies, were, like, fabulous."

"Thank you," I said. "I couldn't have done it without your mom. She helped me so much."

Jason came up to me with his mother. "Your son is so talented," I said.

"I think so, too." She winked at me and gave her son a squeeze.

"*Mom*," said Jason, pulling away.

Priscilla was looking around the room. "Where's your husband, Jenny? I want to meet him."

"My husband?" I said. "Oh, he had to work."

She looked at me. "On a Saturday night?"

"See, he's a scientist, and he—"

Edward said, "What? Jenny's husband didn't come? That's—"

"I didn't know Jenny was married," I heard one of the actors say.

"No, see," I said, "I told him he didn't—"

"Sure, I bet he gets really busy," Priscilla said quickly. "So you guys want to go out after, get something to eat? I, for one, am starving. Jenny?"

"Thanks," I said. "I think I better get home now. As soon as I get all this stuff put away."

The cast and their families helped pack the clothes and stack the chairs.

I WALKED HOME. I had a lot of energy and made it back in a very short time. When I got there, Todd was watching television. "Hi," he said. "How'd it go?"

"It was great!" I told him, going to the kitchen to put my flowers in water. "Everyone did so well. You should have seen them! I'm so glad I taped it. When Clara did her speech, she had this beautiful halo around her head. It was the most amazing effect that happened completely by accident because of the way the

91

fluorescent light hit her hair. But it looked like a special effect. You remember who Clara is, right? She's about seventy-five, just a tiny little woman with a big, beautiful voice, and her hair is all white. I hope that comes across on the video. Do you think it will? And you should have seen Edward. In rehearsals, he was good, but in the real performance, wow, you wouldn't have known him! Of course, you *don't* know him, but you see what I mean. He has this sweetness, this kind of bruised quality that makes you want to treat him tenderly, listen to what he has to say. I think the audience liked it. The applause went on and on. Of course, they were all family. But they didn't look bored or anything." I put the vase of flowers on the coffee table.

Todd said, "I'm glad it worked out. I didn't hear your car. Where did you park?" He moved the flowers to another table. He couldn't see the TV.

"My car? Oh. My car. Whoops. I forgot I drove. I left it at the school and walked home. I guess it will be OK until tomorrow."

"You forgot your car?" Todd looked at me in disbelief. "How could you forget your car?"

"I don't know. I just did."

"Do you want me to drive you back there to get it?"

"It will be all right. It's in a parking lot right in front of the school."

"Sure? Well, OK." He stood up. "Guess I'll go to bed. You coming?"

"No," I said. "I'm going to stay up for a while. I'm still too keyed up."

"Night, then."

"Night."

Todd went upstairs. I kept thinking about the performance, replaying it in my head. If it weren't so late, I would have called my mother in Connecticut to tell her about it. I watched TV for a while without paying any attention. Then I wandered around downstairs, rearranging things—the bathroom towels, the mail, the scraps of paper next to the phone. I still wasn't even close to feeling tired. I decided to walk back to the school to get my car.

n i n e

POSITIVE WAYS TO SAY NO. For those of you who have trouble turning down salespeople, who volunteer too much, or who do far too many things you really don't want to, this class will teach you how to back out gracefully. Tuesdays, 7–9 P.M., beginning September 23, until you can decline our invitation to return. Course cost: $10 per session.

I CHANGED MY SHOES and started off at a fast pace, checking my watch as I left our front door. I was trying to decide what I could do next. I would really have to get a job now. There was no getting around it. A sinking feeling started to spread through me as I thought of the panty hose I would have to wear, the smiling I would have to do, the thoughts I would have to keep to myself, the effort I would have to make to get something I didn't really want.

When I got to my car, Michael was locking the front door of the school. He turned around and walked toward me. "You came back," he said to me.

"I forgot my car," I told him.

He nodded. "So. What next, Jenny Brown?"

"Next?" I said. "Oh, I'm going to go home and go to sleep, I guess, but I'm not tired at all."

"I mean, what's your next project?"

"That, oh yeah. I was just thinking about that. I guess I'm going to have to try to find a job."

93

"What do you do?"

"Banking. Loan applications."

"Hm," he said. He squinted at me. "I can't picture it. You think you'll do that right away?"

"I guess," I said. "I'll have to. So I'll see you, OK?" I opened my car door and got in. "Thanks for everything. Good luck with your school."

"Yeah," he said. "So long." He got into his pickup truck and waited for me to back out of the parking lot.

I drove home. I pulled into the driveway. My finger was on the button to open the garage door, but I didn't press it. I stopped, sat there for a minute, backed out of the driveway. I went to the shopping center and parked. I had my pick of spaces; not much was open, except the twenty-four-hour coffee shop, which was called the Coffee Shop. Now that I wasn't nervous about the play anymore, I was hungry. I went inside, thought a minute about whether I wanted to sit at the counter or get a table by myself or back out and go home.

"Jenny!" someone called. "Hey, Jen!" I looked, and there were Priscilla, Valerie, Jason, Edward, Clara, and Tiffany.

I felt my heart bounce at the sight of them. "You guys! Hi!" I said.

Priscilla left the table and came over to get me. "Come, sit with us. I bet you haven't eaten anything all night. Let me get you a waitress."

I sat down at their table, and a menu came. "Have a burger, why don't you?" Priscilla urged. "Or what about soup?"

"I'll have a cheese omelette," I said to the waitress.

"Does she get toast and fries with that?" Priscilla asked.

"Yes, ma'am."

"There you go," Priscilla said to me. "You'll be all fixed up in a jiffy."

The waitress left the table, and the six of them resumed the conversation they had been having. Priscilla was talking about her family, specifically Chelsea, who spent too much time at the beach and the mall with her friends. "A lot of nights, I don't know where she goes or what she does," Priscilla told us. "She's sixteen and the last one I have at home. All her friends have cars, and you just don't know what they're up to. Before I came out tonight, I dropped her off at home. She said she would stay there, but she could just as easily call a friend to come get her. You don't know what a worry that is when they come home at two, three in the morning."

Edward said, "Two of mine are in college. I worry that they aren't going there to get an education. You know what I'm saying? I mean, are they studying at all? I keep wondering because all they talk about is the parties."

I said, "They probably just don't tell you about the studying part."

"Maybe," Edward said.

"What about you, Jenny?" Tiffany asked. "You got kids?"

"No," I said. "My husband and I decided not to have children."

For just a second, I considered saying that we were both adoptees, then decided it didn't fit naturally into the conversation. The moment to say it was there, and then it was gone. I reached across the table for the Tabasco sauce, poured out a little puddle on my plate, dipped in a french fry, ate it.

"*Decided* not to have kids, huh?" said Priscilla. "Decided. I like that. Young people today think things through a lot more than we ever did. I got married, had four kids in school before I noticed that my husband and I didn't love each other." She laughed dryly. "We've been divorced now for eight years. I'm not complaining. I like being single. Chelsea's my baby. I want to make sure this last one doesn't go wrong. You know what I'm saying."

I nodded. Of course, not having children of my own, I didn't know a thing about it.

Edward said, "You're a good mother. I've seen you with her, and she's going to turn out fine."

"You think so?" Priscilla said. Edward nodded. The two of them looked at each other for a long time. Priscilla took a drink of water.

Jason said, "I have to go. I just w-want to know, Jenny."

I looked at him, waited.

"What p-play are y-you doing next?"

"Next?" I said, taking a bite of eggs.

"Yeah," he said. "Because I want to be in it, and I f-figure if I read it early, maybe I'll have a better ch-chance when it's time for the tryouts."

"Tryouts?" I said, shaking more hot sauce on my food.

"Yeah," said Tiffany, "you know, like, auditions?"

I said, "This was just for one time, you know, because it was sort of an emergency with Rory leaving. I didn't mean to get involved with a play. The whole thing was a big accident. Remember Michael told me I just had to write down the rehearsal schedule? Then before you knew it, I was buying the costumes, telling people what to do, running the ticket sales and the concession stand—it all happened by mistake."

Edward leaned toward me urgently. "Make it happen again."

Priscilla said, "I'll help you with costumes, photocopying, scheduling—anything you want. Put me right to work."

Tiffany said, "I'm going to try out, too. You know what I liked best? The laughs. I got two, and it was, like, so neat to hear people laughing at something I said. I mean, a roomful of people. I keep thinking about that, how it sounded. I always wanted to be funny. And the applause at the end when we all came out to take a bow. I really liked that. OK, it was only family and friends, but they were entertained. They weren't just sitting there to be nice. Were they?"

Jason said, "I can build s-stuff. I'm pretty good at it, if you w-want me to."

I didn't say anything.

Priscilla said, "Oh, now, let's give Jenny a break. She's probably tired. She doesn't want to start all over again with another show right away. Let her recover from this one before we start pestering her about the next one."

I said, "See that bank over there? I used to work at a big desk with my name on it near the window. I recently got downsized out. I'm not—I analyze loan applications. That's what I do."

"For a living," said Edward, nodding. "Sure you do. Hey, I

install faucets, bathtubs, and dishwashers. But this is different. You might need to do this just as much as you need to have money. You might need plays to live, to be alive. I know I do. Now that I've done this, I'm not stopping. It's like I was dead inside, and suddenly I've come back to life. I was *dead* before this show." He tapped his fists silently against the table.

I shook my head and looked at my soda.

"We're counting on you, Jenny," Priscilla said quietly without looking at me. "When you're ready."

I said, "If it's so important to you, I'm sure Michael can find a real director who knows what she's doing. Or he. Someone who has done it before."

Priscilla said, "*You* have. Now."

The waitress came, took my plate, and gave me a check. I shook my head. "Edward, you've done some plays. You've got way more experience than I do. I'm sorry, you guys. This was fun, but I have to be, you know, practical." I got out my wallet.

Edward looked at me, one eyebrow raised, a slight smirk on his lips.

I said, "What? I mean it. I have to get a job right away. Tomorrow, I'm redoing my résumé and I'll be scouring the papers to find places to send it. I have to go. It's getting so late, and I'll have a lot to do tomorrow."

"You'll be back," Edward said.

"I hope so," I told him. "I might take another class at the school sometime. And if you do another show, I'll bring everyone I know."

Jason said, "Th-that's not what Edward means."

"Whenever that place needs something," Clara said, "whether it's chairs or a new building or money or a certain person, it shows up. Poof, just appears out of nowhere."

I said, "It's a very positive place."

"No kidding," said Priscilla. "That's why we all keep going back. I've been taking courses there ever since it opened. I've taken everything from knitting to dream analysis. I can't get enough of the place."

"Same here," said Tiffany. "I want to take Making Magic and Miracles."

"I've done that one," said Edward. "That's the way I found my job. I also found my wedding ring after it had been lost for two years. No kidding. It was in the garage on a shelf next to the paint thinner. I could have sworn I'd looked there a hundred times. You'll love it, Tiff."

"As a matter of fact, I've taken that one," I said. "Only for me, it didn't really work."

Edward shook his finger at me. "You can't say that. Not *yet* maybe. You have to wait sometimes. Remember? Give all three steps a chance to work."

"I'll keep trying," I said.

"It takes as long as it takes," Edward said. "Anyway, I don't know how anybody could walk away from the place."

"I'm not saying that I don't like the school. It's a great place. It's just that I—"

Priscilla said, "If she's supposed to be there, she'll be there. Leave her alone."

"I have to go," I said. "It was a nice surprise to see you all here."

"Yeah," Tiffany said, standing up, "I told my mom I wouldn't be out past midnight."

"Good girl," Priscilla said. "I like that."

"I know your daughter," Tiffany told her. "She's in two of my classes. Want me to maybe talk to her? I could try hanging out with her a little? Maybe I can see what she's up to, check out the kids she spends time with."

"That's the sweetest, kindest thing I ever heard. Yes, I would appreciate that. Thank you very much," Priscilla said.

"I'll see her Monday. I don't know if it will help, but I'll try for ya."

"Thank you," Priscilla said, hugging Tiffany before she left the table.

I stood up, too. "I hope to see you all soon."

"You better," said Edward.

98

Priscilla said, "Don't *pressure* her. If it's right, she'll—"

"Good night, everyone." I went to pay my check.

THE NEXT MORNING I was still asleep when the phone rang. I picked it up. Todd was already gone. I hadn't even heard him leave.

"Did you see the paper?" said a voice. I thought it was a wrong number.

"Who is this?"

"Michael. Sorry. It's Michael from the Institute of Affirmation. We got a review for your show."

"*My* show? It wasn't mine. A review? You did not. I don't believe you. In the newspaper? No way. What time is it?"

"Seven-fifteen. And, yes, we did." Michael said.

I looked at the other side of the bed.

"The *Coastal Current* sent a reviewer! Can you meet me for breakfast? Fifteen minutes?"

"Fifteen minutes," I repeated in a sleepy daze, and he took this as agreement.

"You know that twenty-four-hour coffee shop in the shopping center? I'll be waiting there for you. I'll show you the review."

He hung up. I lay down again and closed my eyes, then forced myself to stand up. I took a shower. I put on shorts and a T-shirt, brushed and braided my hair, got my keys.

When I pulled up in front of the same coffee shop where I had eaten the night before, it was still a little too early for the place to be busy. Michael was waiting, sitting in a booth with a cup of coffee and a newspaper in front of him.

He held up the paper for me to see as I approached the table. A small headline read, AMATEUR NIGHT NOT SO BAD. There was a picture of the cast at curtain call. Some of them had their eyes closed; some of them were leaning over midbow, while others were standing, listing one way or the other, giving an out-of-balance impression that I hadn't noticed the night before. Michael beamed at me.

"Wow," I said, laughing. "This is weird. I called some newspapers after we talked. Four, I think. The *Coastal Current* wasn't one of them. Did you call? I never even heard of it."

"No. I didn't call anyone. Success!"

"Congratulations," I said.

A waitress handed me a menu, the same one I had studied the night before.

Michael said, "Look at this! It's great advertising!" He held the paper in front of my face again. "I'll buy you breakfast. What do you want? Order anything!"

"Actually, I'm not hungry. But thanks."

"We'll do a series of these dramatic productions. What do you want to direct next? It will be great. We'll get as many people involved as we can."

I held up both hands. "Michael, this has nothing to do with me. It was an accident that I ended up in that classroom. I didn't direct it. Don't you remember? My job was to write down the schedule. Then I did a couple of other things, costumes and so on. I just sort of witnessed it happening by itself. I need to get a job. I've been unemployed for weeks now. I appreciate your confidence in me, but I'm going to say no."

He said, "I see. How much time do you need? You find a job, then we'll get started again. I'm patient. I can wait two weeks or so before you hold auditions."

"It's not a matter of how much *time.*... I'm sure you can find someone who knows how to direct. Someone who's done it before."

"I don't want someone who knows how to direct. I want *you.* Now what are you going to eat? How about pancakes? Or they have some very good egg things."

"No, thanks," I said. "I'm not hungry at all. And about the play. No, I really can't do it. No." I shook my head for emphasis.

"Jenny, look at this." He held up the newspaper. "You're a hit!"

"I wouldn't exactly say that this was—"

"Let me put this another way. I *need* you. I need something to draw in some more people. Doing several shows a year might be the answer. We'll list it as a course. People like you; they'll want to be in your productions. Other people will want to watch them blossom under your touch."

I frowned and shook my head. "You're being very—"

"They'll pay money to sit in the audience. Could you please think about it?"

"Um," I said. It took everything I had not to let him get to me. He had this way of making me feel that he was counting on me, that there wasn't anyone else who could help him. I picked up the end of my braid and looked at it. I pictured Todd and his work, the steady, methodical way he moved forward with his life, one experiment leading to the next, one job leading him to another, the people he knew introducing him to people they knew, connections being made that would be useful later. That was how I wanted to be, too.

I took a deep breath and placed the tail of my braid across my upper lip: a mustache. Then I dropped my hair and looked Michael straight in the eye. He had little wrinkles next to his eyes that made me not want to disappoint him. I had to look at the napkin dispenser before I could say, "No. I need a job. I need money. Already my husband is complaining that I've spent too much time—"

Michael interrupted. "But would you consider *thinking* about it?"

"What?" I said. I looked at him again.

"Please," he said. "Just say you'll regard it as a possibility. Just that much. Say, 'I'll consider thinking about it.' Please."

"I guess I could *consider* thinking about it. I suppose I could go that far. But, of course, I'll never agree to—"

"I knew you'd come around," he said happily. "I just knew you would!" He slid a menu across the table at me. "Get something to eat! Have breakfast!"

I wanted to tell him that I hadn't come around, not at all. But I could see I wasn't going to get through. I picked up the menu. I said, "I'll have French toast."

t e n

HOMECOOKING FOR YOUR PET. Fresh food prepared with love is more wholesome for fish, bird, reptile, cat, dog, or rodent than anything you could serve out of box, bag, or can. Recipes and how-tos for all types of animal friends. Please leave animals at home and surprise them with your cooking! Mondays and Wednesdays, September 22– November 19. Course cost: $100.

*T*ODD AND I were invited to Alan Fischburger's for dinner. "He should have won a Nobel Prize," Todd said at virtually any mention of Fischburger's name. Almost two decades earlier, someone else had received the prize for work similar to his, a Swiss scientist who had worked on a smaller scale and published his findings just two weeks before Fischburger's seminal paper. Fischburger was a full professor and something of a celebrity anyway, constantly flying out of town or out of the country for speaking engagements and consulting jobs. He had his pick of graduate students and postdocs to work in his lab, which was the entire top floor of the newest building at the university. When the people in his lab looked up from their microscopes and test tubes, they had a view of the ocean. But they didn't look up very often. Fischburger expected long hours and deep concentration from his people. He was known to dismiss students for taking vacations. He held weekly lab meetings Friday evenings at six so that his people couldn't easily take the weekend off. He made surprise visits early Sunday mornings or the night before a holiday, taking note of who was in the lab working. When he was away, he might call at any moment from Switzerland, Japan, or New Jersey to get an update on a student's work. And he didn't care to leave messages. If you went to his lab at two in the morning or seven at night on Christmas Eve, you would find someone running a gel, injecting mice, writing up results. All the scientists we knew worked long hours, seven days a week, but the hardest workers were in Fischburger's lab.

Fischburger himself had recruited Todd from Tufts, even phoning once from London, waking us up in the middle of the night to ask if Todd had made his decision.

I don't know if anyone at the university realized it during the recruitment process, but for Todd, there was no decision to be made, no list of pros and cons to be drawn up, no comparison of benefit packages and university loan options to think about. There was only the presence of Fischburger at this university and the absence of Fischburger at the rest of them that rendered other variables irrelevant. Fischburger was Todd's motivating force. Even if they rarely spoke, the possibility of Fischburger looking at Todd's work was one of the things that kept Todd so focused and driven. Todd loved Fischburger long before he met him, reading his autobiography, *The Science of Life and a Life of Science*, as soon as it was published almost ten years ago and rereading it many times since whenever he was in need of comfort. The fact that Fischburger was Todd's father figure was so self-evident that to point it out would be like saying, "The universe is large" or "Water is important." Todd's adoptive father had been a dairy farmer who never talked. There was a void, and Fischburger filled it, though the man himself appeared completely unaware of having done so.

We had never been to Fischburger's house before, and Todd was nervous. Some other recently hired assistant professors were going to be there, too.

"Those shoes are too fancy," Todd said when I came downstairs ready to go. "They'll think this is a big deal to us or something."

"It is," I said, going back up for my sandals.

As I came down, he said, "Can we get *going*?" and looked at his watch as he had been doing every thirty seconds all day long. "I don't want to be late."

"I was just—it's not my fault we—yes, come on, let's go."

THERE WAS a new German car in Fischburger's driveway and a sign advertising the type of alarm system he had. From the street, the place looked small, and I was relieved. Fischburger scared me; his legendary status to Todd, his looming influence over our lives, seemed menacing to me. I didn't need a grand-scale California house—doorknobs as big as dinner plates, bathrooms the size of small-town public libraries—to make me feel any smaller than I already did.

Todd rang the bell. Fischburger's wife, Brenda, answered. She was about my age, a tan blonde from some remote part of Scandinavia, who had once been a graduate student in Fischburger's lab. They had started living together before she even defended her thesis. This happened at Berkeley quite a few years ago. I don't know what became of his first wife. Brenda was still working in the lab, as well as overseeing the work of the graduate students while Fischburger was on his many trips. She had on white pants, a white shirt, and bare feet with pink, polished toenails. "Come in," she said. Over her shoulder, she called "Fish! Fish? You're coming?"

"Yes, yes, yes," came the reply. "Give them something to drink."

"Come," said Brenda. "Fish is surfing today, and he is too late."

"Sure, yeah," Todd nodded, understanding, as if he had just finished hastily rinsing off his own wet suit minutes before.

We followed Brenda into the living room, where everything—even the stereo—was white. The two other couples were already there. "Morrison," Todd said, shaking hands with another assistant professor, "you know my wife, Jenny, right?"

The other assistant professor and I murmured greetings to

each other. He was shorter than Todd and a few years older. He came from Cornell around the same time we got here. His wife, who smiled at me now, was a scientist, too. It was one of those package deals where both husband and wife get jobs. This couple worked with yeast.

Morrison said, "Paula, you remember Jenny."

"Hi, Jenny," said Paula.

"I love your dress," I said. Should I have worn a dress? I wondered. No, Brenda wasn't even wearing shoes. Of course, she lived here, and her husband was a full professor with an international reputation.

Brenda introduced us to the third couple. "This is Miriam and Alex. They are coming here from Chicago. Today they saw houses, right, Miriam?"

Miriam applied her fingertips to her temples. "Too many houses."

"Alex is just hired as associate professor, and Miriam is still looking for a job," Brenda explained.

"Oh," I said. "Are you a scientist, too, Miriam?"

"I've been working for a biotech company. There's a lot out here for me, so something will work out."

"Great," I said. "Good."

"Are you mammalian or drosophila or what?" Miriam asked me.

I said, "I'm not a scientist." No one else happened to be talking just then, so everyone turned to listen. "I was working in a bank in a shopping center, but I got fired." No one said anything. "It was one of those downsizing things. So I'm, um, unemployed."

"She's looking for a job," Todd said quickly.

After another pause, "Well, you couldn't have picked a nicer place to be out of work," said one of the men.

I looked out the window. Fischburger's house had a sweeping ocean view framed by two tall palms. This was the first house I had been in since we moved here that had an ocean view. The sun was a big orange ball hanging low over the water, as if trying to resist the temptation to dip in. I could see the small black silhouettes of surfers on their boards, waiting for one last good one before going in for the day. The living room was on street level, but as the house was built on a hill, there was another floor below it. Outside the living room, there was a large deck that hung over the backyard.

"What a view!" Todd said, going outside to the deck railing.

Brenda went out to hand Todd a brown bottle without a label. "Have a home brew." The rest of us went out to the deck, too.

"What?" Todd said, looking at the bottle. "You make beer?"

"Ya," she said. "There's a lot of yeast at the bottom, though; that's the only problem." She handed bottles to the other scientists. Then she held a bottle up to the light. "Next time, we'll do better. It's just like science, like the lab. Beer?" she said to me.

"No, thanks," I said.

"You should try," she said, pushing it toward me again.

"No, thanks," I said. "I just don't drink beer. Thanks anyway."

"Really," Brenda said. "How unusual."

Todd frowned at me. I glared at him. He took a sip from his bottle. "Pretty good." He smiled, impressed all over again at Fischburger's accomplishments, large and small.

Fischburger made an entrance. "Well, if it isn't Mr. DNA!" he said, reaching out to Todd and causing him to blush. From sitting out on the water in his wet suit, Fischburger's hands and face were several shades darker than his arms. His tan face made his hair look even whiter than it was. He had on denim shorts and a white T-shirt. His feet were bare, too. "Howdy," he said to me, extending his hand.

"Nice to see you again," I said.

For a second I saw a look of uncertainty flicker across his face: *Have I met her before?* he was thinking. Then he covered it with a bright smile.

I said, "I hear you've been surfing."

"I get my best ideas out there on the water." He took the beer that Brenda was holding out to him and turned to Alex. "So how did the real estate hit you?"

"Expensive," said Alex.

Fischburger laughed and took a drink from his beer bottle.

Todd did the same. "This is pretty good beer," Todd said. "You *made* this? Whoa. Good stuff."

"Not bad," Fischburger agreed, and took a long drink from his bottle. He looked at Todd. "Well, here we are! How do you like it so far? The department, I mean."

"It's great," Todd said. "I'm happy."

"Good. That's what we like to hear. Hear that, Alex? He's only been here a few months and happy already. And how's the work, Todd?"

"I've got a couple of good students," Todd said. "They *seem* good."

"That's what it takes. Keep them working. Don't let them ease up, and you're on your way. And what kind of projects are you handing out these days?"

"We're still just setting up, you know, getting settled. It takes so long. But there have been a couple of interesting things. I wanted to ask you about something," Todd said. "The DNA we're trying to clone isn't cooperating. I have a feeling it's the enzymes. Could I try some of your enzymes, do you think?"

Todd started describing his recent experiments, a continuation of the work he did at Tufts. Fischburger and Brenda leaned toward him eagerly, listening intently to what he was telling them. Fischburger considered, then talked for a long time about the technical details of a complex procedure that only one lab in the world—it was in Cologne—was capable of executing. Brenda offered a few ideas, people he might contact for information. Alex, Miriam, Morrison, and Paula stepped in a little closer, offering suggestions now and then.

My mother was disappointed with the way I tried to avoid science in high school and college. If she had been born a generation later, she might have chosen the kind of work Todd was doing. So, naturally, she had hopes for me to go into some area of science. Unfortunately, I had no aptitude for it. I had been present at many discussions like the one these scientists were having now, intense technical exchanges in which many of the key words were unknown to me. You might think that I would have picked up some scientific knowledge in all the years that I had been present for these conversations. Instead, at our apartment in Cambridge, at parties, in restaurants, at chance meetings on the street or in the supermarket, I had learned to mentally check out, think about something completely different while Todd and his colleagues talked about their work. While my mind was transported somewhere else, I could continue looking at the speaker, nodding occasionally, smiling when everyone else did, appearing to listen, though often, I wished I'd brought along a book.

The sun disappeared into the ocean, leaving just a purplish glow in the sky. When the sky turned to dark gray, I wrapped my arms around myself for warmth and longed to sit down. Finally, Fischburger said, "Come up sometime and show me what you've got," concluding the discussion of Todd's work. Fischburger turned to me. I could see him struggling to think of something to say, to remember some scrap of information about me that he could use to begin a short, polite conversation that would fulfill his obligation as host. "So," he said, "you're not a scientist."

"No," I said.

He laughed as though I had made a witty observation.

Then Brenda jumped up and said, "Food! I am so interested in these results of Todd that I am almost forgetting."

"Let's get these people fed!" Fischburger said. He went to a gas barbecue in one corner of the deck and turned it on while his wife disappeared into the house. In a minute, she came out again, presenting Fischburger with a plate of marinated swordfish. "You might have something," Fischburger said over his shoulder to Todd. "It might work." He slid a spatula under a piece of fish. "You see that, Alex. You come out here, and things will start to happen."

"Hope so," Alex said.

Todd took a drink from his beer bottle, smiled at me, and took my hand. Eight pieces of fish hissed sharply as each one landed on the grill.

WE STAYED LATE at Fischburger's house. The swordfish was only the beginning. There was salad, corn on the cob, an artichoke thing that must have taken a long time to make. When it got too cold to be out on the deck, we moved inside. In the living room, the seven of them continued their talk of science in a more personal, anecdotal way: funny stories about former graduate students, dramatic findings that turned out to be artifacts, brilliant and funny talks they'd witnessed at conferences. About every ten or fifteen minutes, Todd would say, "Jenny knows him. Remember, Jen? He was the one who brought the Thai chicken to that party by the Charles?" Or, "She worked in Rankin's lab for a while, Jen. Remember? I went to her talk in Colorado." I would nod and say, "Oh yeah, didn't they have twin boys?" or "Was she the one with the Saab that was always breaking down?"

Brenda made some coffee that was almost as strong as espresso, which she served with almond cookies dipped in chocolate. Even after the coffee, I kept feeling that I just wanted to lean my head back against the white leather couch, close my eyes, and be gone from there. But I didn't. I sat up straight, trying to appear alert.

Eventually, it was time to go. "Thank you *so* much," I said to Brenda and Fischburger. "Dinner was fabulous, and I just love your house!"

Fischburger said, "It was such a treat to see you again!"

In the car driving home, Todd said, "That was great. Wasn't that fun? I think they *really* like you."

IT WOULD BE EASY enough to say that I looked at the job listings in the newspaper every day, went to several agencies, and filled out applications at a lot of banks in the area. I could say that the few interviews I had led only to disappointment. Then I could tell you that it was a down time in banking, that the real estate and construction industries in the area were depressed, impacting negatively on the local economy in general and lending in particular. I could say this to you now, and though it would seem plausible, it wouldn't be true. I didn't look for a job. In a half-hearted way, I checked the paper a few times. Then I tried to see myself at a desk doing the jobs I had circled. The picture of Mrs.

Randall, frustrated, accusing, and disappointed, came into my head, and I knew I didn't have the stomach to go back to loan evaluation.

What I did, instead of looking for a job, was check out cookbooks from the library. I served some of the food to Todd and froze the rest. I made Italian-style meat loaf and froze half of it; two nights later I cooked low-fat chicken and vegetables in the Crock-Pot and froze half of that, too. I bought a Weber barbecue for fifteen dollars at a garage sale, complete with a firestarter chimney. I asked my next-door neighbor, a financial planner named Art, how to use it.

Leaning over the fence, he explained it to me. "Stick two pieces of newspaper into the bottom of the chimney. Good. No, don't use any more than that; it will smother the flame. Fill the top part with charcoal. All the way up. OK. Now light the paper and wait twenty, twenty-five minutes, checking every once in a while that it's still lit. Before you cook, every coal has to have at least a gray corner. Then you dump it out on the bottom rack. Don't do it in bare feet, and make sure you have some water nearby."

"OK, thanks," I said. "I guess I can manage that."

"Hey, listen," he said. "You want me to put out a few feelers for you? I know a couple of mortgage people. That might be a nice area for you to get into."

I said, "No, thanks. I'll let you know if I get really desperate. Now, do I spread the coals out or leave them in a pile in the middle or what?"

"Depends on what you're cooking," he said.

"Hamburgers?"

"In a low pile is good."

"How long do I cook the burgers?"

"Five, six minutes on a side," he said. "About. Depends on the size of the burger and how you like them done, of course. You'll get the hang of it. Just takes a little practice."

I made barbecued chicken on the grill, hamburgers, and salmon. Todd kept saying, "Whoa, Jenny, this is really good," with just a hint of disbelief in his voice. He ate everything I gave him.

If we ate dinner together every night, I was thinking, a real dinner, not just take-out or an assortment of things we added boiling water to or heated in the microwave, we would be more like a family. *Pray. Work hard,* I was thinking. Most recipes produced more food than we needed. The freezer filled up with little packets with labels and dates on them. The contents could be removed for easy microwaving at some future time. I considered buying an extra freezer for the garage. I had a friend in Cambridge who had stockpiled food this way before she had a baby. When the baby arrived and she was too overwhelmed to cook, she had the food there to heat up. Once, looking for ice cream, Todd opened the freezer and said, "What's all this?" He looked at me. "Expecting a natural disaster?"

Having dinner together didn't have quite the effect on Todd that I wanted. We didn't have the great conversations that I'd imagined about what we'd done all day, what we wanted to do tomorrow, places we wanted to go together, our dreams for the future. Instead of great conversations and a renewed closeness growing between us, what grew was Todd's appetite. "What's for dinner?" he kept saying with this big grin like the father on some old black-and-white TV show.

ONE NIGHT AFTER cheeseburgers, I woke up in the dark to the sound of Todd saying, "Oh, my God. Oh, my *God*!"

I jumped out of bed, ready to grab for the phone. I thought my cooking had caused some painful intestinal disorder. Todd gasped.

"What?" I said. "What is it?"

Todd said, "What time is it in Germany?"

"Uh . . ." My heart was thumping, and I was trying to get my bearings. I looked at the clock. In San Diego, it was a little after midnight.

Todd looked at his watch, which he wore all the time, even

in the shower and to bed. "Perfect," he said. "I have to make a call. I need some mice!" He hurried downstairs to the kitchen phone. I exhaled. This was about an experiment, an idea he had about his work. Everything was fine, I realized, as my heart rate began to slow to normal. He had just had an idea for an experiment that got him all excited. Wouldn't it be great, I thought, to have work you loved so much that it woke you up in the middle of the night? I crawled under the covers again and listened to a little of Todd's side of a conversation about proteins and some chromosome; I forget the number.

I fell asleep during one of the pauses in the conversation downstairs, and when I woke up, it was light. Todd was sitting up in bed in an unbuttoned shirt and his underwear, scribbling letters and arrows on a piece of paper. "Hi," he said, glancing at me. He stood up and pulled on the pants he had left at the side of the bed the night before. *Like a firefighter,* I thought. Then he got under the covers next to me. He took my hands in his and kissed my nose. "I thought of something good," he said. He kissed my forehead and my ears.

"Did you stay up all night?" I asked him.

"Sort of. I kept thinking of more things. Gieselmann is going to send us some of his mice. Of course, it will be a while. Anyway, I've got to get to the lab. Have a good day."

" 'Bye," I said. "Call me later and tell me how it goes."

"It's going to go great!" he said, already running down the stairs. "But it will take a long time. Weeks, months. See you." The front door slammed, and he was gone.

Wouldn't it be amazing to have something like a lab to go to, work that was calling you every minute you were away from it?

112

e l e v e n

DIARY IN REVERSE. Have you ever wished that you had started a diary as a child and kept it up? Wouldn't you love to look back at your thoughts on your twelfth birthday, remember what you did three days before your wedding? It's not too late! In this class, you will have the opportunity to work backward from today and create diary entries for your great-grandchildren to cherish. Don't remember all the details? Not sure you want to record what really happened? We'll show you how to invent days you'll be happy to share. Who's going to know? 6 Wednesdays, 7–9 P.M., beginning October 15. Course cost: $60. Materials needed: notebooks, pens, and a flexible memory. NOTE: CHANGING YOUR CHILDHOOD is a related course taught by the same instructor but not a prerequisite.

MY MOTHER SAID she wanted to talk to me. I waited for her at the coffee shop at Palomar Airport. She was going to a conference in San Francisco, just for a day and a night, and asked me to go with her. I had clean clothes, a nightgown, a toothbrush, and my hairbrush in a small bag next to me in the booth. She was wearing one of her typical outfits, colors that no one else would wear on the same day: neon green turtleneck with magenta leggings, short turquoise booties with fringes along the sides. I couldn't remember when she got the booties, but her lipstick, most of it wiped off now, was the frosted pink kind that she started wearing in the late sixties, and her eye shadow was a pale blue from the same era. During her flight of several hours, small coils of her hair had escaped from the assortment of pins and clips she used to hold them down, like springs boinging out of the seat of an old couch. She hugged me, sat down at the table, and immediately set to work on refastening her hair. "You look pretty," she said, unsnapping a barrette and transplanting it to a new location. "I love that sweater."

"Thanks. I thought it might be cooler up north," I said. "I ordered you soup and a sandwich. Here it comes."

"What a good girl you are," she said, the same way she had said it all my life, squinting at me, squeezing my hand, marveling once again at her own good luck. When I was looking for my birth mother, I carried a constant leaden guilt about the way the search itself seemed to imply that there was something lacking in the mother I already had. Certainly I had my complaints, but mainly because she was always so delighted with everything I did that I never felt I could veer off course or do nothing at all when my mother was so convinced that I could be reaching the top of something.

A waitress banged dishes down in front of us. "Ketchup?" she demanded accusingly.

"Thank you, no," said my mother.

"Hot sauce?" I said. "Please?" The waitress pursed her lips and went behind the counter to rummage among some bottles. She pulled one out, brought it over, banged it down on our table, and strode off. I removed the crusted top, lifted the bread of my turkey sandwich, and shook the bottle several times.

My mother didn't talk about anything important in the restaurant; she was saving that for the plane. "Looked like storm clouds near Phoenix. I had to go around them. That's why I'm a little late." She looked at her watch. "Still, I made pretty good time. Now, how did you know I wanted French onion soup?" she said, dipping her spoon in.

"Because you never order anything else," I said.

"I guess I'm getting pretty predictable in my old age," she said. "I bet we'll have good weather all the way up."

"You're only sixty-two," I said. "That's not old." We both looked out at the sky. When we'd finished our food, my mother paid the check and led the way to the plane.

Almost as soon as we took off, the questions started. "So, Jenny," she said over Camp Pendleton, "things going a little better with Todd?"

I should have expected this. The purpose of this trip must be to check on me, find out what was going on. After our last one, she was worried. I reached back and pulled up my hair, coiled my braid up on top of my head: a hat. "I guess. I don't know. It was just one of those...kind of..." I trailed off, looking at the mountains.

"Things," my mother finished for me.

I let my hair drop. "Yeah. I don't know why I—anyway, it's just—he seems to be getting over the loss of his student. Or, I don't know if you get over a thing like that so much as you get used to knowing it."

"I keep thinking about the parents."

"Yeah. So does Todd. I have been trying to make things go better. I make dinner so we eat together every night. I try to talk to him, ask him about work. But he's always so preoccupied, so distracted. This isn't the way I wanted it to be. I had this idea that being married would be, I don't know, cozier, not so, you know, empty." My mother took a breath to say something, but I changed the subject. "He got some big idea that really perked him up. He can't wait to get to the lab every morning."

"How exciting. What is it?"

"Oh, I don't know," I said. "Something about brain tumors."

"Yes, well, of course it would be about brain tumors."

I studied the little orange balls below adorning the high-voltage wires strung through the canyons and hills, alerting pilots to the presence of danger.

Then my mother said, "So, Jenny, what are you doing with yourself these days?"

I said, "Well, I directed that play, you know."

My mother was a science-math-business type. For pleasure she read the *Wall Street Journal* and nonfiction books about money or microbes that eat toxic waste or new diseases developing in remote regions of the world. There were some things that were hard for her to relate to: music, literature, film, sculpture, painting, theater. "The play," she said, blinking. "Yes."

"Yeah," I went on. "It was just a short piece at that school I told you about, the adult education place in the old grade school. It all came about by accident, you know, but all of a sudden, I was in charge of something, and it worked out."

My mother pressed her lips together and looked at me. It wasn't a disapproving glance exactly; she didn't do that. It was more of a protective look, the way a mother dog might glance warily at noisy children coming too near her puppies. Quietly she asked, "How much did they pay you?"

"Oh," I said, "pay me. Yeah. Well, nothing. But—"

"I see."

"There isn't any money there. Really. I mean, I'm sure if they *had* any, they would have given me some. These are the most well-meaning people you can imagine. It was a nice break, doing this after the bank."

"And since then?" said my mother.

"Oh, it was just—well, I've been working on my marriage."

"Jenny, don't you think that maybe things would go better with Todd if you had your work life settled? When people are really happy with what they do, it seems that they're happier in general. Now you know that whatever you decide to do, whatever work you choose, is fine with me." She looked straight ahead for a minute, squinting into the distance. She said it was fine, but now it didn't seem so fine to me. It seemed that my activities lately were childish and selfish, things my mother, always focused and determined, would never waste her time on. She put her sunglasses on and took them off. She thought a minute, then put them on again. "So you directed a play," my mother said quietly, trying to understand. "I see."

"It's just something I did *once*." She didn't say anything, so

I went on. "I wasn't planning on doing any more of it. You know, I never liked banking. I'm not the business type. I've tried all these different jobs, and I still have no idea what my career is supposed to be. Sure, I'd like to be happy with my work, but what is it?" I had planned never to get into this subject with my mother. There was no point; I would just be worrying her over something that she couldn't help me with. "I was going against my grain in loan evaluation. I kept having to give money to businesses that didn't need it and turn down people who did. I kept finding myself saying, 'No, you may not open that store that's unlike anything else; we only believe in things that we've already seen happen a million times. No, we will not help your daughter go to fashion design school. Sorry, that idea you dreamed up isn't going to happen, after all.' I hated that. Each job I get makes me more miserable than the last. After that bank fired me, you know what I felt? Relief."

"Against your grain?" she said. "You had an excellent education. You couldn't have been better prepared for a business career. They should have been thrilled to have you at that little shopping-center branch. The problem was you were far too good for them. That's why they had to let you go."

My mother believes that a person's experience shapes her life. Given the right training in the early years, she is convinced that almost any child can be turned into a stockbroker, a physicist, or a trapeze artist. With me, she always emphasized that I should get good grades because she believed that a strong academic environment would secure my place in an excellent university, which would ensure a good job in a rewarding profession, which would lead naturally to a happy life. Her reasoning had a certain logic to it, I had to admit.

Now I have to tell you something. After high school, I attended a famous university in Cambridge, one of the ones you've heard of. I graduated and everything. All my life, my mother had steered me in this direction, believing that once I'd graduated from some high-powered university, I would be safe, secure, and protected from unemployment, poverty, and self-doubt. The same way she yanked me away from curbs and the danger of oncoming traffic as a little girl and made sure that I got all my immunizations precisely on schedule, she also did everything in her power to guide me into a good college, convinced that a career that paid well and had plenty of job openings would naturally follow. But as you can see, her plan didn't completely work out.

Now I said to my mother, "I'm not saying that I was unprepared. I'm saying that it didn't come naturally to me. Maybe that's why I've been an underachiever all these years. I never had much feeling for money and numbers. It was a struggle just to keep afloat. Even back in high school, I had to stay up all night to study for the math tests. You remember that. College was worse. Now that I think about it, I was miserable."

My mother said. "You did very well there. You had the training, and you succeeded."

As I said, I never meant to get into this. "I'm sorry, Mom. It was a lot of money." I got a partial scholarship for the tuition, and the difference was funded by Dr. Brown; it was the least he could do. But my living expenses came from my mother.

My mother said, "A good education is never wasted," then pressed her lips together, peering into the distant clouds, reading what lay ahead.

After a few minutes, she said, "Jenny, there's something I need to tell you. I need to talk to you about something that's happened."

I said, "What? What is it? What happened?" Suddenly I realized my mother had another purpose for this trip, something other than talking about how my life was going. I had unnecessarily confessed to fruitless efforts to improve my marriage, regret about my education, and aimlessness in my work life when I could have been talking about something else. I waited a minute while she checked her instrument panel. "What do you want to talk to me about?" I asked cautiously. If she had waited this long to mention it, it must be bad. Cancer, I thought, or something about my father.

"A birth mother called," my mother said.

You know that feeling you get in your stomach when you think you're alone in the house and then all of a sudden, you hear

118

a noise or see something move out of the corner of your eye? It was a squeezing in my gut and my skin seemed to radiate the dark heat of fear. I took a gulping breath. "Why didn't you tell me this right away?" I said, my voice a squeak. I exhaled. "*Mine?* Is she my birth mother?"

My mother didn't turn to look at me. "Of course, I don't know that for sure. She had a baby girl on March 10, 1962. She was in high school in Wisconsin. When she got pregnant, her parents sent her to New York until the baby was born, then she went back and finished school."

There is no way of knowing before it happens what a person's reaction will be to news like this. I didn't say anything at first, just sat there with my mouth open and my heart pounding. Then I said, "Are we landing soon? I have to go to the bathroom."

My mother ignored my question. "After all your searching, to have her just come to *you* this way!" She shook her head, smiling at me. "I can't get over it. It's amazing, isn't it? She called a few days ago. I didn't want to tell you over the phone. I thought it would be better to tell you when we were together. She said she's been searching on and off for years, then intensively over this past year. She had a lot of questions. She was ready to tell me her whole life story. And she would like to talk to you, of course, see you, especially to find out if you're happy. Funny the way people always think that's a question you can answer with yes or no and then go on to something else. Ultimately, she wants you to get to know each other." My mother was careful to keep her voice even, not to look away from where we were going, not to check my expression or to let her face show more than a small smile.

"What did you tell her?" I asked, turning sideways to examine her profile.

"I didn't tell her anything, of course," she said, indignant at the suggestion that she would betray me. "What did you *think*? Of course I said that I do not have your permission to give her information about you, that I would let you know that she wanted to talk to you. I didn't go any further than that."

"Good." I was getting warm and sweaty. "Don't tell me anything more about her. I don't want to be in touch with her. I can't do it. I'm sorry. This is the worst possible time. You'll just have to tell her I don't want a reunion or any contact at all."

"*What?*" my mother said. "I see. Well!" She waited for several seconds before she said, "Do you want to tell me why? Not that I'd repeat it, of course, I'd just like to know myself—"

"Sure," I said. "I'm a mess. I recently considered leaving my husband, and I don't have a job. I can't have her see me *now*! She should have found me a couple of years ago when I was happier. Bad timing; that's all there is to it."

This would have been a good time to run a few miles or at least walk as fast as I could to the most distant point I could reach; I had the right hormones pumping through me without so much as a warm-up. As it was, though, strapped into the front seat of a small airplane wasn't the best place to be.

My mother said, "She's very determined."

"I told you not to tell me anything else about her! And I'm determined, too," I said. I folded my arms across my chest. "I got it from you, by the way. From your example."

"Thank you," said my mother. "I'll take that as a compliment."

"You don't think she'll find out where I am, do you?" I said. "I mean, you don't know what kind of a person we're dealing with here. Some of these women are relentless. She might even be a little *obsessive*."

My mother said, "I don't think so, Jenny. She sounded quite levelheaded, very calm, kind. I'll tell her you don't want to be in touch."

I held up my hands. "You keep doing that! Don't tell me any more about her. I don't want to know if she's kind or shy or sincere or funny or any of that. I don't want details!"

"All right," my mother said calmly.

I said, "If she calls again, tell her I don't want to hear from her. I'd appreciate it if you'd do that, and don't say anything about me. Don't tell her that I never liked business or banking. Don't tell her that I lost my job recently. Don't let her know that I just tried to leave my husband. Or anything else that's ever happened to me. Couldn't you just ask her not to call anymore?"

"I can. She's going to call me Friday night. I'll tell her that you just don't want to talk to her right now. I'll get her number, in case you change your mind."

"I'm not going to change my mind! I'm telling you, I don't want to speak to this woman. Anyway, she's probably already plastered her name all over every electronic bulletin board there is. I'm sure I could find her in about two minutes flat, if I wanted to. But I don't. You didn't tell her where I went to college, did you? Because that's one very good way to hunt someone down."

"No, I didn't. Jenny, I wouldn't do that. I really don't think that her intention is to 'hunt you down.' I think what she had in mind was a mutually convenient meeting. But I'll tell her that's out of the question. I haven't given her any personal information at all, and I won't. Because you don't want me to."

"Good. I'm sorry. I know you wouldn't. I just—oh, I wish I didn't know this. I really would rather not know. When something like this happens, don't you just wish that you could just rewind back to where you were before?"

My mother laughed. "Jenny, I'm sorry, but I thought you were going to be thrilled. I honestly thought you'd want to call her right away. I mean, you *searched*. Even as a little girl, you asked me all the time who your birth mother was. I thought you'd be jumping at the chance to meet her."

"OK, I'm a little surprised myself. I just don't feel the way I thought I would. I would have been very excited to hear this a couple of years ago, maybe even a couple of months ago. Now everything has just gotten so—I want to meet her when I'm happy or at least have an income, not when she can see all my glaring deficiencies hanging out all over the place."

"Glaring deficiencies? Of course you know that she'll love you no matter what is going on in your life. You're smart and kind and pretty. You have a lovely personality. Her opinion of you will not be influenced one tiny bit by the details of what's going on at a particular moment in your life."

"You're just saying that because you're my mother," I said. "And don't tell me her name. I don't want to know."

"All right, I won't. I can understand how you feel, now that you've explained it to me. And I can see how she feels, too. If I'd given up a baby, years ago, I'd do anything I could to find her."

"You're on her side!" I shouted. "You want us to get together and pour out our life stories to each other. That's what you want, isn't it? You're hoping to chip away at my resolve until I give in and agree to meet with her. Well, I'm not doing it! It would be torture to sit down and look at her face after all this time and compare it to mine and tell her all about my friends in elementary school that she didn't meet and my birthday parties she didn't come to and all the stories I've made up in my head about her coming back to find me. Especially when she sees how I turned out!"

A small airplane is a noisy place. If you're going to yell at your mother, I recommend it. You have to talk pretty loud anyway just to converse, so if you get really upset and crank up your voice a few more notches, she might not be as upset as she would if it happened in her kitchen, say, or in the dressing room of a department store or in a parked car. I tried to get ahold of myself.

"No," my mother said, taking my hand. "No, no, no. I don't want that at all, not if you don't. I was simply delivering a message. A telephone message. A birth mother called. All right? That's it. That's all I have to say on the subject. If you don't want me to tell her anything about you, then I absolutely would not do it. You don't want to see her, talk to her about your life. I understand and support your decision."

"OK. Well. Thank you." I stared at the rivets on the wing and then down at the cars on the freeway below us. We still had quite a while before we would get to San Francisco; we had time to sit there without speaking for a long time. My mother said things into her radio every now and then. I wanted to talk about something else now, something pleasant and trivial, but I couldn't think of anything.

When my mother spoke again, she didn't change the subject. "I didn't mean to upset you," she said. "I honestly thought this would be good news."

"It's just that it brings up everything horrible about my life that I would prefer to forget. Let's not talk about it now," I said. "I went to the library and got all these cookbooks. It's not as hard as it—"

My mother said, "I wasn't aware that there was anything horrible about your life."

"Oh, well, there isn't, except that I'm adopted." I said it quietly, and as soon as I had, I hoped that she hadn't heard me. Quickly, I moved on, hoping to cover this slip. "I mean, except that I'm struggling with a bad marriage and unemployed. I made these great tostadas the other night."

"Hm," she said. "I see." She pressed her lips together and squinted into the bright sky ahead. Unfortunately, she hadn't missed what I said.

She didn't say, "Horrible? Is it so horrible that you lived with an intelligent, competent, patient mother all the time you were growing up, a mother who loved you with all the power and tenderness of her tough and capacious heart, who worshiped and respected you and to this day would do anything in the world to make you happy or help you with any problem, no matter how large or how small? Is that what you call horrible?" She didn't say that. It was worse than that. She didn't say anything at all.

I said, "Mom, I didn't mean what I just said about being adopted. You know I didn't. This birth mother thing has thrown me. I really didn't mean to—"

She said, "Jenny, if I were your birth mother, I would do anything to find you. I would line up everyone on the planet who was your age and look into each pair of eyes until I saw yours looking back at me. And I wouldn't care what you were doing or not doing at the moment. All I'd care about was finding you."

"I know you would, Mom," I said. "I know that." A dark net of misery dropped down over me because my mother was so good and so completely wasted on me. I grabbed at her kindness greedily, used it, then tossed it away, as if it were nothing more than a dirty paper napkin or a plastic bag with a hole in it. My mother took off her sunglasses and began to prepare for our descent, talking on her radio and alternately scanning the ground and her radar.

*T*HE NEXT DAY while my mother was at her meeting, I walked around the city. San Francisco is as pretty as people say it is. On a clear, almost cloudless, fall day, the sky was a dark translucent blue, and the bay glittered more than it did on the 3-D postcards you can buy at Fisherman's Wharf. I looked at the Golden Gate Bridge spanning the water, and it took my breath away. But on this particular afternoon, I couldn't look at the bridge, couldn't take in its strength and simple grace, without thinking of the people who had jumped off it. I kept staring at it, thinking about piercing beauty and pain joined irrevocably in one structure. The sight of that bridge over the water seemed to have an almost physical hold on me. I sat on a bench and stared for over an hour.

Finally, I pulled myself away from gazing at the bridge, walked through Chinatown, ate lunch, and bought a pretty pair of chopsticks for Todd. I wandered around Union Square and went into a big toy store. I didn't buy anything, because I didn't know any children, at least not well enough to give them presents.

My mother and I had dinner at an expensive restaurant overlooking the bay. We hardly spoke, and I hardly ate. My mother had lobster. "Very good," she said to the waiter when he asked. "Delicious. My daughter would like some hot sauce for hers. Thank you."

After the waiter put the hot sauce down for me and left us, I sighed and leaned back in my chair.

"What's the matter?" my mother said. "Don't think about it. Forget it. You don't want to do anything about it, so pretend it never happened."

"Sure," I said, "oh, sure."

My mother rubbed her forehead and finished her lobster.

*B*ACK AT THE HOTEL, I used the complimentary shampoo for bubble bath. In the bathtub, I rolled up my braid at the back of my head and leaned against it: a pillow. I closed my eyes

124

and tried to will something good to happen. *Love, ideas, money,* I thought to myself. *Love, ideas, money.* Something was missing. I opened my eyes. What was the first one? "Something, love, ideas, money," I whispered to myself, trying to remember. I sat still and listened to the bubbles popping, but nothing came to me. "Hope?" I said out loud. "Hope, love, ideas, money?" That wasn't it. "Fulfillment?" No. "Harmony? Peace of mind?" No. I was pretty sure it was just one word, one single word summarizing something everyone wanted. I couldn't think what that could be.

"Jenny? Did you say something?" My mother was watching television in the bedroom.

"If you hear the words, *love, ideas, money,* what's missing?" I yelled to her.

She muted the sound on the television. "What?"

"Never mind. I was just trying to remember something."

"I heard what you said, but I don't know what you mean. Is it a song or a commercial or what?"

"It's a meditation. I'll think of it." The water was starting to get chilly. I let some out and turned on the hot again. I turned it off and leaned back. A drop of sweat trickled down the side of my face. "Love, ideas, money," I chanted. An image of a woman's face came into my head: dark eyes, creased at the corners, a lot of dark hair. She was looking at me, peering as intently as a doctor would. Then she smiled. Despite the heat in the room, a shiver went through me. I opened my eyes, sat up fast, as if waking up from a nightmare. Water sloshed onto the floor.

"Jenny?" said my mother.

"I'm getting out now," I said. I stood up quickly and opened the drain. I grabbed a little too fast for my towel and knocked the shoeshine cloth and my mother's deodorant into the bathwater. When I reached to fish them out, my hand was shaking. I wrapped a towel around myself and opened the bathroom door. "If you want the bathroom, it's all yours," I said, pulling my nightgown out of my bag.

"That was quick," my mother said.

twelve

MUSIC FOR THE NON-MUSICAL. Even YOU can learn
to play the piano, recorder, accordion, or harmonica; sing an
aria; or improvise a blues vocal. Your age, lack of experience,
or bad attitude about practicing will no longer be an
obstacle. One-on-one instruction will bring out your hidden
talents. Class times by appointment with instructor. Course
cost: $45 for three one-hour sessions scheduled at your
convenience.

I MEANT TO TELL Todd about my birth mother trying
to find me. I was thinking about it all the time. The key to making
a marriage work, I had read over and over again, is communication. You have to talk to each other. Very important. On the other
hand, I was worried that as soon as I mentioned it, he would push
me to get in touch with her. Besides, he kept coming home late
or in a bad mood or preoccupied about the new project he was
working on, collaborating with someone in Germany. I knew it
wasn't right to keep something from him that I was thinking
about this much, but I kept putting off telling him. After I had
known for five days, I promised myself I would say it just as soon
as he walked through the door.

When he came home that night, just as I was about to blurt
out the news about my birth mother, Todd said, "My graduate
students are having a party tonight. Let's go, OK? You'll like them.

We won't stay long, just half an hour or so, just to be polite. Then we'll go out to dinner or something."

"A party?" I said. "OK. Let me just go change."

"Don't," Todd said. "They're graduate students, remember."

"Right. Let's go, then."

On the way, in the car, we could talk about it, I thought.

"Should we bring something?" I said.

"Yeah," said Todd. "I'll stop and get some beer."

In the supermarket, as Todd was choosing from the array of imported beers, I was thinking, *I'll start as soon as we get back in the car.* This way, there would be plenty of time to get out the important facts, plus a built-in stopping point to the discussion when we arrive at the party. He chose beer from a microbrewery in Oregon. "Never heard of it," he said as we got in line to pay.

Todd drove. When we were on the freeway, I thought, *Tell him. Now. One, two, three, go.* I took a breath, opened my mouth.

Todd said, "I'm getting good people. They don't work hard enough, but I think I've got a couple of stars."

"How many do you have now?"

"Six. Four graduate students and two postdocs. They sort of came all at once. Three of them are American, one is German, one's Dutch, and one's Japanese."

"That sounds like a lot of people," I said. "I know you were worried about it when we left Cambridge."

"About what?"

"That the best students would go to the big-name East Coast schools, that this area was second-rate, scientifically."

Todd looked away from the road for a second to glare at me. "I never said that. That's just your eastern bias."

"Wait a minute," I said. "I'm not the one who—I don't have an eastern bias. Do I?"

"Sure you do. You think that just because the weather's nice, people don't work hard, that they're distracted by the sun and the surf and the fact that everything is clean and pretty here. But that's not true. I mean, I guess it is for some people, but not the ones I take into my lab."

"Good for you," I said, folding my arms, looking out the window. "You're so open-minded."

"I think I'll get a gas barbecue," Todd said. "Don't you think that would be better than charcoal?"

"A gas barbecue? What's wrong with the one I bought? You mean like Fischburger's? Ours is fine. I do all the cooking on it anyway."

"Maybe if we had a gas one, one that's quicker, more efficient to use, I would cook on it. I might even invite people over so we could have some kind of social life, too, for a change.

"Great idea. A gas barbecue is the answer. It will solve all our problems."

"Problems?" Todd said. "What problems? What are you talking about?"

I folded my arms, looked straight ahead, and didn't answer. Now I didn't feel like telling Todd anything. And we were almost there; I didn't have enough time to say anything big. As we pulled into a parking place, I tried to arrange my face so that it would not be obvious that Todd had made me mad in the car.

The party house was in a neighborhood that had been brand-new thirty years ago but now looked run-down and battered. A young woman in cutoffs and a T-shirt came to the door. "Todd!" she said, smiling, glad to see him.

"Hi, Melissa." Todd turned to me. "This is my wife, Jenny. Jenny, this is Melissa. She lives with Aaron, the postdoc I told you about from Cooper's lab."

"Hi," I said, shaking her hand.

"Come in, come in," Melissa said to Todd. "Aaron is just dying to talk to you. Something's happening with the mice."

"Tumors, I hope," Todd said cheerfully.

"You got it," Melissa said. "I'll take that." She led us through the living room full of people to the kitchen, where she set the beer on the counter. There were candles all over the place and a CD of live blues was playing. The sliding glass doors to the back-yard were open so people could move easily between inside and outside. The house was at the top of a canyon. Fog was rolling in, and a lot of people had put on sweatshirts and jackets. "Aaron was just here a minute ago," Melissa said. She put on a men's sport coat that was way too big. The sleeves came down over her hands. As we followed her around the house, looking for Aaron, I noticed that other women had the same kind of used men's jackets—several of them very wrinkled—over dresses, skirts, and shorts. On some of the women, the sleeves were neatly rolled back, showing the satin linings. "Nice jacket," I said to Melissa.

"Nineteen ninety-nine," she said. "A bunch of us went shopping all together and bought them." She opened it, showing me the inside.

"You all go shopping together?" I said.

"Oh, yeah. We do all kinds of stuff together. Here he is!" said Melissa. "Aaron, Todd's here!"

Todd went over to one of his students, a tall man with long hair, and said, "OK, Aaron, what'd you get?"

"Have some food," Melissa said. She led me to a table filled with all sorts of fancy homemade dishes. There was curried chicken with coconut milk and raisins, rice spiced with rare things that I couldn't name, a plastic container of goat-cheese spread layered with pesto and sun-dried tomatoes, a loaf of braided bread.

"Did someone make all this?" I said. "I should have made something. Have you been planning this long?"

"Couple weeks," she said. "We've got more than we can eat as it is. Most of us like to cook. Being in the kitchen is like doing experiments for us, you know. We have a lot of parties. Want a beer?"

In plastic buckets borrowed from the lab, there were dozens of brown, green, and clear bottles from several countries that I didn't know made beer.

"No, thanks," I said. "Did you know Fischburger and his wife make their own beer?"

"No kidding. There's juice." From a gallon jug, she poured me a cupful of fruit punch the color of a bruise.

"Mmm," I said, taking a sip. "What is this?"

"Mixed fruit. Organic."

"It's very good," I said.

People were standing or sitting in clumps, talking and laughing. I said, "You all seem to get along really well."

Melissa shrugged. "We do. We're together fourteen hours a day a lot of the time, so that's a good thing. We have a lot of parties. That helps."

"Sounds like fun," I said. If I could have joined a lab just for this social aspect, I would have done it in a minute.

"You should come to more of the parties, visit the lab more."

"I can never find a parking space," I said.

Melissa laughed. "Have some food."

I looked at Todd. "I'll just have this juice," I said, as I knew we would be leaving soon to go out to dinner. In some quiet restaurant, I would tell Todd about my birth mother.

A man with red hair came to join Aaron and Todd. He had a ring in his nose, which was connected by a thin gold chain to an earring. I went to stand next to Todd, thinking my appearance might serve as a cue to leave. I was getting hungry.

I gathered that the redheaded man was talking about his mice and their children, or offspring, whatever, and the way they seemed to be dying a lot sooner than he expected. "I mean, granted, they have all these tumors, but I can't help thinking there must be more to it than that." He looked up at Todd, who was taller, and waited for his reply. Todd took a deep breath and went over some possibilities. Aaron listened, absorbed.

I went to the living room and looked at photographs on the walls, the hosts' families. There was a group shot of a lot of people—four generations, it seemed—standing on a dock in bathing suits. I checked for resemblances in the faces and thought I could tell who was a blood relative and who had married into the family. I tried to imagine being one of them, standing there in the group, the shape of my nose matching an older woman's next to me. Now another party guest came to stand beside me. I turned.

"Will," said a man, extending his hand.

"Jenny," I said. We shook hands.

"Are you interested in photography?"

"No, not really. I was just comparing the faces, seeing who was related here."

"Oh, well, yeah. Genetics. Makes sense."

"No," I said, holding up one hand. "I'm not a scientist."

"Oh," he said, surprised. "What are you then?"

I took a deep breath. "To tell you the truth, I'm not sure what I'm supposed to—"

"Excuse me," he said, "I have to get the door." He walked away.

I looked at my watch. We had been there over an hour. Todd was still talking. You'd think they would have had enough of each other after being in the lab together all day. But Todd seemed to need to speak to everyone there, one to one, about experiments. The students had a lot to say to him, too, as if they had been saving things up for tonight. Luckily the music was loud, because my stomach was rumbling.

I sat down on the couch and picked up a magazine. It was *Cell*, and though I knew I wouldn't understand a word of it, I opened it anyway. We had this one at home; I recognized the cover. I leafed through it, as if I might stop at an article that interested me and start to read. After a minute, I got to the last page and put it down.

A young man came over and sat next to me. "So," he said, "nice party, huh?"

"Very nice," I said.

"Can I get you a drink or something to eat? I'm Jack."

We shook hands. "Jenny. No, thanks. I'm fine. I think I'm going to try to drag my husband away in a minute."

"You have a husband? I thought you were alone."

"Todd. Todd's my husband. Maybe you know him." I pointed at Todd. He was holding a napkin against a wall, drawing a diagram on it with a ballpoint pen. He stopped a second to shake it, then wrote some more. Several people were peering close to see.

"Todd?" he said. He stood up fast, as if suddenly discovering that the chair was wet. "You're married to *Todd*?"

"Yes," I said. "What's the matter?"

"Nothing," he said. "I work in his lab. But I never see you in the lab. I just didn't know he was married. Where's your lab?"

"I don't have a lab. I'm not a scientist."

"Wow," he said, sitting down again. "That's amazing. Incredible. What do you guys *talk* about?"

"Oh, just—we, you know, there's more to Todd than just his interest in science."

"There is?" Jack said. "I didn't know that. He's always in the lab. When do you ever see each other?"

"Well, we—" I searched for something else to talk about. "Are you married?"

"No," said Jack. "I live with someone. She's a scientist, too. She works in the same building. She's over there, Deb, see, with the ponytail, standing by the refrigerator. We talk about science all the time."

I looked at his girlfriend. She was frowning, describing something in detail to Todd, who was leaning down toward her, listening. Deb had her first finger and thumb pressed together to indicate something very small. Todd bent lower, as if to see what it was.

"What do you do?" Jack asked me.

"I was just kind of . . . I'm unemployed."

"Hey," he said. "It happens."

Todd interrupted what Deb was saying. Even from across the room, I could hear him shout, "Yes! Hollander got the same result at Yale. I just talked to him this morning! He thought it was an artifact!" He reached into his pocket, pulled out his wallet, and took out a small card. He grabbed a napkin off a table and copied something down to give to Deb.

Jack stood up. "Excuse me. This looks good. I've got to get in on this. See, that's the purpose of parties—ideas, collaborations."

"Yeah," I said. I followed him outside to where Todd and Deb were joining another group of people.

A man was saying, "You know that first paper you had in *Nature*? We read that paper in an undergraduate course."

132

"That was ages ago," Todd said. "You'd have to do more than that now to get a paper." Then he noticed me standing next to him. "Jenny," he said, introducing me. I shook hands with the other man. "This is Robert."

"Hi, Robert," I said, shaking his hand. Robert's eyes focused on me briefly, then went back to Todd, even before he let go of my hand. Todd put his arm around me, squeezing my shoulder, then letting it go. "So, how old were you when you did that work?" Robert wanted to know.

"Twenty-three or so. Right, Jen?" Todd squeezed my shoulder again.

"Yeah," I said. "I think so."

I remembered that the day the paper was accepted, we went out to dinner to celebrate. Before the food came, Todd said, "Now I'm really going to have to work hard. Now I really have to do something."

"What do you mean?" I said. "I thought you could take it easy for a while."

"Are you *kidding*?" he said, horrified at this suggestion. "If I did that, then everyone would think this paper was a fluke, a lucky accident." He shook his head. "If I want to get a good postdoc, I'm going to have to work like a maniac." It took me a long time to clue in to the fact that they all worked like this, seven days a week, all day every day for decades, their whole careers.

Now Todd absently squeezed my shoulder, let it go, squeezed, released, the way people with hand injuries exercise their muscles back into shape with a tennis ball. "Todd," I said, after a lengthy discussion of proteins. "I think it's time to go. I'm really starving."

Todd looked at me. "Go?" he said, as if the word were new to him. "Now?"

"You said half an hour." I looked at my watch. We had been there three and a half hours.

"OK, just a minute, though. I've just got to find out what happened with Will this afternoon. One more thing. He went over to Scripps to get some plasmids. There's all kinds of food here. Get something to eat."

"I thought we were going out," I said.

"Just eat here," he said. "It's getting so late." Todd went back into the house. Through the window, I could see him in the kitchen, interrupting a conversation. A small circle of students stopped talking and laughing, and listened to Todd's question. I went into the kitchen and loaded up a plate with what was left of the food. Everything was cold now, of course, but I was so hungry I didn't care about that.

"That's ridiculous," Todd was saying.

There were no clean forks, but I found a used one on a plate and washed it.

Todd said, "I never heard of anything so stupid. It's already published! What are they being protective about? I'll call them tomorrow. Pisses me off. You guys, I'll see you in the morning."

" 'Bye, Todd," they all said.

"Jenny?" Todd called from the door.

I put the plate down. "Good-bye," I said. "It was nice to meet you all."

I followed Todd outside to the car.

Pulling out of the parking space, he said, "Nice party, wasn't it? Wasn't that fun?"

"Yeah," I said. He was getting on the freeway to go home. "Wait. Aren't we going to eat?"

"Didn't you eat there? I couldn't eat another thing. I'm completely stuffed."

"I thought we were going out. I waited, then I— Never mind. I'll get something at home."

Todd said, "What? What's the matter?"

"What? Nothing," I said. This was my chance to tell him about my birth mother. I should do it now, while I had his attention, before we got into another argument or he started thinking about experiments again.

"Good people, aren't they?" He patted my knee.

"Yes," I said. "Good. Listen—"

"I just wish they'd work harder. When I was a graduate student, I didn't go to half the parties they do. And they take time off in the middle of the day to eat lunch or have coffee. I bet they don't do that in Fischburger's lab."

"They have to eat lunch, Todd," I said. "You eat lunch, don't you?"

"Not for an hour every day. No, I don't do that." He looked over his shoulder and changed lanes. "I mean, some of these guys are gone for a full hour smack in the middle of every day."

"But they stay until, what, ten or eleven at night? They seem to work hard. They don't talk about anything else. I mean, the lab seems to be their whole world."

We passed an exit. There would be three more before we got to ours. Now would be the time to say something. I could still get my news out and have a short discussion before we got home. I looked out at the freeway signs letting me know how far we had to go before each off-ramp.

"And they listen to music all day in the lab. I'm going to hide that boom box they use. I swear I am. I hate that thing. If you want to be a scientist, it has to be *everything*. You have to live it, eat it, breathe it, dream about it. It has to be burning inside you. Do you think Hansen would have tolerated coffee breaks?" Hansen was Todd's boss when he was a graduate student. "We would have been thrown out in about two minutes for that kind of crap."

"You drank coffee. I distinctly remember meeting you at that place with the red tables."

"Only when I was so exhausted I could barely stand up. Some of these guys have regular coffee times." Todd gave a disgusted snort. "Hans goes every morning at ten and every afternoon at two-thirty! And it takes *twenty minutes*!" He shook his head.

We passed two more exits.

"Todd?" As I said his name, I had a mental picture of what his reaction would be to my news. He would become suddenly animated, the way he did when his students told him they had interesting results. He would laugh and shout with joy, congratulate me, tell me how lucky I was, ask me when my birth mother and I were meeting, and what I was waiting for.

"Yeah?" he said, and waited. Then I realized I couldn't face his enthusiasm. I wasn't equal to the task of sorting out the complicated mixture of feelings I had about the news. "What, Jen?"

"Oh, nothing."

"Nothing? What? Tell me. Come on. I hate when you do that."

"I love you. That's all. I know we have nothing in common, and we hardly ever see each other. The thing you care most about is something I know nothing about. I don't know what you do all day or what you think about. But we've been together a long time, and I love you. That's all. I just wanted to say that."

"Well, I love you, too," he said. He turned his head slightly toward me, a question, a worry, passing over him like a gust of wind through a door that opened briefly, then closed again. His hand left my knee so he could turn on the radio. Jewel came on, a song I liked. I opened my mouth to sing along. Todd turned off the radio. "I can't believe that guy at Scripps, refusing to give up his plasmids for something that was published five years ago. *Five years.* Ridiculous. People are so weird." We got off the freeway.

thirteen

DRAWING BLINDFOLDED. In this course, you'll silence your internal art critic and set free your artist by drawing without looking at your paper or your subject. Saturday, October 25, 3–5 P.M. Course cost: $20. No previous drawing experience necessary. Materials: paper, crayons, markers, charcoal, bandanna or other blindfold. "See" you there!

*T*HE NEXT DAY, I was in the bank where we had our checking account, which also happened to be the one I used to work in. I had a lot of change I wanted to deposit—quarters, nickels, dimes, pennies. I'd spent the morning putting all the change I could find into rolls. I tried not to come into this place if I could help it, but this was the only way I could think of right now to make our account balance rise instead of fall. I filled out the deposit slip, waited in line. It was Friday, casual day. All the tellers were wearing shorts or jeans.

"Jenny," said the teller, smiling brightly, when it was my turn. "What can I do for ya?"

I had been hoping to get someone new, someone who didn't remember that I used to work here. "Hi, Wendy," I said. "I'm just depositing this."

"Cleaned out the old piggy bank, huh?"

"Yeah," I said. "Sure did."

She took the money, counted it, gave me a receipt. Her T-shirt, a yellow one, said, THE ANSWER IS YES.

"So where are you working now?" she said.

"Actually, I decided to take some time off."

"Cool," said Wendy, nodding. "Kick back for a while. I hear ya. Well, take care!"

"I like your shirt," I said. " 'Bye."

I turned to leave, and there was Michael from the Institute of Affirmation, leaving the teller next to mine. You think you're a newcomer, a stranger in a place, and all of a sudden you know people and find you've acquired a past.

"Jenny," Michael said. He had on a black sweatshirt with the sleeves cut off, his black ballet shoes, purple bike shorts, and a blue baseball cap.

"Michael. I didn't see you."

"Yeah, well, here I am." He smiled at me.

He held the door open, and we stopped on the sidewalk near the ATM. A woman using the machine glanced sideways at us and cupped her hand around the keypad, as if we might be after her secret code.

Michael said, "Are you ever going to take one of my classes?"

"Dance classes?" I shook my head. "I don't think I—"

"Well—"

"My birth mother wants to get in touch with me," I blurted out suddenly. I didn't plan to say this. I didn't even know I was thinking about it then.

Michael looked at me. "Your birth mother? Really?"

Shifting my braid in front of my shoulder, I wiped the tail over the palm of my hand: a paintbrush. "She called my mother and asked her to tell me she'd like to talk to me. I don't want to do it. I just don't want to bring up all this emotional stuff and go through it. I don't see why I should have to. A lot of adoptees want to reconnect with their birth mothers. For a long time I did, too. You want to see what she looks like, what kind of person she is. But that's not all there is to it. I mean, let's assume that you can get past the fact that you were given up in the first place, which is a biggie in itself. But after that, once you do reconnect, what do you do with that person? I mean, do you have Thanksgiving dinner with someone who gave you away as a baby? Do you buy her a Christmas present? How much should you spend? She is a complete stranger, after all; then again, she's a close relative. I mean, it's not as if I have some disease and need to find a genetically similar person to donate an organ or something. It's up to me, after all, and I choose *not* to meet my birth mother. I believe that's my right." All this bubbled out of me automatically like hot water rising to the surface from an underground spring.

We stood there quietly for a minute. I was a little breathless from saying so much so fast. Michael looked at me. I sat down on the curb. He sat next to me.

"I see what you're saying," Michael said after a few more seconds. "You might be curious about her, wanting to know, say, if she's the source of that thick black hair or the butterfly shape of your mouth." He cleared his throat and looked at the license plate of the car near us: LETSGO, it said. He looked back at me. "But once you satisfied your initial curiosity, there would be a whole lot more to do, wouldn't there? I mean, I guess you can't just take a look and walk away. You can't very well have her send a picture or a video, fill out a questionnaire, and have the whole thing over with, can you? Once there's contact, you've started something. She'd have her questions you'd need to answer, and before you knew it, you'd be having a conversation; a relationship would have begun where there wasn't one before." He looked at me, thinking, nodding. "And that's not what you want?"

"No. Right," I said. "That's what I mean exactly. Yeah. That's it. An adoptee has all these fantasies about her birth mother that meeting her as an adult can't possibly satisfy."

Michael sat there looking at me again. I imagined that he was trying to picture my fantasies.

"I told my mother not to give her my number," I said. "I don't want her to give out any information about me at all."

"Good," he said decisively. He looked at me for a long time and didn't say anything. "You're very clear about it."

"I am?"

He nodded.

"Oh, good." I felt relieved, as if he had solved something for me. I sighed and stood up. "I guess I better get going."

Michael looked up at me, putting a hand over his eyes to shield them from the sun. "By the way, have you thought at all about what we discussed the last time we talked?"

"What?"

"About doing another play?"

"Oh, that. Honestly, no. Not even for a second. I'm sorry. But you'll find someone else. I have considered thinking about it, like you said, but I'm supposed to be looking for a job." I flipped my braid from in front of my shoulder to my back. "I'm going to be just, you know, very busy with that. Soon." Now I felt embarrassed about telling all this personal stuff and then saying no to him.

"I see," he said. "Well. I hope you find a good one then."

"Thanks," I said. "And thanks for listening to my—"

"Not at all."

"See you."

"Sure hope so." He smiled at me.

" 'Bye," I said on the way to my car.

Michael kept looking at me, as if waiting for me to say something else. I waved. He tipped his baseball cap, then walked to his pickup, which was parked in one of the ten-minute spaces in front of the bank.

AT HOME, I went to our computer, double clicked on the icon for our on-line service. I typed in Todd's password. As soon as I was connected, I typed the keyword *Adoption.* I read what other people had to say about their searches. Some of the letters were from birth mothers searching for daughters and sons they had given up. Others were from adoptees searching for birth parents. Most of the people writing, adoptees and birth parents, were women. There were no messages from birth fathers. Some of the adoptees had become birth mothers themselves. One adoptee in Missouri wrote at length about how important it was to take time to get to know your birth mother through letters, e-mail, and phone calls before meeting her in person. I didn't see anything that looked as though it might be about me.

I called my mother. I didn't even say, "Hi, it's me, how are you? Do you have a minute?" I went straight to "I want the number." Though I knew she understood what I was talking about, she didn't respond right away. "I'm going to call her."

"Are you sure?" said my mother. "What made you change your mind? What does Todd say?"

"Mom, I don't want to talk this over. I really don't want to explore the pros and cons, the meanings and ramifications, the ripples it will cause. I'm sick of all that. I'm way past that anyway. I just want the number."

"All right," she said. I heard her put the phone down and open a drawer. I chewed a hangnail, trying to get it off without making myself bleed. My mother came back. "Of course, it's entirely up to you, as I've said. But I'm just thinking, you say you don't want to be in touch with her and then just a week or so later, you do. You might just want to wait a few more days until all these conflicting feelings settle down."

I didn't say anything. Knowing me as well as she did, she could probably imagine the way my eyes were narrowing, the clenched set of my jaw.

"All *right*. Now, I already told her that you had decided you didn't want to speak to her. So, she's not going to be expecting this. Ready?"

I wrote the number in my address book under *B* for birth mother, though her name was Elena Giordano Miller. "Giordano is her maiden name," my mother explained. She spelled it for me. "Got it," I said to my mother. *Italian,* I thought, *that makes sense.* I was Italian American. Of course. The hair, the complexion. Everything fell into place. I remembered that vision or dream or whatever it was I had when we were in San Francisco, the dark woman looking at me. *Elena Giordano,* I thought to myself, *my birth mother.*

"Jenny," my mother said. "Are you sure you want to do this?"

Here is the truthful answer to that question: "No. I'm not.

I'm not sure of anything from one minute to the next." But I didn't say this to my mother; I didn't want her to worry. "Yes," I told her. "It just took me by surprise the other day. That's all. Now I am absolutely, positively one-hundred-percent sure."

"Do you know what you're going to say?"

"I'm going to write it all out," I said, "and practice it before I call."

"That's smart. Take some time," my mother said. "Think it over. Be clear about what you're thinking and feeling. This is an important step. Don't jump into it too fast."

"Mom," I said. "I know. I've been to seminars, read articles and books, talked to people about their searches. I know what to do. Believe me, I know exactly what to do. I'll be calm and careful, and I won't rush into anything. Don't worry, Mom."

"I won't," my mother said. "You've always been very level-headed and cautious."

"Thanks."

"I just don't want you to be hurt or disappointed."

"I promise I won't be hurt or disappointed. OK? Don't worry," I said again.

"Let me know how it goes."

"Sure, Mom. OK. Thanks."

" 'Bye, sweetheart. I love you."

"I love you, too. 'Bye."

My heart was pounding, and I couldn't breathe right. I pushed the button down to hang up and immediately lifted it again for a dial tone. I punched my birth mother's number. I was hoping not to get an answering machine. I didn't want any delays. She answered on the first ring, as if she had been sitting there waiting for my call.

"Hello?" she said. I had heard my birth mother's voice.

"Hello, is this Elena Giordano?" I said.

"Yes," she said cautiously. "That's my maiden name."

She thinks I'm going to try to sell her something, I thought. "My name is Jenny Brown." I waited for this to click, to mean something to her.

"Yes?"

"My mother, Kate Brown, in Connecticut, gave me your number. You called her? I understand that you're looking—"

"Oh, my!" she said. "I'm going to have to sit down. I don't believe this! I thought you weren't going to call. I thought you had decided you didn't want to—" Her voice broke, and she started to cry.

"I changed my mind," I said.

"I'm so happy you called," she said quietly. "I've waited so long. I was so disappointed before, and now this has really come as a surprise. A good surprise. I mean, I'm happy."

"I'm happy, too."

Then we started to talk, both of us asking questions so fast that neither had time to answer. After the first few minutes, we hung up so she could call me back; she insisted that she should pay for part of the conversation. I was afraid to put the phone down, worrying that she might not call back. I did it, though, and the twenty or so seconds before it rang seemed to last a week. When it did, I jumped.

"Hello?" I said.

"Oh, good. Now. Are you married?" she said this as if it were the first question on a prepared list.

"Yes," I said. "My husband is a biologist. He's an assistant professor at a university here."

"How wonderful!" she said.

"Yeah."

"And children? Do you have any children?"

"No," I said. "No children."

"Really?" she said, a little deflated. For a moment, I thought she was going to tell me this was a mistake, that I ought to rethink it. "I always pictured you with children."

These would be her grandchildren, of course. Already, I thought, I'm a disappointment to her. "Sorry," I said. "No children. What about you?"

"I've been married for thirty-one years," she said. "My husband is an investment banker. We live in Pennsylvania." She gave me this information the way she had probably said it a thousand other times. "I've been blessed with three wonderful children." She stopped then, and there was a kind of inaudible thud.

I thought, *Not counting me, she means; she has three children not including me.*

Then she said, "I mean, my husband and I have three. Two girls and a boy, all grown now, of course. My oldest girl has two kids of her own, both girls, and another baby on the way. My other daughter has one boy. My son—he's the baby of the family—isn't married yet. My husband and kids are the ones who encouraged me to search. It was like there was always this big empty space there between me and my life. I was there, and I wasn't there. I had a part of me that no one could get to, not my husband, not my kids, no one. I tried therapy, Bible study groups, and all kinds of things. Finally, my husband brought home a computer for me and talked me into getting on the Internet. It's scary at first. You're afraid of what you might find, that you might end up feeling worse, instead of better. But I got hooked. I was on-line pretty much full-time for about the past two years. I finally got in touch with one of the other adoptees from the maternity home where I was. She was a year younger than you, but she was the key to finding you."

"Rosalyn," I said, remembering an on-line friend from my search.

"Right! She told me you used to live in Cambridge, that you were from Connecticut. Nothing more, though. She was very protective. She kept saying I'd have to get the rest of the information from you. It took a while, but I finally found your mother through the phone book! I must have called a hundred Browns before I got her. Then when I was so close and you didn't want to hear from me, I just about died of disappointment. Well, I finally quieted myself and started to pray. I said, 'Lord, you got me this far, now take me the rest of the way.' Well, I guess He heard me! I'm so glad you changed your mind," she said. "Do you pray, honey?"

"Not very often," I said.

"Really?" She was surprised. "I always pictured us both praying to find each other. No matter. The Lord was watching over you, bringing you to me. He had us both in His care. I knew that if I just kept at it, I would find my birth daughter. Jenny," she said. "Jenny. I like that name. I would have called you 'Anna.' I always thought of you as 'Anna.' But Jenny is nice, too."

Jenny had always sounded childish to me, lightweight. "Anna," I said, and instantly I liked it better than the name I'd had all my life.

"Now, what do you want to do about getting together?" Elena asked me. "Would you . . . do you think we could meet? I'll come to you, of course."

"I want to," I said. "Yes. As soon as possible. If that's OK."

"Oh, this is wonderful," she said, laughing. "I can't wait! I know you're not supposed to jump right into a meeting, but I feel that thirty-five years is long enough!"

"So do I," I said. Now I would know what it felt like to look at a blood relation. At the idea of this, goose bumps rose on my arms. We could find someone to take our picture together. I would get it framed and hang it on my wall, carry a small copy in my wallet. "This is my birth mother," I would tell people. "Yes," they would say. "Oh, yes, I can see that. The eyes, the mouth." "And the hair, of course," I would add. "The hair goes without saying."

"Thirty-five years is plenty," I told my birth mother. "We can do this our own way. We can do whatever we want about getting together! We don't have to listen to anyone."

We decided to meet in three days in San Diego. My birth mother would fly out. She said not to worry about the money. She could handle it, she said, and it would be worth it. I named a restaurant, a Mexican place I had been to with Todd when we first moved here that was easy to find from the airport. Elena made a flight reservation and called me back with a time: two-thirty, Monday.

"Good. Two-thirty, then," I said.

She laughed. "I can't believe this is happening. I mean, it's like on the one hand, I can't quite take it in and on the other hand, I expected it all along."

"Yeah," I said. "I know exactly."

"God bless you, honey."

"Same to you," I said, and hung up. Then I wondered if that was the right response. Maybe I was just supposed to say "Thank you."

I DROVE DOWN to the lab again and waited for Todd in his office. "What, Jen? What happened?"

"My birth mother found me," I said. "She called my mother, and then I called her. She's flying here on Monday." It was easy now, not hard to say at all.

"That's great," he said. He put a hand to his forehead. "Wow! This is excellent news. Let's go outside. Let's get out of here."

"You have time? You don't have an experiment or a meeting or—"

"Nothing that can't wait."

We went outside and sat under a tree. "You needed this," he said. "You deserve this. I'm so happy for you. This will really help."

I guess my face didn't look as pleased as he expected it to. Todd looked worried.

"Jen?" he said. "What's the matter? Are you OK?"

I tried to talk. "It's just so—I don't know—"

He pulled me close and I pressed my face into his T-shirt.

"OK," he said, patting me. "OK. That's it. There you go."

Todd sat there with me for a little longer, holding my hand, checking my face, saying, "OK? Sure?"

I nodded.

"This is going to be the beginning of a whole new phase for you, a bunch of really good stuff. You'll see." He squeezed my hand.

"You better go back now," I said.

"You think?" Todd looked at his watch.

"Yeah, go," I said. "Otherwise, the students are all going to leave their benches and go for coffee. See you at home."

"I guess you're right." He got up and started walking back

to the lab, and I started the long hike to my car. "Jenny!" Todd called a few seconds later. I turned around, and he was hurrying toward me. He held me again, pressing me against him. There was a place in Todd's chest where I always put my head. I did that, and he put one hand on my back and one hand on my hair. "See you at home," he said, letting go.

NATURALLY, I couldn't sleep for the next three nights. I was getting used to the idea that now I knew my birth mother, that I would see her soon. "My birth mother," I whispered to myself in the dark, practicing the sound of it. "My birth mother lives in Pennsylvania. My birth mother said, my birth mother has . . . My birth mother's name is . . . My birth mother and I . . ." I liked the sound of it. I had waited a long time. Todd was right, I had earned this.

I kept flopping around in bed, and I woke up Todd. He understood how excited I was, though, and he was happy for me. "What's she like?" he wanted to know. "What kind of person?"

I said, "She talks a lot and she's religious."

"Religious?"

"Yeah. Honestly, she wasn't exactly what I pictured for my birth mother, but they never are, are they? I mean, how could a real person match someone you dream up in your head? It's just not possible."

"No. Everybody says the same thing. Birth mothers are always a surprise. And talking a lot and being religious aren't bad," Todd said. Better than dead, he meant. But he didn't say that; he was happy for me. Added to the stew of my feelings simmering away inside me, there was a dollop of guilt over the fact that I had a live, healthy birth mother and Todd did not. "Are you going to bring her over here?" he asked. "Maybe you could bring her to the lab. I'll show her around."

"I don't know," I said. I wasn't ready to share her. I wanted to keep her to myself, though I knew this was greedy of me. Todd was never going to get to show his life to his own birth mother, after all. "I'll see how it goes, OK? I don't know how long she's

147

staying or anything. You know what? I like her, and I don't think it's just because she's my birth mother. I mean, we just hit it off really well. I know it's a stupid thing to say, but it felt like I'd known her all my life."

Todd hugged me. "It's not stupid. It's good. I'm glad."

"Me, too," I said, and I kissed him. "My birth mother! I've *talked* to my birth mother!" I squeezed him. "I'm so happy."

We made love. I didn't even have to talk him into it.

I would let him show her the lab. I would have my camera with me and ask one of the students to take a picture of all three of us, a family photograph.

THE MORNING of the day I was meeting my birth mother, I took another class at the Institute of Affirmation. It was about making wishes. The teacher, a young woman in a school T-shirt, talked about all the things you could use to make wishes: the first star of the evening, eyelashes, chicken bones. She had a real cake in front of her as she spoke. "I know some of you have taken this class before. Does anyone have a story for the class about a wish that came true?"

A small woman raised her hand. "I'm Delilah, and I work for a housecleaning company in Lemon Grove. Last time, I wished for a car, and believe it or not, I won a brand-new Chevy Blazer at the supermarket where I shop. You know how they sometimes have a new car out front and they say you can win it. To tell the truth, I never believed they actually gave those cars away to anyone. Well, they gave it to me! So, naturally, I thought I'd come back here. This time, what I really need is—"

The teacher put her finger to her lips to stop Delilah from saying any more. "Don't tell us what you're wishing for this time. As we all know, you can't tell your wishes, or they won't come true. Does anyone else have a story?" She smiled at the class.

An older woman in a sweat suit raised her hand. "I wished to sell my house."

"And did you?"

"In two hours," said the woman, laughing. "It was the craziest thing. See, this couple we kind of used to know—"

"Wonderful," said the teacher. "Congratulations. I know we all like hearing these stories. But we've got some wishes to make. Now I'm going to light the candles on this birthday cake." She struck a match and started lighting the candles. There were about ten or twelve. "Some of you are probably worrying that because it's not your birthday, your wish might not be valid. Rest assured that I have been using this technique for many years, and it does *not* have to be your birthday. That's a common misconception."

We made wishes for a full hour, and each time mine was a variation on the same one: *I wish for everything to go perfectly when I meet my birth mother.* I wished about different aspects of the reunion each time. When we wished on the birthday candles, I said inside my head, *I wish for my birth mother to like me.* When we broke wishbones, I said, *I wish to like my birth mother.* We took a walk to a fountain and threw some pennies in. With one penny I wished, *I wish that from now on, we'll be close and never again lose track of each other.* Another penny was *I wish not to spill anything today or say anything stupid.* Toward the end of the class, when we were walking back from the fountain, I got fidgety and started worrying that I would be late. After the class, some of the students hung around to chat and eat birthday cake, but I went straight home to change.

I didn't know what to wear to meet with my birth mother. I put on jeans and took them off. Too casual. I didn't want her to think I didn't see this as an important occasion. I put on a dress. Too fancy. She sounded like a down-to-earth type on the phone, and I didn't want to seem too formal and stiff. Finally, I ended up in a short tan skirt and white T-shirt with an olive vest over it. I put on a pair of silver earrings shaped like seashells, undid my braid, brushed my hair, and rebraided it. I hurried a little too much, which caused a tangled knot to form in the lower part of my hair. *"Shoot,"* I said to myself. I had to brush it all out again, start over. As soon as my hair was rebraided, I made myself leave the house so I wouldn't have a chance to change my mind again about the clothes.

149

I was fifteen minutes early. I had left too soon and driven too fast. The restaurant was nearly empty. I scanned it quickly and didn't see my birth mother. She wasn't here yet. *Her plane might be late*, I thought. *I should have called the airline before rushing down here.* I sat on a bench to wait.

A hostess in a Mexican peasant dress came over and said, "May I help you?"

I said, "I'm meeting someone. But she isn't here yet."

"Are you Jenny Brown, by any chance?" she asked me.

I nodded, suddenly unable to speak, my mouth dry, my heart pounding.

"She's here waiting for you. I seated her a few minutes ago. This way, please," she said.

I followed the hostess to a table, crossing fingers on both hands, mentally repeating a wish: *I wish for everything to go perfectly when I meet my birth mother.*

"Here you are," she said, pulling out a chair for me.

"Oh!" I said, glancing at the woman at the table. "Wait!" But the hostess was walking away. At first I thought she had led me to the wrong table. The woman sitting there looked pretty and kind, but she could not have been my birth mother. She had blond hair cut in a pageboy and pale blue eyes. Her skin was fair, not freckly like my mother's, but milky white. Her eyebrows, not having enough color or substance on their own, had been drawn in with a fawn-colored pencil. And even sitting down, she looked big, tall, and solid, with broad shoulders and large breasts, beefy upper arms, capable hands as large as an average man's.

"Oh, dear," she said. "Oh, *dear!* Are—are *you* Jenny Brown?"

"Yes," I said. My legs were threatening to collapse under me, so I sat down. "Are you Elena Giordano Miller?"

"Yes," she said. She folded her hands in her lap and sank back in her chair.

"You're not my birth mother," I said, my voice a little shaky. "You couldn't be."

"You're right. It's not possible. You're not my birth daughter. The boy, my—the father of the child I gave up—was a redhead.

So, no, there's no way." We looked at each other for a minute or so, not knowing what to do next.

A waitress came to the table, a thin blond woman also wearing a Mexican peasant dress. "Are you ready to order?"

"No," said Elena. "We're not ready." Her hand was trembling as she reached for a glass of water.

"I'll be back," said the waitress.

"I'm sorry," Elena said. "How could this happen? I was so sure. I went over the details with your adoptive mother, and they seemed to match up so perfectly—the time, the place. I'm very sorry. I've done a terrible thing. I've been thoughtless and cruel. I set up this meeting in the excitement of the moment. It was selfish of me. I didn't think."

"It's not your fault. You didn't know. How could you know? And what about *you*? You spent all this money getting here, dropped everything to come. You must be awfully disappointed. I should have known better. I've been to seminars and workshops and read more adoption literature than you would think possible." And I made all these wishes, I was thinking, I was so sure they would come true. I had to bite my lower lip to keep it from wobbling. Something inside me was giving way, collapsing under a heavy weight. "It's just as disappointing for you," I said. "You must be crushed. I know enough about searching to know I should have stopped us from doing it this way. What's the matter with me?"

"I could have asked for a picture, couldn't I?" she said, getting feisty with herself now. She wasn't going to let herself off the hook easily. "I could have asked you to describe yourself and prevented this very simply. But I didn't. I wanted to experience it firsthand. I wanted to be surprised. Well, I am! I'm about as surprised as I can be. In fact, I'm practically in a state of shock! Just look what I've done!" We sat there for a minute, not knowing what to say. "The Lord doesn't make mistakes," she said, mostly to herself. She opened a big brown purse and pulled out two tissues. Carefully, she laid one on top of the other. Then she dabbed her eyes dry in a way that wouldn't disturb her makeup and softly blew her nose.

I said, "When I heard your name, it kind of clicked with me that my birth mother was Italian. I could be Italian, don't you think?"

"Of course you could!" she said. "Easily." She took my hand in her big, warm, dry one and squeezed.

"But now that I see you, you're not what I—"

"Wait now." She held up the hand that wasn't holding mine. "There's something I haven't told you. I should have. I don't know why I didn't just say it on the phone. After all these years, I should know to just come right out with it, but I never . . . It always seems like the wrong time to say it. And just look what happens." She pressed her hands flat on the table. "I'm adopted, too. That's right. I'm an adoptee just like you are, honey. I probably don't have a single drop of Mediterranean blood in my whole body."

A laugh came out of me then, and suddenly, I liked this woman; we were sort of related after all.

She laughed, too. "Believe it or not," she said, "I was adopted as a baby, just like you were. I'm an adoptee *and* a birth mother. My adoptive parents were Italian American. They've both passed away now. All my life, people have been telling me, 'You don't *look* Italian.' Life's been simpler since I changed my name to Miller."

I smiled weakly. "Do you have a picture of your children?"

"Oh. Well. Do you really want to see it? I have one, yes." She pulled a picture out of her wallet. "An old one. They wouldn't stand for this anymore."

It was a studio photograph, probably taken for Christmas, maybe in a department store. Her children—all blond, two girls and a boy in their early twenties—wore matching dark green turtlenecks. These were some adoptee's half-siblings. "They look very nice," I said. "When you find your birth daughter, she'll be very happy to see that."

The waitress was back. "What can I get for you, ladies?"

Elena put the picture away. "This is terrible. I'm so sorry. We didn't even look at the menu." To me, she said, "Could I at least get you something to eat or drink?"

152

"No, thanks," I said. "I'm not hungry. It's not that I—I'm just not very hungry."

"Coffee? A nice hot cup of tea? Anything?"

"No, thank you." I wanted to want something, just to make Elena and the waitress feel better, but I knew I couldn't face sitting there eating food with someone else's birth mother. "You go ahead, though."

"Maybe in a little while," Elena said to the waitress.

The waitress went on to another table.

I said, "I might as well ask you something, since we're here. When you had your baby, in the maternity home in New York, do you remember any of the other women—and girls—who were there at the same time? Was there anyone you remember who might have looked a little like me? Anyone kind of dark? Maybe Italian American or, I don't know, someone who looked like her ancestors came from India or Greece, South America, maybe."

"Oh, there were all kinds of girls. Let me think. Now this is difficult because for a long time I tried so hard not to think about it. There was only one girl there I became kind of close with. Jo Ann was her name. She couldn't be your birth mother, though, because she was as fair as I am. And I was so depressed that I hardly spoke to anyone else. They kept trying to make you feel that you had done something terrible. Of course, this wasn't very hard to do. We already felt that way before we got there." She closed her eyes, trying to remember. "Certainly there must have been some darker girls. People were coming and going all the time. Not all the girls stayed for any length of time. Some just came in to arrange for the adoption and lived at home until the delivery. When we had our babies, we were with them in the hospital for five days. It was horrible. You held that baby knowing you were going to give her away to someone else. When that time was over, the people from the maternity home turned the babies over to the adopting parents or kept them in a nursery until they found families. We went home with nothing. I was there four months. I was in hiding, of course, because I was in high school and no one from home was supposed to know. But they did.

Where else could I have disappeared to? I wish I could help you. I don't remember many of the girls' names. They had us convinced that all we wanted to do was forget. I'm sorry." She looked at me with her clear blue eyes. "I'll try to think about it some more and see what I can come up with. I should be able to do that much for you. I'll call you if I remember anything. I'm sorry, it's just not the part of the experience that I've focused on."

"It's OK," I said. "Don't worry about it. I already searched for a long time and didn't find my birth mother. I guess I don't really want to start again anyway. Did you ever search for your own birth mother?"

"I never did," she said. "I knew I could only do one search at a time, and it seemed I'd have better luck with searching for my birth daughter. It felt more urgent to me. And as I'm sure you know, the information from adoptions in 1946 is even worse than the information from 1962. Some people tried not to even tell the kids they were adopted. It's almost impossible to find out anything. Of course you know all this. I was an only child. I always wished for a sister. That's why I had three kids. More. Three more after the first one."

"Me, too. I mean, I'm also an only child and always wished for a sister. Or a brother. Or several of each."

"But you don't have any children of your own," she said.

"I had a lot of miscarriages," I said. I just blurted this out. I don't know what made me say this to a complete stranger. I didn't usually like to talk about it at all, but once I got started like that with Elena, I just kept going. "We tried everything to have a baby, but nothing worked. Finally, we decided not to try anymore." I just couldn't stand the flicker of hope that would grow into a small bonfire just before being smothered by disappointment. "This was right before we moved out here, and my husband and I are still— It's been— It's caused a lot of, um...We've been having a hard time. Or maybe it's not just the miscarriages, but other stuff, too. I don't know."

Fortunately, Elena wasn't at all flustered by having a woman she didn't know at all discuss something very private at the table of an unfamiliar restaurant in a city she was visiting for the first time. I told her the whole story of my fertility problems while she listened quietly, her eyes never leaving my face.

"The first time," I told Elena, "I didn't even know I was pregnant until I had a late, heavy period. We had recently decided we were ready to start a family and had abandoned birth control. I was twenty-nine, and it was right after I stopped searching for my birth mother. We weren't using a calendar then or the special thermometer or any of that yet. It was just something we thought we were going to allow to happen. Now, it's almost hard to remember what it felt like before we had seen any specialists or had any tests. But there was a time like that when I assumed I would get pregnant, have a normal pregnancy that ended forty weeks later with the birth of a baby.

"After the bleeding started that first time, I did notice it had happened a bit late, and it was pretty heavy. I went to a gynecologist. They did a blood test right there in the office. I waited a long time in a little paper gown (the first of many), sitting on an examining table. Then the doctor came in to tell me that I'd had an early miscarriage. 'It's more common than people think,' he said to me. 'One in four pregnancies ends in miscarriage, according to some studies.' If I had known then how many times I was to hear this statistic over the next several years, I might have thrown something at him. But there were a lot of things I didn't know yet."

I remember saying, "Really," playing along, as if knowing that I was one in millions made my own experience seem inconsequential to me.

"When I went to my husband's lab and met him downstairs to tell him, he stared at me. He couldn't believe it. '*What?*' he kept saying. 'You were pregnant, and now you're not? Oh, *no!*' He had to sit down.

"I almost couldn't look at him, the way he was looking at me and not blinking, the way I could tell exactly how bad he felt. So I said, 'One in four pregnancies ends in miscarriage, according to some studies.'

"He said, 'How horrible! I can't believe that so many people feel this bad!' "

155

That night, as soon as he got home, he sat down on the couch and pulled me down next to him, just to hold me without speaking for a long time. He kept saying, "Are you OK?" and looking at me closely. What he meant was, "Why aren't you crying?" But he didn't ask that.

"Having a miscarriage was not as simple as I thought it would be. I mean, at the doctor's office they don't just tell you the bad news and let you go home and handle it. You have to go to the hospital and have something like an abortion to clear out any remaining tissue. As I mentioned, that was only the first one. There were four others."

I paused a moment. Elena handed me my glass of water. I took a sip, then went on.

"A pattern developed. The time that I always cried was when I was lying on a gurney in a surgical gown, my hair stuffed into one of those green caps, hungry and thirsty from fasting since the night before, waiting to be wheeled into an operating room and get anesthetized. At that moment, I always felt totally alone. The tears would start to flow from deep inside me out the corners of my eyes down to the elastic of the cap, and there was nothing I could do to stop them." I looked at Elena, and she squeezed my hand. I went on.

"Anesthesiologists and nurses don't always handle this well. You might think they'd all be pretty good with people crying because of all the practice they get. But it doesn't always work out that way. Sometimes one of them would pat me for a minute without saying anything. That was all right. But then there were others who seemed determined to say the wrong thing. 'What's the matter?' or 'You'll get pregnant again and forget this ever happened.' And then there was, 'This happens all the time, you know. As often as one in four pregnancies.' But I remember every single time it happened, five times in all. Each time was different, and each time I had had hope that it would work and also spent every day fearing that it wouldn't. Each time, I was crushed when it was over, and so was Todd.

"The last time I was pregnant turned out to be the worst. By then I was taking these progesterone shots. I was on complete bed rest. I made it almost to fifteen weeks. We had already started to relax, to think that we might be home free. Then the bleeding started. I reminded myself that some women have a little bleeding and still go full-term with a healthy pregnancy. But I wasn't hungry anymore, either. There was more blood, and I started getting cramps. Todd came home to drive me to the doctor's office. An ultrasound showed no heartbeat.

"After I came back from getting cleared out in the hospital that time, I said, 'Todd, I want to stop. I don't want to do this anymore.' So we stopped." I remembered that Todd had sighed the saddest sigh in the world. Just thinking about the sound of it caused a squeezing in my chest. I put my hands over my eyes for a few seconds, trying not to remember the way Todd had said, "OK, Jen." I knew what he meant. He meant he couldn't bear any more of it himself, couldn't stand to see me this disappointed over and over again, either. So we stopped trying to have a baby. But it seemed to me that we had lost even more than the possibility of having a family together. I think we might have lost each other, too.

I didn't tell Elena this part: The day after my last miscarriage, after Todd went to work, I took a paper grocery bag, and I went by myself to collect pinecones to make a cone wreath for our front door. In one of those special holiday issues of a women's magazine, I had seen a picture of what I wanted to make. I honestly thought I was getting busy with something unrelated to what we'd been through, something cheerful that would distract me for a few hours.

The force of my sadness didn't hit me until my bag was almost full of pinecones. Then I looked around through a blur of tears at the place I'd chosen to come on this day of all days, the one place I knew I could find a lot of pinecones easily. It was Mount Auburn Cemetery in Cambridge. A lot of famous people are buried there along with ordinary citizens who were alive a long time ago. Some people who live in Cambridge go there to take walks and even to have picnics. It's big and quiet and has a lot of nice trees like a park. You can take a walking tour. So I didn't immediately associate this place with bereavement, just didn't quite make that connection at first. Until that moment, I had not thought of it as a particularly sad place, had not associated it—or my miscarriages, for that matter—with death.

Anyway, it all suddenly hit me hard. I sat down on brittle, frozen grass and cried and cried. If you're going to cry in public, a cemetery is a good place. When people walked by—not many, because it was a weekday and cold—they seemed to think that it was perfectly natural to see a woman sitting on the frozen grass that covered an old grave, crying. And, under the circumstances, I think now, it was quite the normal thing to do. I had lost a lot, and I was sad.

Eventually, I pulled myself together, picked up my bag of pinecones, and took the bus back to Central Square. Along the way, I made a decision: We were never going to get a pet. I didn't want us to become one of those childless couples who buy little sweaters for their dog or put presents under the Christmas tree for him or give him dessert from a plate and let him sleep in their bed.

I got off the bus at Woolworth's on Mass. Ave. and bought a glue gun and a twig wreath form, some ribbon, and dried baby's breath. (By now, I was fully conscious of the symbolism of baby's breath and bought a lot of it.) If it doesn't fall apart, I'll use the wreath I made every Christmas from now on. And every time I take it out of the tissue paper, I'll remember that day I went to Mount Auburn Cemetery to get the pinecones and cried about the children I wasn't going to have.

"So," I said to Elena. "That's my story. Sorry about this. I didn't mean to unload all this on you. I just— Anyway, thanks for listening. I think I'll go now, if you don't mind." I got up. "It was nice meeting you."

"Now wait," she said. "Sit down a minute. I don't think you should go just now."

I sat down. She said, "I had a miscarriage once. It's a terrible thing. As sad as it can be. I'm sorry, honey."

"What's the matter with me?" I said. "You don't need to deal with all this."

"It's OK," she said. "It's all right."

"It's just so—my husband and I hardly ever even touch or talk anymore. I mean, you know, and I don't—I'm afraid we never—"

"Oh, my dear," she said. "What you've been through." She gave my hand a little squeeze.

"I'm OK," I said. "I know this doesn't look too good right now, me sitting here crying with someone I just met, but really, I'm OK."

She said, "Of course you are. You're strong and lovely and as bright as a penny. You'll be fine. There's absolutely nothing wrong with sitting here crying. We might as well do something together after all this!" She laughed softly, and I managed a watery smile.

We sat there a few more minutes. Finally, I said, "OK, I feel better now. I think I'll go."

"Sure? Really? Let's keep in touch," she said, taking my hand. "I'll call you as soon as I remember anything about the other girls."

"Oh, that's all right. Never mind all that," I said.

Before we left, she put some money on the table for the waitress who hadn't brought us anything.

f o u r t e e n

CHANGING YOUR CHILDHOOD. Most of us had some-
thing about our childhoods that we didn't like: alcoholic parents who didn't love us; intimidating, overachieving siblings;
too many moves to put down roots. You have probably already explored these bad memories all you care to in therapy,
twelve-step programs, and self-help workshops. Now let's
move on! Using your active imagination and a set of specially
designed dolls to represent your family members, we'll show
you how to "remodel" your personal history. Give yourself
wealthy, doting parents; a private school education tailored to
suit your personality and talents; a circle of devoted friends to
play with on a tree-lined street. Employ the much under-
rated, often maligned psychological tools of denial and selec-
tive memory. Saturday, October 18, 9 A.M. to 5 P.M. Course
cost: $50. Materials: Childhood Changer™ dolls (included).
(DIARY IN REVERSE is a related course taught by the
same instructor but not a prerequisite.)

I WENT TO MY CAR and started to drive home, but I
didn't go there. I got off the freeway in Clairemont, went to a gas
station, and called Todd.

"Finally!" he said. "I've just been hanging around by the
phone all day. Are you coming over with her now?"

"No," I said. "Not now."

"Oh. Well, when—"

"I mean, actually, we're not coming, um, at all."

"Why? She's not going back already, is she? Can't she hang around for a few days?"

I took a deep breath. "She had blond hair and blue eyes. And the birth father of her baby was a redhead."

"What? The odds against that would be astronomical," Todd said.

"Right," I said. "Thanks. Even I could figure out that much. Todd, she wasn't my birth mother." I leaned against the wall of the gas station and held my breath. Then I said, "And don't yell at me, OK? Don't tell me I did a stupid thing. Don't tell me that after all the seminars and reading I've done, everyone I've talked to—"

"I wasn't going to yell at you," he said. "It's just that I thought you had already made sure—"

"I don't want to talk about this anymore now. I have to go."

"Where?" he said. "Where do you have to go?"

"Nowhere," I said. "You're right. I have nowhere to go. See you later." I hung up and stood there at the pay phone between the two bathrooms. What I wanted to do was disappear. I couldn't face myself, didn't even want to be confronted with the inside of my own car or house, let alone my own head. I stood there motionless until a man in a suit walked over to ask me if I was going to use the phone.

"No," I said, walking away. "It's all yours."

I sat on my car bumper for half an hour in the hot sun of the gas station. I was sweating, but I didn't move into the shade. No one asked me what I was doing sitting there all that time. I pretended my car was broken down and I was waiting for a tow truck. Two women, dressed up as if to go to work in an office, approached me with a religious pamphlet. "Ma'am," said one of them. "The Lord hears our prayers."

"OK," I said. At that moment, I must have looked like the perfect candidate for conversion, a woman with nowhere to be, alone and disconnected. I imagined Todd and my mother paying someone to kidnap me from some fanatical cult—there were plenty around to choose from—and getting me deprogrammed. In the end, it was the heat that made me decide to get back into my car. I got in and slammed the door. The steering wheel was almost too hot to touch. I started the car and turned on the air conditioner full blast. Air as hot as a blow-dryer's came first, then slowly, it cooled down.

I drove directly to the Institute of Affirmation. I don't remember planning to end up there; on the other hand, I didn't think about going anywhere else first. For a few long seconds, I sat in the car as it ticked in the parking lot, the engine cooling down, the interior heating up again. There were only a few other cars. It was an off time for the school, the late afternoon, but I tried the door anyway. It was open. Maybe I had come here to find someone to talk to, I thought. But there was no one around; the place was quiet. I went to the music room and sat down on the floor near the piano, feeling foolish and sad. Then I went to the bathroom. I looked at my face in the mirror. I said, "Now what, Jenny Brown?" There was no answer. So I went out.

A short distance down the hall, Michael was posting something on a bulletin board.

"Michael?" I said, happy to see another person.

He jumped and turned around to look at me. "Jenny. I didn't know you were here. What a nice surprise."

"I'll direct a play if you want," I said loudly from halfway down the hall. "I've changed my mind. I'll do it." The words just clattered out of my mouth like colored gum balls from a machine.

Michael stood there, looking at me without saying anything for a long moment.

I said, "Oh. Bad timing? You found someone else? You decided not to do a play after all? You don't think I've had enough experience. Whatever. I understand." I started for the door. "No big deal. I don't even know why I said that."

"No," he said. "I think it's fine. I'm glad. It's perfect." He turned around and began to remove the pushpins from the notice he had just posted. He said, "Would you put this in the recycling bin on your way out?"

"Sure," I said, taking the paper from him. It said, WANTED:

162

DIRECTOR FOR A PLAY TO BE PRODUCED THIS FALL. SEE MICHAEL
OR ESTHER.

My mouth opened.

A blush rose to his cheeks. "You want something; it's already
there."

I shook my head. "I keep trying to think that way, but it
doesn't seem to work for me. So what's the play?"

"I don't know," he said. "You're the director."

I said, "You mean just choose whatever I want?"

He nodded. "Yes."

"Oh," I said. "OK, well, I'll start looking, then I'll let you
know what I come up with."

"Perfect," he said, and smiled at me.

"All right," I said. "Well, I guess I better get started." I
turned to leave.

"Jenny?" he called.

I stopped and turned around.

"Did I say thank you? No, I didn't. Thank you."

"You're welcome," I said. "And thank *you*."

BEFORE GOING HOME, I went to the library, found some
anthologies of plays, and checked out the fattest ones I could find.
There were collections of twentieth-century plays, one acts, com-
edies, dramas, musicals, American plays, plays by women, African
American plays, plays by gay men. I didn't care so much about
the playwrights; I was looking for a piece that would be cheap to
stage and had a lot of people in it. I took the books home, sat on
the floor of the bedroom, and began to go through the plays one
by one. I found *Our Town* in a couple of different books. Something like that would be ideal, I thought, with no props or scenery.
The number of townspeople could be expanded to accommodate
the number of people we had. I looked in the beginning for the
copyright information, where I saw the word *CAUTION!* and a
long paragraph explaining that professionals and amateurs alike
had to pay royalties to do this play.

I went downstairs and surveyed the freezer, took out three

bean burritos—two for Todd, one for me—that I'd made a few weeks before, and dropped them with a clunk onto the counter. I crouched in front of a cupboard, looking for something to heat them in. How much could the school afford to pay in royalties? I put the burritos in the oven to heat.

I went back upstairs and looked at more plays: new ones, classics, abstract and avant-garde, conventional and old-fashioned. Maybe there was another way.

Todd came home. "Jen?" he called from downstairs.

"Hi." I pushed the books under the bed. "We're having burritos. Not spicy."

"Good. What are you doing?"

"Reading," I said. If he asked me what, I decided I would tell him about the play. I started to put together an explanation as to why I had chosen to do this, tracing backward to the moment when I'd changed my mind about it, thinking up reasons I thought it would be the right thing to do.

"Are you OK?" he called from the bottom of the stairs.

He meant about Elena Giordano Miller. "Yeah," I said. I pulled one of the books back out from under the bed. I opened it to *Long Day's Journey into Night*. Too hopeless, I thought, and not enough people. I closed it and opened to another. If he comes in, I thought, I'll just tell him. No big deal. He'll be happy I have something to do.

"So are you going to start searching again?" he yelled up.

"What? No," I said. I flipped to *The Glass Menagerie*, which would not be at all expensive to stage. But only four people in the whole thing. And royalties. "I'm done with all that," I called to Todd. "Really." I picked up another book.

"Are you coming down?" he said. "Did any mail come for me?"

"Uh . . . A water bill, a packet of coupons."

"That's all?" He was walking to the kitchen now. "You're awfully calm for someone who just—"

"It's on the table."

"I see it, Jen," he yelled, opening the oven. "I'm starving. Can you check if these are ready?"

"If they're hot, they're ready. If they're not hot, they need more time."

Considering what I knew about the school's resources, I should have been looking for a play that was in the public domain. Shakespeare? No, I wasn't up to that. The thing to strive for would be no royalties. Maybe there was another way to go about this.

I put the book down and picked up the phone from the bedside table, called the school, and asked for Michael.

"Michael?" I said when he answered.

"Yes?"

"Jenny Brown."

"Oh. Hi, I was—"

I thought I heard Todd coming. "Write It Down!" I said quickly, interrupting Michael.

"Uh . . . OK. Let me get a pen."

"No, I mean, the class. There's a class at the Institute of Affirmation called Write It Down."

"That's right. I thought you meant—"

"No," I said. "We could use an original play. Do you think someone in that class might have one? Someone in Write It Down could have written a play. It's possible, isn't it? We could perform it, give a writer a chance, avoid paying royalties."

"Oh, that's—"

Downstairs, Todd called, "Did you say something?"

"A good idea," I said into the phone. "I know. Can you get back to me on this?"

"Sure."

I hung up and went to give Todd his burrito.

A FEW DAYS later, after Todd went to work, I met Michael at the Coffee Shop again. They didn't have cappuccino or iced mocha or latté or anything, just normal coffee from a Bunn machine with two burners, one for regular, one for decaf. Before I got involved with the school, I hadn't been in a place like this in a long time.

Michael stood up when I got to the table. "Jenny," he said,

as if my name were the answer to a question. We sat down. "I got a play." He pushed a stack of paper, a manuscript, toward me.

"That's great! Is it good?"

"Oh," he said, a little startled. "Good? Well, I didn't read it or anything. There was only one writer in the class who had a play. Julie. She had to get it out of a box in her garage. It's from a few years ago. Well, fifteen or so. Some of the students had short stories, some poetry and song lyrics. There were a couple of dream journals, but there was only one play."

"This is it then," I said, taking the script. "I wanted a play, and that's what I've got. Perfect."

"Auditions are set for a week from Saturday. I put an ad in the *Reader*."

"An ad? You did? Oh, my God."

"What? It's free. We'll need fifty copies of the script."

"*Fifty?*" I said.

"You don't think that's enough? We can always make more later. We have an account with the drive-through copy place over in the other shopping center. I'm checking out the performance space this morning."

"We're not going to use a classroom again?" I said.

"No," Michael said, shaking his head. "Jenny, you've got to think bigger. We're going to do it in a *real theater*."

I pictured red plush seats, a sparkling chandelier. The chill of fear crawled quickly through my body.

Michael went on. "Did you know that the school we're in was scheduled to be torn down two years ago? It was built in the early sixties and contains hazardous materials. I talked to some people downtown about delaying demolition. Tearing down a building costs a lot more than you might think. The city let us have it for a very reasonable rent. And it's not that dangerous to us unless we decide to pull down the ceiling or pull up the floor. There's a stage in the multipurpose room. It's a platform, actually. The room used to be the school cafeteria. We've never used that room because we haven't needed a stage or a space that big. But we could. I mean, why not? In the back there's a big kitchen. I've only been in there once. I remember the curtain is in pretty sad

166

shape, and the walls have all kinds of obscene words written on them that we would have to—"

"That sounds great," I said, feeling relieved, smiling at him. Michael smiled back. He said, "I'm glad you decided to do this, after all. I was afraid you were never going to—"

"Oh, well, I got desperate, that's all. I had to do something. Wait. That didn't come out right. I didn't mean that the school—"

"Don't worry," Michael said softly. "You didn't hurt my feelings. I'm just glad you're back."

I took a sip of coffee. It was hot, and it scalded my tongue.

THE PLAY Michael gave me was called *Fields of Love*. It was loosely based on the *Romeo and Juliet* plotline, but set in present day, or rather present day about fifteen years ago. A boy and a girl who lived on neighboring farms fell in love, but their parents didn't want them to be together. The parents felt they should be preparing for their SATs and improving their grade point averages so they could get into good colleges. But Romeo and Juliet wanted to be together, so they met in the hothouse, where Juliet's family grew tomatoes, or in the fields, where Romeo's family grew onions. In the end, instead of committing suicide, they presented their parents with a surprise hybrid of their families' two plant specialties that would revolutionize the Mexican and Italian food industries forever, not to mention unite the two families. Was that possible? I wondered, thinking about how onions grew underground and tomatoes grew on tall plants. On the other hand, there were a lot of characters. Romeo and Juliet came from big families. There were harvest scenes that included a lot of pickers and a Halloween party scene and a final wedding scene with room for as many people as we wanted to use. Maybe I could overlook the agricultural technicalities. As soon as I'd read it, I left a message at the Institute of Affirmation telling Michael that the play would do fine.

I took my copy of the play to the photocopy place that Michael told me about. "Fifty copies, right?" said the woman at the drive-through window. "Michael called. It's prepaid, and I'm supposed to give you this." She handed me a cardboard cup of coffee and a cookie on a napkin. "Monster macadamia and chocolate chip," she said. "Still warm. Michael said to tell you not to wait. He'll pick up the scripts."

"OK," I said. "I've never seen a drive-through copy place that served coffee and cookies."

"You should have seen us before. My sister and I were really struggling with this place, just scraping along. Then my husband and I took an abundance workshop at the Institute of Affirmation. Right after that, we took off like crazy. We owe a lot to Michael and the school. My husband bakes the cookies. Now he also teaches a cookie course at the institute. Maybe you've seen it in the catalog."

"No kidding," I said. "Yeah, I think I've noticed it. I've taken a couple of courses—Make a Wish and the miracle one. Both of them backfired on me. All these bad things happened, and I couldn't help thinking—"

"Try the cookie one," she urged as a car pulled in behind me. "Maybe it's just what you need. Michael said to tell you that he'll pick up the job when it's done."

"Thank you," I said. "I better go. You've got another customer here. Nice talking to you."

AUDITIONS WERE ON a Saturday. I walked to the school. There were a lot of people waiting for the doors to open when I arrived. I had never been to the school this early on a Saturday morning, and I was surprised to see how busy it was. Then I noticed that I knew some of the people who were waiting. Slowly, it dawned on me that all these people were waiting for the auditions. There were twenty-nine of them. Edward, Priscilla, Clara, Roger, Tiffany, Valerie, Denise, and Jason were all there, along with a lot of other people I hadn't seen before. I stood there with them, waiting to be let in. Some of them nodded to me, nervous and self-conscious, as if I were someone important who had what they wanted. Others made a point of not making eye contact.

Michael screeched his pickup into a parking place a couple of minutes late. He had the keys to the front door. He got out with a big cardboard box that turned out to be the scripts and two cups of coffee—one for me and one for himself—balanced on top. He was wearing his dance clothes, as usual. He let me in and asked everyone else to wait outside.

We went into one of the classrooms. "Did you see that crowd?" I said to him. "There were all these *people* out there."

"Yeah," he said. "See that? You'll have plenty of help, if you need it. But you won't. OK, now sit right here. I'll have everyone sit around here. The readers will stand here. I'll ask everyone to sign this piece of paper and put down their ages, so you'll have a list of their names in front of you. When you're ready for the next reader, you just call the next name on the list. When that person is done, draw a line through the name. That's all you have to do. Nothing hard about that, is there? Easy."

"OK. I guess I can do that much. Thanks for the coffee."

"Welcome. You need sugar?" he said. "Here, I have it in my pocket. Spoon? Here."

He hurried out of the classroom to open the doors.

There weren't enough chairs, so some people had to sit on the floor. While they were signing the list, I handed out scripts. Several more people walked in and looked for places on the floor. I said, "Wow, there are a lot of you. Luckily, this is a play that can have a big cast. I'm sure I can find a part for everyone. So don't anyone worry about not making it into the show." There was a round of applause, which startled me; I dropped a pile of scripts, and several people jumped to pick them up. "Thank you," I said. "I can get that. Oh, thanks. So if you want to be in the play, just make sure to register in the front office as soon as we're through here."

Michael reappeared with another cardboard carton. "School catalogs," he said to me.

"Oh," I said. "And if anyone would like a copy of the Institute of Affirmation's catalog of courses, please feel free to take one." Several people stood up and went to the box. Michael smiled and waved at me and went out again.

169

"Please turn to page twenty-two in your scripts," I said. "We will be reading from the line, 'Love is like a tomato' to the next page, where you see the line, 'You can see the whole world in an onion.' Everybody have this section? Good. We'll start with, um," I looked at my list, "Robin?"

A young woman turned a deep pink. "That's me," she whispered.

"All right, Robin, take a minute to read the scene, then you'll be reading with"—I scanned the list for a boy's name—"Sam?"

A short blond boy, who couldn't have been more than fifteen, put a hand to his cheek to cover two large pimples. He rose quickly and started for the front of the room. On the way, he tripped over someone's purse and nearly fell but didn't. I looked down at my script and tried to act as though I hadn't noticed.

We all watched the first hothouse scene again and again until we ran out of teenagers, then we switched to a scene between the Juliet character's parents. More people arrived during the morning, so that we had to return to the hothouse scene to hear some of the late-arriving teenagers, then go back to the adult scene again.

I cast the principals in my head right there at the audition. Tiffany was going to be the Juliet character, who, in this play, was called Courtney, and Jason was going to be the Romeo character, who was called Ryan. Priscilla was going to play Courtney's mother, and Edward was her father. Valerie was Courtney's older sister, and Denise was her best friend. Clara would play the Juliet character's grandmother. Some other people I hadn't met before would play other parts. Real-life husband and wife James and Suzanne were getting the parts of Ryan's parents. They seemed to have done a lot of community theater. In the play, Ryan had three brothers and a sister, and Courtney had three sisters and two brothers. I used up some more of the teenagers in these roles. The remainder of the group would all be townspeople and pickers in the planting and harvest scenes, the party, and later in the wedding. When we finished at twelve-thirty, I said, "I'll be posting the cast list tomorrow morning. You can find out what part you got at ten o'clock."

I stayed for a little while after everyone left, making notes about the actors before I forgot who was who.

Michael came back. "Did you tell those people they could all be in the play?"

"Yes," I said. "I didn't want to turn anyone down. I thought—I'm sorry. I was just trying to—"

"Good idea!" he said. "What are you doing for lunch?"

"No plans," I said.

"I'll get sandwiches."

We went to a grocery store in Michael's truck and bought sandwiches at the deli counter. He drove to a beach where there was a grassy place and a playground overlooking the ocean. We sat on the grass and started eating our sandwiches. I waited for Michael to talk, to say something about the play, the school, his dance classes, whatever. He popped open a can of fruit punch and took a long drink.

Away from the school and other people, Michael didn't say much, just the bare minimum, like "Here you go," "Excuse me," and "How about this?"

To make up for his silence, I began to talk and kept it up without stopping. "It's going to be OK. We'll have a nice production. I want to make sure that each person has something unique and special to do. As soon as I get home, I'm going to call the writer and ask her if she could write a line for each actor, give everyone a name and a job. In the program, I want to list each actor under a character name and not have just a list of townspeople or pickers or whatever. Do you think she would do that? The writer? You know her. Is she nice?" I paused to take a bite of my sandwich.

Michael said, "Seems nice." He nodded and looked at the beach. It was a cloudy, cool day, and there were not many people in the water. The playground was full of kids, though. Two little boys were filling cups with sand and lining them up on the railroad ties that formed the sandbox border. One of them looked at me and said, "Want some lemonade?"

"Sure," I said.

"You can't," he said. "It's *pretend*!" He laughed, as though he had played a great trick on me.

"Oh," I said. "Well, thanks anyway."

I turned back to Michael. "I hope I know how to do this. I guess I'm just supposed to block it all out and then have one or two rehearsals where I tell them the blocking. Or maybe I should start out looser than that, let them kind of go where they want and see how it looks, let them do what feels right. Well no, that's not going to work because most of them have never done this before, either. OK, I'll tell them where to go and get their ideas at the same time. I'll be open to their input. See what works for them, you know, and go from there. They can tell me if it doesn't feel right. Kind of a collaboration. Oh, listen to me yakking away with my mouth full. Where are my manners? I'm talking too much."

"No," he said. "Not at all. I wish I didn't have a class in half an hour so I could listen to you longer."

He had those eyes I told you about, greenish brown ones that were hard to look away from. But after a few long seconds, I had to, because I felt myself blushing.

Down on the beach, an elderly man in shorts and a T-shirt was searching the sand with a metal detector. Several times, he stopped to dig and sift, depositing small items into a plastic bag. From a distance, it was impossible to tell what he had found, treasure or trash, a diamond ring or a pop top.

Now I couldn't think of anything to say.

Michael said, "I've made you self-conscious. I was enjoying hearing your thoughts and your voice, and now I've ruined it."

"I'm not self-conscious," I said. "Not at all." But I still didn't have anything more to say.

Michael finished his sandwich. He folded the paper it came in and put it in his paper bag. "You're married, right?" he said suddenly without looking at me.

"What?" I said, and I felt exposed, as if it were obvious from the way I spoke or dressed or chewed that Todd and I were having problems. "Oh. Yes, I am. Why?"

172

"Just wondered." Michael collected all our trash. "Did a lot of them take catalogs? The actors?"

"Quite a few. Ten or twelve, I guess."

Michael nodded. "Good." We walked to the garbage can. Bees were circling the trash. Michael threw our stuff in quickly. "Juice," he said. I guess he meant that it was juice that was attracting the bees, but he didn't elaborate.

We went to the truck. He unlocked the passenger door. I got in; he got in on his side.

To break the silence, I said, "I think I'm supposed to make a big notebook of the blocking, paste the pages onto bigger sheets and write in all the movements. I guess you need two scripts for that, because, obviously, one side of the page would be glued down. And don't worry. I've checked out some books on directing from the library so even if I don't know what to do, I know where to go for help." He had nice hands. I had an urge to touch one as it held the steering wheel.

Michael reached over and turned on the radio. There was a commercial for a brand of condoms that had been trusted for over eighty years. I looked out the window. He switched stations to Annie Lennox, singing about love and pain. "I wasn't worried," he said. I looked at him, not following his train of thought. "About your directing."

"Oh," I said. "That. Well, good."

When we stopped in front of my house, Michael reached into the space behind the front seat to rummage in a paper bag. He pulled out a script. "Here's a spare," he said. "To cut up for the blocking notebook."

I took the script from him. "Thanks. OK. I'll feel like a real director. Well, maybe not, but thanks. That was fun." He looked at me. "Having lunch with you. Was fun."

"Yeah," he said. He smiled at me. "See you, Jenny."

"So long. Thanks for the company, and thanks for listening to me babble."

"My pleasure," Michael said.

I slammed the door of the truck. But when I started to walk

away, I found that the end of my braid was stuck in the door. Luckily, Michael hadn't started to drive off yet. I backed up, opened the door, then closed it again.

Michael drove away a little too fast, his tires screeching for a second as he plunged out into the street away from our house. Two houses away, a mother in shorts and a San Diego Zoo T-shirt frowned and put her hands on her hips.

Because it was a Saturday, my next-door neighbor Art was out front edging his grass. His ten-year-old was using the slight incline of the driveway to give him speed for practicing flipping his skateboard around. On the other side, Beth and David were reading newspapers in beach chairs set up in the driveway, while three children built a fort out of cardboard boxes, chairs, and old bedspreads. Two of the kids were theirs and one was a friend.

A man was standing on our lawn, looking up at our tree. There were two little girls on our driveway, drawing flowers with chalk.

"Hi," I said to the man on the lawn. "I'm Jenny."

"Brad." The man shook my hand. "How come you guys are the only ones with a tree that grows? Every front yard got a tree when the houses were built. Most haven't grown an inch since they were planted. Some died a long time ago. Mine is half the size of yours, a puny little diseased runt. Look at this! Healthy and big with green leaves. And look at that fat branch, perfectly parallel to the ground. My kids are aching for a swing, and *you've* got the right tree. You don't have kids, right?"

"No kids." I shook my head.

"So what's your secret? What kind of fertilizer do you use? Do you use a chemical pesticide? We don't do any spraying because of the little ones, just soap and water on the rosebushes, coffee grounds, that kind of thing."

"Fertilizer?" I said. "Pesticide? We have an automatic sprinkler system. All I do is hope it's working right. I don't know how to change any of the settings." I lifted my shoulders, turned my hands palms up. "Dumb luck. That's our secret."

He laughed.

"You can put a swing here, if you want," I said. "Your kids

174

can come and swing here anytime. Go ahead. We're not using that branch for anything. Or the front yard, for that matter."

"Are you serious?" he said.

"Sure," I said. "Fine with us."

"That's very kind of you," he said, smiling. "Hear that, guys?" he said, turning to the two girls. "Oh, now, what's this? You can't just go and draw on anybody's driveway. The lady doesn't want that. Here, where's your hose? I'll get that right off for you."

"Oh, don't bother," I said. "It's fine, really." Since I last looked, two rainbows, a heart, and four more flowers had appeared. "Very pretty, girls," I said.

"Thank you," they said together, looking at the cement, not sure if they were in trouble or not.

"By the way," said the father. "We're in the blue house down there with the green van in front."

"Nice to meet you. Well, have fun. I've got to go."

I went inside. In a box in a closet, I found an old three-ring notebook of Todd's full of notes on experiments he did as an undergraduate. I took the notes out, put a big paper clip on them, and left them on his dresser. I filled the notebook with blank paper, took it downstairs, and started cutting apart the pages of the script, gluing them down.

WHEN TODD came home at eight, I was sitting on the floor, whispering the lines to myself, drawing diagrams, and making notes on the pages in the binder.

"Hey," he said. "Who are those kids out there?"

"Kids?" I said, looking up.

"Out in the yard. There's a swing hanging from our tree and a whole line of them waiting to use it. In the dark. There are a couple of parents with flashlights. I didn't think it was our house at first. I drove right by and had to turn around and come back, check the number."

I stood up and went to the window. My legs were stiff from sitting so long. "Look at that," I said. A little girl with a ponytail was sitting on a wooden swing, pumping her legs with everything she had. I opened the door and went out.

A line of six kids stood on our driveway, a safe distance from the little girl's feet. "Thirteen, fourteen, fifteen," all the kids in line were shouting together. When they got to twenty, the girl jumped off and went to the end of the line. A blond boy took her place on the swing, and the counting started again. "One . . . two . . . three . . ." they all shouted.

Brad, the man I met earlier, came over to me. "Sure this is OK with you?"

"Absolutely. This is my husband, Todd. Todd, this is Brad." Todd and Brad shook hands.

"Very generous of you to let us use your tree," Brad said to Todd. "We appreciate it. They're all a little excited, but we'll be getting them home to bed soon."

"No!" shouted several kids.

"I didn't get three turns," said a little girl. "Rebecca got three turns."

Todd forced a smile. We watched the kids on the swing for a couple more minutes, then we went inside.

"How come they don't use their own trees?" Todd wanted to know.

"Don't be so crabby. Apparently, we're the only ones with a good tree. Our branch is perfect."

"What about insurance? What about if someone gets hurt in front of our house?"

"I didn't think of that," I said. "Do you really think the parents would hold us responsible for—"

"Who knows? Is there any food?" Todd said.

"Oh. There must be," I said. I looked at my watch. "Oops. I forgot all about dinner. I'll get you something."

Todd sat down on the couch and turned on the television with the remote control. "So," he said. "Anything happen to-day?"

When you've been with someone a long time, it's hard to tell him that you're going to try something completely new, something he hasn't seen you do, something you never even thought of trying until just now. You have to ask him to see you in a new way, to expand his idea of your capabilities. It's a matter of faith and trust. I took a deep breath, braced myself. "It's a long story. I'm directing a play called *Fields of Love*, an original work by a local writer. I know it's crazy, and I've never done anything like this before. But they asked me to do it, and I decided, Hey, why not? Why not take a chance, try it, and see what happens? There are all these actors who are so grateful to have the chance to be in a play, any play. Kind of like those kids with the swing. You wouldn't believe how many of them showed up for auditions. We have five weeks for rehearsals."

"What?" said Todd. "Sorry. I'm watching a commercial for this car. They go to such extremes sometimes in advertising. I bet it's as intense as science. So what'd you say? What happened?"

Maybe it just wasn't a good time to tell Todd anything big. The kids and the swing threw him a little. I stood up and got some chicken out of the freezer, put it on a plate for the microwave. "Nothing happened," I said. I closed the door and pushed the minutes button—*beep, beep*—and then the start button—*beep*. The light went on inside the microwave, and the fan hummed.

Todd said, "What? Are you mad? You're not mad, are you? I wasn't paying attention for a few *seconds*. God, Jenny, you are so sensitive. OK, now what happened?"

"Nothing!"

"OK. OK. I heard you. No need to yell. Nothing happened to me, either," Todd said. He changed the channel.

fifteen

BAD HABITS SUPPORT GROUP. Are you a smoker? Do you eat lots and lots of greasy, salty foods and far more than your share of sweets? Or are you a seriously messy and disorganized person? Last time we looked, none of these bad habits was illegal. Join one of our groups and spend some quality time with others like you! For one peaceful hour a week, don't fight it! Lay your burden down. We promise not to try to change or improve you. Weekly meetings are as follows: *Smokers*, Fridays, 6–7 P.M.; *Overeaters*, Saturdays, 9–10 P.M.; *Slobs*, Sundays, 2–3 P.M. Course cost: $5 per meeting.

IN THE FIRST WEEK'S rehearsals, I was concentrating on scenes that had just two or three people in them. First, I worked with Tiffany and Jason. The scene was the two of them sitting on the ground where the onion field of Ryan's family stopped and the tomato field of Courtney's began. They meet there by chance. But after some small talk, a spark ignites between them, and the two characters start to tell each other more intimate details of their lives until they reveal their secret dreams for their futures. They are supposed to nearly come together in a kiss when they are discovered by their two sets of parents with flashlights.

As usual, Michael came to the rehearsal. He sat next to me in a folding chair, watching Tiffany and Jason say their lines stiffly with little volume or feeling. When Jason said, "The smell of onions is always with me," he reached out and took a strand of Tiffany's hair between his two fingers. She seemed to come alive when he touched her. Watching them, an electric buzz went through me.

As Tiffany said her line, "Ripeness is critical with tomatoes," she gazed into his eyes and their two bodies came together. This was where the parents were supposed to make their entrance. But they were late. Tiffany and Jason had time to fondle each other's faces, kissing and touching with enthusiasm and abandon barely held in check. They made it seem so simple for two people to come together, a spontaneous and perfect meshing of body and spirit unconstrained by obstacles like poor timing, bad history, conflicting goals, miscommunication.

I looked at Michael.

He cleared his throat. "Chemistry," he said softly.

I nodded. "Yes."

Finally, Priscilla made a late and noisy entrance, waving her improvised flashlight—a rolled-up piece of paper—at them. "There they are!" she boomed. "We have been looking all over for you two!" Tiffany and Jason separated with the exaggerated movements of two cartoon characters. Priscilla dragged Tiffany away by one arm, and the scene ended.

"Good," I said. "Nice work."

"I don't know," said Tiffany, her eyes sliding sideways toward Jason. "Could we do it again?"

"Yeah," said Jason. "I think that needs more work." He touched the metal button holding her overall strap in place.

"Practice by yourselves out in the hall. Now, I need all four parents for act one, scene four. Please."

Obediently, Jason and Tiffany went out in the hall, while the other actors took their places. Through the window in the door, we could see them touching and studying each other's faces.

Michael said, "Well, I have a class. I'll see you later." He left the room.

"OK, everyone?" I called to the actors. "Ready?"

————

AFTER REHEARSAL, Michael and I went to inspect the closed multipurpose room, the place we were going to perform the play. "I hope there's no alarm system they forgot to tell me about," he said, putting a key into the lock on the door. It opened, and we went in. Nothing rang. There was a small platform about three feet above the floor and a pair of velveteen curtains in faded maroon with a lot of rips in them.

"This looks good," Michael said.

Lunch tables were folded back against the wall. There was a door at the side of the stage, leading to the school kitchen.

Michael looked in. "We could use this for a dressing room, couldn't we?"

"Yeah," I said. "We just need a few mirrors, some racks for costumes, and we're ready to go."

"Maybe we can put some screens here to separate men and women. It will be kind of crowded, but this is going to work out fine. Then we'll have to build something along the side of the room so the actors can get from the dressing room to the stage without being seen. Great. Let's see what they have in the way of lights."

"Lights," I said. "I hadn't even thought about lights."

"Very important element," Michael said.

We walked out of the kitchen, back to the stage, and looked up. There were fluorescent tubes on the ceiling. "Well, not much, but we can work with this, don't you think, Jenny?"

"Uh . . . I guess," I said. "I don't know anything about lights. Nothing. Zero."

"You don't need to. I do, and I'll show you," Michael said, looking at me, then up again. "What we need is someplace to hang them. And we'll get that. Soon. We'll need some lights, too, of course. We should get some immediately. I'll handle that."

I examined a rip in one of the curtains. "Could we sew these, or something? At night, from a distance, maybe the repairs wouldn't be noticeable."

"Sure, those will look fine, once they're fixed up a little. You think anyone will see how dirty they are? I don't know how you'd get them clean. They're so big."

There were food spatters on the curtains from years of hanging in a school lunchroom. I had no idea what to do about that.

"There are chairs, too," Michael said. "I wonder why they didn't take the chairs to another school or something. I bet the school district doesn't even know there are a couple hundred chairs here." Folding chairs were stacked on rolling platforms near the walls. "So our audience won't have to sit on carpet squares. Aren't we lucky?"

"Yes. This will be fine," I said.

"Just beautiful," Michael said, smiling happily. "Great." He got out two of the folding chairs and set them up side by side.

We sat down, both of us looking around, not saying anything. I tried to make myself picture what I wanted to do here, how I wanted it to look with a play going on. It wasn't that easy to imagine.

I looked up at the ceiling again. "Like, what kind of thing to hang the lights on? What kind of thing were you thinking of?"

"Scaffolding."

"Oh," I said, "scaffolding. Of course."

Standing up, Michael said, "Yeah, I like this place. It has a good feeling, positive and nurturing, probably because it was a school. Don't you think?"

Again, I surveyed the room. The walls had obscene words and phrases scrawled on them in something brown, which I told myself could easily be chocolate pudding. There was some trash and dirt on the floor and a lot of big, gray dust bunnies. Where there were no bad words, the walls were scuffed and dirty and needed to be painted. The ceiling, acoustic tile loaded with asbestos, was one of the environmentally hazardous portions of the room. This and changing demographics in the area had caused the school district to abandon the building.

"Hm," I said, not agreeing or disagreeing with Michael about the feeling of the room.

"We're going to do something here. We're going to make something out of nothing. You watch."

Something about the way he said it made me think he knew

something that I didn't, something good that I would have to wait to find out. I inhaled sharply, expectant.

"What?" said Michael, turning around to look behind him.

"Oh, nothing," I said. I shrugged. "I was just—"

"Oh. You looked so—I thought you saw a mouse or something."

"No," I said. "No mouse."

He laughed, and I think my face turned red.

WHEN I GOT HOME, I got a meat loaf out of the freezer. The recipe was from the cornflakes box. I should have defrosted it earlier. Meat loaf is hard to warm up in a hurry. I put it in the microwave for ten minutes, thinking about the play as I stared at it defrosting. I was just putting it in the regular oven to heat more when Todd came in. "Hi," he said without looking at me.

"Hi," I said. "How was your day?" I rummaged in the refrigerator for salad stuff.

He didn't answer. He reached past me for the orange juice. He got a cup and sat down at the kitchen table. "I'm dead," he said.

"What do you mean?" I said. "What's the matter?"

"Fischburger came to my office."

"He did?" I said. "What did he say?"

Todd took a moment to stare deeply into his orange juice, then he said, "He told me that I'm a jerk and that I do lousy work."

I said, "What did he really say?"

Todd looked at the floor. "He asked me more about the new stuff I'm working on. I told him about the collaboration with Gieselmann in Germany, our latest results. Then he said, 'You need a publication, man. This isn't the time to start a wild goose chase.' "

"What does that mean?"

"It means he thinks the stuff we're doing is too risky, that it won't work."

"But, Todd," I said. "That's ridiculous. If you don't take

182

chances, how do you ever come up with new findings? Everyone knows how good your work is. You've been published in the best journals."

"A long time ago," he said.

I counted on my fingers. "Ten months ago. What's the matter with you? Do *you* think the project is going to work?"

He said, "Well, I did. I don't know. It's not a safe project. And he's right. There's a lot of funding riding on this. If I'm wrong . . ." He brushed his hair off his forehead. "Maybe I should scrap it."

"I can't believe you're willing to dismiss a great project after one conversation with Fischburger. How much does he really know about what you're doing?"

"Do you really think it's a great project?" he said, looking up at me.

"I know it is," I said firmly, though I didn't know the first thing about it. Todd had never explained it to me. "Fischburger," I said. "Now I see why he didn't win a Nobel Prize! He has no vision. None. He doesn't even have the ability to recognize it in someone else."

"Politics," Todd said.

"What?"

"That's why he didn't get the prize. He deserved to get it. But for some ridiculous political reason—"

"I just mean—"

"I don't *care* what you mean! You don't know anything about it! Stop trying to defend me when you don't even know what's going on!"

"You *asked* me! I'm just trying to be on your side!" I said. "Don't you know kindness and support when you see it? God! Sometimes, Todd, you really make me mad."

I went to the oven. Then I heard a small crash. I turned around. Todd's cup had fallen off the table and broken into a hundred pieces. It lay in a splat of orange juice on the floor.

I looked at Todd, whose face was pinched and pale. It was the dog cup in pieces on the floor. "I forgot it was there," he said. "I knocked it over."

"The dog cup!" I said. "You broke the dog cup!"

"It was an accident," Todd said. "I'm sorry. I know it was one of your favorites, and your mother gave it to us. We've had that cup forever." He looked at it as if reading a message of doom in the shards.

I shook my head. "*Your* mother gave it to us, and I never liked that cup one bit," I said. "It was a terrible cup."

"I never liked it, either." He looked as if he might cry. "I don't know what I'm going to do."

"Listen to me," I said. I bent down and took hold of his shoulders. I wanted him to look up at my face, but he wouldn't. "You do good work. You've always done good work. Fischburger coming to your office to say a lot of idiotic things doesn't change anything about what you've done in your lab or what you're about to do. Does it?" I waited. "Todd? Does it?"

Todd looked at me and sighed, meaning he was tired or he didn't want to even think about it anymore or he wished he had talked to someone else about this, someone who knew something about science. He went to the garage and came back with a dustpan and some paper towels to clean up the mess.

"I just need one publication," Todd said, "just one good thing, and then I'm on my way."

I thought about saying, "You're almost there." Or "Don't worry, everything will fall into place before you know it." But I didn't want him to get mad at me again.

sixteen

HOW TO FIND A BOYFRIEND/HOW TO FIND A
GIRLFRIEND. We'll use a variety of techniques to help
you find someone who's right for you: visualization, group
chanting, hypnosis, matchmaking, and blind dates. Saturdays,
7–9 P.M., beginning October 25. Course cost: $10 per
session, until you've found someone you're crazy about.

*P*RISCILLA AND I were in her pickup on our way to Saturday morning garage sales. Michael had given me some money to buy things for *Fields of Love*. Priscilla had on one of her slippery jogging suits, bright green with blue and purple stripes cutting diagonally across the left side of her chest and the front of her lower right leg. She had a cigarette sticking out of one side of her mouth as she used both hands to steer us onto the freeway on-ramp.

Smoke hit me in the face and my eyes watered. Priscilla was looking over her shoulder, finding a space to move into the lane. When we made the merge, she took a long drag on the cigarette and put it into a special car ashtray stuck to the dashboard of the truck.

"Nice day," I said. I opened my window a little bit, which sucked the smoke straight at me.

"It's almost always a nice day here," Priscilla said. "You should know that by now." She opened her window, too, improving the air quality slightly. "I try not to smoke in the house, so I do it here in the truck. I hope it doesn't bother you."

"Not at all," I said. I turned my face a little closer to the open window.

Priscilla smoked out the side of her mouth closest to her window. "Now, this neighborhood we're going to is really good. I've gotten a lot of my own furniture around here. Garage sales are the whole reason I got the truck in the first place." She took another drag on her cigarette. "Naturally, you have your good days and your bad days. But if it's a good day, we can get a whole load of stuff to use in the play—costumes, furniture, and everything. We're running a little behind schedule, though."

I said, "It's barely seven-thirty."

"Any later than this and you miss all the good stuff."

Priscilla got off the freeway and checked a piece of newspaper she was holding. She slowed the truck slightly to look at a street sign, then sped up when she spotted a bright orange square of cardboard with the words GARAGE SALE on it and an arrow.

At the first house there were a lot of baby things—clothes, toys, equipment—that looked almost brand-new. One woman was loading a lot of it into the back of a station wagon. Under her breath, Priscilla said, "She's a pro. She has one of those stores for secondhand baby stuff, I'll bet you anything." We looked around briefly. A small child, probably the former owner of all the baby stuff, pedaled a tricycle up the sidewalk. "Nothing for us. Let's move on," Priscilla said.

We drove a block farther and found another sale. Before she even parked the truck, Priscilla saw something. "Look at that dresser. For the bedroom scene. Don't you think? You want it?"

The dresser was a small one, brown with three drawers. "That could work," I said.

"We'll spray-paint it white?" she said. "I'll handle this." We climbed out of the truck. "Morning," she said to the man setting up. "You got a perfect day for your sale. Made to order. Looks like you've got some nice things."

"I'm not ready yet," the man snarled. He was wearing a pajama top and a pair of jeans. "You people come too early. I put in the paper eight o'clock. I meant *eight o'clock.*"

"Fine," Priscilla said. "We just wanted a look at that dresser, then we're out of here. How much are you asking?"

"I'm not open yet." He glanced at the dresser. "Fifty."

Priscilla took out three tens. "When you do open, I've got thirty in cash. But when you're ready."

"Forty," the man said, not looking at the money.

"Thirty-five," Priscilla said, pulling another bill out of her wallet. When he didn't answer immediately, she said, "We don't want to be in your way. We'll come back later if we don't find anything else." She took a few steps toward the truck, and I followed.

"Ah, take it," the man said. "Go ahead. Might as well. You're here now."

Priscilla handed him the three tens and a five, which he shoved down into his pocket without looking. He walked into the garage and brought out a basket of kitchen things, a lamp, a rack of clothes, while Priscilla and I got the dresser loaded into the back of the pickup. "Thank you," I called as we climbed into the truck.

At another house, piles of used clothing were spread out all over the lawn. Priscilla had an armload of men's clothes, and I was concentrating on women's. I held up a dress for her to see. "Good. But how much?"

"Two dollars."

"Why not?"

I put it on my pile. I added a plastic bag full of fake flowers that I figured we could use for something. Priscilla found an old radio. We got it all for twenty dollars. At another place, we found a wheelbarrow, some bushel baskets, and some rakes for the scenes in the fields. After nine o'clock, the sales looked as though they already had been pretty well picked over. "It all happens before nine A.M.," Priscilla said. "At nine, it's over. Let's go call Michael to meet us at the school and help us unload. I'm desperate for coffee."

We got into the truck and drove to a 7-Eleven. "You get the coffee," Priscilla said. "I'll call Michael."

When I came out with the coffee, she was waiting in the truck. "Here," I said, handing her a cup.

She took a sip. "Good," she said. She took another swallow, put the cup in a drink holder, lit a cigarette, and started the truck.

"So, is he coming?" I said. "Was he there?"

"Oh, yeah, he's coming," she said. "The great thing about Michael is that he doesn't have a life."

I looked at her.

"No, I mean, you can always find him. You always know where he is, what he's doing. He's either teaching a class, about to teach a class, or the school's closed and he's at home, waiting for it to reopen. The school, the people there, that's it for him. He doesn't have much else. You could call Michael up in the middle of the night and say, 'I have an idea for a new class,' and he would want to hear it. He'd be happy, grateful even, that you woke him up, interrupted a good night's sleep to talk to him about your idea."

"Kind of a workaholic or something, you mean."

"Maybe. But when you think of workaholics, they're usually people who are trying to get themselves ahead. They want more of something—money or fame or something. But with Michael, it's more like he created the school because he needed somewhere to go every day. He needed people around him, projects to work on. He puts his whole heart into it. It's all he cares about. You know that woman who works in the office?" Priscilla went on. "Esther?"

"That crabby woman who's always banging on her computer?"

"That's the one. Last year, she had gallbladder surgery. Michael stayed in the hospital room with her for two nights."

"They must be really close."

"No. That's what I'm saying. He had just hired her two weeks before. The surgery was pretty routine, you know, but her kids couldn't come. They live in Texas or New York or someplace. So Michael went."

"That was nice of him," I said.

"It was nice. You never feel you *know* him very well, but he's very kind." She put out her cigarette.

I was going to ask her what she meant about not really knowing him, but by then we were pulling up in front of the school. Michael was sitting on a low brick wall in front of the building when we came around the corner. "See that?" Priscilla said. "There he is." When he recognized us in the truck, his whole face lit up in a grin. Priscilla said, "No one's been that happy to see me since I used to pick up my daughter at preschool."

As soon as the truck stopped, Michael hopped up onto the bumper and looked into the back of the truck. He opened the tailgate and scooped up a load of clothes. "Looks like you did all right," he said, carrying the bundle into the building. I got the rest of the clothes and followed him, while Priscilla was gathering some of the miscellaneous smaller items. As we walked through the hallway, Michael turned around and smiled at me.

We dumped our loads of stuff in the former kitchen of the school, which we thought of as our dressing room, and went back to the truck. The three of us worked on getting the dresser down from the truck, then Michael and I carried it in, while Priscilla cleared out the last few items and slammed the tailgate. "I'm going to move my truck. We're parked on red here."

Michael and I carried the dresser all the way to the little stage, where it took up more room than I expected. As if reading my mind, Michael said, "I think we need a larger stage area. I'm thinking we could build out a little here. We've got a pretty big cast. What do you think?"

I looked at the surface of the stage platform. "I think more room would be great. Want me to help you? I don't know what to do, but you could tell me."

"After rehearsal this afternoon? About five-thirty?"

I nodded.

"I'm telling you, Jenny Brown, we will make something out of nothing. You will be amazed."

I laughed. "I'm amazed already, just standing here. Sometimes I stop and think, What am I doing? Where am I? What is this anyway?"

"Don't do that," Michael said. "Whatever you do, don't think about it. Don't look at it too closely. We couldn't have that. We want you to stay." I felt my face burn and pretended to be busy with some props we'd bought. Priscilla walked in then.

Michael said, "I'll go get my tape measure. I might have time to buy some wood later this morning." He went out.

Priscilla asked me, "Now where do you want this stuff, Jenny? Here, I'll just lean it up against the wall here for now." Priscilla set the stuff out of the way. "Michael is so sweet, isn't he?" she said. "I'd just love to pair him up with somebody. Too bad he's married." She glanced at me. "I was surprised, too. I couldn't quite believe it at first, but I guess it's true." She took some hangers out of a brown grocery bag that she had brought from home and began putting them into the clothes we had bought. She said, "I've never seen the wife, not even once. I just know she exists."

"He's married?" I said. "I can't picture that. Somehow this is hard to believe. So where is she? If he has a wife, how come she never comes here? I thought you said he didn't have a life."

"He doesn't. I don't know anyone who has seen her. All I know is that she's out there somewhere. Take my word for it."

I said, "Maybe they're separated or something? Maybe she left him and lives somewhere else? Maybe he's divorced?"

"No," Priscilla said, shaking her head. "It isn't anything like that."

Michael always wore dance shoes that made his approach very quiet. So I kept listening for small sounds. I thought I heard a sniff a long way off. Priscilla heard it, too, and stopped talking, continuing to put the clothes on hangers. Michael came back in then and started measuring the stage and the space for the new part that he wanted to build. He pulled a piece of paper from his pocket and wrote down the measurements. "We're going to need an iron," Priscilla said to me.

"I have one," I said. "Brand-new. I never use it. Ever."

When Michael finished measuring, he said to me, "I'm going to go get some wood and supplies before my class. I'll see you at five-thirty, after rehearsal."

I looked at him, trying to picture a woman with him, someone about his age with graying hair and blue-gray eyes that saw right into you. "Right," I said. "See you later," I said.

Priscilla said, "We'll need a costume rack. Now what do I have at home? I'm going to have to think about this." She looked around for something to hang the clothes on. She opened some cupboards and hung the clothes on the tops of the doors. "Say, Jenny." I looked up at her. "I want you to use me in this play. I want to be very busy."

I said, "You want a bigger part, you mean? More lines? I guess I could talk to the writer, but—"

"No, I don't care about how big the part is," she said. "I just mean if there's anything you need—sewing, errands, painting, laundry, running lines—give it to me."

"OK," I said. "Thanks. It's generous of you to offer. We're going to need help with all kinds of—"

"Something happened. I need to be busy. My daughter, you remember we were having all the trouble? Well, she moved to her dad's in Arizona. Monday. I woke up, went to her room, and she was gone. Everything was neat and in its place. Right there, that gave me the chills, seeing her bed made and all her things put away like that. I don't think it ever happened before, not even once. I knew something had happened, something big and terrible. There was no note or anything. I had to just sit and wait to hear from her. Naturally, I spent the day imagining accidents and abductions and all kinds of terrible things. But with that room looking that way, I had a feeling she was physically all right. But gone. Then my ex-husband called me from Arizona to say she was there with him. He's enrolled her in a local high school. I can't tell you how that makes me feel. I think my heart broke, right then and there. You know, I think I feel worse than I did when I was still married to her dad and I found out he was cheating."

I went to her and put a hand on her shoulder. I stood there a minute next to her, patting her back. She leaned on me for a long time. When people come to you for support, somehow it makes you feel as if you might have what they need, something you didn't know about before.

After she'd leaned on me for a few minutes, she stood up and started sorting through costumes. I watched her a minute, her shoulders sagging in her bright jogging suit with the weight of her sadness. Her hands were trembling a bit as she fussed with things that didn't need to be adjusted. I said, "Wait. Don't fold those shirts." She looked at me, biting her lower lip, as if on top of everything else, I was about to criticize the way she put away clothes. "Put them in that basket over there. And could you take them home and wash them? I'd really appreciate it. Also, look them over for rips and do any mending that you think is necessary. You know, we didn't find a nightgown for Tiffany. I don't think there's anything we can use for that bedroom scene. Do you think you could find one for me? A long one, not too revealing, but not too demure, either, white if possible. And remember how small she is. Of course, we don't have much money, so see what you can get used. I need it tomorrow, if you can manage it."

She nodded. "I'll see what I can do."

"I need a wardrobe person, someone to keep track of who wears what, to make lists of what we're missing, arrange to get things washed, figure out the sewing. Would you do it?"

"Yes, I will."

"Now there are a lot of clothes here for the younger characters, but I think we're going to need more for the older generation, don't you? And Clara. Let's not forget we need some grandmother clothes."

"Absolutely," she said, a weak smile forming on her lips. "This isn't anywhere near enough. I'll get to work on it right away."

"Thank you," I said. "I knew I could count on you."

"Thank *you*, Jenny," she said. "I'm so glad you're doing this show!" And she started to go through a bundle of shirts we'd bought, pulling out each one and giving it a fierce shake before assigning it to a pile.

seventeen

YOUR MESSAGE HERE. Tired of expensive TV and radio spots and not sure if they're really working? Explore the limitless possibilities of wearable advertising. T-shirts, hats, aprons, and more can boost your business and change your life. We'll help you write a slogan and design a garment to get you started. Saturday, November 8, 9–12 A.M. Course cost: $15. Materials: one T-shirt, sweatshirt, or hat.

*I*T WAS the first time we were to rehearse the Halloween-party scene with everyone in costume. I had left it to the actors to decide what to be and to get their own costumes. As long as they wore masks, I told them, pretty much any costume would be fine. "I'll give you exactly five minutes to get dressed," I announced, looking at my watch. "By the time we open, we're going to have to be a lot faster. Ready, set, go!"

Twenty-three minutes later, most of the actors were ready. Priscilla had dressed as a pumpkin. She had on a puffy orange suit, green tights, and a green beanie with a stem. Edward looked like a fat cat from a cartoon in a black sweatshirt pulled tight over his round belly, a tail made from a stuffed black stocking, and a mask with glued-on whiskers. For ears, he had glued triangles of felt to the hood of the sweatshirt.

At first, it was hard to spot Tiffany and Jason. Several of the teenagers came as superheroes. I couldn't pick them out of the crowd with their masks on. But then after staring at the group for a long time, I realized they were both dressed as Batman. They looked startlingly similar. Both were thin and about the same height. I finally figured out that they were the ones holding hands and staring into each other's masks. Momentarily, I considered having one of them switch to some other costume. Instead, I had the parents do a little wordless scene, getting mixed-up about which of the teenagers was theirs. It was funny. I laughed at my own joke. All the other actors laughed, too, and I liked having an audience for something I thought up.

As we finished our rehearsal, Michael returned, bringing in wood from his truck. "Before we leave for today, would some of you please help Michael bring in the wood for the stage?" I said to the actors. "Thank you. Tiffany, please work on that speech a little more for next time. It's coming along, but I'm thinking there's something missing. Maybe once you get the words down, we can develop what you're doing with it."

Tiffany nodded.

"You may all put your costumes back here in the kitchen, which will be our dressing room. Priscilla's going to be in charge of wardrobe. She'll find us a rack and some more hangers. Meanwhile, you can just fold your things and mark them with your names. Here's a marker. Then put them on the lunch counter here. Thanks. Nice work today, everyone." The actors went into the kitchen. I could hear them commenting on the costumes Priscilla and I had collected earlier.

"Cute."

"Wonder where they found this."

"Oh, my God," someone said. "I hope that isn't for me."

Michael was busy organizing the lumber he'd brought in. Edward carried in sawhorses from somewhere; Jason brought in a power saw, glue, and nails. "That's it, Michael," Edward said, tossing Michael his keys. "You need some more help with this? I've got to go home now, but tomorrow I could—"

"Thanks. I'm all set," Michael said. "I've got it."

Edward said, "Are you sure you don't want—"

"Absolutely. Jenny and I will take care of it, but thanks so much for offering."

Gradually the room emptied until just the two of us remained. Michael studied the stage, consulted his drawing.

I said, "Do you want me to do something?"

"Yes," Michael said. "I do."

"OK, what?"

"Or do you have somewhere you need to—"

"No, no, but I—"

"Have to go?"

"No, not—I just—"

"If you can stick around, I could use someone else here."

"OK, sure," I said.

Michael studied his drawing. "Priscilla told me you were married." As soon as these words were out, I wanted to take them back.

"I am married. I am," he said. "Priscilla was right." He laid a sheet of plywood across the two sawhorses, measured, then drew a line down it, using a metal ruler as a straightedge. He plugged in the saw, turned it on, began to cut.

I said. "Where's your wife?" I didn't even try to stop myself.

Michael turned off the saw. "What? Did you say something?"

"I said, 'I don't think I've met your wife, have I?' I was wondering if she ever comes to the school."

Michael said, "No, you haven't seen her." He turned the saw back on.

"Well, how come?" I said. "Is she completely involved in something else, her own career that takes a lot of time?"

He turned off the saw. "I didn't hear you."

"Does she have a demanding job and work long hours?" I said.

"No," he said. "It's not like that. She just can't get here." He turned on the saw.

"And look at me, I can't stay away."

Michael turned the saw off. "Pardon?"

"But she's going to come for the play, I hope."

Michael pressed his lips together. "No." He turned on the saw.

"That must hurt your feelings. Does it make you feel sad that she doesn't care about what you do? Do you wish she would be with you more, be more involved in your life, more of a partner, a friend?"

"What's that?" Michael said, turning off the saw again.

"Don't you want her to see your work?"

He shook his head. "She really can't be here. She's—" He was going to tell me something and stopped. "She's unable to come." He turned on the saw again and cut a long straight line down the width of the board.

When he turned off the saw, I said, "I don't understand."

He put the saw down and sat on the floor. "OK, let me explain. She's not well. She's mentally ill. She lives in a full-care facility not far from here. She's on medication all the time, but she's not high-functioning. She can't be out in the world. It's too much for her. She has hallucinations. Sometimes she can come out for a brief outing. But even that is hard on her."

"Oh," I said. "I'm sorry. I see."

"No, you don't. I don't understand it myself, and I've had almost twenty years to get used to it. We were both dancers. We went on tour in Europe with a small company. That's how we met, dancing. While we were over there, we got married. We were both pretty young. She was only nineteen; I was twenty-one. Three other couples got married, too. It was very romantic, being in Europe in this low-budget dance company. Everything seemed heightened and super-intense and so interesting—the food, the clothes, the old buildings, the weird bathrooms. I remember really believing that this was what our lives would be like forever, touring around the world with other dancers. My wife—her name is Charlotte—had some difficult moments even back then, bouts of paranoia and almost paralyzing anxiety. I was egotistical and naive enough to think I could help her through all that. At the time, I truly believed that love and compassion were the solution to everything. One time she couldn't leave the hotel room for three days, and I stayed with her while the others went on, did our pieces without us. Another time, she sort of fell apart onstage. I thought it was fatigue or being away from home or something.

"When we got back, these weird moments got longer and

more severe. It turned out that her mother had committed suicide when she was little. She hadn't told me that. She didn't know where her father was. So it was up to me to get her taken care of. And that's what I've been doing. She doesn't have anyone else. I never went on another tour. That was the only one. The other two couples who got married when we did broke up within two years. But they didn't have mental illness to hold them together." Michael winked at me without smiling. "I taught dance at the university for a long time to support us. But I grew out of that. I wanted to do something of my own. So I started the school. Nobody knows about Charlotte, by the way. I don't talk about her. It's better for me if people don't—"

"I see," I said. "I wouldn't say anything."

"I know," he said. "I know you wouldn't."

He stood up and turned on the saw again. I held the boards while he cut. We didn't talk much after that. I had already asked too many questions, and Michael was concentrating on building the stage. I glued some of the pieces together, held some parts steady while he worked on them, suggested some steps be added on one side both to ease entrances and exits and to add interest to the design.

"Steps?" Michael said. "Steps would be good. I'll build you some steps."

"Thanks," I said.

It was after nine when Michael said, "Let's get something to eat."

I helped him put his tools away. "Your tape measure," I said, handing it to him.

"Thanks," he said, taking the tape measure. He dropped it into the toolbox and clicked it shut.

I got a broom for the sawdust.

"Leave that," he said. "I'll have to come back anyway. Let's go," he said. Ever so lightly, he put his hand on my back as I walked out the door.

We went in Michael's truck to get food. When he had parked at the shopping center where all the food places were, he turned to me and said, "Japanese or Mexican?"

"Mexican," I said. And we both stepped out into the dark. We ordered food and ate it, walked back to the truck. He drove me home.

" 'Bye," I said.

"Good night, Jenny," he said.

"Night," I said. I slammed the door of the truck.

WHEN I CAME IN, Todd was pacing around the family room with a pair of Walkman headphones on and no music playing. For just a few seconds, I thought that maybe he had been worried about me because I came home late without calling. "What's the matter?" I said. "What happened?"

"Nothing," he said. "Nothing at all. That's the problem."

"What do you mean?"

"Nothing is working. No results. No data. No papers. And everything takes too long! We're losing a lot of time. Robert's experiment didn't work. Three months wasted. I've been counting on that one. I was *sure* it would. I can't figure out where we went wrong."

"You can't expect—"

"Everything to work out? I don't. I just want *something* to work out! Just one thing. Anything! Other people who have been here less time than I have are way ahead. Fallows got tenure already. You met him. Can you believe it? He got a job offer from a university in France, and—boom!—tenure. Well, OK, he was an associate for a couple of years, but still. His projects are *average,* Jenny. *Safe and dull!*"

"I guess you've just got to be patient, keep going."

"Yeah, yeah," he said. "I need a miracle. You know that, Jenny?" He gave a little sarcastic snort. "Nothing short of a miracle could save me. I've got a bunch of talented people working long hours every day. Maybe not as long as I'd *like* them to. But they're there. I've got good, new equipment. But we're getting nowhere. We've got nothing. Thousands and thousands of dollars in grant money, in work hours invested. And what?" He looked at me as intensely as if he were scrutinizing a piece of DNA for mutations. "What happens? *Nothing* happens."

There was a long silence. Todd sank down onto the futon couch, forgetting how hard it was and landing with a jolt. Then he put his hands to his forehead and exhaled.

I sat down next to him. "Is this about what Fischburger said?"

Todd slumped backward into the cushions. "He was right. I don't know what I'm doing. I never should have become a scientist."

"You never should have listened to Fischburger. That's your problem."

"I need a miracle," Todd said again.

"There's a course in miracles at the Institute of Affirmation," I said. "It's called Making Miracles and Magic."

"What?"

He had used the word *miracle* as a figure of speech. I knew that; of course I did. But I continued anyway. I said, "People *say* it can be just amazing the way things work out in your life after you take this course. I guess that's not everyone's experience. But anyway, you have this little notebook for writing down your miracles. And then they happen. Or at least for some people they do. You write something like, 'Miracle Number 1: My experiments have all worked out. Miracle Number 2: I have tenure three years early. Miracle Number 3: Uh, well, you know, like, I am happily married to the right person. Or whatever thing you're working on. It can be anything you want. You write down the things you want to have happen to you, but you write it as if it's already true. Under each one you leave space for writing how the miracle came about. It might happen the same day you write it down or it might take more time. You work on three miracles for the course. You can have more later, but this is just to get you started."

He glared at me for a few seconds. "Oh yeah? How much is this course?"

"Just five dollars, actually," I said. "Per session. Of course, some people go several times. It's only an hour, so they wouldn't want to charge too much. But so many people go to it that I think—"

"Three miracles?" Todd said, moving his eyes sideways to look at me. "Five dollars. Not bad, except for the fact that the whole thing is *deceptive* and *preys* on people who are probably desperate!"

"Do you think so?" I said. "To me, five dollars seems like a small price to pay to get hope back when you've lost it. I guess you have to assume that people know what they're doing when they take a course like that."

"Jenny, I have a *Ph.D.*! I have worked a lot of years to get where I am. If you actually believe that a session in wishful thinking could help my situation, then you must think I'm an even bigger loser than I do myself."

I chose not to mention, at this particular time, that there was also a course in making wishes.

"You're not really getting sucked into this crap, are you?" Todd said. "I mean, what if they got someone in there with a really serious problem? It wouldn't be right to make this person think that a little notebook could help."

I said, "But I've heard all these stories from people I know at the school about miracles really happening to people. One woman really wanted to go to Europe. It was her deepest wish that she would get to go to see the Michelangelos in Italy. So she put this down as one of her miracles, something like, 'I am in Italy looking at the ceiling of the Sistine Chapel.' She had played the lottery every week of her life and never won anything. The very day after she made her miracle notebook—"

"She won," Todd finished for me. His eyes were closed. He didn't open them to speak. "She got exactly enough money to go to Italy." He tipped his head back against the couch, placing his hands over his face.

"More, actually. How did you know?" I said.

"More. Right. Of course. Way more." Todd stayed slumped on the couch. "Now listen to me," he said, opening his eyes. "If you think about it, chances are that *some* of the people will have their wishes come true or miracles happen or whatever you want to call it. That's just a matter of chance. If you're going to use that as evidence that the course works, then you have to *also* look at how many people's miracles *didn't* happen and how many people had amazing things happen to them that *weren't* what they wished for, that weren't written down in their notebooks. Do you have any data on that?"

"I just thought it sounded—"

"You don't! You see? They're giving you lousy data! And you're drawing conclusions from it!"

"It's just a very positive approach, that's all," I said quietly. "I just like the way they try to get people to see that their wildest dreams are possible. I like to think that when you're stuck in some tangle of a problem, there is a solution, a way out will present itself. Or something really good that has always been out of your reach is suddenly right there in front of you to take, hold in your hands because it's yours. I like that. I think it helps. That's all I'm saying." Just to give myself a reason to walk away, I picked up an empty wastebasket and went to the kitchen to turn it upside down over the garbage can.

Todd said, "I suppose writing down three things that you really want could be useful for defining your goals. Sure, OK, I'll go along with you that far. Maybe that's how it helps some of the people in the class. By writing down what they want, putting it into words, they might become aware of what they're after, which enables them to do something about getting it. But writing things down doesn't make them happen! No. That can't be." Todd was shaking his head at me, *no no no.*

"No," I said. "I'm not saying it does. It's not just the little notebook. Of course not. You have to meditate, too," I said. I didn't want to use the word *pray* when Todd was in such a bad mood. "And work. Hard. The woman who went to Italy said she was chanting, 'Yes, yes, yes,' silently to herself when she bought the lottery ticket. And she had taken a second job to save money. But then she won the lottery, so she didn't need—"

Todd slapped his hand against his thigh. Then he got control of himself and tried to help me. "Jenny," he said. "Listen. They're stealing money from these people. OK, so five dollars isn't much. But desperate people who have real problems could be taken in by this. It could hurt them. You do see that, don't you?"

"Well," I said, "To me, it just seems—"

"It seems impossible!" he said. "And it seems even more impossible that intelligent people pay money to sit in a room and listen to this crap! I don't care how cheap it is!"

"Don't yell at me!" I said. "I don't agree with you! We think differently! We don't see things the same way!"

Todd let out a long sigh. "I'm going to bed."

"Fine," I said. "Good night." I folded my arms across my chest. "And you're wrong, by the way."

"No, I'm not," he said from the stairs. "I'm right, and *you're* wrong. Good night."

ALL AFTERNOON on Sunday at the Institute of Affirmation, we rehearsed scenes with a lot of people in them: the Halloween party, the picking scenes, and the wedding scene at the end of the play. But no matter what we worked on, it always seemed there was something else that was a bigger disaster. As soon as I felt I had one scene under control, another one fell apart. I had the actors practice that until it improved, then went back to the first scene, only to find they had forgotten how to do everything that we had worked on.

Clara said, "Are you sure this show is going to be ready to open on time?"

"I wish the story made a little more sense," said Edward.

"I keep forgetting the order of the scenes," Priscilla said. "And what I'm supposed to do in them."

"I just need to know what to say and stuff, and then I'm there," said Tiffany.

"Th-there are a lot of s-scenes, and it's hard t-to believe we'll be able to get th-them all ready."

"There's a simple solution to all this," I said. "We need more rehearsal. Clara, Priscilla, Edward, Tiffany, Jason, Suzanne, and James." The principals looked up at me. "We'll be rehearsing tonight after dinner." There hadn't been a rehearsal scheduled for later. I felt like a crabby teacher, asking them to stay in for recess, so I said, "Let's have it at my house. We'll get some food and bring it over to my place first. OK? Is everybody free?"

They all looked at each other before they began to nod in agreement.

"What about your husband?" said Suzanne. "Is he going to mind?"

"My husband?" I said. "Mind? Oh, he always works late. OK, everybody? My house?" They nodded. "So we'll all go get food and meet at my place at"—I looked at my watch—"six? Good." I wrote my address on the small chalkboard near the kitchen door that must have once announced the cafeteria menu. "See you at my house," I said as they left.

I WENT STRAIGHT home to make sure I was there to open the door when they arrived. They all arrived at once, carrying bags of food from take-out places in the neighborhood.

"How come there's no furniture in here?" Tiffany wanted to know.

I said, "We used to live in a small apartment before we moved here. We don't have very much furniture."

Tiffany nodded. "Could you, like, buy more?"

"I guess," I said. "For now, we're going to have to sit on the floor. We only have four chairs at our table in the kitchen."

Priscilla said, "We don't want to make a mess, though. Looks like this rug has never even been walked on. Where do you keep your sheets, Jenny? I think we should sit on something, don't you?"

"Upstairs. Closet at the end of the hall."

Priscilla went quickly upstairs and came back down with a white flat sheet, which she spread out on the living-room floor. The actors brought their food to the sheet and sat down. The doorbell rang, and Edward opened it. It was Michael.

"Hi," I said. "I thought you had a class. How did you know we were here?"

"Oh. Is it OK? I saw the address on the chalkboard."

"Of course. Come in," I said.

"I brought my dinner." He held up a bag. "Got you some, too. In case you hadn't had a chance to get anything."

"Thanks," I said. "I didn't."

Michael looked around, turning his head from side to side like a curious bird. "Nice place," he said. "Very open." There was the slightest pause in the conversation as he walked into the living room.

"Well, now," Priscilla said. "Isn't this nice!"

I turned on the radio and there was a song on that Tiffany and Jason knew by heart. They sang along loudly, while the rest of us smiled and ate our food. I wanted to join them and sing along, but I didn't know the words.

"OK," I said, turning off the radio when the song finished, "now let's get to work. We're going to start with the scenes that are in the worst shape, go through them one by one, and then see how much time we have. I don't want to go past, say, nine o'clock."

I stood at one end of the room, where we would have put a dining table and chairs if we had had one. "This will be the stage. OK?"

The actors went there, waiting for me to decide which scene was first. It was hard to choose a scene because if I had been really honest about it, I would have had to say that all the scenes were in terrible shape. So I started from the first scene that didn't involve a crowd, and we worked our way through the script as quickly as possible, not improving anything appreciably, but at least becoming that much more familiar with it.

Michael and I were sitting on the floor in front of the actors. We were the audience. I looked around at the people in my living room, and I felt happy, glad to have them there with me. This was so much better than being by myself.

"Does Tiffany know *any* lines?" Michael wanted to know.

I shook my head. "I'm sure it will come together."

He nodded.

"We still have time," I whispered.

"Oh yeah," he said. "Plenty. It's like, almost two weeks."

There was a clutching feeling in my throat then as I realized how much we had to do. "Yeah," I said. "Twelve whole days. Well, eleven, now. No problem."

"Right," he whispered, looking at the actors.

We went on to a different scene, a dinner at the Juliet character's house. They all sat on the floor and mimed eating food. Tiffany had her script in her lap, and she was reading from it. In a way, I liked the look of the scene without the props and furniture. I could see the appeal of *Our Town*: the simplicity, the uncluttered feeling of just the words, ideas, and emotions bouncing around in the room between and among the people, like balls inside a racquetball court or neutrons, protons, and electrons whirling around inside an atom.

We all heard the sound of Todd's key in the lock. The actors paused for a moment as the front door opened and Todd walked in.

I said, "Don't stop."

Tiffany said to Priscilla, "I just want to be happy. Is that too much to ask?"

Priscilla said, "Happy?"

Standing baffled in the entryway, Todd said, "Hey! Jenny?"

I whispered, "We're rehearsing." The actors stopped, embarrassed. I stood up. "We're practicing our play," I said out loud.

Michael said, "Maybe you'd like to watch. Jenny is doing some incredible work here. I'm Michael."

"This is my husband, Todd, everyone," I said.

"Oh," Todd said. He kept looking at Michael. Then he looked at the others, one by one, as I said each person's name.

"Tiffany, Jason, Clara, Priscilla, Edward, Suzanne, James."

"Hi, Todd," a few of them mumbled.

"Hope we're not intruding," Priscilla said.

"No," Todd said. "Not really." He looked at me.

Now that Todd was there, the actors looked a little different to me. There seemed to be more of them than there were before, a crowd, and they were filling the whole living room. Priscilla's clothes seemed extra bright, and Edward seemed plumper and balder than he ever had before. Clara looked tiny and frail, really *old*. On the other hand, Tiffany and Jason seemed too young to be out without their parents at this time of night. But it was Michael who held Todd's attention the longest, with his purple clothes, pink ballet slippers, tight muscles, and his sweat-stained hat that he hadn't taken off when he came inside. He smiled at Todd in a way that struck me as goofy, and I had to look away.

When I looked back at Todd, I noticed how pale he was, how faded and worn his shirt was, how badly his hair needed cutting. And I wondered how long his glasses had been slipping down his nose the way they were now, making him look like a cartoon of an absentminded professor.

It was Michael who broke the silence. "So were we just about finished here for tonight, Jenny?"

"Uh, I guess so," I said. "Thank you, everyone. Nice work."

Loudly, Priscilla said, "Let's not forget to clean up here."

We picked up all the trash from our take-outs and unintentionally formed a line on our way to the kitchen to throw it away. Priscilla picked up the sheet. "Look at that," she said to Todd, as if to reassure him. "Not a spot on it." She folded it, put it at the foot of the stairs, then picked up her purse, which today was a white vinyl backpack. All the other actors began to pick up their things, too.

"Good work tonight, everyone," I said. "I think we're getting there. See you tomorrow."

"See you tomorrow," Tiffany said, and Jason echoed.

Michael said to Todd, "Nice to meet you. You should come down to the school sometime and take a class. We have something for everyone." Michael pulled a school catalog out of his dance bag, and Todd accepted it as though it were a used tissue he had been asked to throw away. "Good night, Jenny," Michael said.

"Good night." I closed the door after them and waved out the window.

Todd said, "Whoa."

"What?" I said. "What do you mean by 'whoa'?"

"How much time are you spending with these people?"

"What do you mean? Per day? Sometimes three hours, sometimes eight. I don't know. It depends. Why?"

206

"I don't know," Todd said. He just stood there, staring at me for a minute, like one of those people in a movie whose loved ones' brains are being controlled by aliens. I was tempted to reach up and slide his glasses back to the bridge of his nose where they belonged.

"Well," I said. "I think I'll go upstairs."

Todd said, "I'm going to watch some TV."

eighteen

HOW TO DEVELOP YOUR INTUITION. Psychics and skeptics alike can benefit from this course that awakens and exercises the sixth sense. Learn to read tarot cards, tea leaves, Ouija board, or your own dreams. Become more aware of your inner "voices." When you're finished with this course, you may want to open a fortune-telling business or simply be more attuned to other realities. Monday–Friday, November 10–14, 7–9 P.M. Course cost: $30. Materials: package of loose tea, tarot cards, and Ouija boards welcome but not required.

I WOKE UP in the middle of the night with a feeling of panic and fear. Something was terribly wrong, and for a minute, I couldn't remember what. I was sick. I checked for symptoms. No, that wasn't it. We were broke. Wrong again, I thought, remembering Todd's job. My mother was—no, I had just spoken to her before I went to bed, and she was fine. Then I remembered: *Fields of Love* was going to open in a week, and nothing was right about it. The actors didn't know what they were doing, the costumes weren't sewn, the sets were not finished. There were supposed to be lights. Michael had a friend who said he had some we could borrow, but so far, he hadn't come through.

I thought about the bank where I used to work. I pictured getting dressed up again, driving to the shopping center, staring at my computer all morning, printing out letters to loan applicants, going to lunch, then going back to my desk and having an afternoon that was nearly indistinguishable from the morning. Looking back on it, I couldn't quite remember what was so bad, why I had disliked it so much. A wave of nostalgia washed over me; working in the bank seemed like a happy time that I just wanted to go back to.

Lying there in the dark, I tried to think of ways I could stop the play. I could get the cast together and confide in them. It was all my fault: Because I didn't know what I was doing, there was nothing right about this production. It would be best for all of us if we faced that now and did not try to go on with it. But I knew I couldn't come up with anything that wouldn't break hearts and cause severe loss of hope. I would just have to carry on, as if it were possible to pretend that I hadn't created a big ugly mess, as if no one would notice. I would just have to behave as though I believed there were a way this could work and hope with everything I had that the cast wouldn't hate me too much when, inevitably, it didn't.

"OK, TIFFANY," I said in rehearsal the following afternoon. "Let's go over the bedroom scene again. There were a couple of things that could have been smoother last time. I want you to tighten the pace, close those gaps. There were quite a few pauses that shouldn't have been there."

Tiffany went to the stage. Priscilla stood in the doorway of the set to say her few lines at the beginning of the scene. Tiffany looked anxious, biting her lip, shifting around. Jason took his place, ready to start walking, look up, notice Tiffany. "Priscilla," I said, and she started the scene.

"Get a good night's sleep. Tomorrow will be a busy day," she said in character.

"Night," Tiffany said.

Priscilla mimed closing the door. We were supposed to be getting a door. A set-design class was working on this, but it wasn't there yet. Tiffany lay back in the bed, turning over a couple of times to indicate restlessness, then she got up and went to the window to begin her soliloquy. We had a window. It was a sample of a discontinued brand. Edward had retrieved it from a Dumpster at a store where he bought plumbing supplies. Right now it was held up by an open frame of unpainted two-by-fours. But it was a start. First Tiffany sighed, then she said, "Ryan, where are you right now? I wonder. I can't believe my luck. The only boy I like is the son of my father's biggest competitor. This is totally unfair."

Jason lifted his head to the level of the glass. "C-courtney, is that you at the w-window?" he whispered.

"Um . . ." Tiffany said, trying to keep a smile on her face, to stay in character. She had forgotten her line.

The slightest aberrations in a person's neurological hookups can cause differences in behavior. Some people have a natural knack for mathematical concepts and numbers; others can become proficient in a foreign language in a remarkably short time. Some kind of unique wiring, ever so slightly different from normal, gives them a single, highly developed ability. On the other hand, some people transpose letters as they're reading and mix up the simplest words: *was* becomes *saw*. It's wiring again. Todd could argue quite convincingly that most of our personality traits, the very things that make each of us unique, turn out to be genetic, built into us from the beginning. There are those who can't memorize the simplest nursery rhyme or phone numbers they dial every day. Tiffany was one of these.

It was just the way things were hooked up inside her. It wasn't that she didn't practice. It wasn't that she didn't *try*. Often, I had heard Jason whispering cues to her behind me when I was rehearsing with other actors. I saw her lips moving as she repeated the words to herself, waiting to rehearse. Now you might be thinking that she was not the right person to play a lead role in a play. But I thought, way back four weeks ago, that she had plenty of time, that with a lot of help, she could do it. Now between Jason's stutter and Tiffany's poor memory, the many scenes between them were long and difficult to listen to, instead of being quick and absorbing, the way they should have been.

"Ryan, is that you?" I prompted Tiffany.

"Ryan, is that you?" she echoed.

"I've only seen you twice, but I recognize your voice," I went on without having to look at the script.

"I've only seen you twice, but I...I remember...um..."

"Recognize your voice."

Tiffany snapped her fingers. "Oh, yeah. Your voice. Uh... then what?" She looked at me for help.

I walked over close to the stage. "Tiff," I said. Tiffany looked at the floor. "I want to help. We all do. We need to find a way to get these words out. You have to say the lines or we don't have a play. Without the words that Courtney has to say, there's no story."

She looked up. She was crying. "I know," she said. She put her hand to her heart. "Am I dropped? I was in *Children of a Lesser God* once, a little part, and they got someone else right before it opened. Same thing with *Our Town*. I wasn't Emily or anything, just a townsgirl, but I couldn't remember my line. The director gave it to another kid. Are you going to get someone else to play Courtney?"

"No," I said. I waited for someone to say something. Tiffany and Jason were avoiding looking at me. Jason looked at Tiffany, sending her waves of empathy; Tiffany looked at the floor.

"In school," I said, "I bet you've had to memorize things sometimes." She didn't look up. "You must have developed some strategies over the years, some tricks you count on to remember things you have to learn. Multiplication tables? Poetry? U.S. presidents?"

Tiffany shook her head. "I'm no good at that. In fifth grade, I had this teacher who said she wouldn't pass me if I didn't know the capitals of all the states. She made me stay after school on a certain day, just me, and say all the capitals to her. That was my test. One mistake meant another whole year in fifth grade. Old bag."

"So, what happened? Did you learn them?" I held my breath. "Did you have to repeat fifth grade?"

"I made it."

"Good." I exhaled. "So how did you do it then? Whatever it was, we'll do it here. I could find someone to coach you, or give you a tape player to repeat your lines, or maybe you—"

"That's not how I did it," she said.

"So what did you do? How did you pass? Did you just repeat them over and over all day long until they stuck?"

She looked up at me. "I cheated. When she wasn't looking, while she was checking a late homework paper for someone else who was in trouble, I taped a list of the state capitals in alphabetical order to the front of her desk. When she tested me, I sat in my seat in the third row and looked at it. I looked around the room, too, so it would seem like I was thinking, trying to remember. Acting. I was very real. I'd get the city, then look at the flag or the calendar or the author-of-the-month bulletin board, like I was thinking. I didn't get caught. She thought I knew them all. When it was all over, she said, 'You see how well you can do when you try? You're a smart girl. You just need to apply yourself.' I walked over to the desk, smiling, and peeled the tape loose. I said, 'Yeah, you're right. You were right all the time. Thank you.' Acting again. When I turned around, I stuffed the list down my pants and walked out fast. After summer vacation, I went to sixth grade with all my friends."

"I see," I said, disappointed. "I'm glad you made it. We'll think of something here, too. But right now we've got to get on to other things. We've only got a week to go here, and we've got several big problems to solve. We're a long way from ready." For the rest of the morning, we worked on scenes involving the townspeople. When Michael stopped by, I said, "Are we getting those lights any time soon, do you think? I don't mean to pressure you. I know your friend was doing it as a favor, but the thing is, I need to get stuff kind of, you know, organized, a little more certain."

"Right," he said, looking around. "I kind of thought they were already here."

"You did?"

"Last Friday I talked to him, and he said he could drop them by. Did he—you didn't see him?"

"No," I said. "And we're running out of time."

"I'll go call him." Michael left the room.

A short time later, Michael came back with his baseball cap in his hand, rubbing his face. "Uh. Bad news."

"What happened?"

"Uh. He's in Hawaii until March."

"Oh," I said. "Is there any way we could—"

Michael shook his head.

Priscilla said, "Don't you know someone else who—"

Michael exhaled. "No."

"All right then," I said firmly, making a decision. "No lights. Forget lights. We won't have lights."

"No *lights*?" said several people. I heard someone say, "Are you kidding? This is going to be totally lame." I recognized the voice. It was a high school boy named Dylan who played a townsperson, someone who didn't always make it to rehearsals.

"Uh," Michael said. "You know, Jenny, there are some things you can't really do without. One is actors, another is a script—sure you can have improvisation and all, but you do need a story of some kind—and a third is lights. Lights are kind of critical. Even if they're very simple, you have to have something." He looked at me. "In my opinion. But you're the director. You should do it your own way, of course."

"So, what do you suggest?" I said.

He stood there for a minute, sighing, scratching his head, looking around the room, maybe for inspiration. "If you'll excuse me for a little while, I'll just go call everyone I've ever met." He left the room.

I said, "Let's take stock of how our production is going here. Some things are probably in better shape than we think. Right? No need to get discouraged." I was hoping that my voice wouldn't shake, that I wouldn't break down in front of everyone. "Priscilla, how are the costumes coming along? You'll be ready a week from today, right?"

She looked at me blankly. "A week? It's two, isn't it?"

"No," I said, growing warm. "It's one. We open in one week."

"Oh, my God! I thought it was *two*," Priscilla said. "I've been

213

so busy with the props and scenery that I've had to stop work on the costumes for the last little while. I'll, we'll, um, anyone know how to sew?" There was no answer. "I can teach anybody. All I need is a few volunteers." No one said anything. "Man, woman, boy, girl? Anybody. I'll bring my machine in, and you just step on the pedal, run the fabric under the needle. That's all there is to it. I'm going home to get it now." Priscilla started to leave. "Anybody who's worried about working on a sewing machine can do the handwork. While you're sitting around waiting for your scenes, you might just as well be sewing on snaps, hemming skirts. Be right back." She started out.

"Wait," I said. "You mentioned working on the scenery. What about the flats? Are they done?"

"As a matter of fact, no. There was a little mistake."

"Mistake?"

"They weren't using the right scale, so things came out a little small. They just started over yesterday."

"Small? I don't understand."

"Jeff somehow got the idea that this was going to be for a, well, a puppet show. That's what he's always done in his class before, you see. Puppet scenery. It's cheaper to build small stuff, you see. And he somehow got the idea that this play was for puppets, instead of, you know, actors. That's what he's always—I guess no one mentioned to him that we're using live human beings in all the roles. Little Tiffany here would have been taller than the oak trees that were supposed to shelter her from the rainstorm. Jeff said the new materials would be there today. Or tomorrow, maybe. Day after tomorrow at the latest."

"Oh," I said. "Oh, boy." I put my hands over my eyes. I wanted to wake up and find out that this was all a nightmare. I could almost feel the relief that would spread through me as soon as I realized that I was safe at home in my bed and that none of this had really happened. I took a deep breath behind the darkness of my hands, then came out to face everybody still looking at me. "I don't see how they can build everything from scratch in a week. Less than a week, by the time they get the materials."

214

Michael came back. "Something could come through on the lights any time."

"You mean you found somebody who might have some for us?"

"Well, no, not yet," Michael said.

I said, "Thanks for trying."

I called the cast together. "Now listen, everybody. We have only seven more days. In order for us to be ready, we're going to need more help. If you could do some sewing with Priscilla, please raise your hand." No hands went up. "Sewing?" I said. "Anybody? Because one woman can't sew the clothes for all of you by herself in the time we have left." I waited. No volunteers came forward. "OK, well, what about set building? I know they're going to need some help with that. They've got three or four people signed up for that class, but that isn't enough to build everything, is it?" The room was quiet, much quieter than it ever was for a rehearsal. "Um, OK, listen. It seems to me that if you want this show to happen, you're all going to have to be willing to help."

Quietly, Tiffany said, "Jenny, my mom's already upset that I'm spending so much time on this play when I should be doing homework."

"Same here," Jason said. "We're, like, in high s-school, and we have to get into c-college, or we're dead m-meat."

"If I stay down here any more than I already am," Tiffany said, "my parents won't let me be in the show at all."

I said, "All right. I see what you mean." I sat down on the new part of the stage that Michael had built.

"I've already taken a lot of time off work," Edward said. "I really can't afford to do it anymore."

"I understand," I said.

"My kids are furious at me," said Suzanne. "Most nights when I get home, they're already in bed. I never see them these days. Sure, I could help out more. But it wouldn't be my time I'd be using, it really belongs to my kids."

"OK, OK," I said. "I get it." With a sinking feeling, I realized they didn't have any more time to give, even just for a week. I looked at their guilty faces alternately staring at me and looking away. I said, "You're right. You should all go home now, be with your families, do what you have to do. I'll try to work something out." As an unemployed childless person with a spouse who was never home, I was the most likely candidate to do more.

Quietly, they all gathered their things and shuffled out. Tiffany said, " 'Bye, Jenny. Sorry I couldn't—"

I said, "You're doing a lot. I'll find a way to make this work." I didn't believe this, and I don't think I convinced anyone else.

"If you want," Edward said, "maybe I could come back at eleven or so, after I go over some figures for my job."

"When are you going to sleep?" I said. "And maybe we're not as far behind as I think." I smiled weakly at him. "Maybe I'm just feeling a little pessimistic?"

Edward shook his head. "I don't think so. We're not even close. See you tomorrow."

When everybody was gone, I sat motionless for a little while, trying to assess what the most urgent problem was. I called Todd and told him I would be late. Then Priscilla returned from home with her sewing machine, a box of supplies, and an armload of clothes. "I have a couple of personal days I can take off. I'm going to do it. I'm off tomorrow anyhow. Maybe a couple of days off next week to be here and sew wouldn't be a bad thing."

I said, "What if you need those days later?"

"I need them now. Do you know how to hem?" I shook my head. "I'll show you," she said. "Then I've got a pile of stuff for you to work on." She put on her little half glasses and showed me the stitch.

"I think I can manage that," I said.

I hemmed a whole dress. I made the stitches big so it wouldn't take too long.

"Not too big, now," Priscilla warned, "or she'll catch her heel and pull the whole thing out."

I stitched a little smaller. Then I sewed buttons on shirts. I knew how to do this from home ec in seventh grade. I repaired a couple of rips and hemmed another dress. Priscilla did the more complicated work, sewing pieces of half-made clothes together.

There was a white satin wedding dress for the final scene that she worked on for a long time. We got it in a Salvation Army thrift store, but it had to be altered to fit Tiffany. As soon as the wedding dress was finished, she picked up another one. This one was for Suzanne, who was playing Jason's mother. The two of us hardly spoke. Priscilla just kept handing me things to do, and I had to concentrate hard to get them right.

Finally, Priscilla said, "I'm going to stop now, or I'll be useless tomorrow."

I looked at my watch. It was almost two in the morning. I said, "We've been sitting here for five hours. That's not possible!" I looked at the pile of clothes that still needed work and it didn't look any smaller than it had when we started. Priscilla looked at the pile, too.

"It's a big cast. What time did you think it was?" Priscilla said.

"About eleven, eleven-thirty."

We put down our sewing things without putting anything away. We would resume our work as early as possible in the morning. Priscilla gave me a ride home.

I got into my nightgown without even turning on a light and crawled into bed. I was so quiet that Todd didn't turn over to ask me where I'd been all this time. In the morning, he left before I woke up.

At nine, I got out of bed, put on clean clothes without taking a shower, and drove to the school to see how the sets were coming along. Michael was there already, banging nails into wood, making a frame for a flat. When he stopped to get another nail, he looked up and said, "Do you know how to build a flat?"

"No," I said. "No idea."

"I don't, either. I'm sort of making this up as I go along. Jenny, I'm sorry, but I don't see how we're going to make it," he said. He put down his hammer. "There's no way this play can be ready in time."

I sat down next to him on the floor, sighed with everything I had, relief as big as the sky radiating from me through the room. "People are going to be disappointed when we tell them we're canceling the show. I mean, what about the writer? She's going to be so heartbroken when she finds out that her play isn't going to happen, after all. And Tiffany. She tried so hard. And Priscilla. Of course, she's much older and she's used to disappointments—you know the way you get when they just keep coming at you, sort of immune or something. All that work she put into the costumes and getting all the stuff. You know her daughter went back to live with her ex-husband. That was such a blow to her. She asked me to keep her busy with things to do for the play. So I've had her doing all this stuff, not only costumes, but running around to get things, copying stuff, collecting props. And stopping dead right now is going to be hard for her. But I guess you have to figure that the experience served some kind of purpose, that it wasn't a waste, that it was worthwhile somehow. We all learned a lot and achieved a closeness that was really positive. For everybody. That's worth something. Isn't it? To me, it is."

"Jenny?" he said.

"What?" I looked at him, hoping I wasn't about to make a fool of myself, jumping up and down, laughing hysterically, thanking him repeatedly for getting me out of this mess.

"I think you misunderstood what I said. We aren't going to cancel. We can't do that."

"What?"

"We can't cancel the play. I said I we won't be ready on time, but that's not the same as saying we're going to cancel. Ready or not, we're opening this play when we said we would."

Deep fear grabbed me by the throat. "*What?* Why? It will be horrible, an embarrassment, a humiliation for each of us individually, all of us as a group."

Michael considered for a moment. "It has even less chance of working out if we don't do it."

"Why would you want to do this when you know what bad shape it's in?"

"Because this is the Institute of Affirmation. 'The answer is yes,' remember? *Yes* is at the core of what we're about. Canceling would be a big *no*. We don't do that here." He stood up and started hammering again.

"Michael, this is a mistake." I had to yell at him over the banging. "We have to stop now, admit defeat. I mean, I understand the value of following through. Of course, I do, but you have to admit, there are times when you need to face the fact that a project just hasn't worked out the way you wanted it to, that following through would be worse than giving up on it."

He shook his head, stood there looking at me. "Sorry. Can't do it. It would be against our philosophy, and—"

"That's nuts," I said, raising my voice again, though he was no longer hammering. "Of course you can. Just say, 'We are extremely sorry, but this production did not work out.' *I'll* say it. I'll tell everyone, if you don't want to. I'll take full responsibility. 'I'm very sorry, but I don't know how to pull this together. We all did our best, and we can be proud of that, but we didn't make it this time. We had insurmountable problems.' People will thank me for not causing them public shame." Michael was shaking his head. "What? Are you saying no, you won't save your school, your students, from embarrassment, humiliation?"

"I'm saying whatever the problems are, we have to do it anyway."

"We don't have lights! The costumes aren't made! The lead actress doesn't know her lines! The set isn't built!"

"We have some things to resolve before Thursday," Michael said. "Big things, some of them. But there's another reason that we can't cancel."

"What's that?"

"We've sold tickets," he said. "It's a big cast with large families and a lot of friends. We sold tickets, and the money, well, it came at just the right time, because I had to pay a couple of bills."

I opened my mouth to argue with him, but I couldn't get any words organized. My hands went up at my sides and then flopped down again. I said, "You mean—"

"I mean," Michael said, "the show is going to open. I'll help you in any way I can, but it absolutely has to happen, in some form or other. The ticket money is gone."

"Well," I snapped. "I guess that settles that!"

nineteen

PET PIX. Learn how to photograph your animal friends like a pro! We'll show you how to choose a background, suggest cute pet costumes for the willing pet, list outdoor settings around town for that "pet-in-the-wild look," and show you ways to sneak up on your pet for those priceless candid shots. Friday, November 14, 6–9 P.M. Course cost: $15.

I HAMMERED some flats together, put several of them in place myself. When I stood back to look at them, I felt more discouraged than ever. One was leaning to the left; one tipped backward. They didn't line up. Jason stood next to me, tilting his head, squinting at what I'd done. "Lousy!" I said in disgust.

"B-but it's something!" Jason said. "It's there, and it wasn't there b-before!"

"Did Michael tell you to say that?" I scowled, folding my arms and frowning at him.

"M-Michael?" he said, confused. "No. He's not here, is he?"

I said, "Well, no. It just sounded like something he might say."

Jason smiled. "Really? Th-thanks."

"Jason," I said.

"What?" He put a finger under his hat to scratch his head.

"See that big rip in the curtain? And that smaller one over there?"

"Yeah," he said, tipping his head sideways again.

"Could you please get some of that gray tape and repair all the rips? You're going to have to close the curtain and look it over carefully. They're all over the place."

"OK," he said, picking up a roll of tape. "Don't worry about a thing. I've got this handled."

"Thank you." I went to the back of the room to iron a pile of clothes that Priscilla had finished working on. After a couple of dresses, I looked up to check on how Jason was doing.

"Jason?" I said.

"Yeah, Jenny?" He smiled at me.

"Do you think maybe you could put the tape on the *back* of the curtain, instead, the part the audience *doesn't* see?"

"Hey! Good idea!" He looked at the curtain for a minute and scratched his head. "Should I take off the ones I've already d-done?"

"I think so. Then maybe people won't notice that we repaired the curtain with tape."

"G-got it," he said, giving me a thumbs-up sign. He started tearing tape off the curtain.

I sat next to Priscilla at the sewing machine. I said, "Sometimes I have these bad dreams where I'm trying to do something and the more I try, the more I can't do it. I have guests, say, a roomful of cranky important scientists, successful middle-aged men with attitudes."

"Mm-hm," Priscilla said with pins sticking out of her mouth.

"And I have to be nice to them because they might give Todd a job or review a paper he's written or write him a recommendation or something. I am trying to serve lasagna, but all the plates are in the dishwasher and I have to wash them one by one. The utensil drawer is stuck shut. I can't find the spatula and have to use a knife. The lasagna keeps sort of melting and sliding off the knife and down the gaping garbage disposal. Hours pass and I still haven't served the first plate. Do you know what I'm talking about? Did you ever have those dreams?"

"Oh, sure," said Priscilla, biting off a thread. "Only I'm running late and I have to get to a parent-teacher conference. I've got a run in my hose and it's my last pair. So I decide to wear something casual. I put on a top and discover it has a big stain down the front. The phone rings. I answer and can't get off. It goes on and on. I hate those dreams."

"Yeah," I said.

"What made you think of that?"

"This," I said quietly. "The play."

"Oh," she said. "Oh, dear."

I said, "Priscilla, do you think we can make it?"

"Now, you shouldn't even ask that," Priscilla said. "You've got to think like Michael. He's always so convinced that things will work out, and, by God, for him, they always do."

I said, "Maybe it's just the way he interprets what happens, though. He processes it in a way that makes it look good. And when it works out for him, does it work out for everyone else at the same time? I don't know." Just then Tiffany was walking through the door of the multipurpose room. "I think I'm about to get more bad news."

"You've got to start working on the yes thing," Priscilla said, "Just say 'yes, yes, yes,' over and over to yourself."

I stared at Priscilla. She cupped a hand around one ear.

"Yes, yes, yes," I said in the flattest, most defeated voice I had ever heard come out of my own mouth.

Tiffany walked up to me. Her head was down, and she was shuffling. She had something to tell me. As bad as things are, I thought, they're about to get worse.

"Jenny?" she said. "Can I tell you something?"

"Yes," I said. "Yes."

"I can sew. My mother can, too. We have a machine at home."

"Oh," I said, "really?"

"I couldn't offer before because I had this big research thing I had to do for my government class. My mother said if I got it in on time, she would do all the sewing you want, and I can, too. I turned it in today, on time, so now I can sew for you. I'm fast, and I've had a lot of experience."

"I see," I said. I looked at Priscilla. Her mouth was open.

"Well, that's *good* news, isn't it? Priscilla will give you some stuff to take home tonight, won't you, Priscilla?"

"I will," Priscilla said. "Yes, yes, yes."

"Thank you," I said.

"You're welcome," Tiffany said. "I'll go help Jason."

"Good idea," I said.

"Did you see that?" Priscilla said. "Now, what did I tell you?"

"I did see that," I said. "Did that just work, or was it a co-incidence? OK, I'm going to start rehearsal now." I went to the front of the stage, where Tiffany was tearing strips of tape and Jason was sticking them to the back of the curtain. "We'll have to finish that later, OK? It's time to start rehearsal. We're starting with act one, scene one, and we're going to try to make it through to the end of act one today. Let's see how far we can get without stopping."

We didn't get very far. We had to stop so many times for Tiffany to get her line that we only made it through half of act one before I had to let everyone go for the day.

THE MORNING OF our run-through, I woke up with a feeling of dread. I thought about the miracle class I took and the one about wishing. Maybe if I tried those things again, really applied myself this time, I might see some improvement. There might be some kind of shift somewhere; something might give. I made a new notebook with just one miracle: "Our play is a brilliant success." Writing it, I wanted to crawl into a hiding place and never come out.

I got some pennies out of my purse, filled up the bathtub, and threw them in one at a time. "I wish Tiffany would learn her lines"; "I wish the sets would be ready on time"; "I wish we had lights"; "I wish the costumes would be ready"; "I wish the curtain would be repaired to perfection"; "I wish something, anything, would work out right"; "I wish I would have a run of excellent luck"; "I wish for a breakthrough." I kept going until I ran out of money. There was a lot to wish for, once I got going. Then I took a bath in the water, shoving the money to the sides of the tub and leaning back, closing my eyes to focus better on my prayers and wishes.

WHEN I ARRIVED in the multipurpose room, Michael was on a ladder with a wrench in his hand. He was putting up a light fixture, hanging it from a wooden frame.

Was this *it*? I wondered. The miracle?

"Where did you get those lights?" I asked Michael. "Want me to help you with the others? Where are they? I'll bring in the rest of them."

He turned around to speak to me. "This is all. I only got two, and that one has a short somewhere. Keeps going out," he said. "This other one is more or less stuck in one position. I guess we'll just have to do what we can to hang it so that it points the most useful way, then leave it there. A guy I know was throwing these out. This one has a short and sometimes turns itself off. Now you're going to have to do this, get these things pointed where you want them, so let me show you what to do." He climbed down the ladder, handed me the wrench.

Climbing up, I said, "It's like Santa came during the night and left us a present."

"Right," Michael said. "You're not afraid of heights, are you?"

"Heights? Not at all," I said. He was holding the ladder steady. I was at the top now.

"Good. Now you see that sort of knob on the side there?"

"This thing?"

"Yeah. That's what you're supposed to loosen to move the light. It's pretty stuck. Try the wrench."

"OK, yeah." I put the wrench around the knob. "Did the light move at all? Maybe a fraction of an inch?"

"No. I don't think so. It's sort of pointing at the back wall. You'll see when I turn them on. I'm not sure that's going to help us. The gels go in that square thing. A gel is the colored plastic that changes the color of the light."

"Here? Oh, I see," I said. "It opens. OK. I'm going to have to fool around with this a little until I get the hang of it."

"All you can really do is change the gel and turn it on and off. Unless you can somehow get it unstuck. When's your run-through?"

"Seven o'clock," I said, coming down the ladder. "We're not ready." I had said these words so many times now that they came out almost without my thinking them.

"You will be," Michael said. "You will."

Tiffany came in then. "How did the sewing go?" I asked her.

"Sewing?"

"The basket of stuff Priscilla gave you to take home and work on with your mother?"

"Oh, that, yeah. We're going to try to do some of it this weekend."

"Tiffany," I said, putting my hands on her shoulders, looking into her eyes. "It's Tuesday. The play opens on Thursday. We need the costumes finished." I let go.

"OK, OK," she said. "I hemmed a dress. I only slept for, like, seven or eight hours," Tiffany told me. "Did you?"

"What? Sleep? No, not much," I said. "I've kind of given that up."

"I thought so," she said. "You've got these dark circles under your eyes. Want to borrow some makeup? I've got tons in my backpack."

"No, thanks," I said. "I've given that up, too. I don't take showers or eat meals, either."

"You don't need makeup," she said. "You're pretty without it."

"Ha!" I said too loudly. Edward and Suzanne raised their heads from the sewing they were doing. "Priscilla will give you something to work on right now. If you're not going to do that stuff she gave you, I want you to bring it back here."

"Whatever," said Tiffany.

Priscilla had set herself up in a corner of the room. She had pulled out one of the lunch tables that folded down from the wall for laying out fabric she had to cut. Two girls were cutting out dresses there, while Priscilla sewed on the machine. Edward had learned how to baste. He was sitting cross-legged on the floor at Priscilla's feet, a pink satin dress spread out across his lap. The tip of his tongue was sticking out as he stitched two pieces of cloth together for Priscilla to sew on the machine. "You know, I may have missed my calling. I think I like this better than plumbing."

"From the sound of it," Priscilla said, without lifting her head from her work, "you like almost anything better than plumbing."

"True," Edward said. "How's this?"

Priscilla took her foot off the sewing machine pedal to look at Edward's work. "Look how neat and even those stitches are. It's like you've been doing this for years."

Edward smiled to himself with satisfaction.

"Tiffany hasn't finished the stuff you gave her," I said to Priscilla. "She didn't bring it back with her."

"What?" Priscilla said, feeding cloth under the foot of the machine. "How far did you get, Tiff?"

"I hemmed my dress for the pizza scene," Tiffany said.

Priscilla stopped the machine and looked at Tiffany. Then she said, "Why don't you give Robin and Stephanie a hand with those dresses they're doing?"

"OK," Tiffany said, going to join two of the girls who played pickers and Halloween-party and wedding guests.

Jason, Clara, and Edward went to try on their costumes for the wedding scene. Tiffany put on the part of hers that was done, and two of the other girls had theirs finished. I turned out the lights at the door to the room and went to the light board that Michael had just finished connecting. "This slider is the way you control how much light they give out," he said. "Push this down. Good. Now back up. See? Easy."

"Can I use the lights one at a time?"

"No," he said. "Sorry. They're both on or they're both off."

"Oh, well," I said. "Fine. That simplifies things."

I went back to the ladder. I wanted to see if I could get that light to move. I took a few gels up with me, a pink, a blue, and a yellow. I tried yellow first. A golden circle appeared on the back wall. Nice. I tried the pink, studied the rosy glow. I put the wrench around the knob and tried to move it again. It didn't give. I took the wrench off and then put it back again, trying with both hands this time. It still didn't move. I climbed down.

Then I called to the actors, "OK, let's do just one scene from the beginning and see how this looks. Now that we've got some lighting and some costumes, I bet we're going to be amazed at the difference it makes. Onion family, I'd like you to take your places now for the dinner scene. Tomato people, be ready."

The actors took their places. Jason had the first line. Standing at the front of the stage, he was in almost complete darkness. There were no sleeves on his costume. Suzanne came onstage to say her line, which was supposed to be, "Come in now, it's time for dinner." But before she said it, she tripped over a box of tools that Michael had left on the stage. "Sorry," she said. "It's just so dark. Oh. I forget my line. What scene are we doing?"

There was silence while everyone waited for me to say something, and I was just standing there looking at the stage. Finally, I said, "OK, let's try this. In half an hour, we'll start the run-through. We're going to start at the beginning of the play and keep going, no matter what. Priscilla," I said, "I want as many of the actors in costume as possible. Get your props set before we begin. In half an hour, it's act one, scene one. Any questions?"

Priscilla said, "A lot of costumes are at Tiffany's house."

"Use whatever you have. Jason, go get changed for the first scene."

"R-right, ch-chief."

"Over here, everyone," Priscilla said. "Let's get some clothes on you. Come on now, hurry. Jenny wants you dressed in something before we start the run-through."

As long as I had the ladder, I thought I might as well take the whole curtain down so that we could get to the rips we hadn't been able to reach before. I climbed up and unhooked the curtain, let it drop. I climbed down again and gathered it into a big pile to have it out of the way.

I let down all the venetian blinds in the room and turned out the room lights, except for the lamp that Priscilla had over by her sewing machine. I climbed up the ladder with the wrench. The knob on the side of the light was still not moving. I took hold of the wrench with both hands and put more of my weight against it. Then the ladder shook.

Priscilla and Edward were on the stage, Edward on his knees pinning Priscilla's costume together. Clara was collecting dishes for a dinner scene. Jason was listening to Tiffany say one of her speeches, while she pulled a dress over her head. If I asked one of these people to hold the ladder for a minute, I would delay everything. We were not going to be ready on time, as it was.

Michael walked across the stage and looked up. He said, "Be careful up there."

I said, "I am being careful." I put the wrench in my back pocket and reached up to try to work on the knob with my hand. Now that the lights had been on for a few minutes, the metal was hot. "Ow!" I said, pulling back sharply and upsetting my balance on the ladder.

Then I fell.

I remember falling. I remember thinking on the way down, *Wasn't I wishing hard enough? Where exactly did I go wrong?* I even had time to silently say, *Yes, yes, yes,* a few more times. But I don't remember landing. Several people have mentioned the sound my body made when it hit. "A muffled, sickening thud" was the way Priscilla described it. "A cantaloupe hitting the sidewalk," Edward told me later, and shuddered. Tiffany added, "We thought you were dead! You didn't move or open your eyes!"

*Y*OU KNOW what happened after that. I opened my eyes in a hospital bed. I had a bad headache. Michael was with me. Priscilla and Edward were there, and I was trying to tell them that I was all right. Next thing I knew, Michael started kissing my face. "You're my angel! You know that, don't you?" He took my hands in his. "I love you, Jenny!"

Then Todd was at the side of the bed, not saying anything.

I tried to get up. "We're supposed to be in the middle of a run-through! I've got to get out of here!"

"Jenny, don't!" Michael said. "Just rest now." He put a hand on my shoulder.

Todd hurried out of the room.

I heard myself say, "Wait!" too slowly. My brain was working in slow motion. No one spoke for a few seconds.

"All right now," said the nurse. "We'll be taking her down to X-ray now. You'll all have to wait in the lobby downstairs."

A young boy who could have been Jason's brother pushed a gurney into the room.

Priscilla said, "I'll be right downstairs, Jenny, OK? Michael and Edward, you go back to the school to tell everyone Jenny is all right. Send the actors home."

"No! I want to go back, too!" I said. "I can't stay here. And don't send anyone home. We need that run-through!" I tried to get up and walk away, but I found that I was attached to an IV. "What is that for?"

"Fluids," said Michael. "I asked. It's just saline."

"That's ridiculous," I said. "Why don't they just give me a drink of water?" My head felt like an elephant had been practicing a dance routine on it.

The nurse said, "Your friends may come back later or tomorrow. Right now we're taking you down to X-ray."

"Tomorrow!" I said. I looked at Priscilla, Michael, and Edward. They were all looking back at me helplessly. "I'm not staying here!" I said to the nurse. "We're in the middle of putting on a play. It opens day after tomorrow. It needs a lot of *work*! I have to get out of here *right away*!"

"Don't worry about the play," Priscilla said. "You just get better. Just rest."

"*Rest*? Are you kidding me? This is a hospital!"

I KNEW no bones were broken, but no one seemed interested in my opinion. I had a big bruise on my cheek, a headache, and a black eye, but otherwise I felt perfect. A technician named Lynda took a lot of X rays anyway. I waited for the films to get developed. Then someone took me to another room, where I had blood drawn. Finally, a technician called for someone to take me back upstairs.

"Well, how am I?" I asked Lynda.

She shook her head.

"*What?* What's wrong with me?"

Lynda said, "I'm not allowed to discuss results with patients."

I kept looking at her, waiting.

"All right," she said. "But don't tell anyone I said this. Unofficially, no fractures."

"I knew it," I said. "I want to go now."

"You'll have to wait for your doctor to release you."

"What doctor?" I said. "I don't have a doctor. I just moved here a few months ago. I hadn't gotten around to being sick yet."

"They give you one," she said, smiling at me, as if I were someone's cute but annoying younger sister.

A wheelchair arrived to take me back upstairs, this time to a different bed. Truthfully, I knew enough about hospitals to realize that I had to let a certain amount of procedure unfold before I could do anything about leaving. Still, I wasn't going to just lie there like some injured patient. I made sure I was sitting fully upright on top of the covers, with my legs crossed under me Indian-style, so that if a hospital employee happened to walk in at any time, there would be no mistake about the fact that I was healthy and fit, ready to jump up and be gone. It was a double room with a view of another hospital across the street. I had a roommate named Janine, who had just had abdominal surgery and who didn't talk much because of the anesthesia and pain medication. She had a lot of flowers all lined up on a shelf on the wall. Her daughter was with her. Priscilla came in and sat in the visitor's chair next to my bed. "Where's Todd?" I asked her. "Did he come back?"

"No," Priscilla said. "He will, though, I'm sure. Don't worry about it now, hon."

I looked at the door, expecting someone to walk through it, Todd or a doctor. "A doctor is coming to talk to me about my X rays and blood tests. Then I'll be able to go. I'll get everything all straightened out, the play and, well, just everything. As soon as that doctor gets here," I told Priscilla, "we'll leave."

"Trauma Team, Emergency Department," the PA system called. "Trauma Team, Emergency Department." I groaned and leaned back against the pillows for a minute. "It's going to be a long wait," I said to Priscilla, as the announcement repeated over and over.

"How do you know?"

"I just know. My mother's a nurse. It's like traffic or water drainage. A backup in one place slows down the whole system."

A volunteer, an elderly lady in a yellow smock, brought me dinner. "Thank you much," I said. As soon as she was gone, I pushed the tray away. "I'm not eating this," I said. "We'll get something on the way back to the school."

"I don't know, Jenny," said Priscilla, looking at her watch. "It's getting pretty late."

I glanced at the food. "I couldn't eat that if I tried."

"Why not? Are you nauseous? Sometimes with a head in-jury—"

"I'm not nauseous," I said.

"Are you sure?"

"Positive."

"Then why can't you eat? What's wrong, hon?"

"No hot sauce. I can't eat without hot sauce."

"Oh," she said.

Then, just to prove to her that there was nothing wrong with me, I ate the whole dinner, everything, even the orange Jell-O with the little flower of fake whipped cream on top.

When I was finished, Priscilla pushed the tray to one side and turned on the TV. We watched a couple of sitcoms without laugh-ing. I got up a few times and went to the door to look down the hall for a doctor who might be coming to see me. I was holding my gown shut in the back with one hand, clutching the pole of my IV on wheels. "I hate this," I said. "It feels like the play is getting worse and worse every minute I'm here."

"Get back in bed, would you?" Priscilla said. "You should just be thankful you didn't get badly hurt."

231

I dialed Todd's lab. A student told me Todd wasn't there. I called his office and got his answering machine. I called home and got my own voice, saying I would call back as soon as I could.

Very late, long after my roommate's daughter had gone home, my nurse marched in quickly from the hall. Her name was Christine. She had red hair cut short and a pink top over pants. On her hospital name badge, there was a little pink heart. Under her name, it said, 14 YEARS OF CARING. Quickly, she told me, "You're staying. Doctor just called with orders. He won't be in tonight. I've got to go start a couple of IVs and give some pain medication before I leave. I'll be back."

"Why do I—," I began, but she interrupted.

"I'll be back!" she said, and left the room.

"They can't make me stay," I said to Priscilla. "Obviously there's nothing wrong with me or they'd be putting a cast on something or doing surgery or whatever. Don't they *tell* you anything? Who *is* my doctor anyway? What if I don't like him? I refuse to stay here without a good reason!"

"When she comes back, we'll ask her for more information," Priscilla said. "It's probably just to make sure."

"To make sure of what?" I wanted to know. "Well, if it's just to save their butts from a lawsuit, I'd like to get out of here!"

The phone rang loudly and scared us both. Priscilla got it. "Hello? Yes, she's right here. Just a moment."

"Is it Todd?" I whispered before taking the receiver.

Priscilla shook her head.

"Hello?" I said.

"Jenny? It's Mom. What happened?"

"I was just—" I began, and had to stop, because I burst into tears. It was her voice. She could do that to me. Just hearing her voice when I was the slightest bit vulnerable and—boom—I was crying. Tears rolled quickly down my cheeks. "I was trying to—" I had to sob, gulp, gasp in some air.

"Never mind now. You can tell me when I get there. I'm at the airport. In San Diego. Todd paged me. I was on my way anyway. I was going to surprise you and get there in time for your opening. I'll get a cab to the hospital. It's all right. Don't cry, sweetie pie. I'll be right there."

I sniffed, sobbed, blubbered. Helplessly, I gave Priscilla the phone back. "My mom," I managed to splutter out. "She's coming. She was coming for our opening." I choked on the last word.

"That's good. That's just what you need." She sat on the bed and held my hand. "And don't you worry about anything."

"I'm *fine!*" I cried.

"I know. I know that." She smoothed my hair and got me some tissues.

I HEARD FOOTSTEPS, and then I saw my mother. It was morning. She was wearing an orange sweatshirt with sparkly designs on it and royal blue pants. She was never going to get colors right. "Hi, treasure," she said, and came over to hug me. She smelled good: a little perfume and behind that, the soft feathery smell of *her*, my mother. "How do you feel?"

It was odd to have her there in the hospital to see me instead of me coming to see her working in one. "I slept here," I said.

"You did," she said. "Most people don't sleep very well in a hospital, but you did. I don't think we talked for more than fifteen minutes before you were out like a light. How's your headache?"

I tilted my head left and right. "Better. Where did you sleep?"

"In that chair right over there. You know me. I can sleep anywhere. Do you need any pain medication?"

"Are you my nurse?" I said.

"No, I'm your mother, remember?"

"I remember everything. I mean, are you officially taking care of me or is there someone else in charge?"

"You have a lovely nurse named Susan Kennedy. I told her I would take care of you. She had a couple of difficult cases last night. So if you need something—"

"I don't need anything." I smiled at her, hurting my face. I put a hand up and touched my cheek where it hurt. It was puffy.

"All your X rays and tests were normal. I checked them over

myself as soon as I got here." She went to the sink and filled up a plastic basin with water, then pulled the curtain around my bed, as if she were on duty. She brought the basin to the side of the bed, set it on a chair, dunked a washcloth, squeezed it out. She helped me sit up and untied my gown in the back, rubbed the warm washcloth over my skin. My mother was good at this, gentle but firm. I had bruises that she didn't bother too much by washing.

"Let's take this off, and I'll put on a fresh one," she said, untying my gown.

"Where's Todd?" I said. "Is he coming?"

My mother didn't answer right away. She focused on my left hand, wiping the washcloth over the fingers, one by one. "No," she said. "I don't think he's coming."

"Sure, sure," I said. "I get it." I exhaled, letting out all my air, like a deflating balloon.

"Some people have a hard time with hospitals—" my mother began.

"Right," I said, reviewing the scene at the bed when I first opened my eyes, Michael kissing me and saying that he loved me, Todd running for the door. I lay back against the pillows. "OK, I give. I surrender. I tried everything I could think of and it all backfired. Everything. Now I give up. I tried to talk to Todd about his work, I prayed, I wished, I visualized, I even cooked dinner for him a lot of times, and look what happened! Well, I'm done now."

"Ah, sugar," my mother said. I stared at the ceiling while she ran the washcloth up the length of my arm. "Things can seem a little dark—"

"And I give up on the play, too! I worked and worked and it ended up a disaster. I tried to think positively and work hard. I gave it everything I had, then I fell off a ladder and missed a run-through. I'm stuck in a hospital, and I can't get out. I wanted everything to work, but it just wouldn't cooperate."

My mother washed my other hand. "I see," she said.

I felt my body go limp. I closed my eyes. I didn't feel desperate or anxious anymore. I was satisfied to give up on everything. I didn't really care what happened to me next. I could lie here in this hospital forever, for all I cared. I just lay there not moving while my mother washed me. I let her put a clean gown on me and tie it closed in the back. Then I lay down again and curled into a ball with my eyes closed. I felt very peaceful, a tremendous weight lifting off me at last after a long struggle carrying it up a craggy mountain.

"Good morning," said a male voice.

I jumped, opened my eyes. There was a man in a white coat with a stethoscope around his neck standing next to my bed.

"I'm Dr. Victor," he said, shaking my hand.

"Jenny Brown," I said.

"And I'm her mother, Kate Brown," my mother said.

"Pleasure," said the doctor, shaking her hand. "Hear you're a nurse. The nurses on this floor sure appreciated your help last night." He took my chart out of the holder at the foot of the bed. "Says here you fell off a ladder?" I closed my eyes. I heard him turning the pages of the chart, not saying anything for a long time. Then he said, "Let's take a look." The doctor examined me. I had to bend things and straighten them, walk to a chair and back, follow a light with my eyes, touch my toes, stand up straight. "How do you feel?"

"Terrible," I said. "Everything hurts. I have a headache. I'm tired."

"Any injury in particular you're concerned about?"

"My elbow," I said. I showed him a bruise. "And my head feels like it's going to explode. I have a stiff neck. I can only turn my head this far." I showed him.

"Yes," he said. "OK, good. If that's all, you may go. Sorry it took so long. We had a busy night. So long." He started out.

"I can leave?" I said. "Right now?"

"Yep," he said, writing on my chart. "Be more careful on your ladder next time."

"That's all? You're not even going to—"

"You've been here longer than you should have already. Have a good day." The doctor left the room.

I sat there not moving for a minute. I lay back on the bed

and closed my eyes. I thought about the run-through and Todd. I put my legs under the covers, pulled them up to my chin. I was really quite comfortable here in the hospital. I had become fond of the bed, the water pitcher on the nightstand, and I didn't want to leave the little white TV that hung over my bed. It had become almost a friend.

"Jenny," said my mother, "let's go."

"My elbow," I said to my mother. "Did they x-ray my elbow? I don't remember. It's really killing me. It's way worse than yesterday."

My mother said, "That's normal."

"My knee hurts, too. This one. It really aches. I don't think I can move it," I said.

"Getting up and around will be the best thing for it."

"What about internal bleeding? Did they check for that? Because what if I get up and start—"

"They checked. I looked at the results of all your tests. You're fine."

"Oh."

My mother said, "I'll get your clothes."

t w e n t y

FINISHING WHAT YOU STARTED. Bring in any project
you keep putting off and our instructor, an expert quitter/
procrastinator herself, will help you get it done—finally! Get
out that sweater you started knitting for your high school
boyfriend twenty years ago, the dresser you said you'd
refinish for your baby who just left for college, the hundreds
of photographs you swore years ago you'd put into albums.
Daily meetings at 6 P.M. until you finish. Course cost: $5 per
meeting. Sign up today—don't put it off a moment longer!

WE TOOK a taxi to my house. Walking in the front door
I felt a hollowness in the house, and I knew that Todd was gone.
He had left me. Maybe he had been planning it a long time, and
the scene he witnessed in the hospital finally helped him to make
up his mind. Or maybe it was just that one incident that suddenly
made me impossible to live with. Maybe he had been having an
affair for months and now felt justified moving out. He might even
have talked it over with my mother. For now, she and I didn't
discuss it, as if nothing had changed, as if there were nothing to
talk about.

I went upstairs. The bed wasn't made, and some of Todd's
drawers had been left open. It seemed as though he had done this
on purpose, to make it absolutely clear to me: *I have taken my
things. I am gone.* As I walked by on my way to the closet, I

pushed the drawers back in. I got out some clean clothes and changed.

The phone rang. *Todd,* I thought.

It was Michael. "You're home!" he said. "You're OK! I called the hospital and they said you had been released."

"Yeah," I said. "They said I could go home. You know, if I'm really careful."

"Great. So, tell me. What do we have to do first?"

"Uh . . ." I said. "First? Well, to be perfectly honest, since I fell, I really think—"

"I understand completely. I'll climb the ladder for you. So that will be the first thing. My morning class isn't until ten-thirty, so I have some time. I'll meet you at school."

"Michael, do you really expect me to go through with the play after all that's happened?"

"Oh," he said, surprised. "You mean you have some injuries that I didn't know about? I'm sorry. If you're physically unable to do it, then you're right, we shouldn't."

"I'm not physically *unable* exactly. I really wasn't badly hurt. I just—"

"Good. The whole accident looked worse than it was. I'm glad. You don't know how scared we were. So I'll meet you at school in, say, ten minutes. Twenty?"

"OK," I said. "As soon as I can." With Michael, it never seemed as though I had a choice.

THE SCHOOL smell hit me first—the sweat of anxiety, pencil shavings, old food inside a brown bag—and my spirits lifted a little, a bird flapping its wings inside my chest. I felt as though I had been away a long time—months, years maybe—as if the people I knew here might be gone now or not remember me because I had changed so much. My mother was following me. She had set aside this time to visit me anyway. The multipurpose room was empty. "It's early," I said.

"It's not even nine o'clock," my mother said.

The ladder stood there waiting patiently, and the curtains

squatted in a velvet heap on the stage, a big lump the color of drying blood. Luckily, there was no actual blood for me to confront. But just looking at the ladder made me queasy.

"Mom," I said, "I'm just going to go up on this ladder and try to move that light I was working on. I didn't have a chance to finish last night."

My mother didn't answer. When I looked at her, her face was white and her lips open slightly. Generally, my mother tends to be gutsy and fearless where her own safety is concerned. And goodness knows what kinds of mangled messes she's found some of her patients in before she pulled them through. But she's a wimp when it comes to me.

"It was an accident," I said loudly to make myself sound confident. "It happened once. This time you'll hold the ladder steady for me, and I promise nothing will go wrong. Come on." My heart was pounding as I looked around and found the wrench in one of the folds of the curtain where it must have dropped out of my pocket.

My mother did as she was told, gripping the ladder tightly with both hands while I climbed up. I didn't look down. It's just a light, I thought. How scary can this be? I put my wrench around the knob and prepared to yank at it with all my strength. It turned. Unprepared for it to move, I wobbled slightly on the ladder.

"Jenny!" my mother said sharply.

"It turned," I said. I loosened the knob, moved the light. "I can't believe it moved!" I tipped the light down, guessing at the right angle tightening the knob, but not too much. "Now, Mom, go to that board over there. There are two sliders. Move the one on the left all the way up. Yes. Let go of the ladder. I promise I won't fall off."

"Oh, Jenny, I just can't—"

"Go, Mom. I need you to help me out here."

She went to the board, turned on the light, scurried back.

"OK," I said. "Now, stand on the stage just in front of that table. Good. OK, stay there." The light was still a little high. I moved it so that her face was lit and without shadow. "Now come forward about three steps. Good. Now walk over in front of that chair. Perfect." There were still a couple of dark spots, but this was the best that I could do with two lights. "OK, I'm getting down now." My mother rushed over to steady the ladder as I climbed down. Michael walked in.

"Michael!" I said. "The knob turned."

"I thought I was going to do that," he said. "I oiled it this morning. I guess it worked."

"Oh. I thought it was a miracle or something."

Michael shrugged. "You changed your focus?"

At first, I thought he was talking about my thinking about my life. Then I realized he meant the lights. "Yeah. Right. I'm just guessing, really. I might have to reset tonight when I can see what I've done. This is my mother, Kate Brown. She's going to help us today, aren't you, Mom?"

My mother said, "Oh. Well, all right. Sure." She and Michael shook hands.

We put the ladder away. I didn't hear my mother heave a sigh of relief as much as I felt it. "What's next?" I said to myself.

Michael was getting out the flats to look them over. One of them was just halfway painted. "What's this supposed to be?" he said, not critically but just because it was hard to tell from the slashes and globs on the muslin. "And where's the paint?"

"It should be in the boys' bathroom. That's where I was having them leave all the messy stuff. It's supposed to be on newspaper in there. And could you bring the pile of newspaper back with you? We don't want the floor messed up before opening night. Any more than it already is. My mother will paint that."

"I will?" said my mother, an edge of panic in her voice.

"Yes. As soon as we decide what it's supposed to be."

"I've never painted anything in my life," said my mother. "I mean, of course, I've painted a few doors and living rooms, but nothing, I mean, I have no artistic ability whatsoever. None."

"Look at this one." I held up a flat to show my mother.

"I see," said my mother. "Oh, dear."

"Do you know what it is?" I said.

"A motel? A car? A fireplace?" She threw out a few wild guesses like a contestant on a game show.

240

"It's a door. Of a barn."

My mother looked relieved. "I suppose I could paint as well as that," she said.

"Nothing to it," I said.

I looked at the pathetic flats and thought longingly of *Our Town* again, the way the stage would have looked so clean and uncluttered. I said, "Wait a second! *Stop!*" I guess I yelled this. Michael froze in the doorway. My mother stood still. "Could we save the flats for something else and do without them this time? I don't know why I didn't think of this before."

Michael thought a minute. "Could we *do* that?"

"Why couldn't we? It's our play. We'd keep the props and furniture and the costumes. And the window, of course. But we'd mime the opening and closing of doors, the way we've been doing all along and do without the set. What do you think?"

"Good. Good," Michael said, his eyes flashing. "I like it."

"You mean I don't have to paint?" my mother said, brightening.

"You don't have to paint. Nobody does. We're not using flats." We all stood there for a minute, picturing it. "And Michael?" I said. "I want to get that curtain out of here. If you want to use it for something, fine, but we don't need it."

"You—" Michael looked stunned for a second, then a smile spread across his face. "Consider it gone," he said, and went to get the curtain. "The Tuesday-night quilters will thank you, I'm sure."

I turned to my mother. "The more things we get rid of, the fewer problems we have."

"Well, I guess you're right," she said, a little startled at the force of my conviction.

"I have to go make a phone call," I said.

My mother followed me to the school office.

I called Priscilla. "Hi," I said. "It's me. Now I just want to know where we stand, costumewise. Do we have a long way to go before tonight? Is it totally impossible? Or do you think we still have a chance? Because if you don't think we—"

"Jenny?" Priscilla said. "For a second you sounded exactly

like my friend Jenny Brown, but she's in the hospital recovering from a bad fall. Who is this?"

"Sorry, I forgot to say that I'm out of the hospital and I'm fine," I said. "I bet you're still in bed. Michael and I are down here at the school and even my mother. So can you come, or do you have to work?"

"Oh, my God. You're not kidding. You *are* down at the school. Let me just get some clothes on and a big cup of coffee, and I'll be right with you. Are you sure you're all right? The doctor said this was OK? Are you sure you should be up so soon?"

"I'm fine. And my mother's a *nurse*," I said, as if this gave me some kind of a waiver.

"I'll be right there," Priscilla said.

I set up my mother in the school office with Esther. The two of them called everybody else who was working on the play to tell them it was going to happen after all. Those of us who didn't have jobs or school or small children to take care of worked all day on the things that still had to be pulled together. In the afternoon, there was a rehearsal. Actors ran from the sewing machine or the ironing board to do their scenes.

About every fifteen minutes someone asked if I was feeling OK and told me to sit down. I kept saying that I was fine. Once when I was washing my hands, I looked in the mirror and found that my face was black-and-blue on one side. After that, I made it a point not to look. From other classes, people who had heard about my fall brought me food, herbal tea, and wheatgrass shakes. Irwin, the visualization teacher, came up to me during rehearsal and handed me an audiocassette. "This is a wonderful tape for visualizing perfect health and happiness. I want you to start right away. An accident is no accident, as I'm sure you know."

"You're probably right," I said. "Thanks for bringing this by. But this kind of stuff doesn't work for me." I shook my head and handed the tape back to him quickly. "Besides, I'm really busy right now."

He said, "Then with your permission, I'll visualize *for* you. Now, usually I charge fifty dollars per quarter hour, but for you, it will be my pleasure to perform this service for free."

I held up my hands. "Irwin, please don't," I said. "I just have the wrong kind of, I don't know, energy for this. Every time I try it, something bad happens. I step in something or someone gets hurt or I fall off a ladder. Really, don't. OK? Please. Thank you. I appreciate it and all, but whatever you do, don't visualize about me!"

Irwin smiled. "Jenny, Jenny. There's no such thing as the wrong kind of energy."

"Well, thanks anyway for offering. Now, if you'll excuse me, I have to keep this rehearsal on track. Jason? Tiffany? Where are you guys? Can we get to that love scene?"

"It's up to you, I guess," Irwin said on his way out.

"Thanks anyway!" I called. "Tiff, I need you now."

Naturally, Tiffany still wouldn't know her lines. Before my fall, this seemed to be a catastrophe. Now I thought we would just have to think of something; no use trying to force something that wasn't happening. Jason and Tiffany approached the stage area. "So," I said, "are you ready?"

Tiffany looked at the floor. Jason put a finger under his baseball cap and scratched his scalp.

I said, "I was thinking about the way Tiffany learned those state capitals, and I think we'll do something like that here. We'll tape Tiffany's lines to the set."

"That's it!" Jason said, snapping his fingers. "Yeah! Let's d-do th-that!" As usual, he had his hat on backward, the adjustable plastic band and the hole above it framing the pink skin of his forehead, wrinkling now as his brows rose with enthusiasm.

"For each scene, the lines will be preset, like props."

Tiffany said, "Like, you'll have the lines I have at the window taped to the sill or something? The lines out in the field could be on one of the haystacks? Like that?"

"Exactly," I said. "Is my mom still here? There she is. Mom, would you please go to the office for a new copy of the script, a pair of scissors, and some tape? Then we'll start cutting out Tiffany's lines."

"All right," said my mother, hurrying off to get the script.

"So what if in most plays the actors memorize their lines?" I said to no one in particular. "We don't have to follow every single convention to the letter, do we? For now, Tiffany, get your own script and read from it."

"OK," Tiffany said. She smiled at Jason, a pink glow of relief entering her cheeks, making her radiate. Jason smiled, too, and put his hat on Tiffany. Without the hat, he looked a little naked, and his brown hair was dented in a ring around his head. Half of Tiffany's face disappeared under it, but we could still see her smile, hear her laugh.

While they worked on their scene, I quickly cut the script into pieces and taped them to the furniture. Just to be sure, I highlighted Tiffany's lines in pink. Tiffany and Jason ignored me, as I worked, and continued through their scene. The play went on, while I kept taping pieces of the script to the backs of chairs, bales of hay, a vase, her pillow, and the windowsill in the bedroom.

At the close of a scene, I said, "Let's take a short break now, please. Ten minutes. Tiffany," I said, "could I see you please?" Tiffany joined me on the stage. "Go to the pillow on the bed."

"Great!" she said. "OK, now where should I look in the dinner scene? My plate! Good. And when I put the flowers here, and I talk about the party, I just look at this. I get it. I can do this! I was so worried! Now I can breathe again. I think it's been a month."

"Well, good. We wouldn't want you to go any more than a month without breathing. We should have done this a long time ago. We could have saved ourselves a lot of worry. I guess I needed to fall off that ladder. It knocked some sense into me." For the next several minutes, Tiffany went around the set by herself practicing delivering her lines from various places on the stage.

My mother whispered, "Isn't the audience going to be able to tell that she's reading her lines?"

I shrugged. "Probably."

Michael brought dinner for my mother and me and sat with us while we ate it. We kept on with the run-through. Around ten, the high school kids started to get sluggish, and I worried about whether or not they had tests the next day. After Tiffany's soliloquy, which she read beautifully from the windowsill, I said,

"Excuse me. We're stopping now, everyone. I know we're not finished, but I don't want you all to be tired tomorrow." Some people ignored me and kept on sewing or gluing. I said, "Everybody, put down what you're doing, go home, and go to sleep. Right now. Tomorrow, you can pick up right where you've left off."

Michael, my mother, and I herded everyone out, then we left, too. The room was a mess, but we didn't pick anything up or put anything away. Michael closed the door and locked it behind us.

At home, I found an extra blanket, sheets, and a pillow for my mother to use on the futon downstairs.

"Good night, Mom," I said.

"Good night, dear," she said. "Sleep well."

Upstairs, I took off my clothes, got into bed, and fell asleep before I had time to think any more about anything. Much later the phone woke me up. *Todd,* I thought, and I heard my mother answering and talking a few minutes before hanging up.

A minute later my door opened. My mother whispered, "Are you awake? It was Todd. He said to tell you he won't be coming back—"

"Don't!" I said. I folded the pillow around my ears. "I don't want to hear his message!"

My mother stood there for a minute. She might have said, "I see," but I didn't hear because of the pillow. Then she went downstairs.

I went back to sleep.

THE NEXT DAY was more coffee and more running around, a series of small disasters that made opening seem impossible and then got resolved suddenly. My mother helped, doing errands for me and standing by at rehearsal to pitch in where she was needed.

The play was scheduled to start at seven. Michael and I didn't have time to go home and change. I hadn't taken a real shower in a couple of days, and there was paint as well as a few different varieties of food stains and dirt on my pants. But no one would be looking at me, so it didn't matter. I borrowed some lipstick out of Tiffany's box, brushed my hair, and rebraided it, and I was ready.

As soon as I sat down at the table we had set up in the hall to sell tickets, people were standing in front of me with money out. I had a feeling in my stomach—thrill and dread—as I watched them put their money down or take a numbered ticket out of a wrinkled envelope.

Because we had never done a complete run-through, we were all surprised at how long the play was, almost three hours. Most people stayed to the end. I saw one man taking notes in the dark. I thought I recognized him from the Write It Down class, but I wasn't sure. During the curtain call, as I was clapping like crazy at one side of the stage, Michael pushed me out with the actors. The lights I had worked on were shining in my eyes and I thought how terrible I must look in my dirty clothes and black eye. The actors were clapping for me as Michael handed me a bouquet of pink roses. *When did anyone have time to buy these?* I was thinking as I looked at them. And I liked it out there in the bright lights with a roomful of people smiling and clapping for me. I thought, I will do anything I have to in order to make this happen again.

AFTERWARD, in the former kitchen of the school, there was a lot of hugging and retelling the highlights, reviewing the moments when the play seemed about to go wrong and what the actors had done to save it. They took off their makeup and hung up their costumes for the next night's performance.

"Jenny," Tiffany said, removing the clips from her hair. "You know those lines I have in the kitchen? I was thinking, could you move them to the inside of the refrigerator? Then when I open it to look for the leftover pizza, I'll already be looking in the right place."

"OK," I said. "Good point. I'll move that then." I made a note of this on a pad I was carrying around.

Priscilla said, "Shall I pick up more food for the party scene?"

"No, I'll do that." I wrote down "Party food." I said, "Anything else?"

246

"How many people came?" Clara wanted to know.

"Fifty-seven," I said.

"Whoa," Tiffany said. "Huge crowd."

MY MOTHER and I stayed until everyone else had gone. I reset the stage and the props for the next night's performance and straightened the chairs in the audience. Michael was typing something in the office when I left.

"Jenny," he said when I came to say good night. "You're still here."

"I'm leaving now. Thanks for the flowers."

"Those were from Esther," he said.

"No kidding. That was nice of her. I'll see you tomorrow."

"Good night. And good night, Kate."

"Good night," my mother said.

At home, I couldn't find anything to put my flowers in. I was too exhausted to do anything with them anyway. I put the stopper in the kitchen sink, filled it with cold water, and stuck the stems in, leaning the bouquet against the side. Then I went to bed.

twenty-one

COOKING, SEWING, AND LAUNDRY FOR MEN. Finally! A home economics class to make up for what we guys missed out on in junior high! Whether you're newly single, a longtime bachelor, or your wife has threatened to leave if you don't pitch in, together we'll all become more proficient homemakers. Mystifying tasks, such as sorting laundry and rolling socks, become as easy as apple pie—and we'll teach you how to make one of those, too—in this valuable and fun class. Enrollment is limited, so sign up early! Saturday–Sunday, November 15–16, 10 A.M.–4 P.M. Course cost: $30. Materials: apron, sewing basket with assorted needles and thread; small, sharp scissors; two large baskets unsorted, dirty laundry; soap; latex gloves.

*I*N THE MORNING, I picked up one of those giveaway papers off the driveway and paged through it, as I did every week, looking for coupons before dropping it in the recycling bin. A picture and a paragraph caught my eye. It was a listing of our play and a sort of review in the "Things to Do" section.

"FIELDS OF LOVE"—*Large and Little*
An original play, a stumbling saga of agricultural ro-mance, opened last night at the Institute of Affirmation. The play is enormous (39 cast members and nearly three hours in duration), but depth is limited, focus minute,

scenery nonexistent, and the cast seems completely inexperienced. Director Jenny Brown has made a silk purse from a sow's ear, turning an unwieldy amateur production into a sparkling evening of wit and warmth, humor and heart. Seeing this play is like finding a diamond ring in the lint trap of your clothes dryer, a shining jewel discovered in the most unlikely place. Don't miss it! Thursday, Friday, Saturday performances at 7 through November 8.

I looked at my name again. It was really there along with the playwright's and the names of all the actors. There was a picture of me standing between Michael and Priscilla on the stage, holding my flowers, not very flattering, but my bruises were hardly noticeable. I had never had my name and picture in a newspaper before. Seeing it there, a thrill ran through me, lighting me up like electricity.

My mother joined me on the driveway and read over my shoulder. "Look at that!" she said. "My daughter is a celebrity. They're right, you know. I don't know how you did it. When you see the rehearsals, everything all in pieces, you don't see how the thing is going to pull together."

"You sure don't," I said, shaking my head.

"I meant *me*. *I* don't. You obviously did. You masterminded the whole thing."

"I wouldn't say that," I said. "A lot of it was, you know, accidental. Are you all set?" I was driving her to Palomar Airport. She was going to Wyoming this morning to start a new job.

"All set," she said.

I carried her suitcase to the car and put it in the trunk. On the way to the airport, I was grateful that she didn't interrogate me about what I was going to do with the rest of my life. She commented occasionally on the landscape and left it at that. I parked at the airport and went with her to file her flight plan. "I'll call you when I get there, angel," she said to me.

"Yes," I said. "Have a good flight."

"If there's anything you need, I'll come right back."

"I'll be fine, Mom," I said. "Really."

We hugged, and she walked across the blacktop to get into the plane. I read the back of her yellow T-shirt as she walked away: NOW, WHAT'S YOUR QUESTION? it wanted to know. Michael had given it to her after the play. She was wearing it with her burnt-orange pants. I stood there and waved while she taxied down the runway, then watched her plane take off, and then shrink from a toy to a dot to nothing.

A lump rose in my throat and I tried to swallow it away, but it just got bigger. This always happens whenever my mother leaves me.

So this was the way things were going to end up, I thought, as I drove away. Todd had left *me*, instead of me leaving him. It was only logical that Todd must have been as unhappy with me as I was with him.

I WENT TO the Institute of Affirmation to get things ready for the night's performance. I moved Tiffany's lines to the refrigerator, checked props. I went to the grocery store to buy more food for the party scene. In a little more than an hour, I was finished with everything that had to be done before the second night's show.

Esther was sitting in front of her computer in the school office. The screen was dark. "I've asked you politely," she said to it. "I've begged you. Now I'm commanding you: WORK." She pushed a button on the keyboard. Nothing happened.

"Esther," I said. "I want to thank you so much for those beautiful flowers last night."

"My pleasure," she said. "You're such a lovely person. Now, don't ask me for any comps for tonight, because we're sold out."

"I wasn't going to ask for—we are?"

"Well, what did you expect? You're in all the papers."

"We are?"

She showed me. Three more giveaway papers had run a picture and a brief description of the play. One of them read, "Anything is possible at the Institute of Affirmation, even the marriage of an onion and a tomato. *Fields of Love,* weekends through November 8."

"We're so lucky!" I said to Esther.

"Lucky? Well, that's one way of looking at it."

"So, people saw these reviews and called up or came over to get tickets. Wow."

"That's the way it works. Plus you've got some cast members with big families. Edward's got a party of twenty-five coming down from Costa Mesa tonight. We're sold out tonight and next weekend is going fast." She grabbed her computer with both hands and gave it a shake. "Know anything about computers?"

"About how to fix them? Sorry." I started out, then stopped by the door. "Esther? Is this supposed to be plugged in?" I held up a plug.

Esther grabbed for her computer cord, which pulled the one in my hand. "You know, I think it is!"

"I think so, too," I said, squatting to plug it in.

Esther's computer started making quiet fan noises and her face turned slightly blue from its light. "Now how did you even notice that?"

"Just lucky," I said. "It must be my lucky day."

"Thank you," she said. And for the first time since I came to the Institute of Affirmation months ago, I saw Esther smile.

"I'm going to see if I can squeeze a few more chairs into the multipurpose room so we'll have more tickets to sell."

"That would be good," Esther said. "I hate turning people away, especially when we owe on the electric bill."

I managed to fit eight more chairs in the back and six on the sides. Michael came in as I was realigning all the chairs, making sure they were as close together as possible. I froze, staring at him. My skin got prickly. This was the first time we had been alone together since the hospital.

"Hi, Jenny," he said. "Hey, you don't have to do the chairs. Leave it. I just wanted to ask you if this music is OK with you for the party scene." He showed me a tape.

I looked at him, looked at the tape. "Music?"

"Seems a little flat without music, don't you think? It wouldn't be loud or anything. Some people are very picky about this sort of thing, and I didn't want you to feel—"

"Oh, no. Not at all. I never would," I said. "What? Feel what?"

"That the music didn't go with the play."

"Oh. I see. No, that tape will be great. Fine. Use it."

"OK," he said. "And leave the chairs. Take a day off. Go to the beach or something. Let someone else do the—"

"Michael," I said.

He looked at me, and I looked at the chairs again.

"Yes?" he said.

"Oh," I said, "well, I was—I just—my husband left. We broke up."

He bit his lower lip, shook his head. "I'm sorry," he said quietly. "Oh, Jenny." He put his hand to his heart. "He seemed like a nice guy to me. Sweet. Maybe you can still—"

"Oh, no, it's way past any—"

"Really? You're sure about that? Too bad. I wish I could—" He walked over to me, putting an arm around my shoulders. "Let's sit down over here." We went to the edge of the stage, the part I had helped him build. He kept his arm around me for a long time. He said, "Jenny, may I tell you something? I hope this isn't the wrong time to say this. You're a dream come true to me. Do you know that? I tried to tell you this in the hospital, but you were in no kind of shape to—"

I looked at him, waiting.

"What I mean is," Michael went on, "I don't think you re-alized how bad things were for this place before you came along. I mean, this place lost money from the moment the doors opened, a little over two years ago. And I tried everything to turn that around, I assure you. Advertising, local celebrities teaching courses, lowering class prices, free T-shirts. But the place was go-ing nowhere. Now, we did have a loyal core of students who kept coming back, who brought their friends in and so on. I'll always be grateful to them. But there just wasn't enough of a build, you know? I had to give up, admit that the school was not going to turn a profit.

"The day I came into Acting for the First Time, I had already told the city we weren't going to renew our lease. I was going to start teaching a Saturday-morning ballet class to six- and seven-year-olds at a friend's studio. It was all I could find! I was hoping to add more classes as time went on. And you know the copy place where I sent you to get the scripts copied? They offered me a job, and I was going to take it. But then you came to that class, and everything changed. When I saw you working with that class, I realized you had a gift. You didn't even know it yourself, did you? We got almost forty people in here just for the auditions for this show! Did you know that the fifty-dollar registration fee from each of them was going to be the turning point for this place? Of course not! The actors got their friends and families to come to the show—more cash flow for us! We gave out twenty-two course catalogs at last night's show. And then there are the reviews in the newspaper, reaching thousands of people.

"But it's not just the bills we've been able to pay. It's more than that, because, well, I'm crazy about you, Jenny. We all are. Priscilla and Edward, all the actors. Esther loves you, too. I just hope that you'll stay with us, that you'll continue to work here. I'll do just about anything to keep you. I know this is a hard time for you, but I want you to know that you have a home here. You're our angel!" He smiled at me, pressed my body hard against his, then let me go. "I knew that something would come along to save us. I just didn't know it would be a small woman with a long, dark braid and big ideas. You've pulled us through, and we love you for it!"

I looked up at him, and he was smiling. "Oh!" I said. This wasn't what I expected at all. "Well, thanks," I stammered. "That's very nice of you. Really."

"I know this is a big dose of bad news about your husband. It's got to be disappointing as anything, no matter how bad that relationship was."

"Oh, well, it wasn't *bad*, exactly. Or, I guess, yeah, it was kind of bad, but not—"

"I just wanted you to know how much you mean to us."

"Sure, OK. Thanks for saying all that. And I'm really OK. I guess I might even be glad about Todd. You know? It's probably a *good* thing. It's—I'm *happy* about it." My eyes filled with tears then, my chin wobbled, and my shoulders began to shake.

Sometimes you can stop yourself from crying. When you're watching a sad movie with someone you don't know very well, say, you can kind of build a dam inside yourself to keep the tears from starting. But then other times, it's like a waterfall in the mountains during the spring thaw; then all you can do is stand back and let it flow.

"Jenny?" Michael said. "Oh, Jenny, you're— Gosh, I'm sorry about this! What can I do? Here I'm celebrating our good fortune and you're as sad as you can be!" He hugged me. "Did I just make it worse? I was trying—"

Esther came in then. "Michael, there's someone from the— What's this? What's wrong? Jenny! What happened?"

I couldn't speak at that moment, but just sobbed and sputtered, tears pooling at the tops of my cheekbones before cascading down my face.

Michael said, "Her husband has left her. And I'm afraid I've just said all the wrong things. I was just going on and on about the school, how we—"

"Oh, *honey!*" Esther hurried over to pat me. "I'm sorry. I'll just go take care of the phone, and I'll be right back with some tissues for you, angel."

I sat there crying for a few minutes with Michael sitting silently beside me, his arm draped heavily over my shoulders, not wanting to say the wrong thing. Esther returned to pat my back and sit with us while I cried, saying things like, "It stinks. It just stinks like all get-out. But don't you worry, sweetheart, we're here for ya." People can surprise you. I didn't know Esther could be so sympathetic. And I wouldn't say this to anyone else, but to be honest, I was a little disappointed to learn that Michael wasn't in love with me, to find out that he was just relieved that his school didn't go belly-up and grateful for my part in its financial turn-around. You can see how that was kind of a letdown, can't you?

After a few minutes of sopping up my tears with tissues, when I thought I could manage to speak again, I said, "Esther, Michael, you don't have to—I mean, what about the office and the phone and—"

"Oh, sweetheart, just never you mind. That's what answering machines are for," Esther said. She took a turn hugging me and told me that I would find someone else before I knew what hit me. She said that I should know that everyone here at the school thought the world of me. "Michael, for instance, is just as happy as he can be about this play of yours. He thinks you're tremendously talented. Don't you, Michael?"

"She has a gift. She sure does. I was just telling her."

Esther went on. "I promise that one day you will be thanking that husband of yours for getting the hell out of your life." She hugged me and kissed the top of my head.

I pulled a new tissue out of the box and blew my nose.

I DROVE to Todd's lab, where I found eight people hard at work, including two I'd never seen before. "Hi," I said to the one with the ring in his nose. "Is Todd here?" He looked at me as if trying to recall where he'd seen me before. "I'm his wife?" I said. I didn't mean for it to sound like a question. "Hem," I said, clearing my throat. "Wife," I added more firmly.

"Right," he said. "He's in his office."

Walking to Todd's office reminded me of all the times I had to go to his lab to tell him that I was having a miscarriage; there was the same dark dread in the pit of my stomach. It had been a relief to get out of Cambridge. When Todd got this job, it was so much easier not to have anyone corner us at a party or in the video store and look deeply into our faces, asking, "So, how *are* you?" a congratulatory smile slowly dropping into an expression of condolence. Naturally, we planned that from the moment we moved things would start going better for us. We didn't expect that Todd's first student would die or that I would get fired and lose interest in finding a regular job, then start questioning what I was supposed to be doing with my life, or that we would each decide to leave the other.

I found Todd at his desk, typing something on his computer. I stood in the door a minute before he noticed me. He had made a nest for himself in the corner of the small room. There was a sleeping bag and a lamp that had disappeared from the bedroom. A book with pictures of magnified gray cells lay open beside the sleeping bag. There was a plastic cup of water on the floor next to the pillow. Some clothes were stuffed into a plastic bag at the foot of the sleeping bag. If I pulled open one of the desk drawers, I'd probably find his toothbrush, razor, deodorant. "Todd?" I said.

He jumped. "Oh."

"Hi," I said, testing. "I just came to . . . see you."

"OK," he said. "Your mom left, I guess."

"Yeah," I said. "This morning." I walked in, closed the door behind me. "So," I said, and stopped.

"I slept here."

"I see that."

He clicked save on the computer and then looked at me. "How's your head?"

"Good. It's good," I said, touching the back of my braid. "My play opened. It got in some of the newspapers. Well, mostly they're the ones people recycle without reading. Still . . ."

"One of the graduate students showed me. They all bought tickets. Congratulations. I'm sorry about not being there last night, but I was so worried about the mice that I—"

"What mice?"

"The German mice."

"What German mice?"

"The German mice I had to pick up in L.A."

"You didn't say anything about any German mice in L.A."

"What? I called and told your mother. I had to go to LAX and pick up my mice that the guys in Cologne sent me. I had to. I've been waiting forever for those mice. You knew that. Giesel-

256

mann's mice. It took way longer than I thought. Those USDA people have no sense of urgency, you know? I had to stay in a motel in Los Angeles because they didn't finish the paperwork in time. Your mother said she would tell you that I was staying overnight."

"I guess I didn't let her give me the message." Now I remembered the pillow over my ears.

"Well, then when I got the mice back here, they looked terrible. I mean it was more than just the tumors. Now I think they just had jet lag or something. But I was so worried I slept here so I could check on them during the night. I went home to get my sleeping bag and stuff, but you weren't there. They're fine now. All nice and stable. I told your mother the whole story on the phone."

"I believe you," I said.

"Where did you *think* I was the last two nights?"

"I thought you left me," I said quietly.

Todd looked blank for a second. Then he stood up and hugged me. "Ah, Jen," he said. "Sometimes—" and he couldn't think how to finish.

I kissed him. Sometimes relief is the closest thing to pure joy. I put my head against Todd's chest. I could hear his heart. He put one hand on my back and one hand on my hair. He held me tight, and all our years together, our whole story, every last detail was there in one squeeze. We kissed for a while, and Todd laughed softly.

"What?" I said. "What's so funny?"

"Why did you think that?" Todd said.

"Because we've been having such a bad time. You never say anything to me. You're never home. Well, I guess you were never home before, either. But then you ran out of the hospital when I was there with Michael, and I thought—"

"I hate hospitals. You know that. By mistake I looked at that IV tube going into your arm, and I didn't want to throw up or faint in front of all those people. I can handle medical procedures on mice, but my own wife—that's a whole other deal entirely.

That's why I had to call your mother and get her to come and take over. She called me here a couple of times. She said you were fine. You are fine, aren't you?"

"Well, yeah."

"Good. Why would I leave you? Why would I *do* that?"

"Incompatibility? Because we have nothing in common? Because we have a lousy sex life and poor communication?"

"But I *love* you," Todd said. "I love you, and I can't live without you. The rest is just details. Temporary details. It wasn't like that before with us, and it's going to get to the good part again."

"Yeah, well."

Todd said, "A bunch of lousy stuff happened to us. We were just trying to keep afloat, Jen, deal with each thing as it came along. You have to step back a little and look at the big picture. It's been good more than bad, right?"

I nodded. He was still holding me and I could smell his skin through his T-shirt: straw. I love that smell; it was like home sweet home to me. If you stay with someone long enough, it's quite possible that you will fall out of love with him. And then if you stay just a little longer, you might just fall back in.

"I'm not worried about us," Todd said. "Never was."

We didn't say anything for a few minutes. The fax machine yelped and then a sheet of paper came out of it. Todd didn't look to see what it was.

He said, "Are you ready to talk now? You notice I haven't brought it up all this time, but since we're going over all this other stuff, maybe we could—because I really can't wait any longer." Todd let go of me so that he could see my face.

I just stood there, blinking.

Todd said, "I've been patient, don't you think? I haven't brought it up, not even once since we've been in California. Did you notice that? I haven't been pushy at all, have I? Of course, not talking about it meant not talking about a lot of other things because they might have led to talking about it. Maybe that's what you mean about poor communication. For instance, I never brought up the subject of where we should move after this year because then we would have had to decide whether or not it was important to live in a good school district. I mean, when you think about it, not talking about this one thing has meant not talking about much at all. So now I'm going to talk about it." He took a deep breath. "I have to. I can't stand not talking about it anymore. I want to adopt a baby."

This, of course, was exactly what he would have said months ago before we stopped talking about it, before we moved here, before I exploded one day and said, "Todd, you are nagging me! You are whining and pressuring and harassing me about this. You are driving me nuts. I keep telling you, *I'm not ready to discuss it!*"

And Todd put his hands up in a gesture of surrender and said, "OK. OK. I hear you. I'll wait until you're ready."

When we gave up on getting pregnant, Todd had begun his adoption campaign the very next day. He had researched it, gone over the options on agencies. He had done all that knowing that I wasn't ready to consider it. "But why?" he kept saying. "We'd be perfect."

"Perfect or completely wrong," I told him. "And how do we know which?" I didn't want to bring a load of unresolved adoption issues of my own into parenthood. He wouldn't stop, wouldn't leave it alone, until I yelled at him not to bring it up again until I was ready. He was right when he said that when you aren't talking about one big thing, there are lots of other ones that are closed off, too. And there's another thing that he didn't say. When you've unsuccessfully tried for a long time to have a baby, the idea of making love starts you thinking about the human life that you're not going to begin between you. Believe me, it's easier to just not go there, not to get that close, even if it does leave you feeling isolated and abandoned.

I looked at him sitting there now, and I said, "So how's the work?"

He didn't answer right away. He sighed. Then he decided to let me change the subject. He said, "Something happened. I got something, something big."

"You did?" I leaned toward him, listening, waiting.

"Well, yeah. And it's good."

"That's great, Todd. Congratulations." My heart was starting to pound. "So what is it?"

"Oh, it's more brain tumor stuff, but with general applications to other kinds of cancer."

"So now you're writing it up?" I said.

"No, no. It's not publishable yet. And listen. Wait. Everything seemed to be happening just so I could get these results. You could almost hear all my years of research finally clicking together like puzzle pieces. Then I just found out—this morning right before you walked in here—that a guy in London is working on the same project. He's ahead. I might not make it." He shook his head.

"How do you know?"

"Well, I know how far they are, how far we are." He put his hands over his face for a second, then let them drop to his sides.

I sat down on a chair, the one his students sat in when they came in his office to be interviewed to work here or show him their data or complain about their projects or whatever.

"I had this nice feeling that what I was doing had meaning, a direction. Even Fischburger telling me that he didn't think my project was any good seemed to have helped me get where I was going. Now I'm not so sure again." He sat still for a minute, thinking. "Let's go. Let's leave, get out of here for a while."

"Todd!" I said, shocked. "It's the middle of the day. You can't just leave!"

Todd laughed. "All these years, you've been telling me to take time off, and now you don't want to just go out and get a coffee or something."

"Coffee? *Coffee?* You should be in the lab, working!"

"Jenny." Todd shook his head.

"Go! Stand up! Walk! Get to the lab right now! You're in a race, and you're just sitting around doing *nothing*. Come *on*. If you hurry, you could win."

Todd smiled. "No, see, really, races like this take place over a period of months, *years* sometimes, not hours and minutes. Scientists who are competing to get results are not actually *running* around a lab."

"Maybe not. But it would help to work fast, all the time, put everything you have into this. I really think you should get going now. I'll help you. Even though I hate the smell, I'll do whatever you want to help you get the project finished fast. Let's go." I stood up and started out.

"Jenny, I didn't mean, I'm not even sure if—"

I spun around on the heels of my sneakers and faced him. "You don't have to be sure of anything; that's not part of your job. You just have to finish the work. I happen to know for a fact that you have everything you need to make this project succeed. It's all there waiting, ready to go."

Todd looked at me, a little stunned. "Where are you getting this stuff?"

"I just open my mouth, and out it comes. Let's go." I walked fast out the door.

Todd followed me to the lab. I stopped in front of his bench. "OK," I said. "Now what do I do?"

twenty-two

HOW TO GET MORE OF WHAT YOU WANT. See it. Reach for it. Grab it. Hold on tight. We'll teach you how to get more friends, work, satisfaction, success, fame, money, hope, respect, laughs, space. Saturday, November 29, 9 A.M.– 3 P.M. Course fee: $30.

I NEVER WOULD have imagined how many things a person could do in a lab without knowing the first thing about science. It was a good thing I was unemployed, because Todd needed help. Sometimes I sent Federal Express packages to the lab in Cologne that Todd was collaborating with. Other times, Todd showed me real lab things he needed done, like sucking up liquid with those plastic pipette things and transferring it to different containers. We worked all the time that we weren't asleep, eating, or driving to or from the lab. After a month, Todd had the results he needed to write up his paper. He submitted it to *Nature,* the scientists' favorite journal. After a few more weeks and some minor revisions to two of the tables and some rewriting of the discussion section, it was accepted. It would be published in two more months. Meanwhile, a lot of new projects had developed from this project. Everyone in the lab was busy all the time. Two new students were coming from Cologne to work here and one was on her way from MIT.

The scientist in London Todd had been worried about would have his work published a few weeks later in the same journal. His project was not as similar as Todd had heard; it had to do with a different kind of cancer.

"See that?" I said to Todd the day his paper was accepted. "What did I tell you?"

"What did you tell me about what?"

"That things aren't always what they seem, that even when you think everything is falling apart, it can still work out in a surprising way. Or no, wait. Let me get this right. The biggest miracles happen when a tremendous problem turns out never to have existed."

"I don't remember you saying that."

"I thought I did. I was thinking that, anyway."

"Oh, well, it's a good thing to remember," Todd said.

IT WAS ALMOST Thanksgiving. Todd's students were having a dinner in an apartment in graduate-student housing. "We won't have to cook!" Todd said enthusiastically.

"Have we ever cooked a Thanksgiving dinner?" I wondered out loud. We both thought about it and finally shook our heads. "Never."

"We won't have to start this year!" he said.

"What time do we have to be there?"

"Noon," he said.

"Good, because there's a dinner at the Institute of Affirmation, too, and it starts at four."

"You don't *have* to go, right?" Todd said.

"I want to," I told him. "I do. We're both going. The two of us, together."

"Why? I don't want to spend my holiday with a bunch of weirdos and misfits."

"Neither do I, but I'm going to yours," I said.

"Jenny," he said, trying to be patient with me. "These are my *students*. That's different. You know it is." I stared him down. "OK, it's the same. It's exactly the same." He threw up his hands and let them drop. "All right. I'll go. But I'm not getting dressed up."

"Dressed up?" I said. "You are kidding, right? Talk about weirdos and misfits."

AT THE GRADUATE students' Thanksgiving dinner, most of the guests were from other countries: the Americans from the lab had gone home to their families in Los Angeles, San Francisco, or El Paso, not for the *whole* four-day weekend or anything, because they had experiments to do, but for a day or two.

Planners of the dinner had not concerned themselves with sticking to a traditional menu, if they were familiar with it in the first place. Instead of turkey, the main course was a choice of steak or a lentil-vegetable pilaf. I chose the pilaf. Next to it was some Gorgonzola cheese and a bowl of popcorn. On another table was a chocolate torte with marzipan fruits on top. There was also a bean-and-tortilla dish garnished with jalapeño peppers, as well as the usual varied assortment of international beers. I had brought an apple pie, which didn't seem to belong on the same table with the other food. We all got plates and sat on the floor around the coffee table. Only five other people came, so there was plenty of food and plenty of room.

I took my shoes off and got up to get more of the pilaf. Now that I had worked with these people for a few weeks, I felt more comfortable with them. "So, Coby," I said to a Dutch woman, "what do you like best about being in the States?"

"De beef," she said. "De meat is very good and so cheap. Et home, you never eat good meat like dis."

"Ya," said her friend Inge from Germany. "But da coffee dat you get in restaurants is terrible. Chust as bad as da meat is good."

"Really," I said.

"Et home de coffee is incredible so good," said Coby.

"You will see after," said her boyfriend Jan. "We will be hevving coffee after de food."

"I'll be looking forward to that," I said.

"They place a great deal of emphasis on coffee," Todd said to me. "Maybe if they didn't drink so much coffee, we'd get more work done in the lab." He said it as though he were joking, though we all knew he meant it.

"My mother sent you some coffee from Holland," said Coby, handing Todd a foil pouch with Dutch writing on it, decorated with a red bow. "Maybe when you hev dis, you can take a coffee break, slow down, relax a little bit."

Todd said, "Then where would we all be? If I relaxed. Besides, I always thought coffee was to speed you up, get you going." I glared at him. "I mean, thank you. Tell your mother thank you."

I got up to get some dessert. I didn't take any of my own, which looked so plain. Instead, I let Coby cut me a large piece of chocolate torte. I said, "That's huge."

"Ya," she said, "but you are fin." She put a dollop of whipped cream on top, which dripped down the sides of the cake.

"Thank you," I said, taking the plate. I sat on the floor and ate all of it without speaking. When I was finished, I looked up. The rest of the guests, including Todd, had been watching me. "What?" I said. "It was good."

The coffee was good, too. "I see what you mean," I said. "Wow. I don't think I would've left Holland if I were you." I took another sip. "Gee, how do they do it? I mean, what's the difference between good coffee and bad coffee?"

"De beans," said Coby, "en how much water you use."

"Oh. Yeah, I guess it would be."

"Are you doing more feeder?" Jan said.

"Pardon me?" I said.

"Coby and I liked your play so much. We used to be involfed in de feeder in Holland. We used to be enjoying it very much. But den we got into science, and we didn't hev time to go to de feeder so much anymore. I liked your staging, de elaborate costumes with no curtain or scenery. Interesting contrasts. I like productions dat take risks."

"I'm glad you enjoyed it," I said. "It was sad when it ended. You work so intensely with these people for several weeks, then suddenly, it's over. We're seeing some of them later today, though."

Todd said, "We better go. Thank you very much for the dinner."

I gulped down the last of my coffee and stood up quickly. "Yeah, thanks. So nice of you to include us." We shook hands with our hosts.

In the car, I said, "How come we had to leave so suddenly?"

Todd said. "I have to refresh my cells."

PRISCILLA HAD organized the Thanksgiving dinner at the Institute of Affirmation, assigning foods to all the participants to bring. There were sweet potatoes with melted marshmallows, carrots with honey sauce, creamed green beans, Parker House rolls, and cranberry sauce that held the shape of the can it came from on a paper plate with a cartoon of a smiling turkey. Tiffany brought the plates; Jason was bringing the napkins, but he wasn't here yet. Michael was bringing the tablecloth, but he wasn't here yet, either. Priscilla had brought a microwave from home and set it up on a table. There were a lot of tables in the multipurpose room. And, of course, there were excellent cooking facilities for preparing meals for large numbers of people, except that the gas wasn't turned on.

I brought pie to this one, too, and set it on the table with the other food. I was aware of Todd standing next to me, not speaking. "Todd," I said, "You remember Priscilla."

"Hi, Todd," Priscilla said. "Glad you could join us."

"Hi," said Todd.

"And this is Edward over here," I said, "You've seen him a couple of times, too."

"Howdy," said Edward, setting his sweet-potato-and-marshmallow casserole on a table. "Glad to see you." Todd gave a little nod. Edward pulled a big spoon out of a paper bag and set it down next to the sweet potatoes. "I hope this is still hot enough. Priscilla, we better eat soon, don't you think?"

"Not everyone is here yet. We can't eat without Michael. And what about Jason?"

"What about my sweet-potato casserole? It's getting cold."

266

"Microwave?"

"It's in a metal dish!" Edward said.

Priscilla said, "I can't help you then."

"I always make it in this dish!"

"Here's Michael anyway," Irwin said. "Hey, who's—" He stopped putting plastic forks into a paper cup and stood still.

I followed his gaze to the doorway where Michael was standing with a woman I hadn't seen before. She was wearing silver platform sandals, old ones from the early seventies, with a pair of sweatpants and a quilted jacket. Her hair hung in her face, and she wore no makeup. She was staring fixedly at the light switch.

"Hi," Michael said. "Everyone, this is my wife, Charlotte."

"Hi," said Irwin. "Welcome."

"Happy Thanksgiving," Priscilla said.

"Happy Thanksgiving," a couple of people chimed in.

Charlotte didn't reply but continued to look at the switch plate.

Michael handed me the tablecloth. "Sorry we're late. All the patients were signing out at the same time, and it took forever."

"You didn't miss much," I said. I took the cloth over to the table. It was a white cloth one, fancy and antique with heart-shaped lace cutouts. I said, "You don't want to use this, do you? It's so . . . so beautiful and good. What if we spill gravy and cranberry sauce on it?"

"Uh, well, I'll have it cleaned," Michael said. "I've had it a really long time, and I never use it. I wanted to use it."

Tiffany felt the lace. "If my mother had one of these, she'd keep it in a plastic bag and not let anyone touch it."

"That would be too bad," Michael said.

I looked at Priscilla, as if for her permission to go ahead. She nodded at me. With a big toss, I flung the cloth out to its full length. It covered a lunch table big enough for twenty kids.

"Ha!" said Charlotte. But when I looked, her face hadn't changed, and she was looking at the floor.

We started putting the food on the table. Jason arrived. He was wearing an enormous pair of overalls and a baseball cap on backward and carrying a cardboard carton with two covered dishes in it. He said, "Happy T-turkey Day! My mom said to give you these beans and onions."

"Thank you. Those look good." Priscilla took Corning Ware casserole dishes out of his box and put them on the table: green beans with almonds, creamed onions.

"The napkins are in here, too. She always makes too much. It was just the t-two of us today. My sister's in Idaho with her family. Couldn't get here this year."

"Did your mother want to join us?" Priscilla said. "Go call her."

"Thanks, but she's not h-home," Jason said. "She went to a movie with her b-boyfriend."

Tiffany glided over to Jason and fit herself sideways under his arm. She tipped her face upward, and he kissed her.

"Want to help set the table?" Priscilla said. Holding hands, Tiffany and Jason put turkey paper plates and cups at each place.

I said, "Tiffany, did your mother make a big dinner today?"

"Yeah," she said. "I have to be home by seven to eat it. We've got relatives coming."

"Who brought the flowers?" Tiffany said.

"I did," said Suzanne. "Do you like them?"

"Totally," said Tiffany.

"We're waiting for Esther, aren't we?" I said.

Michael said, "She told me she was coming."

"We'll wait then," I said.

We set all the dishes on the table, and everybody took a seat. "Sorry I'm so late," Esther said from the door. "I couldn't find my keys." She took a seat next to Jason. She put two different kinds of bread down on the table and pulled off the plastic bags. "Who's this?" she demanded.

"Esther," I said. "I'd like you to meet my husband, Todd."

"Nice to meet you, Esther," Todd said. "Happy Thanksgiving."

"Happy Thanksgiving. Now what are we waiting for?" She picked up her fork, and we all started to eat.

With everyone sitting down, it looked like a bigger crowd than I thought it would be. We didn't separate couples. Michael sat with Charlotte, putting food on her plate for her, speaking softly to her while she kept her eyes down, consuming all her food without seeming to prefer one dish over another. Tiffany and Jason stayed together, laughing a lot, sometimes exploding into hysterics over almost nothing. Priscilla and Edward sat together, too. I thought of them as a couple now; they spent so much time together. Todd sat on my left, Edward on his other side. Somehow, they hit it off, though I wouldn't have expected this. Todd explained what he did, and Edward explained how to make his sweet potatoes. Irwin was carrying the turkey platter around the table, making sure everyone had enough.

Across from me was Clara, who said, "I love this. This is great. Nobody's fighting, nobody's drunk. I hope we do this every year from now on. This is what I call a holiday!"

If you didn't focus too well, or if you looked into the room quickly, then away again, you might be convinced that this was a big extended family, all having Thanksgiving together. And in a way, it was. What is a family anyway? To me, I guess it's the collection of those people you choose to be closest to.

Just as everyone was finishing a final helping of the main course, I said, "Todd?" He didn't hear me. There was a lot of conversation going on all at once, and there was music playing, a CD of seventies disco hits that Priscilla had brought. I put my hand on Todd's arm. He turned to me, waited. Then he leaned down closer. I said, "Now I'm ready. I'll talk about it now."

"What? Now?" he said. "You want to talk about it right now?"

"Yes. Let's go ahead. I'd like to adopt a baby." No one else heard me. It was just a private conversation between Todd and me. Then we had dessert.

twenty-three

CREATE YOUR OWN CLASS. You've got a great idea, and we want to hear it! We'll show you how to create a course people will want to sign up for. Join us! We've been waiting for someone like you to come along! Saturday, December 20, 10 A.M. to noon. Course cost: Free.

A COUPLE OF WEEKS ago, I found the notebook with my "miracles" in it. In the spaces I had left blank, I wrote how each miracle came about.

I am happily married to the right person. There was a time when I never would have guessed it would turn out to be Todd. But it did. What makes it work now is part shared history, part common background because we're both adopted, part chemistry. And a significant chunk of our happiness at being together now is gratitude and relief that the hard time we had is over. It was like after a winter of looking out your window at cold dirt, all of a sudden, tulips and daffodils show up, something good you believed in once, then forgot was possible.

I love my new job. I'm theatrical director of the Institute of Affirmation. I get paid and everything. Since our first show, the school has become quite profitable. Last year, the school moved to a new location in a shopping center, where in addition to the office building that Michael had converted to classrooms, we took over an old movie theater for our stage productions. Two or three days before a show opens, it still seems like a chaotic mistake. This happens every time. The difference is that I've come to accept this as part of the process. I get a deep thrill when things finally click into place and work out in surprising ways. It always seems like a miracle. We do one play per season during fall, winter, and spring, then two in the summer. I got tired of hearing myself say I didn't know what I was doing, so I took a couple of theater courses at the university, then a few more, until in just a little over two years I had earned a master's in theater.

About the time I completed my degree, we adopted a baby girl. Waiting for our daughter was just about the hardest thing we've ever done. While we were waiting, I kept saying to Todd that we should have started sooner, years ago, way back in Cambridge. And he would always remind me, "You wouldn't have found your job. And you wouldn't have had time go back to school. We just weren't ready until now." Of course, he was right, but it was hard to admit at the time.

Our adopted daughter's name is Lacey. She has curly brown hair, green eyes, and freckles. Of course, she doesn't look like anyone in our family. She gets that from both her parents. She is almost two now.

While we were waiting for Lacey, something else happened. I discovered I was pregnant. Of course, Todd and I both expected another miscarriage and braced ourselves for it. I continued working and going to school. Our daughter, Lily, was born a week after her due date, within just a few days of her sister. We had heard about this kind of thing happening to other couples, but we never expected it to happen to us. Lily has straight dark hair like mine, and she is tall like Todd. Even though the two girls don't look anything alike, almost every day someone asks us if they are twins. We always say yes.

Now I've cut way back on my work schedule. At the moment, I just teach one workshop at a time and hire guest directors for the plays. With Lacey and Lily and a little teaching, every day is completely full from beginning to end with a million things that need to be done right away. I just love that. I plan to go back to directing when the girls go to first grade.

Even though I don't see him every day the way I used to,

Michael has a way of showing up out of the blue at exactly the right moment. I don't know how he does it. A couple of months ago, both girls had runny noses, ear infections, and fevers. Todd was in Germany, speaking at a conference. I had just realized that I was out of Children's Tylenol and almost out of milk. Lacey was crying, and Lily was asleep. I was trying to figure out how I was going to manage a trip to the store when the phone rang. It was Michael. He said he was at the grocery store and wanted to know if I needed anything. Another time, I got a flat tire on the freeway. Both girls were with me. Who do you think was about ten cars behind me? Michael again. It almost seems as though he's hovering in the background, keeping an eye on me.

My birth mother and I are reunited. You know this part. My half-sister searched for me from her home computer in Mexico City, finding my non-identifying information and a description of me and what I do listed with a couple of search services. She e-mailed, asking for a picture, which I sent. As soon as she saw the pictures—the one of me standing on the stage with the cast of *Fields of Love,* and a few close-ups that Todd took—she drove straight to your house to show you. You said the minute you saw the pictures, you knew I was your birth daughter. She gave you my e-mail address. You wrote me a long letter about your life.

You wrote to me about attending an acting school in New York for two years, beginning when you were only eighteen. You wrote about the affair you had with an acting coach there, the association that was not only completely against your upbringing and religious beliefs, but also strictly prohibited by the school, which threatened dismissal for any personal relationships that developed between teachers and students. I know you didn't even consider an abortion, though the teacher would have paid, would have gone with you and seen you through it.

You could not return to Mexico and your parents with a baby, either. It would have been such a shock and disappointment to them after all they had done for you, all they had given up to get you to New York. You said in your e-mail that, in fact, the teacher probably would have married you if you had said that was what you wanted. But it wasn't that simple. There was his wife, the three children he already had—one of them was almost your age—and the important fact that you could not see yourself spending your life with this man. In your heart, you knew it was not possible, that you would be hurting a lot of people to get something you did not truly want. The decision to have me and give me away was entirely yours, you said. You finished school a few months pregnant, lied to your parents about wanting to spend more time in New York to take an additional course, had me, gave me away, and returned to Mexico.

Soon after your return, you started acting professionally, working in several soap operas until you finally settled into one permanently as an ingenue at first, then later as a young mother, transforming briefly into a conniving vixen, returning to your former sweetness via a life-threatening brain operation. In your third year of working on this program, you married one of its directors. The two of you have two children, both in their late twenties now. You are still in touch with the acting teacher, my birth father, who continues to teach, though he is quite elderly now. You have stayed friends, which you find strange, but you believe it is only possible because you were never really in love with him and have hardly seen him since you were nineteen. He was kind to you when you were lonely in a strange country. Your husband doesn't know that you still hear from him, but I do, and I appreciate your sharing this secret with me.

You never searched for me. You were aware of the many adoptees and birth mothers searching, but you had made your decision a long time ago. You believed it would be wrong to disrupt my life by reappearing and asking for a reunion. Of course, you had wondered about me every day since I was born. On each of my birthdays, you made a donation of toys and a check to an orphanage in Mexico City.

You knew as soon as you saw my picture that I was your birth daughter because we look so much alike. You said seeing a photograph of me was almost like looking at a picture of yourself somehow unearthed from a past you didn't know you'd had. You even used to wear your hair this way, in a long single braid. But that was years ago, before New York, even. Occasionally you have seen women working in a shop or passing you on the street that you've thought might have been your birth daughter. Something about the expression or the eyes looked familiar. But until you saw my picture, you never had this feeling of absolute certainty that this stranger was a blood relation.

So that's it. That's my story. I'll see you a week from Friday at the AeroMexico Terminal at four-thirty in the afternoon. My mother, Todd, Lacey, and Lily will be with me. I think Todd and my mother are almost as excited and impatient about this reunion as I am. And I'll look forward to meeting my half-sister and half-brother and your husband. You'll know me right away, but just to make it as easy as possible, I'll be wearing a purple T-shirt that says, THE ANSWER IS YES.